BAEN BOOKS
by
ANDRE NORTON

Time Traders
Time Traders II
Star Soldiers
Warlock
Janus
Darkness & Dawn
Gods & Androids
Dark Companion
Masks of the Outcasts
Moonsinger
From the Sea to the Stars
Star Flight
Crosstime

CROSSTIME

BY
ANDRE NORTON

BAEN

A Baen Books Original

Baen Publishing Enterprises
P.O. Box 1403
Riverdale, NY 10471
www.baen.com

ISBN 10: 1-4165-5529-3
ISBN 13: 978-1-4165-5529-2

Cover art by Stephen Hickman

First printing, March 2008

Distributed by Simon & Schuster
1230 Avenue of the Americas
New York, NY 10020

Library of Congress Cataloging-in-Publication Data
Norton, Andre.
 [Crossroads of time]
 Crosstime / by Andre Norton.
    p. cm.
 ISBN-13: 978-1-4165-5529-2
 ISBN-10: 1-4165-5529-3
 1. Science fiction, American. I. Norton, Andre. Quest
crosstime. II. Title. PS3527.O632C75 2008
 813'.52--dc22
                           200704727

Printed in the United States of America

10 9 8 7 6 5 4 3 2 1

Contents

THE
CROSSROADS
OF TIME

prologue

The office was bare of all furniture except for a seat pulled drawer fashion out of the softly glowing wall. The report shining in fiery script up at the Inspector was on a desk. Or perhaps those letters only appeared fiery because of the possible conflagration to come, masked in the official idiom of his particular security section. As long ago as his third month in the Service, a time now he found difficult to recall, he had ceased abruptly to believe that any operation could run smoothly. In past experience the most placid landscapes hid the nastiest traps.

Now he leaned back in the seat which accommodatingly changed shape to fit his middle-aged bulk at the new angle. Though his expression had not changed, he ran a finger tip nervously back and forth along the edge of the reader plate on which the message still stood. He had already wasted too much time on this, but—

CLASSIFIED REPORT: Division 1 Plus Information

PROJECT: 4678

NATURE OF OFFENSE: Attempt to influence
                        other level history.

AGENTS:

Section Leader: Com Varlt, MW 69321

Crew: Horman Tilis MW 69345 Fal Korf AW 70958
          Pague Lo Sig AW 70889

PROGRESS TO DATE:
   Traced subject—Kmoat Vo Pranj—to Levels 415-426 inclusive. Established prime base on likeliest world (E641— marked, on survey of Kol 30, 51446 E.G. as "culturally retarded, critical, forbidden, except to sociological investigators, rank 1-2"). But subject may be on another world of this grouping or engaged in hopping.

COVER:
   Have assumed credentials and background of members of native law enforcement body, national in scope (Federal Bureau of Investigation).

TYPE OF CULTURE:
   · Dawn atomic—inhabitants on this level appear to possess no psi powers—highly unstable civilization—just the type to attract Pranj.

REMARKS:

There was the meat of it, entered under "remarks." The Inspector's eyes lifted to the restful, unbroken glow of the opposite wall. They were getting all too many of such "remarks" at Headquarters lately. Why, when he had been in the field force—He shook his head and then had the grace to laugh at his own dawning pomposity. The important point was—the man in the field *knew*. He read the final sentence on which his decision must be made.

REMARKS:
   Must term operation "solution dubious"—critical plus—require extreme powers under 202 classification.

                              Com Varlt, MW in charge.

Com Varlt. The Inspector triggered a button with one of those nervous finger tips. The report flashed off and in its place was a series of code symbols. Hmm, that agent had a rather impressive record all the way along. The Inspector's hesitation was gone. He pressed a second button and smiled almost grimly. Varlt had asked for it—now he had his wish. Only "solution dubious" had better turn out "Solution Satisfactory"! A new report clicked on the reader and the Inspector turned to consider another case.

Chapter One

The window was a square of gray light at the narrow end of the small hotel room. Blake Walker regarded this evidence of another day with an odd detachment. He moved—to snub out a cigarette in the tray beside the bed. Then he collected his watch from the table. A minute past six. And what he had been waiting for the past hour must be very close now—

He pulled his six feet of lean muscle and fine bones out of the bed and padded into the bathroom to plug in his razor. From the mirror his own eyes, tired and dark, stared back at him without curiosity or interest. In the artificial light his thick cap of hair appeared as black as his brows and lashes—but in the sunlight it would be red, so dark a red as might rightly be termed mahogany. Only his skin was not fair, but a smooth and even brown, as if before birth he had acquired a permanent sun tan.

Shaving was a perfunctory business, conducted mostly from force of habit, since his area of beard was small and grew slowly. His black brows twisted together now in a familiar frown as he wondered, for perhaps the thousandth time, if he did have Asiatic blood. Only, who had ever heard of a red-haired Chinese or Hindu? Not that he could trace his parentage. Detective Sergeant Dan Walker had brought the resources of an entire city police force to bear on that problem some twenty years ago, after he had stumbled on the "alley baby." Patrolman Harvey Blake and Sergeant Dan Walker had found him

and later Dan had claimed him for a son. But he would always wonder about the two years of his life before that.

Blake's well-cut mouth became a grim line under the pressure of
memory. Sergeant—now Inspector—Dan going into the First
National to buy traveler's checks for that long-awaited trip—running
into a holdup in progress. Dan Walker had been shot down and it
had not lessened Molly's heartache to know that he had taken his
killer with him. After that there had been the two of them, Molly
Walker and Blake. Then Molly went to bed one night and did not
awake in the morning.

So now he was alone again, cut off from the only security he had
known. Blake put down the razor carefully as if that motion was a
part of some intricate and necessary action. His eyes were still on the
mirror, but they saw no reflection there, certainly not the lines of tension suddenly aging his face. It was coming—it was very close now!

The last time that feeling had driven him into Molly's bedroom
and his painful discovery there. Now it was urgently pushing him
toward the hall. He listened, knowing of old that there was really
nothing to hear—this he could only feel. Then, with quiet cat's feet,
he went to the hall door without snapping on the room light.

With infinite caution he turned the key and eased the door open.
He had no idea of what waited on the other side—he only knew that
some action was being so forcibly demanded of him that he could
not disobey even if he wished.

For one moment he stared. Two men stood, their backs toward
him, one behind the other. A tall man wearing a loose coat, his dark
hair still glistening with the sheen of sleet, was fitting a key into the
door on the opposite side of the corridor. His companion held a gun
jammed against his back.

Blake, his bare feet making no sound on the carpet, moved. His
fingers locked about the gunman's throat and he jerked the fellow's
head back. Instantly the other man whirled. Almost, Blake thought,
as if he had known what was about to happen. His fist swung up and
connected with just the right point on the threshing captive's jaw;
then Blake was supporting the full weight of an unconscious man.
But the other took hold, waving Blake back into his room, following
him quickly, the prize in tow. Once inside he dropped his burden to
the floor without ceremony and locked the door.

With a doubt or two, Blake sat down on the edge of the bed. Why so little fuss on the part of the suddenly released prisoner? And why come in here with the captive?

"Police—?" His hand went to the phone on the bedside table.

The tall man turned. He brought out a wallet and flipped it open for Blake to read the card inside. Then the younger man nodded.

"No police?"

The other shook his head. "Not yet. Sorry to barge in on you, Mr.—Mr.?"

"Walker."

"Mr. Walker. You helped me out of a tight hole there. But I'll have to ask you to let me handle this my own way. We won't bother you for long."

"I'll finish dressing," Blake got up.

The Federal Agent was squatting on his heels by the slumbering gunman. And Blake was knotting his tie when a scene, reflected in the mirror, drew him back to the bedroom. The self-introduced Kittson was searching his unconscious prisoner and the oddness of that search intrigued Blake.

Slowly the Federal man ran his fingers through the oily hair of the other, apparently in quest of something on the skull beneath. Then with a pencil flash he examined both ears and nostrils. Last of all he explored the gunman's half open mouth, withdrawing a dental plate. He made no sound but Blake sensed his triumph as he freed from underside of the plastic denture a small disc which he wrapped in his handkerchief and stowed away in an inner pocket.

"Care to wash now?" Blake asked casually.

Kittson stiffened. He looked up, straight into Blake's eyes. And his own eyes were strange ones—almost yellow, unblinking, like those of some hunting feline. They continued to bore into Blake—or to try to—but he met stare with stare. The agent got to his feet.

"I would, for a fact," his voice was mild, deceptively so, Blake believed. He was certain that in some way he had surprised the man, had failed to respond as the other had expected him to.

When Kittson was wiping his hands there came a knock at the door.

"My men," the agent appeared as certain of that as if he could see through the wall. Blake unlocked and opened the door.

Two men stood outside. Under any other circumstances Blake might not have given them a second glance, but now he watched them with double intentness.

One was almost as tall as Kittson and his wide boned, freckled face was surmounted by a thatch of bright red hair only partially concealed by his hat. The other, in contrast, was not only short but small, delicately boned, almost frail. They gave Blake flickering glances as they passed him, and he felt as though he had been measured, catalogued and filed for all time.

"Okay, chief?" asked the red haired one.

Kittson stepped aside to reveal the man on the floor. "He's all yours, boys—"

Between them they brought the gunman to partial consciousness and took him out. But Kittson remained and, when they were gone, locked the door for the second time.

Blake watched this move with raised eyebrows. "I assure you," he kept his tone light, "I have no connection with the departed."

"I am sure you have not. However—"

"This is a matter which should not concern me—is that it?"

For the first time Kittson's tight lips moved in a shadow smile. "Just so. We would rather no one knew about this little episode."

"My foster father was on the police force. I don't talk out of turn."

"You are from out of town?"

"I'm from Ohio, yes. My foster parents are dead. I came here to enter Havers," Blake answered with the exact truth.

"Havers—so you are an art student?"

"I have hopes," Blake refused to be drawn. "But five minutes of checking on your part will support all my statements."

Kittson's shadow smile broadened. "I don't doubt that at all, young man. But tell me one thing—just why did you open your door at the crucial moment? I'll swear you couldn't have heard us coming up the corridor, not through these walls and—" He was frowning now, watching Blake with that same hunting cat intensity, as if the young man presented a problem which must be solved.

Blake lost a fraction of his assurance. How could he possibly explain those queer flashes of foreboding, which he had had at intervals all his life, warning him of danger to come? How could he explain to this man that he had been sitting in the dark for at least an hour certain that trouble was ahead and that action on his part was necessary?

Then, moved perhaps by that unblinking, demanding stare, he plunged: "I just had a feeling that something was wrong—that I must open the door."

And those tawny eyes held his as if they would bore into his skull and lay bare every one of his thoughts. Suddenly he resented that suggestion of invasion, and found he was able to break away from that odd hold, that compulsion.

But to his surprise Kittson was nodding. "I'll buy that, Walker. I've faith in hunches. Well, it was a good thing for me that yours—" He paused, froze into immobility except for a gesture with one hand which held Blake as quiet. Kittson might be listening, but though Blake strained his own ears he could hear nothing at all.

A second later there was a discreet tap at the door. Blake got up. Kittson was as still as a hunter waiting for prey to come within striking distance. But his head turned to Blake and he shaped words with such exaggerated lip movements that the younger man could read them.

"Ask who?"

Blake went to the door, his hand dropped to the catch but he did not release it as he asked, "Who's there?"

"Hotel security officer." The reply was prompt, only slightly muffled by the barrier. A hand came over his shoulder with a scrap of paper. Block letters read, "Say—check with desk."

"Let me check with the desk," Blake called. He flattened himself against the door. There was no objection, no answer from without. But, after a moment, Blake heard the faint footfalls of someone moving away. He went back to his seat on the bed.

Kittson had preempted the single comfortable chair and was gazing out into the air shaft as if he found the brickwork beyond of absorbing interest.

"I take it that that was *not* the hotel dick?"

"No, he was not. Which puts us all in a jam of sorts." Kittson took out a cigarette case, offered its contents to Blake, and snapped a lighter for them both. "That was an attempt to discover what had happened here. Unfortunately it means that you have now been linked with us. And that leads to complications all around.

"There are good and sufficient reasons why we do not want our actions to become public. We shall have to ask you to cooperate with us."

Blake stirred. "I'm just an innocent bystander. I didn't come here to play cops and robbers. And I'm not even asking what I'm mixed up in—which I believe shows some restraint on my part." Again Kittson smiled faintly and Blake continued, "I just want to go about my own business. . . ."

Kittson tossed his hat on the desk and leaned back his black head to blow a perfect smoke ring. "And we'd like nothing better than to see you do just that. But I'm afraid it's too late for second thoughts now. You should have had those before you opened your door. Others have taken an interest in you, and that might prove—at the best—embarrassing. At the worst—" his eyes glinted like gem stones through the smoke and Blake felt an odd chill, almost a suspicion of that same uneasiness which had drawn him into this adventure. Kittson was implying things, and the force of his implications was heightened by the very vagueness of his words.

"I see that it begins to dawn on you that this is serious. When must you report at Havers for classes?"

"The new term begins next Monday."

"A week. I'm going to ask you to play along with us for that period. If we have any luck this case will be settled by then, or at least your part of it will. Otherwise—"

"Otherwise I might be taken care of for my own good and yours?" Blake demanded. But he recognized the voice of authority. This man was used to giving orders which were obeyed without question. If he said "Remove Blake Walker and put him on ice," Blake Walker would be removed with the same speed and efficiency as the gunman had earlier been extracted from this room. No one ever gained by ramming a stone wall head on. Better follow orders—at least until he could learn more about the setup.

"All right. What do I do?"

"You vanish. Here and now. How much luggage do you have?"

Kittson was on his feet, across the room to open the closet before Blake really understood that reply to his question.

"One bag." Something, perhaps the power of the other's personality swept Blake into action he would not have considered an hour before. He snapped the suitcase shut and took out his wallet to count out some bills on the top of the chest.

"I take it that we do *not* check out formally." It was more a statement than a question and he was not surprised as Kittson swiftly agreed.

The gray light outside the window had brightened very little. It was five minutes after seven, but the dusk within the room was that of evening as the agent snapped off the light. Blake shrugged into his top coat, picked up his hat and bag, ready to follow as the other beckoned him out into the hall.

They did not take the turn leading to the elevator, but instead went to a firedoor. Stairs, five floors of them, silent and deserted as the hall had been—then Kittson paused for a moment before another door, giving the impression of listening. Down another flight of stairs, narrower, not so well lighted, threading through a place of storage compartments to more steps going up. They emerged on the open street with the chill drizzle of sleet in their faces. Blake was sure that his guide not only knew exactly where he was going, but that they had been unobserved throughout that flight. His belief in the efficiency of the agent's organization was settled for all time as a taxi came in at the curb almost as they crossed the strip of pavement. Kittson opened the door and Blake obeyed the implied order. But to his surprise the agent did not join him. Instead the door slammed shut and the cab pulled away.

For the moment Blake was content to follow orders and see where all this stage managing would leave him. But, as he had more time to think and was out of the range of Kittson's electric personality, he was surprised at his own compliance with every suggestion the agent had made. If this wasn't some weird dream it came very close to it. Undoubtedly the wisest thing for him to do would be to stop this cab and disappear on his own. Only he had a very strong suspicion that Kittson would sooner or later catch up with him again and that then their relationship would be on a far less easy footing.

The taxi wove through the narrow roads in the central park in a shuttle pattern which completely baffled Blake's scant knowledge of the city. Then they came out on the main streets once more. Morning traffic was on the move and the cab rounded busses, bored between trucks and private cars. It slowed at last to whip into a narrow alley running between blank walled buildings which might be warehouses. About three-quarters of the way down this the driver pulled to a stop.

"Here y' are."

Blake reached for his wallet. But the driver said, without turning around, "It's already paid, Mac. You go in that door, see? Elevator there. Punch the top button. Now make it snappy, Mac, this here's no place to park!"

Blake went on in to be confronted by the glass frosted panel of a self-operating elevator. He punched the top button and tried to count the floors as he moved upward creakily, but he was not sure whether they came to stop before nine or ten.

Beyond was a scrap of hall, hardly more than standing room before a single blank door. Blake knocked and the portal opened so speedily that he thought they must have been awaiting him.

"Come in, Walker."

Blake had been expecting Kittson. But the man who greeted him was the elder of the agent by at least ten years. He was shorter and his hair was brindled with gray threads among the dark brown. But, as inconspicuous as he might have been in a crowd, there was a quiet distinction in his air. He was as much a personality in his way as the more aggressive Kittson.

"I am Jason Saxton," he introduced himself. "And Mark Kittson is waiting. Just leave your things here."

Deftly separated from coat, hat and bag, Blake was ushered into an inner office where he found not only Kittson but the red haired man who had helped remove the gunman in the Shelborne.

The room was bare except for a wall range of files, a desk and three or four chairs. There was not even a window to break the gray walls, matched in shade by a carpet under foot. And the lighting came from a concealed source near the ceiling.

"This is Hoyt," Kittson indicated the redhead abruptly. "You made the trip without incident, I see."

Blake wanted to ask what kind of an "incident" Kittson had expected him to encounter, but he decided that his wisest move now was to let the other fellow do the talking.

Hoyt was slumped down in his chair, his long legs stretched out, his hands, with their fringing of coarse red hairs, finger-laced across his flat middle.

"Joey knows his stuff," he observed lazily. "Stan will report if any-one showed undue interest."

"I believe you said your father was a policeman. Where? In Ohio?" Kittson paid no attention to his colleague's comment.

"In Columbus, yes. But I said my foster father," corrected Blake. He was on guard, aware that every word he spoke was being noted, weighed by all of the three fronting him.

"And your real parents?"

Blake told his story in as few words as possible. Hoyt might have dozed off during that recital, his eyes were closed. Saxton gave it the courteous attention a personnel man would grant that of a job applicant. And Kittson continued to study him with those hard, amber eyes.

"That's it," he ended.

Hoyt arose in one lithe and strangely graceful movement. His eyes, now fully opened, Blake noticed, were green, as vivid in color and as compelling when he turned them on one, as were Kittson's.

"I take it Walker is staying?" he asked of the room at large.

Instinctively Blake glanced at Kittson; the final decision lay with the agent he was sure. And on the desk he now noticed something new. In the middle of the green blotter was a small ball of crystal. Some movement of the agent's must have disturbed it for it began to roll toward Blake. It had almost reached the edge of the desk when he put out his hand and caught it.

Chapter Two

Its weight suggested that it was a natural crystal. But when he reached out to replace it on the desk there was a change in it. He had caught a clear ball, what he now held was a globe in which swirled a blue-green twist of vapour. As he continued to hold it that vapour grew more dense, thickened, until the color was solid.

The change was uncanny. Blake set it down as if the ball seared his flesh. Now the blue-green was fading once more. But Saxton was on his feet, crowding forward against Hoyt to watch the transformation. Kittson's hand covered the sphere. The blue-green was gone. But had there been the beginning of another change? The agent dropped the globe into a drawer. Not before Blake was certain that in a few short seconds that the other's fingers had been in contact with the crystal an orange-red mist had begun to collect within. Before he could ask a question a warning buzz from a plate set in the wall was an interruption.

There followed the hum of the elevator and Hoyt answered the door, admitting his small comrade of the early morning.

"Everything satisfactory?" That was Kittson.

"Yes," the voice was light, musical. He might have been a boy hardly out of his teens, until you saw his eyes, assessed the very faint lines about his almost-too-well shaped mouth. "There was a tail: that squat punk from the Crystal Bird. You'd think they wouldn't use the same men so often."

"The supply of proper material may be strictly limited," suggested Saxton.

"For which we should give thanks," Kittson caught him up. "One raid, if we could be sure of getting all the dupes together, would put our friend out of business here."

"To send him hopping," Saxton's slow voice was clearly warning. "Better keep him on this level." His eyes touched Blake and he was abruptly silent.

The young man who had just come in shrugged out of his coat and draped it across a chair. "Roscoe isn't too bright. I left him nosing a cold trail. We needn't worry about him for an hour or so. Walker's in the clear for the time being."

Kittson leaned back in his chair. "That may be. But they'll back-track on him when it dawns that he's given them the slip." He turned to Blake. "Did you tell anyone at the hotel that you were going to attend classes at Havers?"

"The doorman. I asked him about a bus to get out there. But he's used to questions about transportation; he must be asked a hundred a day. He won't remember just one."

The others, by their expressions, did not agree with that hope.

"People have a way of recalling just what you want them to forget, when it is made clear to them that it is important," Kittson remarked. "We'll keep you here a couple of days, until we can assess the amount of excitement your disappearance causes—that's the only way to check their interest in you. Sorry, Walker. You need not remind me that this action is undue interference in your private life. I know that as well as you do. But sometimes situations develop when innocent bystanders have to suffer for the general good. We can give you comfortable quarters and your stay is for your own protection as well as for the safety of our investigation."

"I think," Saxton got up, "that our first gesture of hospitality might be to offer breakfast."

And Blake, rising to that bait readily enough, followed him through the second door in the office into an astonishing suite of rooms. The furniture was modern in monotones of gray, green and odd, misty shades of blue. There were no pictures and in each room the lighting came from the ceiling. A TV set of some size stood against one wall and a great many books, papers and current magazines were profusely scattered in piles on tables, and stacks on the floor, within easy reach of each chair.

"Our quarters are a little cramped," his host informed him. "You will have to share my sleeping accommodations, I'm afraid. In here—" He opened a door off a short hall to display a sizeable room with twin beds.

"And here breakfast awaits."

There were no windows. Blake puzzled over that as he took his place at a table and Saxton went to the wall, pushed aside a panel and lifted out a tray which he put before his guest, bringing out a second for himself.

It was a hearty meal, excellently prepared, and Blake enjoyed it. Saxton smiled.

"This is one of the cook's generous mornings." He pushed aside a pile of books.

They were all histories, some English and some American, and they bristled with small paper markers as if some program of intensive research was underway. Saxton indicated them.

"They represent a hobby of mine, Walker. It is also, in a manner of speaking, connected with my employment. You are perhaps yourself a student of history?"

Blake took time to think as he swallowed a bite of ham. Either he was jumpy or Saxton had purpose behind this line of conversation.

"My foster father collected books on criminal history—famous trials, things like that. I read those—and diaries and letters—Pepys' eyewitness accounts."

Saxton held his coffee cup poised, studying it as if it had suddenly turned into a precious bit of antique china. "Eyewitness reports—just so. Tell me, have you ever heard of the 'possibility worlds' theory of history?"

"I've read some fantasy fiction founded on that. You mean that idea that two complete worlds stem from every momentous historical decision? One in which Napoleon won the Battle of Waterloo, say, and our own in which he lost it?"

"Yes. There would be myriad worlds, all influenced by various decisions. Not only by the obvious ones of battles and political changes, but even by the appearance and use of certain inventions. A fascinating supposition."

Blake nodded. Sure, the idea was interesting, and it was manifestly Saxton's hobbyhorse. But at the present moment he was more absorbed by the predicament of one Blake Walker and *his* possibility worlds.

"There are points of departure even within the past few years," the man across the table was continuing. "Conceive a world in which Hitler won the Battle of Britain and overran England in 1941. Suppose a great leader is born too early or too late."

Blake's interest was sparked. "I read a short story about that once," he agreed. "How a British diplomat in the early 1790s met a retired Major of artillery dying in a small French town—Napoleon born too soon."

"But suppose," Saxton had set down his cup and now he leaned forward his eyes alight, "suppose such a man, born out of his time in his own world, were given the ability to move from one possibility line to another—would he not be doubly dangerous? Suppose you were born in an era in which your own society stifled your particular talents, giving you, as you thought, no proper outlet."

"You'd then move to where you could use them." That was elementary. But Saxton was beaming at him as if he had been a bright pupil coming out of a quiz with honors. There was definitely something behind all this—what? His warning sense had not been alerted, but he had a feeling that he was being carefully steered along a path Saxton had chosen for him and that it was being done under orders.

"That might be a good idea," he added.

But that was *not* the right answer this time.

"For *you*," Saxton rapped out. "But perhaps not for the world you moved to. That presents another side to the problem doesn't it? Ha! Erskine! Come and join us."

"Any coffee left?" It was the slender, blond man. "No? Well, press the button, Jas. I need reviving after a rugged morning.

When he dropped onto the bench beside his older colleague he smiled at Blake, a flash which wiped the boredom from his face and gave his well-cut features warmth and life.

"We're to stick around here," he announced. "What did you do with the paper, Jas? I want to see the TV program. If we have to be cooped up we might as well enjoy it."

He removed a fresh jug of coffee from behind the panel and loaded his first cup with two heaping teaspoonsful of sugar. When they returned to the sitting room Erskine seated himself before the

TV. There was something odd in his absorption in the very ordinary entertainment offered, almost as if TV were a new toy which enchanted him. As the program signed off he sighed.

"Amazing appeal for such primitive stuff—"

Blake caught that murmur. But the show had not been some ancient movie. It was a "live" and fairly well done production. Why the application of "primitive"? There were tiny threads of "wrongness." A suspicion triggered by Saxton's table conversation crossed Blake's mind only to be smothered by sane reason.

They were undisturbed for the rest of the day and evening though without windows it was difficult to say whether it was day or night. Erskine and Saxton played a card game which Blake was sure he had never seen before. They ate heartily of the meals which came from behind the panel and Blake browsed amid the wealth of reading matter. It was predominately historical or biographical in subject. And the spiking of reference slips continued from book to book. Was Saxton planning to write an article on his hobby? Blake continued to think about the problem the other had proposed that morning.

A man born out of his time on his own world, but able to visit a new one in which his particular talents could bring him the power he craved. He found himself producing some fantasies of his own based on that.

Who were his companions, or maybe it should be *what* were they? He was still thinking lazily of that as he drifted off to sleep some hours later.

He awoke in the dark. There was no sound from the other bed. Blake wriggled out from between the covers and investigated. The other bed was rumpled but empty. He went to the door and opened it a crack.

Kittson, one arm about Saxton's shoulders, was being supported down the hall. There was a dark stain on his shirt and his feet stumbled as he went. A moment later both men passed through the door at the far end and it closed. But on the carpet a shiny spot rested like a coin. Blake stooped to touch it and his finger came away both wet and red. Blood!

He was still waiting for Saxton to return when sleep overcame him. When he roused again, the lights were aglow and the other bed was smoothly made. Blake dressed hurriedly. Kittson had been hurt, but why the secrecy?

As he went out into the hall he looked for the stain. It was gone as he had thought it would be. But when he ran his fingers over the pile they detected dampness. Someone had made a thorough job of cleaning, and not long ago. It was now he consulted his watch, half-past eight, Tuesday morning. And he had some questions to ask.

Jason Saxton was alone in the living room, a topheavy pile of volumes resting on the coffee table before him, a secretary's notebook half-filled with minute script on his knee. He glanced up with a smile so open that Blake curbed his impatience.

"I hope that I did not disturb you this morning, Walker. We're short-handed and I'm to take over the office. So you'll be more or less left to yourself today."

Blake murmured an agreement and went on to the dining room. Erskine was there before him. His smooth face was drawn and tired, and there were brown smudges under his heavy-lidded eyes. He grunted something that might have been a greeting, and waved a hand at the panel. Blake withdrew a tray and sat down to eat, leaving it to the other to initiate conversation. But Erskine was apparently not one of those souls who felt their brightest in the morning. After he drank his coffee he got up.

"Have fun!" he bade Blake almost sardonically.

"I shall," the other assured him. And then wondered if he had given his plans away by his inflection. He was almost sure Erskine had shot a doubtful glance at him before he left the room.

Blake lingered over the meal, wanting to have the apartment to himself for his own purposes. He made sure the office door was closed behind both men when he readied for action.

In the center of the living room he stood still, listening. Then he crossed to put his ear to the panel of the outer door. He could hear, very faintly the murmur of voices, followed by the opening and closing of file drawers. A rumble—surely that was the elevator. Cautiously he tried the door and was not in the least surprised to find it locked.

Blake went back to the hall off which opened the bedrooms and got down on his knees. There was more than one damp spot in the carpet. And they led to the door through which Kittson had been helped the night before. This, too, was locked and he could hear no sound from beyond. But the next room was open for his inspection and it was very similar to the one he shared with Saxton. Both beds were smoothly made; there was no sign of luggage. Bureau drawers opened to display neat and innocent piles of clean shirts and underwear, socks and neckties.

There were an unusual number of suits in the closet and they ranged from well-cut tweeds, through ultra-conservative business wear, to Levis and semi-uniforms such as delivery men might use. Apparently the inhabitants of the apartment were sartorially equipped for every occasion. Well, that might be demanded of F.B.I. agents. As yet he had discovered nothing to suggest that they were not exactly what Kittson claimed them to be.

But Blake was not satisfied. He found a small automatic in the drawer of a night table. But that could not be evidence of what he sought. The few toilet articles were well-known brands such as could be bought in any drugstore. He did note hair dye which again could be easily explained.

After ten minutes he had searched all the easily accessible places. Dare he really tear the place apart without leaving any evidence of his investigations? He was sure, after surveying the meticulous neatness of the bed making, that he could not. But he did empty every drawer and turn it upside down to see if anything had been taped to bottom or sides. The worst of it was that he had no idea of what he was looking for except that he wanted some concrete answer to certain fantastic suspicions.

He went through Saxton's half of his own room with the same thoroughness, finding nothing. After that he did not try to search the living room but he did check the office door; it was still locked and very quiet as if Saxton, too, had now gone out.

No one joined him for lunch, and boredom drove him to the books. He could not rid himself of speculations concerning Saxton's time traveler, inventing a few possibility worlds which might attract such a man. How would it feel to step into another such level? Suddenly he was cold, chilled and apprehensive. What had seemed an exercise of the imagination began to take on sinister connotations.

It was easy enough to accept the idea of a civilization being upset by a single man with an overwhelming belief in his own destiny and a power of character; his world had had its share of earthshakers and movers native born. The driving force of those men had been a vicious appetite for power.

And that was a human drive right enough. Unite it to the supreme type of egotism which does not brook any opposition and you get a Napoleon, an Alexander, a Caesar, the Khans who almost smashed Europe as well as Asia.

And picture such a man frustrated in his own world but able to move on to one ripe for his rise! Suppose that *had* happened in the past. Blake reined in his imagination and forced a laugh which echoed too hollowly in the silent room. But he did not wonder at Saxton's absorption with the theory.

He put aside his book and stretched out on the wide couch. It was getting on into the afternoon. Would they let him go by Friday? Hush-hush stuff. Grade-B spy thriller.

His mind and body tensed. He stared up unseeingly at the ceiling. Something was on the way. All that warning which had been pulling at him in the hotel yesterday was now flooding back a hundredfold. Vague discomfort shaped speedily into the sensation of being hunted, of danger approaching.

Blake sat up, but he did not stoop to put on his shoes. This was stronger, in its way worse, than any of the attacks he had known before.

He went down the hall to the door through which Kittson had gone. The last time he had experienced this it had been associated with the agent. The door was still locked. He rattled the knob, knocked as his discomfort grew. There was no answer from within.

Blake returned to the living room and there the menace was intensified. As a weathercock influenced by an unseen wind he wheeled toward the office door, pressing against it, very sure that whatever was coming had its source in that direction.

He not only heard the rumble of the elevator but felt the vibration of its rise. Its passenger must now be in the small hall outside the office. Was Saxton waiting to receive the invader?

It was in that moment, without knowing just why, Blake ranged himself on the side of the four men whose quarters he now shared. They had told him very little; there was much which needed explanation—yet now he was one with them, and this newcomer could only be defined as the enemy.

There was no click of the door, no movement within the office. Then he caught the faintest of scratching sounds as if someone were working at the lock. It lasted for only a moment. The stranger might be as intent upon listening as Blake was.

But he was totally unprepared for what followed. Suddenly he was conscious of an intangible presence, a personality without body or substance. It was as if that other listener had projected an emanation of himself past the barrier he could not force. Through that utter silence the intrusion provoked panic.

Blake backed away from the door, some inner core rebelling against possible contact with that—that Thing! But a second later he returned to his post, positive that if the other got into the office physically, he was going to know it.

For a space that weird sensation of another's presence persisted. But he was certain that it was not yet in turn aware of his occupancy of the room. He was becoming adjusted to it, able to relax for a second, when, with a cat's leap it struck straight at him.

Blake's hand went to his head. Contact had come as sharply as a blow, a blow which addled coherent thought. With the other hand he clung to the door knob, with a queer feeling that the one sane and ordinary object between his fingers would keep him safe against that foul onslaught.

For, having once established touch, the thing—power—personality—however it could be identified, attacked viciously. It was a spike ground in between Blake's eyes, striving to force a path to his brain.

As he held to the knob with a frenzied grip, gray blurs of pain veiling the room, his body shook with long nervous shudders. No physical torture, he thought, could ever equal this. He was meeting a test as out of place in his time and world as the personal Devil of the middle ages might be.

The agonizing pressure faded, but Blake did not dare to believe that it was retreating for good. And his refusal to believe in escape was justified, the other had not abandoned battle. For the attack swept in a second time, prying, biting in search of an easy victory.

Chapter Three

Blake endured as the floor rolled in sickening waves under his feet. There was no measure of time. He could only hold to reason and sanity typified by the door knob sticky with his sweat.

He was dully surprised that his ears could still catch the sound which brought an abrupt end to that malevolent assault: the buzz of the warning within the office. There was an instant withdrawal on the part of the enemy. Blake heard the sound of the elevator.

Erskine or Saxton returning? If so, were they about to walk in unwarned upon the danger lurking out there? There was nothing he could do, no way he could prevent it.

The elevator bumped to a stop, paused, and then began a jerky descent. And it took with it the presence which had haunted the room. The whine thinned, to be followed by utter silence—that other had gone.

Blake was on his knees, his forehead resting against the door, his stomach churning. He started to crawl. With the aid of the nearest chair he got to his feet and staggered on, making the bathroom just in time. Weak with retching, he leaned against the wall. For the worst of that attack had been the feeling of being utterly befouled.

When he could keep his feet he pulled off his clothing and stepped into the shower. Only when the water had alternately cooked and frozen his flesh for long moments did he begin to feel clean once more. Dressing was a task. He was as tired as if he were moving about for the first time after a long and serious illness.

Blake wavered out into the living room to collapse on the couch. So far he had concentrated on the obvious, on being wretchedly sick, on bathing and dressing. His mind refused to be pushed beyond those immediate actions. But now to think about it made him sick again. He began to repeat random lines of poetry, slogans, anything with rhythm. But between one word and another, oozing over and through and by those lines his lips shaped, he recalled painfully that strange attack. He was alone now; he would swear to that. And yet the invisible slime left by that visitor was thick in the air he drew into his lungs. He could almost smell its stench.

That sound—the elevator again! Blake tried to sit up. The walls whirled. He clawed wildly at the fabric of the couch. Then he blacked out.

He awakened in his bed, hungry and oddly alert from the second of returning consciousness. From somewhere came the murmur of voices. He got up. Doors were open in the hall and he listened without shame.

". . . canvassed the whole town, up, down and sidewise. His story is true. Foster child of the Walkers. Found in an alley by two cops . . . the whole fantastic thing. He's well enough liked but he seems to have no very close friends." There was no mistaking Hoyt's drawl.

"Found in an alley—" Saxton sounded thoughtful. "I wonder. Yes I do wonder."

"Any signs of substitution and erasure, or applied false memories?" Kittson's demand cut through.

"Nobody I met showed them. I don't see how he could possibly be a plant—"

"Not a plant, no," that was Saxton again. "But perhaps something else. We aren't all knowing. No close friends. If what we suspect is true, that would inevitably follow. And the evidence of the selector was certainly emphatic enough. We can't afford yet to take the position of 'who I don't know is against me.' And he did come to Mark's aid at the Shelborne."

"Just how do you rate him, Jas?" Erskine asked.

"Latent psi, of course. Which bothers him as it naturally would.

Intelligent with something else I can not put name to yet. What are you going to do with him, Mark?"

"What I'd like to know," Erskine again, "is what happened here this afternoon. He'd blacked out; perfectly limp when we found him. Took both of us to stow him in bed."

"What would happen if a psi with the sort of barrier that lad naturally possessed met a mind probe?" Kittson inquired with chill dryness.

"But that would mean—!" Saxton's voice was a shrill protest.

"Certainly. And we'd better begin thinking about Pranj's being able to do just that. I want to ask that young man some questions as soon as he is awake. You did give him a restorer shot?"

"About third strength," Saxton assented. "After all, I'm not sure of the reactions of his race. I'm not even sure about his race." The last sentence might have been a thought spoken aloud.

Blake walked into the room. All four of them eyed him without surprise.

"What do you want to ask me?" he spoke to Kittson.

"What happened here this afternoon?"

Choosing his words carefully, trying to keep all emotion out of it, Blake detailed his adventure. There was no disbelief around that circle. A little of his belligerence ebbed. Were they *used* to such attacks? If so, what in the world—or who in the world—was this quartette of hunters trailing?

"Mind probe," Kittson was definite. "You are sure he did not physically enter the office?"

"As sure as I can be without having watched him."

"Well, Stan?" Kittson's attention shifted to the boyish Erskine who was curled up on the couch.

The slight blond man nodded. "I told you Pranj was an adept. He did a lot of experimenting the Hundred never knew about. That's why he's so deadly. If Walker hadn't been psi, and a barrier psi at that, he'd have sucked him dry like this!" He snapped his fingers.

"What is psi?" Blake broke in, determined to have a few answers which would make sense as far as he was concerned.

"Psi—parapsychological powers—is extrasensory perception in different fields, abilities which mankind as a whole has not yet learned to exploit." Saxton had turned schoolmaster again.

"Telepathy—the communication between one mind and another without the need for oral speech; Telekinesis—transportation of material objects by power of will; Clairvoyance—witnessing of events occurring at a distance. Prevision—foretelling of events to come; Levitation—the ability to move one's body through the air—these are phenomena which have been recognized in part. And such attributes may be latent in an individual; unless he is pushed by circumstances into using them, he may not know that he possesses psi abilities."

"Why," Kittson broke into the lecture, "did you open your door on Monday morning, Walker—just at the right moment for me?"

Blake answered with the truth. "Because I thought that I had to—"

"Did that compulsion come suddenly?" Saxton wanted to know.

Blake shook his head. "No. I'd been feeling—well, uneasy for about an hour. It always works that way."

"Then you've had it before. Does it always foretell danger?"

"Yes. But not danger to me—or at least not always."

"And afterwards," Kittson was addressing Saxton now, "I was unable to take him over because of his natural shield."

"I don't see why we should be surprised," Hoyt contributed for the first time. "It stands to reason that since we were the same stock in the beginning, we're going to discover latents here and there. We're lucky that so far we haven't run into any true power men—"

"Do you mean," Blake selected his words carefully, "that all of you have such powers and can use them at will?"

For a long moment they were silent, the other three looking to Kittson as if waiting his decision. He shrugged.

"He knows too much; we'll have to take him all the way. If Pranj's men pick him up now . . . And we can't keep him under wraps forever, though this is beginning to look like a long term job." He held out his hand and the package of cigarettes lying near Erskine's knee floated lightly across several feet of space to make a neat landing on his palm.

"Yes, we have control over some psi powers. The degree varies as to the person and his training. Some are better telepaths than telekinesists. We have a few teleports—people able to project themselves from one point to another. Precognition is common to a degree—"

"And you *aren't* F.B.I. agents!" Blake added.

"No, not agents of the F.B.I. We are members of another law enforcement body, perhaps just now more important to the well being of this world. We are Wardsmen. Jas has told you of the possibility worlds, only it isn't his hobby or only a theory but cold fact. There are bands, levels, whatever you wish to call them, of worlds. This world has been reproduced innumerable times by historical events. My race is no older than yours, but by some chance we developed an extremely mechanized civilization several thousand years ago.

"Unfortunately we possessed the common human trait of combativeness and the result was an appalling atomic war. Why we did not end by blowing ourselves out of existence as other level worlds have done and are doing right now, we shall never know. But instead of total destruction, the result, for a handful of widely scattered survivors, was a new type of life. Probably the second generation after the war was largely mutant, but we learned to use psi powers.

"War was outlawed. We turned our energy to the conquest of space, only to discover that the planets in our system were largely inimical to man. Expeditions left for the stars—none have yet returned. Then one of our historian-scientists discovered the levels of 'Successor Worlds' as we term them. Travel, not backward or forward in time, but across it, became common. And, because we are human, trouble developed too. It was necessary to keep a check on irresponsible travelers, prevent criminals from looting on other time lines where their powers gave them vast advantage. Thus the organization we represent came into being.

"We maintain order among travelers but in no way may we interfere with action on another level. Before we take a case we are given a complete briefing on language, history, customs of the level on which we must operate. Some levels are forbidden to anyone except official observers. Others no one dares to enter—civilization—or the lack of it—there has taken such a twist that it is unsafe.

"There are dead, radioactive worlds, worlds foul with man-made plagues, worlds held in subjection under governments so vicious that their inhabitants are no longer strictly human. Then there are others where civilization is poised on a trigger edge, where the mere presence of an outsider might wreck the status quo.

"Which brings us to the case now in point. We are after—well, by the standards of our culture he is a criminal. Kmoat Vo Pranj is one of those super egos who craves power as an addict craves his drug. We no longer have nationality divisions within our world, but we do have differences of race due to barriers caused by the atomic war of the past. Saxton and I represent a group descended from members of a military unit which was cut off for several hundred years in the extreme north on this continent. Hoyt's ancestors took to living underground in that island known to you as Great Britain, developing a separate culture of their own. While Erskine, like the man we hunt, is a member of a third grouping, limited to less than a million, all springing from a handful of technicians who remained in a compact community in the South American mountains, working for expert control of psi powers."

"In addition to which," Erskine's voice was colorless, remote, "we also produce from time to time variations of the stock who have the unpleasant natures of our remote warlord ancestors. Pranj wants a world to conquer. Not being able to realize that ambition on our level, in fact now that he is recognized for what he is, he will be subjected to corrective treatment, he seeks an outlet for his energy elsewhere. He played the role of a normal so well that he was able to enter our Service and mastered training to the point of level travel without supervision.

"Now he is in search of a level where civilization is ready to allow him full scope. Having found such a world, he will build up an organization and make himself ruler of the planet. Part of his unbalance is a super self-confidence. He lacks all elements of self-doubt, remorse or any softer virtue. Our purpose is not only to take him into custody but to repair any damage he might have already done."

"You think he is here—right here?" Blake had passed the point of accepting or not accepting the fantastic story; he was merely listening.

"You may have met him this afternoon—if not face to face," was Erskine's sober and apparently sane reply.

Kittson produced a small cube of some clear substance. For a moment it rested on his palm, then it lifted, to sail across to the hand Blake extended rather gingerly. Through the clear envelope he looked down at a tiny figure, bright with color, glowing with a life-like hue as if the cube did encase a living manikin. The tiny man had the same sharply marked cheekbones, delicately cut thin lips, blond hair which were Erskine's. But there was in addition a subtle difference and the longer Blake studied the figure the more marked the difference became. Erskine was aloof, his air of detachment must be inborn, yet one sensed that there was no malice, no assumption of superiority in his manner. This statuette was of a man who was ruthless. There was a shadow about the corners of the lips, a slight shade about the eyes. It was a cruel face, an arrogant face, and a very powerful one.

"That is Pranj—or rather as Pranj was before he disappeared," Kittson explained. "What type of disguise or cover he may have assumed we do not yet know. We have to locate him in spite of it."

"Is he working alone?"

Hoyt shook his head. "You met one of his dupes at the Shelborne. He has recruits, none of whom, we think, know the real truth. He provides some of them with varied gadgets which tend to make it harder for us."

"Any one of us," Kittson took up the explanation, "can master mentally the types Pranj draws to him, if they are unshielded. That thug in the hotel was wearing a shield to protect his mind against mine."

"That disc you found in his mouth?"

"Just so. Luckily an essential ingredient in those can be obtained only on our level. And Pranj can not have too many to scatter around."

"Let us get back to this afternoon," Erskine cut in. "I think we can be sure Pranj made us a visit. Somebody used a probe on Walker and we didn't. Pranj—do you agree?"

Saxton sighed. "We must move. Such a pity."

"But we are lucky in this much," Erskine had not finished. "What if he had come when all of us were gone? We might never have known until too late that he had spotted this place. So we're ahead there. What about it, Mark, do we move?"

"Yes. I'm sure that this level world is his main objective. If he is hopping for safety, he'll come back to fight. And he can't have his way here until he removes us, a job which we shall make as difficult as possible. Now," he turned to Blake, "it's up to you. Frankly, you know too much for our comfort. You'll *have* to come in with us."

Blake stared down at the carpet. Big of them to offer him a choice, he thought wryly. He did not doubt that he would be efficiently dealt with if he said "no." But after this afternoon he found that he had not the slightest idea of replying in the negative.

"I agree."

They accepted that without thanks or comment. He might have said that it was a pleasant night out. And then he was forgotten as Kittson gave orders:

"We'll move tomorrow after Jas has a chance to check on number two. Hoyt, you patrol the Crystal Bird beat. There's no hope of getting at him there, but try and discover how many of the attendant goons are wearing shields. Erskine—"

The blond man shook his head. "I've a job of my own. Today I thought I spotted a Ming-Hawn throat jewel in one of those antique jewelry shops along the parkway. The store was closed, so I'll have to make sure the first thing in the morning."

"Ming-Hawn!" Saxton's voice trailed off into a breathy hiss.

Kittson studied a smoke ring. "Might be. If Pranj's hard up for ready cash, a few things of that nature sold in the right places would be a good fund raising project."

"But any expert seeing it would ask questions! And he doesn't want exposure any more than we do!" protested the other.

"I don't know about exposure. Not all Ming-Hawn pieces are so distinctive that they would be recognized as alien art. You weren't absolutely sure yourself, were you, Stan?"

"Almost certain. I want to handle it. But it's worth investigating. Suppose I take Walker with me."

For one anxious moment Blake was afraid that Kittson would refuse. But reluctant or not, the agent finally agreed. And when he woke in the morning, after a dream-filled night, Blake was aware of an inner excitement which was not a warning.

With Erskine he descended to the basement of the building, traversed a dingy pawn shop there. The proprietor of this daw's nest did not even look up as they went out his front door. They reached the corner just in time to swing on board a bus. Before they had gone five blocks they were in another section of town with wider streets and smarter shops. And having crossed to thriving intersections Erskine signalled to leave the bus.

"Second from the corner."

The shop Erskine indicated was aristocratically somber in black and gold paint. There was a wrought iron grill covering the lower part of the show window to protect but not conceal the display within. Erskine pointed to a piece close to the glass.

It was a pendant of a silvery metal set with discs of black, on the surface of each of which were intricate patterns in enamels. There was something vaguely oriental about the piece and yet Blake could not place it as belonging to any Eastern art he had ever seen.

"Ming-Hawn right enough. We've got to find out how it came here."

Erskine went into the shop and addressed the man who had risen from behind a desk to greet them.

"You are Mr. Arthur Beneirs?"

"Yes. There is something I may show you gentlemen?"

"I am told that you buy as well as sell curiosities, Mr. Beneirs?"

The man shook his head. "Not from the general public, sir. I am sometimes called in to bid upon objects which must be sold to settle estates. But otherwise—no."

"You would, however, value an art object?" persisted Erskine.

"Perhaps—"

"This, for example?" Erskine held out the crystal ball Blake had himself held two days before.

"Rock crystal," Beneirs turned it about. But to Blake's amazement this time there was no change in the color of the sphere. It remained clear and uncloudy.

Then, without a word, he put it down, went straight to the window and took out the pendant. When he handed it to Erskine he spoke rapidly, as one reciting a memorized lesson.

"This was brought to me two days ago with other antique jewelry by an attorney, Geoffrey Lake. I have often had dealings with him before in estate sales. He did not tell me from whom he had received it, but I think it was given to him to sell privately. Lake is a man of good reputation—his office is in the Parker Building, suite 140. The price I paid was two hundred and fifty dollars."

Erskine brought out a wallet and counted out some bills. With almost mechanical movements Beneirs picked up the money while Erskine put the piece in his wallet. He then pocketed the crystal. Beneirs, as if they were now invisible, went back to his seat behind the desk, paying no more attention to them.

Chapter Four

"There must be some simple explanation for Mr. Beneir's remarkable cooperation," remarked Blake mildly as they went out.

Erskine laughed. "Simple is right. The sphere not only proved that he had no psi powers, but enabled me to take him over and he responded by telling everything he knew. Beneirs won't even remember us. He'll have some vague memory of selling the Ming-Hawn piece, but if he has to report back to this Lake, he will not recall any of the details of the transaction. So now we're one piece ahead in the game, having a line to Lake."

"But what is Ming-Hawn?"

"Who, rather than what. Ming-Hawn was an artist in enamel, a form of art peculiar to his successor world, who did his best work at the end of the 18th century. He inhabited a world which exists as the result of a successful Mongol conquest of all Europe occurring in the thirteenth century. Refugees from that invasion, Norman, Breton, Norse, Saxon, fled westward by ship to Viking colonies in Vinland. Their descendants intermarried with Indians from the spreading native empires in the southwest and formed the nation of Ixanilia which is still in existence on that level. The present civilization is not an attractive one, but it offers possibilities which might attract Pranj. However, now we want Lake."

Erskine turned into a drugstore and made his way to the phone booths. He picked up the classified directory and pushed the other to Blake. "See if his home phone is listed."

Blake was still searching when Erskine made a call. He emerged from the booth frowning.

"Lake's ill—in the hospital. Lives in the Nelson Arms."

"No number listed there for him," Blake answered.

"Hmmm." Erskine produced a second dime and this time his voice reached Blake faintly from out of the booth.

"Geoffrey Lake, attorney, Nelson Arms. We want the usual report as quick as you can make it. Yes." He hung up. "Now back to our hole-in. This is moving day."

"Somebody will check on Lake?"

"We pay an investigation agency for such routine. If Lake's straight we can work it one way; if he's crooked he may be sitting in Pranj's pocket. Then we'll have to be more cautious."

They did not return through the cellar pawn shop, but made their way around the block. Erskine grinned at Blake.

"More than one door to a fox den. You'll have to learn 'em."

"You've a rather elaborate set-up. Wasn't it difficult to arrange?"

"Not so much. In the worlds we visit constantly for trade or study we have permanent bases manned by our people under a good cover. This is a makeshift, but it coincides in space with one of our shift bases and, being a warehouse, it was easy to lease and make our own interior changes."

Erskine led the way into the dingy lobby of a small office building. The white haired man lounging on a stool before the open door of the elevator put aside his tabloid and smiled at Erskine.

"'Lo, Mr. Waters. Good trip?"

"Fair, Pop. The boss ought to like the sales report. How's the back?"

"'Bout as usual. All the way up?"

"All the way. The boss must have pigeon blood, he likes it so high."

He gave the elevator operator a cheerful grin as they creaked to the top floor.

"You off duty at four as usual, Pop?"

The old man nodded. "If you ain't through by then, you walk down," he warned. "But you never are, are you, Mr. Waters?"

"Not while the boss is watching. But it's easier to walk down than up. Take care of yourself, Pop."

There were two doors in the hall, and one bore flaking lettering across its ground glass surface. But when the elevator sank out of sight Erskine unlocked the plain metal one leading to the roof. They mounted a half flight of stairs to the open air. Before them was the canyon of the alley. Erskine lifted a board to the parapet, swinging it out until the other end rested on the warehouse roof.

"If heights bother you," he told Blake, "just don't look down."

Once across, they descended a stair into a dusty corridor. There Erskine stopped, spread both hands flat against the wall, and under his pressure a panel moved, letting them through into one of the bedrooms of the hidden suite.

"Did you get it?" Hoyt stood in the doorway.

"Got it—*and* a lead. Beneirs, the owner, bought it from Geoffrey Lake, estate attorney. I put J.C. on to him."

"What's this about an attorney?" Kittson called from beyond.

Erskine made his report.

"Suppose he is really ill? Or could it be a stall?" Hoyt wondered.

"Pranj knows that we're here. But I'm inclined to think he sold that Ming-Hawn piece before he discovered that. He must need cash and need it badly; so I want to know a lot more about this Lake—especially about Lake's contacts, any visitor he's had since he went into the hospital." Kittson swayed back in his chair to study the ceiling. "Mr. Lake is ill. It is the proper time for Mr. Lake's dear friends to be thoughtful."

Hoyt got up. "Fruit, flowers, or the bonded stuff routine?"

"Flowers suggest the feminine touch. We don't know enough to venture that. Fruit is nicely middle of the road. A medium sized offering and you might put Mr. Beneir's card in it."

"What about moving? Are we going now?" Erskine asked as Hoyt went out.

"Sooner or later. Wait 'til Jas has checked the other place. No use settling in there only to discover there are watchers about. We have some advantages including unlimited funds. And the type of henchmen Pranj has to enlist demand their pay on time. If he's taken to selling other level loot, it proves that the Hundred were able to seal off his resources back home."

The phone rang. Kittson listened. "Good enough. The usual fee will be mailed to you." He hung up.

"J.C. on Lake. He's middle-aged; from a family who have run the same law firm for four generations, conservative; most of the business is handling estates and trusts; a bachelor, nearest relative is a sister in Miami; had an operation two weeks ago; no direct contact with Pranj's men."

"Kmoat can be very convincing," Erskine pointed out.

"We'll let Hoyt learn what he can at the hospital. I want to know if Lake is shielded. And I have a feeling that from now on we may have to move fast."

He was interrupted by the buzzer, and then Saxton came in. He shed a conservative homburg and a well cut tweed top coat before he sat down.

"Everything is in order for the move. But our alley here is under observation. I had to use the roof route."

"Who's in the alley ?" Erskine wanted to know.

"A muscular person we last saw supporting one of the walls of the Crystal Bird with his shoulders. He's one of their strong-arm boys. Do you know," Saxton took a cigar case from his pocket and made a careful selection from its contents, "the cleverest move for Pranj to make at present would be to involve us in some disagreeable incident which would focus upon our activities the attention of the local law? That would gain him time and force us to temporarily withdraw from this level."

To Blake's surprise he discovered that all three were looking to him. Kittson spoke first.

"What charge would you select to make us trouble with your police?"

"Considering your semi-secret set-up here," he answered slowly, "they might say gambling—or drugs. Either would get you raided. And a hint to a Syndicate contact that you were operating some new racket in a closed territory would bring them down on you too."

Saxton pursed his lips in a silent tut-tut. "In other words he could make us plenty of trouble now that he has run us to earth. I would say move and at once!"

Kittson nodded." All right," He took a small map out of a drawer. "The Crystal Bird is located in the basement of that converted brownstone. Some apartments over it, aren't there?"

"Three, two occupied by members of the club staff," Erskine supplied.

"TV antenna on the roof?"

"At least one."

"Then we'll do the repair act."

"When?" Saxton wanted to know.

"Now. Send a messenger through to clean out this place."

"Can't we eat first?" Saxton sounded plaintive and Kittson agreed after a short hesitation. They were gathered about the table when Hoyt returned.

"Boy friend in the alley and another keeping his eye on the sky route," he announced, "or is all this stale news?"

"Lake?"

"Well, he hasn't a shield. But I didn't get to see him. His sister is due in from Miami on the four o'clock plane—"

Kittson looked at Erskine. "A pleasant encounter between one lady and another out at the airport might lead to bigger things," he mused in a mild voice.

The slight man sipped his coffee slowly. "The things I do for the Service! For this job I shall put in for the Star and Cross Bars."

Kittson's smile was ironic. "'It is necessary at all times,'" he was plainly quoting, "'to select the agent to fit the job, and not the job to fit the agent.'"

"A beautiful bit of pass-the-buck if I ever heard one," Erskine remarked. "Meditation will supply me with a fitting retort. Also deeds, not barren words are the order of the day. I only hope that what I learn from this flying female is going to be worth going into skirts." He left from the table.

An hour later a fashionably dressed woman wearing a tailored suit with a mink clutch cape left the apartment accompanied by Saxton. And twenty minutes after that departure, Blake was a member of the second exodus. Neither Kittson nor the others had done any packing and it appeared that he himself was expected to abandon his belongings, a casual disregard for economics which bothered him.

Wearing the coveralls of repairmen, the three took the elevator to the basement. Hoyt's thick hair was now brown and there was an odd alteration in his jaw line, squaring it more, while two front teeth protruded a little in squirrel nakedness below his upper lip.

By the same mysterious means, Kittson's features had coarsened.

The hawk sweep of his nose was thicker and displayed a reddish flush. The same craft made his eyes seem a little too close together, and he walked with a lumbering gait.

They did not go through the pawn shop but in the opposite direction, winding up through an air shaft court and a second door into a parking space. There was a panel truck, the sign on its side reading: "Randel Brothers, TV-Radio Repairs."

"You can drive?" Kittson asked Blake.

"Yes."

"Take the wheel; Hoyt'll direct you." With eel-sinuosity the tall man coiled up in the limited space behind.

"Straight on to the street and turn right."

Blake proceeded with caution down the narrow way.

"This is one bolt hole they didn't find," Hoyt commented as the truck edged into traffic.

But he was answered from the van. "Shielded mind not more than a half-block behind—"

Hoyt tried to look back. "We'll take the long way around just in case. They following, Mark?"

"Yes. I can't locate which car—too many on the street."

Blake wondered why he was not uneasy. Either the precognition which these others had insisted was his was not working on schedule, or they had nothing to fear.

"A green delivery truck, but it's turning off a block back," Kittson added to his report.

Hoyt's attention went to Blake. "How's the hunch working? Are we heading toward trouble?"

"Not as far as I can tell."

"That truck may be delivering another shift of stakeouts for duty, to watch an empty mousehole," Hoyt mused. "To be on the safe side, we'll lay a fancy trail. Turn left at the next corner, Walker, then straight on five blocks to the ferry."

"It's close to three o'clock." Kittson sounded a warning.

"Ferry takes about five minutes to cross. We can cut over the end of the freight yards and hit the highway at Pierce and Walnut. Make it back into town at the Franklin bridge. Use up about forty minutes, but if that doesn't foul up any tail, nothing will."

"Very well," Kittson sounded resigned.

On the ferry they changed drivers and by inspired mastery of his vehicle and a knowledge of routing, Hoyt brought them back into the city from another direction in five less than his forty minutes.

From the crowded business section they passed into a district which had been fashionably residential fifty years or so earlier. Tall brownstones were built about an iron fenced park. But now many of the houses had fallen to the indignity of small grayish signs of "Rooms" in the lower windows and several had been converted into shops. Hoyt pulled up at the end of a block. The steep stairway leading down into the half-basement was covered with a curve of awning and a neon sign flashed on to notify the world that this was the Crystal Bird.

The thick winter dusk was gathering in and there was a hint of worse weather to come in the steady sifting of large snow flakes. As far as Blake could see, save for their truck, the street was clear of both cars and pedestrians. But after he had stopped the motor, Hoyt did not get out; he remained where he was as if listening. When he spoke, it was hardly above a whisper.

"Two shields in the club. But I think the house is clear."

"Yes," assented the unseen Kittson. Then he scrambled out of the back as Hoyt gave Blake his orders.

"Be ready to pull out in a hurry if we have to run."

Kittson came around and held out a comic book. "Stay in character but don't get too interested in the literature."

Blake slumped down in the seat, and over the edge of the comic watched the other two climb to the front door and be admitted by a drab woman.

More lights winked on through the dusk—dim ones in the "Rooms" houses, brighter ones in the shops. Now there were more people on the street. One man, his head bared in spite of the snow and rising wind, took the steps down to the entrance of the club with a speed suggesting he was late for an appointment. Blake wondered how it would be to reach out and read the thoughts of those passing.

Then came something he did understand—Danger! A smothering pillow of danger pressing down upon him. He could taste it—feel it! Not since his encounter with the presence had Blake been so shaken. His fingers curled about the wheel and he forced himself to look about to try and discover the source of the warning.

He could see nothing new in the house containing the Crystal Bird. The neon blazed, a light or two was visible in the windows above. From that point his gaze traveled slowly down the block, appraising each house: no people, no cars. Wait!

On the other side of the square a delivery truck had stopped before one of the shops—a green truck.

Hoyt had ordered him to stay at his post. But over there he was sure was the source of his warning. If he got out—walked only a foot or two. . . .

Only the building tension held him in the driver's seat. On impulse he started the motor. He looked back at the club. A tall shadow flitted around the side of the house making for him; a second followed the first. Then the one to the rear stopped beside a rubbish can, grabbed off the lid and groped in its depths, just as the first reached the truck and climbed into the van. Blake gunned the motor. The man by the can thrust something into the front of his jacket and joined them with a couple of running leaps. As Hoyt got in Blake gave the warning:

"Green truck—there on right—!"

Hoyt leaned out as they swept past. "Denise, Gowns," he read aloud. "Pranj disguised as three yards of silk and a belt buckle. Perhaps—"

But Blake's attention was divided between his driving and the overwhelming sense of menace.

"Turn right!" Hoyt snapped.

Another street of old houses. Street lamps made wild white whirls as the snow fell through their beams.

"Left, here—"

He drove automatically by Hoyt's direction. There was no sound from the rear where Kittson had gone to cover. A series of turns brought them out on an avenue bordering the large park which almost bisected the city.

"Get into the park and then let me have the wheel."

Blake eased through the growing rush of homeward bound traffic and brought the truck into the obscurity of tree and brush which made an effective screen against city lights; then he changed seats with Hoyt.

They went on, switching from wider ways to narrow ones until at last they came out on a cindered parking lot beside a white theater-restaurant closed for the season.

"All out!"

Blake hit the cinders in time to see Kittson slam the back door.

"Come on!" The agent turned away.

"Where?"

"We get out of the park at 114th street. You cross the avenue there and wait on the opposite corner for the 58 bus. Take that and get off at Mount Union, about a forty minute ride uptown. Walk down Mount Union to the first street—that's Patroon Place. Go to the service entrance of the third house—the one with the wall around the yard. Knock twice. Got that?"

"Yes."

They did not speak again during the walk out of the park. And once outside the other two left Blake without a goodbye, speedily lost in the crowd on the pavement.

He crossed the street and joined the group at the bus stop. Fifty-Eights were, he discovered, not too plentiful, and he had to squeeze into a jammed one. The massed buildings of the lower city gave way to private homes set in yards.

There was a drugstore on the corner of Mount Union, a brilliantly lighted super mart of its kind. But the block he was to walk was dark, the lamps far apart. One block down and Patroon Place. He counted houses.

Number three had a row of lighted windows. The gate to the drive was open and recent tire marks slicked down the snow. Sound was muted here. As Blake stepped over the beginning of a drift to reach the back door the wind drove a flurry of flakes into his face. He rapped as instructed. The door opened and Erskine drew him into light and warmth.

Chapter Five

Warm, dressed once more in his own clothes which had appeared mysteriously in an upstairs bedroom, Blake came into a small room furnished with the heavy pieces of an earlier century. Hoyt sprawled in one of the massive chairs.

He was watching with doting care a very small black kitten absorb chopped raw meat, and when he noticed Blake's arrival he indicated his feline charge.

"Meet the Missus. She sure can tuck it away, can't she?"

The tip of the kitten's tail flicked as if in acknowledgement of the introduction, but she continued to chase scraps of beef with single-hearted devotion.

"Did you take her out of that ash can?"

Hoyt's smile vanished. "She was tied up in a sack and left to freeze."

The kitten, her center section ball-round, sat down to make washing dabs with her paw. She paused to look up at Hoyt, her baby eyes blue circles. Then with a spring she landed on his knee, kneading his slacks with thumb-sized paws, singing a song of content.

"She's going to be a help." Hoyt drew a finger around the furry head, rubbing all the right spots behind ears and in the angle of her jaw. "This level doesn't realize the possibilities of its natural resources. Cats and dogs and some birds can be contacted mentally if you try. Yes, Missus here is going to be a help. The more since

Pranj," his grin was no longer pleasant, "hates all her kind. I wouldn't be surprised that it was by his orders Missus found herself exiled today."

The kitten relaxed in slumber and a drowsy feeling of well-being enveloped the room.

When Blake awoke in the morning, it was to the soft hiss of snow against the window pane. Outside drifts ridged high. Thursday; Blake counted off the days since this wild adventure had begun. It seemed longer.

The garage was open. Down a path shoveled from the house, two foreshortened figures, whom he was sure were Erskine and Saxton, went to get into the car and drive off.

Blake did not hurry. Who were the owners of this house, he speculated, as he went downstairs. There were two servants, a cook and a maid, who kept to themselves. Who had welcomed the agents here, and why?

Kittson was alone in the small dining room watching the snow swirl outside the pane. And the kitten sat on the sill, making dabs at the glass, as absorbed as its human companion. The radio had been turned on and the newscaster was announcing that the snow level was rising, that the city was fighting to keep the main streets clear. There followed some ominous comparisons to the big blizzard of five years back and the two-day tie-up of services which had ensued.

"It's getting worse," Blake ventured.

Kittson only grunted and the other realized then that the agent was in one of his trances of concentration. Were each one of these strangers in themselves receiving sets tuned in on message lengths they alone could pick out of the air?

Hoyt came in, his shoulders still powdered with snow. "It's almost as bad as glue," he informed them as he picked up the kitten. "Out this far they've given up trying to keep the side streets clean."

"If we're tied down by the weather," Kittson moved restlessly from window to chair and back again, "so is Pranj."

Hoyt shrugged and sat down, turning his attention to the kitten. If he had not witnessed what followed Blake would not have believed it. He had always heard that cats could not be trained to do tricks, that their innate independence kept them from obeying any will but their own. But in some manner the big man established contact with the minute bundle of black fur. Round kitten eyes stared into Hoyt's and the tiny feet moved, the small body climbed or ran, or little jaws closed upon a scrap of paper and carried it the length of the room to drop into a waiting hand. But kittens tire, and after a few moments Hoyt allowed his pupil rest.

It was mid-afternoon when Blake decided to go out. Both of his companions were in the peculiar trance state, perhaps they were in contact with action elsewhere. He was not only restless but in some way resentful, feeling as if he had been deliberately shut out.

The cook was standing by the back door. "Do you think you could get as far as the drugstore?" she asked abruptly. "Agnes has one of her headaches and will be good for nothing the rest of the day if she doesn't get her drops. The silly girl waited too long to have her prescription filled." She had a paper in her hand.

"I'll be glad to get it," he plunged out into one of the whirls of wind driven snow.

There was a holiday mood inside the store. Highway workers were gathered there drinking coffee, exchanging good and bad news with such customers as had fought their way in. Blake listened as he waited for the prescription to be filled. This was real—the way life was. The fantastic world he had inhabited for the past three days was a dream.

How could one believe in other level worlds, in criminals hopping from one to the next, in psi men who could turn life upside down and shake it while you watched them? If he had any sense he would walk out now—away from the house on Patroon Place, out of the reach of Kittson. He could do it if he was not again nagged by the thought that it would do no good, that escape from those forces was impossible. Real world, dream, he was trapped in this.

But he was still rebellious, as he had been since waking that morning. He suspected that he was as much a tool in his way as the kitten Hoyt now trained. They would use or lay him aside as they thought expedient. It was a parent-child relationship and it aroused antagonism.

Was that resentment recognized and fed by something outside himself? Had he during those hours been deliberately prepared for what was to happen? Afterwards Blake sometimes believed that he had been so conditioned for the kill.

Outside the grayness of the afternoon had deepened into a

premature night. Blake stamped off clinging snow between strides. Then he saw that other figure ahead. There was no mistaking, as he thought, the slim outline, the quick walk—Erskine.

A car came slowly along the cleared way. And with it a twist of apprehension hit Blake. Danger—danger for Erskine in some way. Blake shouted, plunging on. But the other, bending against the push of the wind, neither saw nor heard.

The car pulled up beside him, two dark forms dropped from it and went at Erskine in a rush. Blake's feet struck a slick patch of ice. He fought for balance, but at that moment a bolt of mental pain blasted him into utter blackness.

There was a throbbing ache beating in his head. Blake tried to remember what had happened. He was gagged, his mouth filled with cloth, tape across his lips. It was dark and his hands and feet were tied. When he jerked in his bonds he learned that the man or men who had put those on knew their business. He tried to roll over and discovered that he was inside a container, his knees cramped up against his chest.

Erskine! Had the other been taken prisoner, too? For all their powers the psi men had their limitations. Kittson had been unable to escape from the shielded thug in the Shelborne. Blake wished though that he had one of the others' powers. If he could only communicate now with Erskine! He was still aware of his own private warning system, but he had met its prod so often lately that he was familiar with such uneasiness.

He was not dead so the kidnappers must have a use for him. How had they managed to get on the trail so quickly? Or had they been after Erskine and collected him as additional bonus? How long would it be before Kittson and Hoyt would discover and come to the rescue? (That they would not make any move on his behalf never occurred to Blake.) Could their mysterious "Listening" inform them of this disaster?

No use asking himself questions to which he had no answers. It was more profitable to concentrate on what *he* could do . . . which was nothing at present.

Blake had no way of telling how long that trip lasted, but he felt the jerk of their stop. There were low voices. The box which held him was propelled forward and fell, jarring him painfully.

Warmth now and more voices. Something else. He caught a trace of perfume. At last a bump deposited the box on the floor and feet retreated. Warmth. Perfume. Blake strove to fit pieces together. The green van—the dress shop across from the Crystal Bird?

His cramped limbs were numb, he could do no more than move his head from side to side. There was a crack of light and from time to time he could hear muffled conversation.

When they did let him out he would be a sitting duck, too numb with cramp to put up any resistance. But—Pranj was psi. And any-one raised in an environment where psi powers were the norm would depend upon those powers consciously and unconsciously, considering those who did not have them inferiors.

Blake had sensed a trace of this same attitude in the agents, although they had been conditioned to live as ordinary citizens of non-psi worlds. In the process of training they had lost their conscious superiority. But Pranj would have no reason to conceal his talents. Would not his dependence upon them blind him, lead him to undervalue opponents except those from his own world?

In spite of his aching head, Blake forced himself to study the situation with what calmness he could muster. What did he have: a latent psi power of precognition of dangers and a strong mental shield. Very small advantages to set against Pranj's arsenal of invisible weapons. But the shield—it had held during his first encounter with the outlaw. Suppose such an attack would be leveled at him once more? Could he build on that barrier a false set of memories to be read by the enemy?

His body might be immobile but his mind raced, exploring that possibility. If he only knew more! Could he make Pranj believe that he was only an innocent bystander? With a few alterations he might tell the truth and it would bear that out.

What if he still believed that the agents were from the F.B.I, tracing a normal criminal of this world? The story would fit his actions and might satisfy Pranj into believing he was relatively harmless.

Without more than a vague idea of what he was trying to accomplish Blake set to work. He recalled the details of his life back home—that he had come to attend classes at Havers. That was true—it could be checked. In his hotel room he had been startled by a sound, he made himself remember that sound. He helped Kittson to escape the thug.

Kittson had shown him identification. They had made him join them. Ruthlessly he tried to overlay true memories with false. The visit to Beneirs, the assault on Tuesday, the story the agents had told him; he must forget those. And as he fought that strange battle in his own mind Blake was surprised. It was almost as if his efforts, crude as they were, awakened new skills, new and keener insights.

The light outside flashed off. For a moment Blake's preoccupation was broken by a wave of real panic. Was he going to be just left here? It was difficult to breathe, the cramp was crippling. Could he stand hours of such confinement?

That touch of hysteria was frightening until the new part of his mind, the section which observed and evaluated, saw how it could be put to use. To be afraid was the correct reaction. And fright in a way was telepathic, might be picked up by the enemy. Fear would add to his protecting cloak.

Blake had come a very long way since he had been taken prisoner, made a journey down a path he had not even known existed before. Shock was stimulating growth and he was no longer the same Blake Walker who had been taken captive on a snow-drifted street. He never would be again.

The light went on again; there was the heavy tread of feet. A cover was ripped off and he blinked up into brightness before he was sprawled out helpless on the floor. A kick twisted him around and he stared up at two men. Neither of these, even disguised, could be Pranj. Swiftly Blake thought bewilderment and fear.

"Yeh, he's one of them all right. And he's awake."

"Told you he was." The smaller man spat out a chewed matchstick. "What yuh gonna do with him?"

"Take 'im to th' boss. Git them ropes off his legs. We ain't gonna lug him."

The smaller man produced a switch blade and sawed at the cords about Blake's ankles. When he saw that the captive was watching him, he displayed rotting teeth in a grin and stabbed threateningly. Blake allowed himself to flinch and both men laughed.

"You be good, sonny boy, or Kratz'll cut more'n ropes."

"Sure thing," the other replied. "Me—I'm good with the sticker. Can carve you either neat or messy. Don't ask for it—see!"

Blake was dragged to his feet and slammed against the wall with a grip which kept him pinned in that position. The numbness in his legs gave way to the torture of returning circulation. As he was enduring this, a third man came in, a curious twist of his upper lip in a cruel dark face showing the points of two fang teeth.

"Take him over the lower way." One glance disposed of Blake.

"Sure, Scappa."

Between his captors Blake was hurried along in the wake of Scappa, down a dark hall and a flight of stairs. There was a well opening in the floor and Scappa descended into this followed by Kratz. Then Blake was lifted and dropped casually. He nearly blacked out with the force of his landing, but he was not allowed to lie in peace. The big man came down, picked him up, and bore him on.

Through an opening in the wall they came into a second cellar. Blake was placed on a chair, jammed against it so that his bound arms were crushed and a muffled grunt of pain forced out of him. The big man looped a strand of rope about him, anchoring him firmly to the seat.

Scappa jerked a thumb at his henchmen. "Get out!"

To Blake it appeared that the other two were only too glad to mount the rough wooden stairs and vanish through a trapdoor. Scappa, once they had gone, spread a handkerchief on a step and seated himself, lighting a cigarette. He had the air of one waiting for a curtain to go up on an eagerly anticipated theatrical performance.

When the assault came it was not the stabbing probe Blake had met before, but slow, inexorable pressure—a pressure which warned that this time the enemy meant to be the victor.

Blake held his thoughts to the selected memories he had prepared. It was easy to allow self pity to creep in also. Why should he be dragged into this battle. Slowly, under the prodding of the door, he revealed the meeting with Kittson and what had happened afterwards.

He no longer saw the cellar nor Scappa lounging there. In an odd way his sight was turned inward. Even his fear must be carefully nourished, but it must not reach deep enough to endanger the wall of his edited recollections. The invader must not realize that there *was* a wall!

Blake had no way of knowing whether he was standing up to the test or failing. The probes were sharper, deeper, as if the mind launching them was growing impatient. Wearily Blake held to his story and the weird interrogation continued in utter silence.

Then the mind touch of the other withdrew. Blake shuddered. Again he was left with the sense of defilement, violation. But he had also a spark of hope. The barrier had not been assailed with the strength he had feared. Did that mean that Pranj had accepted him for the innocent, normal world dupe of the agents? He was aroused by a slap which rocked his head. Scappa's features set in a sadistic mask flickered through a red haze.

"Come and get this punk!"

The big man clattered down the rickety stairs. Kratz followed.

"So what do we do with him?" the knife man wanted to know.

"Whatta yuh think? Unload him back with the gunsel. Then we can forget about him."

"Sure." The big man fumbled with the rope. "Big Boss git what he wanted?"

Scappa's grin faded. "Big mouths talk too much. Git him outta here!"

"Sure, sure!" the big man was instantly placating.

He propelled Blake through the opening in the wall. Halfway along the tunnel he stopped and Kratz shone a circle of light on a metal door. Drawing bolts he opened the portal just wide enough for them to boot Blake inside.

"Ask the gunsel to untie yuh punk!"

Blake tripped, to slide along the floor, his face saved from a skinning only by the tape which held his gag in place. When he was able to twist his head around, the door had closed.

The dark and silence combined into a crushing weight. Perhaps he could inch his way to the wall and struggle up with his back against it. But now he was too tired to try. The chill from the pavement crept up his sweat bathed skin.

"In with the gunsel." He had been deposited in some private burial place. They had not retied his ankles, but his arms were a dead weight. Get up—move! But he was so tired; he ached with weariness.

Blake froze. There had been a sound out of the darkness. It came again from the other side of the unseen chamber. The gunsel. Blake controlled that thought. Something was moving now.

"Who's . . . who's there?"

Blake chewed on the gag which prevented him answering that hollow ring of voice.

"Why—why don't you answer me?" There was fear in that. "Answer me! Answer—!"

Movement again—toward him.

Erskine? Instantly Blake repudiated that. No matter what the ordeal he could not imagine Erskine's voice holding that note. He heard footsteps broken by pauses. Then a foot caught under his knee. With a scream the other tumbled across Blake, driving most of the breath out of him with the impact of their bodies. There was a flick of light, followed by an exclamation. Fingers explored his face, pulling at the tape.

With a cruelty which might be born of terror, the other ripped that away. The cloth was pulled out of his mouth and he was able to move his tongue. He wanted water more than anything he had ever desired in his life.

"Who are you?" demanded his companion querulously. "Why did they put you in here?"

"To get rid of me," Blake whispered huskily. "Can you untie my arms?"

He was unceremoniously turned on his face. His arms rolled, dead weights to his side, and he asked a question of his own.

"How long have you been here?"

"I don't know," the note of hysteria was stronger. "I was knocked out—woke up here. But . . ." Fingers dug into Blake's shoulder, pulling him up, "there may be another way out. They said something—"

With the assistance of the other Blake won to his feet.

"We go along the wall," he was informed. "There are only five matches left. And in the middle's a big hole."

The grip on Blake's shoulder urged him on that strange journey.

"You said 'another way out'?" he prompted.

"They said, earlier, before they threw me in. Something funny about it—they laughed—kinda nasty. But anything's better than this!"

"Take it slow," he admonished a second later.

How long that inch by inch progress continued Blake could not have told. But he was sure that the chamber was a large one. Then that other spoke again with a trace of excitement.

"This is what I found jus' before they dumped you in. Step up!"

Blake's chin scraped against a rise about a foot above the pavement. He went down on one knee and explored the surface by touch. It was slick, almost greasy smooth. Metal? He stepped up on it.

"I found something stickin' out at this end; it feels like a crowbar. If we could twist if off then we'd have a go at the wall over on the other side. Some of the stones are loose there. But yuh gotta help me git this lever loose first."

Blake was tense. Through every nerve and muscle the warning shrilled.

"Don't—!"

He got out only that one word before he was thrown from his feet as the surface beneath him shuddered. A faint greenish glow gathered and he saw that he shared a small platform with another dark figure whose hands clasped a lever protruding from the surface under them.

Chapter Six

The radiance was accompanied by sensation: wrenching, twisting, wringing which might be inside Blake, or actually heaving the raft on which they crouched. It seemed to him that this small square was the only safe refuge in a world gone suddenly mad.

Now that his eyes had adjusted to the light, dim as it was, Blake could see walls—if they were walls—billowing like smoke beyond. The green glow was about them on four sides and beyond that was utter chaos.

Other lights flickered, blazed, and were erased by patches of dark, all the blacker in contrast. Once a cone of cold blue, somehow deadly, roofed them in for a space. Blake caught glimpses of other things, and he dared not believe them real. Strange vehicles flashed by and several times the platform was in open country—once a countryside where a war was in progress, judging by the flares of red, the roars and concussions which rocked the raft and deafened the two clinging to it.

The other whimpered in fear, burying his head, but his hands did not release their hold on the lever. Blake wavered to him. That bar must control this impossible journey. If they were ever to stop, his companion must let go. Under him the carrier vibrated with a life of its own, and always outside the green bubble weird scenes developed and broke. Blake crawled to the other, pulled at his arm. But the grip with which the frightened man clung to the simple control was so frozen that Blake could not break it. Finally he had to bend the other's fingers loose one by one.

As the hands dropped, the lever snapped up. There was a whirling, a sickening swing. Blake slumped, bumping his head as the flitting shadows outside the green solidified.

"Wake up! Wake up!" Fingers raked painfully across his skinned face.

"What—?"

There was a real light on, a steady glow, softer than that of the electricity he knew. And he could see the man who was bending over him. A small man, thin to the point of emaciation, with an unruly lock of dull brown hair flopping down to his wide, wild eyes. Hands jerked at Blake, trying to pull him up.

"Wake up, damn you!" There were tiny white flakes of foam at the corners of the other's mouth. "Where are we—tell me, where are we?" His voice shrilled to a half-scream.

Blake levered himself up and looked around. They were still on the metal platform but it was apparent that they were not in the underground prison to which Scappa had consigned them. This was a large room and the floor was paved with blocks of a rust-red, the same shade tiling the walls. There were no lighting fixtures he could see, the glow appeared to diffuse from the ceiling. Long bench tables ran around three of the sides, tables covered with a multitude of objects Blake associated with a laboratory.

Except for the two on the carrier the room was empty, but a flight of stairs led up into unknown regions. Blake edged toward the rim of the platform, eluding the grab the other made for him.

"Don't go!"

"Look here," Blake turned on him, "as long as you don't fool around with that lever we're staying here. But I want to know where we are."

Level travel was the only logical—the only sane—explanation of what had happened to them. And when the other looked at the control stick as if it were a flamethrower pointed at him, Blake thought that he could be trusted not to touch it again.

Blake dropped his feet to the floor of that strange laboratory. He had half-expected that act to break the illusion—that everything would vanish when he tried to prove its reality. He stood up and moved a full step away. Nothing happened. It was solid under foot as the streets of the city where he had walked earlier. The faint plop-plop which had registered for the past moment or two proved to be the drip of water from a pipe running into a basin.

Water! Blake lurched across, catching at the table to regain his balance, to hold his hand under the leaky tap. Liquid ran over his dirty palm, trickled between his fingers. There was a row of buttons in the wall above the pipe. Made reckless by his thirst, he pushed the outer one on the right. The drip became a warm stream.

On the edge of the basin was a small cup, clean and dry. Blake filled it to the brim, gulping the tepid water. His thirst satisfied, he washed the grime from his puffed and swollen hands, allowing the water to run refreshingly over the deep purple gouges about his wrists before he splashed it over his face, where it stung in the scraped skin of his mouth and cheeks.

"Where are we?"

Blake looked around. The man had moved to the edge of the carrier and was staring about, curiosity plainly battling his fear. He was younger than Blake had first judged him, perhaps not beyond his own years, and his clothing consisted of a ragged pullover and a pair of dirt streaked corduroy pants. His brown hair needed clipping and his thin hands were never still, either pulling at his clothing or brushing that lock of hair out of his eyes and rubbing his chin.

"You know as much about it as I do," Blake countered.

The fellow did not look formidable, not that he would improve upon closer acquaintance either. But because they had made that queer journey together they were now united with an invisible, if uneasy bond.

"I'm Lefty Conners," the other introduced himself abruptly. "I'm a runner for Big John Torforta." He watched Blake narrowly as if trying to measure the effect of that announcement.

"Blake Walker, I was kidnapped by Scappa."

Lefty shivered. "He got me, too. Said I was workin' in his territory. That big goon of his put me to sleep and then I woke up in that cellar. Who you workin' for?"

"Nobody. I was with some FBI men and I think Scappa wanted to find out what I knew about them."

"Feds, yet! Whatta yuh know!" Lefty's interest was colored by awe. "Scappa's got th' Feds after him! Big John'll give a bill to hear that. But—" he glanced around and remembered, "we gotta get outta here first. Only where's 'here'?"

"We came when you pulled the control on that," Blake indicated the carrier.

"I couldn't!" protested Lefty vehemently. "I tell you I walked all around that place we were stuck in—all around. And there wasn't nothin' like this—nothin' at all!"

"What's your explanation then?" Blake silenced the other effectively. His own version of what had happened to them was one he had no intention of voicing as yet. He had been in the hands of Pranj's dupes—and this was, without doubt, Pranj's means of traveling to other time levels. It looked as if someone had imprisoned them in the "contact" point on his world and Lefty's meddling had wafted them through a whole series of successor levels, which would account for the strange things Blake had sighted.

But how much of this dared he pass along to his new comrade-in-misfortune? Suppose by some miracle they could return to their own world? Then all that he told Lefty would cancel out his claim of ignorance. He decided to keep his mouth shut at least for the present.

"How about that hole in the floor you mentioned?"

Lefty, clearly startled, looked up at the ceiling. "You mean this here's some kind of an elevator, and we came down?"

Weak as that was, Blake took it. "Your guess is as good as mine. At least we're out of that cellar."

Lefty brightened. "We sure are. And there ain't none of those goons hangin' round neither. What you say we have a look-see up them stairs? Geeze, jus' let me outta here and Big John'll pay plenty for an earful about this. Whatta silly lookin' joint this is. Whatta yuh suppose they do in here?" His nervousness was fading fast as his interest in his new surroundings grew.

"I'd say this was a laboratory."

"Like where they make atom bombs? Geeze—is that why the Feds are after Scappa? Maybe we'd better make tracks outta here but fast!"

Blake wanted to explore, he agreed with Lefty that far. But should they leave the vicinity of the carrier, their one link with their home world? He hesitated as Lefty, his self-confidence increasing with every stride, started toward the stairs.

"Get a move on, can't yuh?" the impatient whisper floated down as Blake followed, still reluctant.

He climbed into a short hall from which another stairway led up a second flight, and a half open door offered an invitation. Lefty was half crouched by the latter post of observation.

"It's some kinda store." But he did not appear too sure of his identification.

Shelves lined the walls beyond, crowded with small boxes and jars. The light was subdued and did not extend clear to the front of the room. Blake ventured in.

More shelves, save for where the door broke the pattern. There were no counters but a series of small tables with stools filled the main part of the open space. It might be a restaurant or cafe.

Blake tiptoed across to the front. There was another, wider door, perhaps giving on the street. His hand, resting on its surface, felt movement and he pushed aside a small panel. Yes—a street outside!

Snow lay in ragged, dirty patches, tinted blue by the rays of curious lamps fixed irregularly to the walls of neighboring buildings. He could see no tall structures and the street was narrow. Distinctly this was not the city he knew.

"Get away from there!" Lefty's hand clawed at his shoulder. "Want some cop to see us? We could get picked up for a break-and-enter job jus' bein' here!"

Blake closed the panel. Lefty was right; he had no desire to attract attention. But he had to learn where they were. This must be played slow and easy, without Lefty catching on for as long as possible.

If he could find a newspaper or its equivalent—some clue. Blake turned to the nearest shelves and picked up one of the containers, looking for a label. The pot was earthenware, beautifully molded, the cone top peaked into a knob. And the knob was a small head. Blake brought it into the light.

A head, right enough, but the head of nothing which had ever lived on any earth he could imagine—a hideous, grinning devil's head. Something like a gargoyle with a voodoo mask added. He put it back and explored farther.

There were no labels on the jars and they were tightly sealed. But there were variations in the head knobs which perhaps identified their contents to buyers. The horned and grinning one was lined up with ten identical fellows. But next to that regiment was a colony of long fanged, wolfish things, and beyond them a collection of a dozen or so he recognized almost with relief as owls, very realistically portrayed. A swift inventory showed demons of various sorts and a few more animals and birds.

"What's in them things?" Lefty did not venture to touch the jars, but paced along the shelves surveying them.

"No way of telling."

Why didn't Lefty question their surroundings—this building? Surely he was not so stupid that he could not see this was extraordinary.

"Say!" Lefty stopped short, "D'yuh know—I think this is one of them ritzy beauty shops where rich broads get their stuff straight from Paris."

"Could be." But Blake doubted if any woman would care for a jar of cosmetics enhanced by some of the gargoyle visages he could spot.

"Well," Lefty reached the door, "we ain't gonna get out this way. I bet if we laid a finger on the front door we'd raise an alarm to bring half the precinct boys down on our necks. Those ritzy places ain't never push-overs. Let's case the rest of the joint."

He went back into the hall and started up the second flight of stairs. Blake would rather have returned to the carrier. That platform had brought them here and if they were ever to return, it must return them. Was now the time to tell Lefty the truth? But something inside him still urged caution.

The stair gave on a second hall, longer than the one below. Blake surmised that the shop occupied only a limited portion of the building. Spaced along the wall were five doors, but none were open and there were no visible knobs or latches. The faint light coming from a blue line which ran along the molding made that clear. Lefty inspected the first with open surprise.

"Where's the knob?" he asked.

"The door might push to one side." But Blake was in no hurry to test his own suggestion. The last thing in the world he wanted to do was to walk into the private quarters of some other-level native, and try to explain not only who he was but what he was doing there in the middle of the night. With a faint shiver he imagined what would happen in a reversed situation in his own world—a marooned time traveler forced to account for himself before an assembly of indignant householders and police.

But Lefty was troubled by no such worries. He pushed at the nearest door, and when it resisted his efforts, went to the next and the next.

"What th'—!" As he reached the last door it did not wait for his touch but slid smoothly back into the wall.

A trap? Almost it had the appearance of one. Lefty made no move to enter the dark space beyond. Were they now expected? Blake wanted to sprint for the uncertain safety of the carrier. But Lefty still teetered in the doorway. Curiosity was battling his caution.

He crossed the threshold and let out a frightened squeak. Lights had flashed on. A photoelectric cell control? Blake was hazy about these things, but it could be. He looked over Lefty's shoulder into what was without doubt a sitting room. There were chairs, rugs, a table, ornaments on the walls. And the fact that there was a subtle difference about each one of those did not greatly concern him now. The main fact was that the room was empty and there was something in its perfect order which suggested that it had not been in use for some time. Heartened by this, Blake pushed past his awestruck companion.

The carpet underfoot was very soft, so yielding that Blake thought it closer to fur than any fiber. The chairs were barrel shaped, made of a light gray wood, each cushioned with a pad of silky fur. There were no lamps, the light came from a slender tube running about the four sides of the room at the join of wall and ceiling. Squares of opaque substance probably masked windows. Between these and over the long, fur-covered lounge were a series of masks hung like pictures. They were strikingly life-like, though Blake did not believe that they were meant as portraits. The eyes were exaggerated, set with gleaming stones in a flat, almost menacing, stare. Blake, after a single glance at them, preferred no closer study. If they *were* portraits he had no inclination to meet the originals. There were cruel curves to the mouths, promises of strange and evil knowledge in the staring eyes.

Along the full length of one wall was a case holding books, books encased in the same gray wood as formed the furniture. To his left were two other doors, both open.

Lefty, seeing that Blake had come to no harm, now sidled farther in. He stared about him as if the oddness of the place made an impression.

"Geeze—" was his acceptance of what he saw. "Some joint!"

He drew a finger across the cushion of the nearest chair. "Whatta yuh know—fur! And why all them faces plastered up on th' wall? This guy must be a headhunter!" He started to laugh at his own flight of imagination but the laughter died away as he took a second look at the masks.

"This sure is a screwy joint. I don't get it."

There was no sound from the other rooms. Surely if the apartment was inhabited they would have roused someone. But the feeling that the suite was deserted persisted, and his own private warning system gave him no hint of danger.

Blake went into the next room. Again lights flashed as he crossed the threshold, and he saw he was in a bedroom. The bed was low and wide, built into a corner, bunk fashion. One of the soft carpets—this time pure white—covered the floor. And the bed was spread with an embroidered cover glowing with color, sparks of gemlight reflected from points in the pattern. A chest of ebony wood inlaid with a design of leaves in red and gold was against one wall and above it hung a silvery mirror.

Catching sight of his grimy, disreputable self in that mirror, Blake was more than ever glad he had not blundered in upon a native. But the room was empty and again he had the undefinable feeling that it had been so for days.

"Geeze—" Lefty paid his favorite tribute. "Class, real class! Big John's dump ain't like this. Real class!"

The artist in Blake longed to examine the jewel-sewn cover, and all the rest of the treasures, but there was no time; to linger was foolish. They must get back to the laboratory and make an effort with the carrier even if it meant a return to the cellar where Scappa had imprisoned them. Something in the very air here suggested that Scappa, as bad as he was, might not be the greatest peril one could encounter along the worlds-traveling route. The masks had shaken Blake more than he cared to admit even to himself.

"We better get back—" he was beginning.

"Back where?" Lefty wanted to know. "Sure; I know we gotta get outta here."

Whether Blake could have carried his point about return to the carrier he was never to know, for at that moment there was a subdued chime, the first sound they had yet heard.

On the wall by the hall door was a round plate, resembling a porthole in a ship's cabin. But this was no longer dull gray. Three flashes from it riveted their attention. Lefty, with a cry close to a scream, simply turned and ran blindly out into the hall as a pattern began to form on the disc.

Blake stood his ground. There were lines of script—totally unfamiliar. And yet he felt they were allied to something he had once seen—that somewhere he had glanced over pothooks not unlike them. He roused from his study just in time to see the hall door close, sealing him in and Lefty out. He jumped for it, but there was a sharp click and for all his pushing it remained sealed.

Daringly he hammered on its surface, calling upon Lefty to release the catch by stepping in front. But, if the little man was still in the hall, he made no move, and the door continued to withstand Blake's efforts.

By the time he accepted the fact that he was now a prisoner, the message plate had gone dead. And he was very sure he could not depend upon Lefty to free him. He had been all wrong in keeping the full meaning of their journey from the other. Lefty wanted to get out of the building. Suppose he did leave—he would be an object of suspicion to the first native of this level whom he met. And the farther Lefty strayed from the laboratory, the more certain was their capture.

Chapter Seven

It must be well into the early morning hours, Blake thought. He now might have only a short time left before someone appeared to open the shop below—before workers were in the laboratory. He must get free!

He discovered a second door into the hall from the bedroom, but it resisted his efforts. The third room proved to be a kitchen. The sight of the appliances there, strange as they were, triggered his hunger. For a moment he wondered about a search for food, but common sense warned against that.

There was only one possible exit—a window. Breaking two finger nails he managed to loosen the panel which closed it. Still between him and freedom was a clear surface. Glass? No. Under his touch it bulged. He labored to force the second barrier, then he breathed air tainted with the usual city smells and some exotic new ones.

Blake's luck continued to hold. Some five feet below a ledge ran along forming a stepping stone to the offset roof of a first story projection. If he could worm through the window. . . .

It was a tight fit and he had to shed his jacket before he could make it. Then he stood shivering on the ledge before jumping to the offset. The bluish street lamps were far away but he could see a little. Here were none of the towering skyscrapers he knew in his own city. Few of the buildings were more than four or five stories high.

He looked down into a pocket of dark which was either a court or a backyard. Once there he might be locked out of the building and be even farther from the carrier.

As he hesitated, Blake saw two orange-red globes move majestically through the night sky, swinging in a circle above the city. Aircraft of some type? He turned to follow their flight and saw another light flash up in the building he had just left.

At the far end a window was a bright square in the dark. In fact it was so bright that Blake believed it must be open. If he could get in. . . .

He pulled himself up on the ledge once more, advancing toward that gleam. Had Lefty managed to get into another room? Then he could help Blake in; and this time he would be told the truth so that they could retreat to the carrier.

But innate caution made his approach to that light a stealthy one. And after he glanced inside, Blake stiffened.

Lefty was there all right. But an altered Lefty, a Lefty at perfect ease in his surroundings, a Lefty who bore only a very superficial resemblance to the frightened crook who had shared Blake's escape from the underground room.

The nervousness, the stare, the twitch of the lips no longer contorted the thin face which was now set in lines of calm force. The untidy hair was slicked smoothly back from a high forehead and there was an odd smile pulling the slack lips into firmness. He lounged in one of the barrel chairs and between his fingers he rolled a brownish cigarette. Lefty waiting—for what? Lefty at home? Here?

Only—the right answer shook Blake—this was not Lefty, not the frightened creature to whom he had felt so superior these past hours. He had been assured that only Pranj knew of the level worlds. Which meant, though the weedy little man in there bore little likeness to the image he had been shown, this was Pranj! A Pranj so able to fit himself with a new character that no suspicion of disguise had troubled Blake.

Then—they had not landed in this world by chance. This was a level Pranj already knew, a world in which he had contacts and a base of operation, a world in which he could dispose of Blake at his leisure, after getting out of him all that he knew. And now the outlaw would believe that his victim was safely waiting his pleasure.

Blake's hands balled into fists. He might not be a match for the psi powered criminal now. But let him reach the carrier—if he could, before the other realized that he was no longer locked in that suite.

A sound from the street sent Blake a step or two farther along the ledge to investigate. There was an egg-shaped vehicle drawing to a stop. From a hatch in its top three men stepped to the pavement and entered a door. Blake hurried back to the window.

On the wall before Pranj, one of the vision plates lit up with a message. He arose to press a button in the frame under the disc. And a minute or so later the three men entered.

Blake studied them. They were all tall and their dress accented the fine muscular development of their bodies: tight breeches with soft boots laced to the knees, jerkin-jackets buckled from throat to belt. Two of them glittered with embroidery of gold and silver, and their buckles and belts were gemmed, as were the guards and hilts of the knives they wore. The third man, who had a short shoulder cape of bright scarlet, remained by the door, his attitude that of a servant.

They were all dark skinned and their hair had been shaved to two narrow strips running from forehead to nape, leaving wide bare spaces above the ears. There was an arrogance about the two who seated themselves without invitation, the assurance of those whose will had never been disputed from birth. If these were members of some native nobility, it was a virile and dominant caste.

Since they were settling themselves as if for a conference, there was no indication that Pranj would be troubled about Blake for a time. Now he should move.

But he would gain nothing by returning to the locked suite; this left the street door through which the visitors had entered. Blake dropped to the offset, sped across it. The street looked deserted; in any event this was his only chance.

He landed with a jar, which brought a grunt out of him. It was to be hoped that the three had been the only passengers in the queerly shaped car. No one hailed him as he sprinted to the door.

It was closed but under his push it began to glide into the wall. Hardly daring to believe in his luck he entered, and not too soon for it snapped shut, catching a fold of his jacket. He tore savagely at the garment with no result; it was wedged fast. For the second time he had to slip it off, but this time it remained behind, a tell-tale sign of his passing.

That clue would shorten his time of grace. Blake sped to the foot of the ascending stairs and listened. There was no sound from above. So encouraged, he hurried down the other flight. The laboratory was just as they had left it, the carrier in its center. Blake remembered that he lacked a weapon. If he were to return to his own time and the care of Scappa, he wanted one.

Swiftly he made the rounds of the tables. Something which could double as a club if he could find nothing better. He was reaching for a small hammer when he saw another object, a dagger similar to those worn by the native noble men. The ten inch blade was razor sharp, the needle point a threat. He thrust it into his belt, but before he left he selected another piece of loot, a smaller edition of one of the demon-headed jars, which he crammed into the front of his flannel shirt with the vague idea of using it to identify this base of Pranj's if and when he ever caught up with the agents again.

Blake scrambled up on the carrier and reached for the control. In this light he was able to see as well as feel a series of small notches along the bar. Using his thumb as a measure he was able to assure himself that its position when they landed here had been at the last of those nicks. Another must stand for the world from which Pranj had originally fled—that of the agents. To get there might be a good idea. The inhabitants of that level would require no explanations and they would be in sympathy with his quest. He need only report to the agents there. He counted the notches again: five—six—Would it be the top one, since this was the last?

A shout carried through the building, jerking him around. He pulled the lever—first notch it would be. But the control did not yield to his tug. He twisted it; and there was the pound of feet on the stair. A second cry with a note of triumph in it. They must have found his jacket!

Blake worked feverishly at the rod and then threw himself down to examine the shaft from which it projected. There was a catch there! And it held stubbornly.

A clatter of feet on the stair. Blake pried at the catch with the point of the dagger and someway touched a spring. It gave, and with both hands on the control, he looked up. They were strung out along the stair: the red cloaked men in the lead and Pranj in the back as if he were a commander who led his armies from headquarters well to the rear. But of them all, Blake was most conscious of the fury on the changed face of "Lefty."

The red cloaked man raised a tube, sighting along it as if he were aiming a rifle. Blake had no time to pick or choose. He simply thrust the control forward, but in that second a numbing blow struck his shoulder and his left arm dropped useless to his side.

Once again the humming, the rise of the green globe of light to encase the carrier. There was Pranj and the others, the three natives open-mouthed with astonishment, Pranj displaying the cold and deadly anger of one who has underestimated an opponent and so lost an important move. Was he exiling Pranj in this world? Blake speculated with a soaring sense of triumph.

Then the laboratory was gone and the stomach- and nerve-wracking journey through the light and dark began. Blake lay flat, his head pillowed on his good arm, his deadened left one along his body, content to rest and leave his escape to the machine he did not understand.

Lights. Dark. Lights. Blue fog. Lights. Dark. The carrier no longer quivered under him. His voyage was ended, and he was in darkness. But with that, exhaustion conquered and Blake slept.

He awoke cold—cold and stiff. His eyes opened and he did not understand. There was a pallid light, a splotch of weak sunlight spotting his hand. Sun!

Stiffly, every muscle protesting, Blake raised himself on his right elbow. Moving his left shoulder sent a thrust of burning agony down his back and breast, tearing a little cry from his raw lips. And, when his head cleared, he stared about him in horror. He had thought himself free!

But this was not the underground room he had left sometime the night before. (Was it only yesterday?) Time no longer had much meaning. He hunched together, supporting his left arm across his knees, gazing dully at what encircled him.

Walls of stone, rough hewn in misshapen blocks, but fitted together with an engineer's precision which left no cracks, spiralled dizzily upward. The carrier rested in the bottom of a dry well was his first confused thought.

But about six feet above there was a break in that wall through which the sun shown, promising a way out. Blake, a little light-headed, got to his feet. The carrier was not steady under him, rocking a little when he moved. It rested on a mass of blackened stuff, from which protruded the jagged and charred end of a beam. And now he noted that the walls about him bore traces of an old fire, fire which must have eaten out the heart of the structure—perhaps in the far distant past, because when he ventured to kick at the beam it powdered away to dust.

This was certainly not Scappa's cellar; nor was it, he was quite sure, the world from which Pranj had fled. Unless the outlaw had chosen to operate out of a ruin far from the main settlements of his race.

Moved by that thin hope, Blake paced about the circumference of the wall. His feet sank almost ankle deep in the charred debris, but, as far as he could see, there was no opening in the stone surface at this level. Any entrance must have been made from above. He eyed the break; it was surely wide enough to provide an exit. Whether he could make it with the use of only one hand was another matter.

Blake sat down once more on the carrier. His hunger was now a gnawing ache in his middle; he ran a dry tongue over dryer lips. He wanted food and water. Should he trust again to the blind chance of the carrier, hoping to land either in his own level, or that of the agents, or should he explore further here?

If Pranj had established bases along the line the carrier was geared to, he might find trouble awaiting him anywhere he dared to stop. And he remembered the agents' warnings concerning level worlds where even their trained investigators dared not venture—the radioactive worlds, and those where humanity had taken other and more desperate roads for survival.

It was quiet here and the ruins suggested that this might be a deserted and relatively peaceful pausing place. He could rest, collect his wits and do a little planning. But first—food—warmth—he shivered as a breeze licked down at him through the shattered wall.

Blake went to the wall. Somehow he made that climb, hitching his way up and over. But a weary time later, shaking with weakness, he stood on the ground looking dazedly around.

There was pavement under his feet, uncovered in places where the wind had scoured away the snow, which in other spots drifted about the bases of towers, the boles of stunted and wind carven trees, now barren of leaf. But that pavement was not any civilized street—instead it was a circle of flagstones with withered clumps of grass and winter-dried brown weeds pulling block apart from block. It was plain that no one had walked this way for a long time.

Blake went down on one knee, scooped up a handful of snow and licked it from numbed fingers. But his eyes swept from one tower to the next, from trees to wall of brush. No tracks of either man or animal patterned the snow. Except for the whistle of the wind playing hollowly across the broken towers there was no sound.

Painfully he dragged clumps of the withered grass free from the frozen soil, and then went farther afield for fallen branches, half rotten sticks. He would have to have a fire—warmth. There was a book of matches in his pocket—he held a tiny flame to the withered grass twist. It seemed, Blake decided with a wry grin, that he was not altogether helpless in his Robinson Crusoe guise.

The blaze caught; the flames were warm on his half frozen body and blue hands. Blake became aware that some measure of feeling was returning to his left arm as the heat of the fire struck in. But whenever he tried to move it, pain streaked out from the point on his shoulder. He could see no blood, no sign of a bullet.

Clumsily he unfastened his upper shirt, the clothing underneath, trying to find the wound. Just below his collar bone was an angry red patch which resembled a burn. Well, there was nothing he could do about it now.

Instead, as he rebuttoned his clothing, he gave his surroundings a second and more intent study. The ruined towers, he could count at least ten within easy sighting, did not appear to be arranged in any consistent pattern of streets or a city such as he could recognize. And there were no other buildings except the tower form to be seen. Towers, which could only be entered from above, which did not even possess slitted windows. That suggested defense—a needed defense of the most serious kind. And yet that tower from which he had just climbed *had* been stormed, stormed and burned.

A people who had been so hard pressed by some enemy that they had lived in a constant state of siege—a people who must in the end have fallen victim to that same enemy a long time ago.

But the enemy? Had the invaders, or besiegers, having won their victory withdrawn, content with the total destruction of the conquered? He could see nothing to suggest that there had been any attempt to rebuild from the tower ruins.

Blake licked more snow from his hand. Something to eat. This place had gone back to the wild. Rabbits, birds, were everywhere. He had never hunted, and how efficient he would be with only one usable hand he dared not guess. But he had fire and a knife. And if man had long vanished from this place not only should there be small animals prowling among the ruins, but they should also be unafraid and so the easier to bring down. He kicked at the frozen rubble and chose some stones which fitted into his hand. When a man knew how to pitch a baseball, he ought to be able to aim at a rabbit.

He fed the fire with a couple of large chunks likely to last for a while and plotted a path toward a more distant tower whose crown was broken into two parts rather like a pair of teeth gnawing at the morning sky. With that as his goal, and a keen eye for the spoor of game, Blake started off.

The weird sighing of the wind was disconcerting. Sometimes it raised to a scream as it forced across the empty throats of the towers and through gaps from which stones had fallen. Twice Blake sprang for cover, sure that the sound he had heard *had* come from some human throat. But he saw nothing.

He was heartened by the unmistakable tracks of a pigeon in snow, and then, at the foot of another tower, the paw mark of some small animal he was not woodsman enough to identify. But at that moment any animal meant only meat and he followed the trail.

It led straight to another tower where a large portion of the wall had collapsed. He caught a stale whiff which spelled den. But that did not interest him as much as something else.

Inside there had been another and more recent fall of masonry. And it had broken open an ancient storage place. Blake was deafened by the whirr of wings as pigeons and other birds beat out at his coming. Piles of grain had trickled from the stone coffer, offering such bait as he did not count on existing. He was sure the birds would return. Scooping up a fistful of the stuff, he chewed it as he flattened back into the protection of the remaining wall to wait.

He was right; the pigeons returned first, greedy for the treasure. Blake knotted small stones into the opposite corners of his handkerchief. There was a plump white bird right along a line of scattered grain. . . .

An hour later Blake made a rude toilet in the snow. Meat without salt, even when toasted to take the rawness out, was not the most appetizing dish in the world. And the dusty, gummy taste of the grain he had chewed still clung to his tongue. But he was no longer hungry. Not only that, but deep inside him he had a new satisfaction. He had been moved about by the agents in the game against Pranj. And in turn he had been fooled by the outlaw.

But he *had* escaped from Pranj. And here, without tools or any real knowledge, he had managed to achieve food and warmth. No thanks to anyone but himself. Some measure of confidence had returned to him.

What had finished off this city? War certainly. But what kind of war? Who had fought whom? Had the tower people been of his own kind—overwhelmed in their refuge by savages who had no wish to follow up their advantage? Had this been the last stronghold of civilization on this world?

Curiosity tugged at Blake. He wanted to explore—to learn. He reached mechanically for more wood and then paused. Why build up the fire? He ought to return to the carrier to try it again. . . .

He stiffened, so startled he did not remember the dagger in his belt. Above, the wind screeched in rising fury. But Blake heard nothing, saw nothing but the thing which had crept up through the brush, its eyes reflecting the light of the flames.

Chapter Eight

The dragon of Teutonic folk lore, the very personification of nightmare crouched there. It was about seven feet long, and jointed, a bulbous head stretched for a third of its length above it many-footed body. And the fire was reflected in glassy eyes, which were the only features in that noseless, mouthless face—if you could term it a face.

Blake retreated step by step as the thing crept as cautiously forward. He could not tell as yet whether it was attracted solely by the fire, or whether he was the bait. It moved, slow as its pace was, with a fluidity which suggested that its attack might be hard to counter.

His shoulders pressed against the stone of the tower wall, sending a thrill of pain shooting down his back and injured arm. And that red agony broke the spell. He drew his dagger as the creature half-crouched before the fire, staring with the same bemusement into the flames.

Blake drew a long breath. Each segment of that silver-gray length wore armor sheathing like a beetle's shell, and the thing twisted and turned upon itself with a worm's ease. So far, it had shown no interest in him, nor could he say that it was a danger. If it would remain where it was—enchanted by the fire—he might be able to run to the carrier and safety.

The round head of the creature turned; it gave the impression of listening intently. Blake, however, heard no sound except the ever present whistle of the wind. And then his warning sense went into action. It had not heralded the approach of the worm, but now. . . .

Too late for him with his crippled arm to climb the wall; the worm could pull him down. And the creature was moving around the edge of the fire. Under some of its feet, stones rolled and it slid to one side. A clang as of metal against stone sounded when the thing brushed a large block. Metal!

The worm flashed around the block as if the small mishap had angered it, and now it coiled before him, its head raised, the round red eyes regarding him without expression or life. They were like glass bulbs. . . .

Glass. . . .

Blake had been so intent upon the worm that he was not aware until now of the figure which had approached noiselessly from the same direction. Not until the stench, which cloaked it as a garment, brought his head up. A worm-dragon, and now—an ogre! Again he returned to the tales of his childhood for a description to fit.

Mats of filthy hair covered a skin which might remotely have been whiter than his own, but which was now so caked with ancient dirt that it had a dull gray cast. The thing was not wholly animal, though he wished that he could so classify it. Not quite an animal. For about its middle was a kind of kilt of untanned skins, rotting in tatters from the thong which served it as a belt. The creature crouched in what was probably a perpetual stoop, strings of hair half masking the vacant horror if its face. But the worst of all was that it was so plainly a female!

The worm made no move, nor did it turn to acknowledge the arrival of the other. It remained in position as if holding Blake at bay according to some order.

But the hag was content to hunch down by the fire. Until suddenly she raised her frowsy head and looked straight across the flames at Blake. Her eyes were no longer as vacant as those of her worm-hound, but feral, the eyes of a carnivorous hunter. The slack lips folded back from teeth which could not have budded in any strictly human jaw, fangs which would better serve a wolf or a mountain lion.

Ropy muscles moved under the scaled and warty skin as almost lazily she raised hands ending in the hard and pointed talons of a beast.

"No!" Blake did not realize that he had voiced that protest until the word was echoed back to him from the hollow towers.

And, as if his cry had broken some last restraint, the hag opened her slavering mouth and howled a challenge. For the first time she arose to her full height and her stringy leanness gave such an impression of menacing strength and avid hunger that Blake tensed, ready to meet the rush which would bring her at his throat.

But the worm moved first. With a lithe uncoiling of its limber segments it reared up and forward. From somewhere under its belly shot tentacles which snapped about Blake with bruising force, pinning him to the rough stone of the wall. And the touch of those limbs burned! The thing *was* metal! There was no mistaking that—just as the red orbs now on a level with his own eyes were not natural organs of vision at all.

He was as helpless as he had been when bound and gagged in the hands of Scappa's goons. The worm—thing—machine made no move to crush him. It only held him, waiting for an order from the crone.

Again that creature voiced her howling challenge, or was it a summons to others of her kind? Blake shivered and then he struggled vainly against that hold—the only result unbearable pain from his shoulder. His whole being shrank from any physical contact with the hag, yet now she was shambling about the edge of the fire toward him.

There was another sound—a sharp snap. It could have been a stick breaking under an incautious foot. But it was not.

From the matted hair on the hag's breast a bright blue shaft protruded. Dancing, she uttered a series of eerie shrieks until blood frothed between her lips, then crumpled down, her hands and feet scrabbling on the ground in her last struggles.

The worm did not loosen its grip; it did not even turn its head to watch the death throes of its mistress—if that was the relationship between them. It merely stood its ground, locking Blake to the stone, the chill of its metal body icy.

Out of the same patch of brush which had masked the arrival of the worm came another, walking with the assured tread of one who is master of his environment and has little or nothing to fear from the world about him.

Eskimo? Blake's first confused thought identified the fur clothing, the parka-like upper garment. But the hood of that parka was flung back and who ever saw an Eskimo with the features of a South Seas Islander? Features embellished with tattooed patterns in dark blue, patterns supplying with graceful spirals and dots the beard lacking by nature.

The fur clad Polynesian halted a step or so away from the hag. He surveyed Blake with open curiosity, paying no attention to the worm. Then he stopped, selected a piece of rough stone, and came around the fire. The worm did not move, nor did it show any interest in the newcomer—it might now be a part of the tower.

With no concern the fur clad hunter brought his stone down to smash one of the red globes sprouting from the worm's head. Then with a speed which left Blake a little dizzy, he struck at the second organ. There was the tinkle of breaking crystal but still the worm did not move, made no defense against the attack.

The hunter put out his hand and jerked at one of the tentacles which imprisoned Blake. At first it clung, then it gave and the creature crashed to the ground, plainly out of commission. The hunter laughed and toed it with his fur boot before he went to pick up his weapon—a form of crossbow. He ground this between his feet as he turned to face the other. His bare hands were held up in the universal sign of peace—empty and palm out.

Shakily Blake hurried to copy that gesture. The stranger voiced a question in a liquid trill. Regretfully Blake shook his head.

"I do not understand," he answered slowly.

The other listened carefully, his mobile features registering surprise, as if a different language was the last thing he had expected to hear. But he did not show alarm. Instead he made an inquiring gesture to the fire, giving an exaggerated shiver. Blake stood away from the wall and tried to put all the good will he felt into a sweeping invitation to enjoy the heat.

It was accepted, the stranger squatting down to hold his hands to the blaze. Blake, still shaken, sat down on a block of stone. This Eskimo, or Hawaiian, or whatever he was, seemed disposed to be friendly. But would that friendliness continue if Blake tried to reach the carrier? And flattened against the wall, in the climb he would present a perfect target for the other's crossbow.

The man across the fire was working on his weapon, rubbing the string of the bow between thumb and forefinger. He smiled at Blake and spoke again as if the other could understand. Then he got to his feet in one graceful movement.

Before Blake could protest he began putting out the fire, smothering the flames with snow. When Blake shook his head, the hunter laughed and pointed to the worm and then to the warmth he was destroying, suggesting that the fire would draw such.

The worm was a machine. Blake was now sure of that. But any civilization which could produce so intricate a robot as that and then paired it with the beast-hag. . . . He could not fit the two into any sane companionship. Nor did the worm fit the civilization which had built the towers, at least from casual inspection it did not. And it certainly was not connected with the hunter or he would not have destroyed it so quickly. Thoroughly muddled, Blake longed to make a break for it—back to the carrier.

When the last spiral of smoke died, the hunter went to the crone, performing an act of such savagery that Blake, shuddering, retreated once more to the wall, trying to figure a way of winning over it while the other was engrossed in his butchery. For the hunter deliberately smashed the jaws of the hag, groping among the bloody splinters to bring out a couple of the animal fangs. He rubbed these clean in the snow with a business-like dispatch and then stored the trophies in a pouch swinging from the broad leather band that belted-in his parka.

With a grin, into which Blake was no longer so quick to read friendliness, he turned and beckoned the other to join him. Determinedly Blake shook his head. He had no doubt that the dagger was little or no protection against that crossbow. But neither was he going to be tamely led away from the carrier into a world which certainly had more than one lurking danger.

The smile faded from that elaborately tattooed face. The eyes narrowed. Good nature had been wiped from the tough mask of a fighting man who was and always had been top dog in his particular section of the earth. The crossbow came up, its sight on a line with Blake's chest.

And Blake could not forget that bright blue dart which had killed the crone, the unhurried and practical way the hunter had disposed of the worm—as if each act was an everyday occurrence. Now Blake presented a good mark. Again the hunter perked his head in an order, his hands sure on his weapon.

The wind which had howled over their heads now carried snow with it: a powdering of small hard balls, and Blake shivered as it lashed through his clothing. With the fire out and the other impatient to move, with no common speech in which to explain or appeal, Blake realized the folly of resistance. If he antagonized the hunter it would only make his situation worse.

He moved, circling the snuffed out fire, avoiding the body of the hag. And the hunter fell in behind him, cradling the crossbow on his arm but leaving Blake in no doubt that he would use it should the other prove stubborn.

They forced a crackling path through the brush as the snow fall thickened. Blake tried to mark the trail, note the position of the towers within sight, locate any guide which would bring him back to the carrier if and when he managed to elude his captor. He had no longer any desire to explore here . . . Escape—even to Scappa—to a world where he could in a small way predict danger to come was better than this.

On the other side of the thicket they came upon a well-beaten trail worn a foot or more deeper than the surrounding ground, but so narrow they would have to travel it single file. The hunter motioned Blake to the north, waiting for him to step into that slot before he followed.

The path wound, purposelessly as far as Blake could see, about the bases of several of the towers, sloping downward. Here the wind was shut away by a strand of trees. A branch way curved from the track, running to a tower which was largely a tumbled heap of stone. Blake's nose wrinkled at the sour-sweetish stench issuing from that dark hole.

His captor gave a soft exclamation and Blake saw the other spit at that opening, loathing plain to read on his face. He had stopped, and now he fumbled with one hand at his belt, loosening a small box clipped there. He gave that to Blake with an order the other could not translate. But, since it must be connected with the box, he snapped up the lid.

The interior was lined with clay blackened and baked and a small coal winked red. Blake glanced up to find his companion making gestures—pulling up a handful of the withered grass. Apparently Blake was expected to build another fire—right there and now. The why he could not understand, but he gathered from the other that it was in some manner vitally important.

On an open space not far from the lair, he achieved a small blaze. The hunter moved no closer to the heat. Instead he was alert, watching, his attention for the mouth of the den. Plainly the blaze was intended as a lure—for what? Another worm—another nonhuman crone?

The wind died and they were caught in an odd pocket of quiet. Through that stillness Blake heard a clinking, the click of metal against stone. A worm! He looked about for some rocks. Now that the hunter had demonstrated the proper way to deal with the things he would be prepared.

But it was no seven foot monster of gleaming metal which crawled to their bait. A small glittering thing darted to the fire from the shadow of the den and then another and another!

Blake, prepared for a dragon, was faced by a handful of centipedes less than five inches long. Young! But that metal creature he had seen was manufactured. A robot; he was certain of that. It could not have reproduced its kind.

The hunter stalked forward and brought his heel crunchingly down on one of the glittering things, motioning Blake to join him in that act of righteous destruction. Blake struck with a stone and then picked up the smashed body. His blow had broken it open and he was right—inside was intricate machinery, too delicate and involved to study without time—it was truly a robot. One more mystery to be added to all the others this level offered.

His fur clad companion was searching about the edge of the fire, prying up loose stones, hunting for more of the small worms. But, save for four smashed bodies, the ground was bare. At last, with a grunt, he began to put out the fire.

With the satisfaction of one who has done his duty, he motioned Blake on once more when the blaze was out. The worn trail led away from the towers now and there were no more breaks in it, no more lairs of the metallic monsters and their subhuman mistresses.

They came out on a headland and Blake looked over an arm of the sea. It wore its gray winter guise and there was a rim of ice along the shore below. The path they followed so far now became a series of hand and footholds leading ladder-fashion to the beach. Painfully Blake made the descent, given no choice by his guard. He was able to use his left hand now, but the resulting pain brought cold dampness to his forehead and made him bite hard on his underlip.

On the beach, back against the cliff wall was the hunter's camp. A queer, blunt-bowed boat fashioned of skins drawn tightly over a frame of light metal and smeared with a thick and shiny substance, was drawn up on the sand well away from the reach of the waves. While a shallow indentation too shallow to be termed a cave had been enlarged as a shelter by the addition of a projecting brush roof and walls making a snug lean-to cabin snug for one, cramped for two.

Hides were stretching on boards against the cliff and wraps of fur strips cut fine and then woven into blankets covered a bed of springy pine branches. There were strong smells from the raw pelts, and the wood smoke, but none of the filth-born stench which had wafted from the tower lair.

Now that he had Blake in his own territory the hunter relaxed his watchfulness, stowing away his crossbow before stirring up the fire and preparing a meal. The appointments of the camp were a queer mixture of civilization and the primitive. For the fur blankets, intricately woven as they were, might belong to a forest dwelling barbarian. While a set of nested bowls, almost translucent as the finest china, yet of some incredibly tough substance, bowls which could safely be placed on hot rocks in the center of the fire without melting or cracking, were beyond any product Blake knew of in his own world.

The hunter shed his parka, as if to prove that he himself was a study in contrasts. For under the thick fur he wore a shirt of some silky material which molded itself to his powerful chest and shoulders almost as if painted on his skin. It was of a flaming scarlet with a pattern of dots and circles, such as formed the tattooing on his face.

Savory steam arose from the bowl over the fire and Blake swallowed. The musty grain and the half-burnt, half-raw scraps of pigeon he had downed earlier were very remote memories.

His host ladled stew into a small bowl and then produced a horn, carved and embellished with inlay, from which he drew the stopper to pour a small portion of its contents into a handleless cup he tendered to Blake with some ceremony.

Blake's hands were shaking so that he had to use both of them to raise that cup to his lips. He gulped a mouthful. First it was bland on his tongue; then it came awaking to warmth in his throat and then to fire in his middle—a fire from which a glow spread throughout his cold and starved body.

The hunter took back the cup, refilled it to the same mark and uttered a sentence before he tossed it off with a single draft. Then he drew a knife from his belt and fell to spearing chunks of meat and unidentified vegetables out of the stew. Blake pulled out his dagger and followed his example.

As his hunger was appeased and he was relaxing in the warmth of the small cabin he was troubled once again by the paradoxes of this level. Was this one of the bases set up by Pranj, or had chance—chance and the shot which had numbed Blake's arm—brought him into an unknown, unexplored world? And what historical event of the remote past had produced the fallen towers, the subhuman hags and their mechanical serpents—this fur clad islander?

Speculations had to be wild to cover all the points. He would like to show Saxton this level and ask for a logical explanation. Blake's eyelids seemed weighted. He leaned back against the side of the bed. The hunter had taken up one of the stretching pelts and was working over it. Blake's eyes closed in spite of his struggles and he fell asleep.

Chapter Nine

The boat on the beach was marked by a mound of snow, and the white stuff had drifted high about the entrance to the cave-cabin. Blake pulled the hood of the parka, which had been flung over him while he slept, higher about his ears and wondered if this was the time to cut and run, if he could make the carrier before his host-guard caught up with him. The hunter had left some minutes earlier; Blake watched his exit from beneath lowered eyelids, trying to play the man deep in slumber.

But he was reluctant to face the storm without. He kept telling himself that in that whirling white curtain he would lose all track of landmarks, that he would quickly be lost and unable to find his way to the tower which held the carrier.

During the past hours he had tried to discover whether Pranj had visited this level. Though he was no nearer solving the mysteries of this world and he probably never would, he had established a limited communication with the hunter. The latter was named Pakahini; his true home lay to the westward across the arm of sea which lapped this island; he had come here to trap for the fur of a variety of animal numerous on this site but greatly prized in his own community. With pride he had displayed his catch: creamy white skins Blake could not identify. He had almost completed this particular trip, and was now gathering in his traps and bundling his take, preparatory to returning to his own people.

But to all Blake's halting inquiries concerning the hags and their worm-hounds he replied with shrugs so the other did not know if he was not making his questions clear, or whether the other refused to discuss the subject. Blake suspected the latter.

To his surprise the hunter had his own explanation for Blake's appearance, one to which he had only to agree, when the other stated it, to have it readily accepted. He was, in the other's belief, the victim of a shipwreck. And, Blake thought with a wry grin, that was one way of looking at his arrival by carrier. His alien speech and dress to Pakahini meant that he came from overseas, which argued that the hunter had met travelers from the East—or had heard of them—and so was able to accept that idea readily.

But Blake did not accept, in his turn, so easily the present plans of Pakahini. Both of them, he gathered from a long speech the other had made that morning, were to return in the boat to the town of his people. Blake's clothing had been fingered with appreciation, his belongings examined. Proof that he was from a highly civilized community was plain, and Pakahini wanted to display him to his tribe.

The hunter's own degree of culture was, Blake guessed, on the upward grade. His people were thirsty for new skills, for anything which would add to their advancement. They were not of the race which had built the towers. Pakahini had managed to give the impression that the towers were already old ruins when the first tribes of his race had penetrated into this section. And his people did not work in stone at all.

But all this, Blake told himself, was not solving his own problem. If he remained in this camp Pakahini would return. And eventually he would find himself in the boat out there, being paddled north to become a trophy for the hunter to show off in his village. Once off the island, the American might never be able to win back to it. He would have to move—and right now!

Blake raised his left arm as high as he could, flexing the fingers of that hand grimly in spite of the pain all movement brought. The stiffness was going, but he still did not dare to put much weight upon it. That climb to the trail above—he wondered if he could make it. The alternative was to walk along the shore and hope to discover an easier slope. With the danger of being lost by venturing too far from the trail at the top of the cliff.

He finally decided on the shore path. If he overtaxed his arm now, what of the climb into the tower? He might reach his goal only to be baffled in the last few feet!

Snow beat about him and he pulled the parka hood over his head. He tramped along so close to the cliff wall that his shoulder brushed now and again against the rock, his guide in the storm. One good thing about the snow: it would cover his trail speedily. If Pakahini was gone long enough, he could not track the runaway upon his return.

Already the hunter's camp was hidden, not only by the storm but also by a turn in the cliff wall. Blake pushed on, glad that the wind was at his back. He had no way of measuring either time or distance but finally he found what he sought, a break in the walls, a staircase of rock ascending from a flat platform of stone running out into the waters of the bay. Some relic of the tower people he supposed.

The broken and crumbling steps were coated with ice where spray had frozen. He eyed them doubtfully and then solved the problem in his own fashion by seating himself on the nearest and then rising to the next—"bumping" up as in babyhood he had "bumped" himself down a more familiar stairway. It was an odd way to make the climb but the safest that he knew, and it put little strain on his shoulder.

Twice he skidded and saved himself on the very edge of a downward slide. And he breathed a sigh of relief when he reached the top. Now if the day were clear, or he had more of a woodman's training he might be able to strike straight across country for his tower. But with the blizzard hiding most of the landscape, he did not quite dare that. He must retrace a path along the top of the cliff until he connected with that game trail.

Only now he must face the force of the wind, and he had to fight a blast which left him gasping for breath when it met him head on. Blake paused, a little frightened. That had been enough to sweep him off the cliff. He did not dare to keep on in the open.

If the island followed the contours of the one in his own world, the one which was one gigantic city, then it wasn't too long. But half a block in this storm could completely bewilder a man. He should find a tower and hole up, wait for the fury of the wind and snow to abate. Pakahini might think him lost and not search at all and make his scheduled departure. The more Blake considered that idea, the more sensible it seemed. Now—to find a tower. . . .

He could follow the wide way inland which led from the head of the staircase. Sooner or later that should guide him to a tower.

Unlike the scattered, purposeless planting of the towers he had seen, this route ran with a mathematical thrust toward the heart of the island. And he had not gone far before towers did loom out of the murk. But all of these were intact, unbroken, affording no shelter in their round bases. They were also larger than the others. He went on, staggering when the wind struck at him cruelly.

It was cold. Through the slacks, the boots which had been protection enough against storm on his own level, the chill struck him. His hands, covered with the mittens which were attached to the parka sleeves, he stuck into his arm pits, huddling in upon himself, making his wavering way from one rock mass to the next, hunting a hole which was never there.

The shriek of the wind was now deafening. It could have covered the advance of a whole regiment of metal worms and their ogrish owners. Blake paused every few strides to stare about him. But the white blanket rising now well above his ankles showed no breaks.

He came to another flight of steps, broad enough to be a series of ledges. And at the top of that ascent was a wide expanse open to the sky, scoured clean of drifts by the wind. He dared not venture out there, but climbed down once more to make his way about the platform. The pavement ended there; there was no other guide to follow.

Blake leaned against one of the intact towers. The ruins where he had entered this world lay to his left—he had retained that much sense of direction. Should he strike out now that way, trusting to luck to find a den in which to sit out the storm? This couldn't keep up forever!

There was a tower. He could go as far as that one and still win back to this point. Blake made that, then stumbled ahead to the next, to be faced by a wall of thorn bush half-hidden in a snow bank. He could thread his path from one to another, around the barrier of the brush.

He was panting, his head beginning to whirl, when he at last was brought up (literally blown against it with bruising force) against a tower which did afford a refuge. There was a large gap, an opening into blackness. Blake had remnants of caution, enough to hold him in the opening sniffing, afraid of another lair. But the foul odor was missing and he stumbled in, scuffing through the charcoal residue which marked the defeat of the fortress. The black dust sullied the snow as Blake perched on a projecting ledge and sat staring dully out into the storm.

But as the chill crept up his body he was conscious of a new danger. Either he must keep moving or have fire. His fine plan for hiding out during the storm was stupid. He should have had more patience, have maneuvered Pakahini into leading him back to the carrier. Now he was lost, without a fire, imprisoned by the storm.

Not yet was he aware of the full extent of his folly. He made himself walk back and forth across the circumscribed space. A certain amount of snow shifted down from time to time from the roofless reaches above, but the walls did hold off the wind.

Time had no meaning, but he suddenly realized that the howling of the wind no longer blasted his ears and when he peered out the snow had ceased. A lull—or the end of the storm? Either way it was a signal, or he accepted it as such, to make the best of the break and start for the carrier.

He was sure he had been heading in the right direction when he blundered in here, or he made himself believe that he had, a little off the direct course because of the brush wall.

The snow was now as high as his knees, and plunging through the drifts was cruelly tiring. Insensibly Blake altered course, choosing a route where the drifts had not formed, protected by towers or trees.

Now and then he halted, not only to rest, but to examine the ruins in search of that particular tower with the fanged top which marked the vicinity he sought. There were strangely shaped pinnacles in abundance now that they were no longer hidden by the storm, but none showed the right outline.

Blake was struggling through a last high drift, making for a cleared space between two towers when his head snapped up and he listened. That frenzied howl was not born of the wind. He had heard it too clearly before—the screech of a hag huntress!

He looked back. Sound was distorted here by echo. Was that cry from one nosing on his own trail? Or had some crone cornered other prey? Pakahini?

The hunter had shown so little fear of the hag and her worm when he had disposed of them to rescue Blake that the latter could hardly believe he would allow himself to be attacked. But suppose a man fell here, it would be easy to break a leg, twist an ankle in this place of ice and snow and rolling stones. And unable to move he would be sure prey for the worm and its mistress.

Pakahini? Blake shifted from one foot to the other. He owed the hunter his life. And if their positions were now reversed and Pakahini needed aid . . . But he could not be sure, perhaps the worm was slinking along behind *him*! And he had no way of deducing from which direction the scream had come.

Sense dictated an advance. But Blake turned back, quartering toward the right, padding into a run wherever the ground was bare enough to allow haste. His breath hissed between his teeth as he listened, over the pound of his own heart, for a second cry.

Here the towers were farther apart, and the tangled bushes between them forced him into wider and wider detours from the track he had marked for himself. Then he started, rubbed his mitten across his eyes, and looked again. He was right! There was the fang-topped tower. Chance had brought him back to the very place he was seeking!

And swift upon that recognition came again the howl which had drawn him there. He slowed pace, for with the sound his own warning struck. Danger ahead!

A third howl, so swift on the dying echoes of the other that he was certain it had not come from the same throat. A pack of crones gathering in for an easy kill?

Blake skinned the mitten from his right hand and reached for his dagger; then set the steel blade between his teeth while he looked about him for a rock to hurl. He advanced cautiously, slinking from the shadow of copse to the protection of a pile of rubble, until he rounded the fang tower.

From there a cleared space led with only the thinnest screen of stunted and leafless brush to the tower he sought, the one which hid the carrier. But he forgot about that when he saw what was happening before him.

A fur clad figure was pinned to the ground by the shining length of a worm. And over it struggled, talon against talon, tooth against tooth, two of the hags, tearing and gouging at each other in an elemental determination to each have the kill for herself. In almost automatic reflex Blake's arm went back, and the stone he had found sped through the air to strike against the skull of the nearest with a horrible, hollow sound. The hag he had brained went limp in her opponent's grasp, and the other took advantage of that chance, burying her teeth in the now flaccid throat.

Blake sprang across the clearing. There was a chance that the victim was not yet dead. For the first time in his life he used a knife to kill, experiencing an odd shock as it entered flesh and bit deep into body wall. The hag raised a dripping mouth, gasped at him with wild eyes. He leaped aside as the worm stirred and struck for his legs. Then the wild woman seemed to shrivel in upon herself and collapsed. And the worm remained as it was, rearing to grasp at Blake but not quite making it as the will which had powered it died.

Methodically, as Pakahini had done at their first meeting, Blake smashed the eyes, saw the metallic creature fall clatteringly to the rock. And then he turned to the hunter on the ground. A single glance was enough. Only by the torn and befouled parka could Pakahini be identified now. Even the manner of his entrapment and death would remain a mystery, as Blake could not bring himself to touch that horribly mangled body. Had he come here hunting Blake and been trapped? Perhaps—but now Blake wanted nothing but to be out of this world.

He pulled himself up the tower wall, swung down into the dusky interior. Snow had drifted a little over one corner of the carrier. Mechanically he brushed it off and then dropped down crosslegged before the control with its row of notches. He had no idea where he was or which of those would bring him to a time and place where he could find help, or even manage to survive. He could only guess.

Blake put out his hand to the control. Second notch—a blind choice, but this time if he had made the wrong selection he would not allow himself to be separated from the carrier. He tugged the lever loose and pulled.

The lights, sounds, spells of darkness. He closed his eyes against their dizzying whirl. The vibration ceased and Blake sat for a long moment, his hand slipping from the rod. Then he was aware that he, too, was sliding slowly along the platform. He opened his eyes.

He was out of the tower—that was true. But the carrier was canted to one side, because around it rose walls of broken brick from which projected jagged spikes of rusty metal. Overhead was a roof pocked with ragged holes through which a sun shone, a sun without warmth.

Pockets of snow were cupped in the rubble. A trickle of sandy gravel whispered and he whipped around, knife ready. Across a barricade of debris a rat, bloated, obscene, too tame and confident, watched him.

Ruin and desolation. Blake got shakily to his feet and then over a pile of blackened stone. Food. Water. It seemed a long time since he had eaten with Pakahini. He flinched from his memory of the hunter. When he wavered to his feet he was dizzy and he suspected he was close to the end of his strength. Dared he take the carrier on and perhaps plunge into some trap of Pranj's?

The platform had brought him into what was the more cluttered end of an underground room and, as Blake clawed his way through the piles of rubbish which had cascaded from above, he smelled smoke—wood smoke. There was a fire!

It had burned down to a single smoldering brand: the charred wood enclosed by a circle of bricks. Blake stirred the coals to life, feeding the fire from a pile of wood in which he discovered both broken furniture and splintered packing cases mingled indiscriminately. The graceful leg of a period chair puzzled him and he surveyed it dully, turning it about in his hand. He had seen its like in a decorator's shop of his own world. Its presence here hinted at some major disaster. But he was cold, tired, weak, and still suffering from the shock of the last scene in Pakahini's world.

Several blocks of concrete had been placed as if to serve as seats. And in a corner was a pile of ragged blankets and strips of torn cloth which could be a bed. But Blake saw no signs of food, nor could he guess who or what camped here.

". . . sure," the voice shrilled and cracked outside, "he's the one, Manny. We saw him come outta here just before the Limey hider picked him off. Then Ras shot the Limey. He's the one who's been raidin' our cache. . . ."

Blake, in a panic he could not then master, wavered back to the carrier. He made himself small behind a landslide of brick and watched for the arrival of the newcomers. But the fact that they spoke recognizable English was an overwhelming relief.

There was a clatter of feet on stone and a small figure tumbled down through the opening which served as a door. Blake blinked as the other advanced into the sunlight.

Chapter Ten

He was a boy, perhaps just into his teens, dressed in a ragbag collection of patched clothing. And in the crook of his arm was a rifle ready for use, the muzzle of which swung threateningly as he slowly pivoted to survey the interior.

"Empty," he called. "Jus' as we thought, Manny. He was goin' it alone. We said so." There was a tone of accusation in that.

"Yeah?" The answer from the outside was dubious. "Well, that ain't exactly how the Sarge heard it, kid. And it pays to use your brains, as you oughtta know by now. Ras, you stand guard while we see if we can flush us out another bird."

A second figure entered. This was no boy, but a small, very lean man with gray hair and suspicious eyes alert to every feature of the basement. His arm also cradled a rifle and not one but two knives hung from his belt.

"How long ago did you say that hider picked this guy off?" he demanded, his eyes still cataloguing every detail of the sorry camp.

The boy squinted at the patch of sunlight on the floor as if that were his timekeeper. "Two, maybe three hours ago, Manny. This here fella came out with his water can and the hider sniped him neat. We was on point duty, workin' our way down here for a look-see. Then Ras—he used that ricochet trick you learned us—got the Limey. I did a squirm and saw they was both dead. This fella got it in the head and the Limey took it in the middle. But they both had it—right enough!"

"Then how come this fire's burnin' so good?" Manny asked.

The boy spun around to stare at the flames. "How do I know? We've been makin' point around here for two days now and there wasn't no one here but this one guy—nobody! I did a squirm when he was out yesterday and this place was empty. No sign of another guy holin' up here. I don't care what Long did tell the Sarge—there's only bin one fella here since we've been on point! Go'n ask Ras if you don't believe me!"

Manny scratched a finger through his thick crop of brindled hair.

"Well, you and Ras look around for the cache stuff. I'll take point 'til you're through."

He went out, to be replaced a few minutes later by a second boy not much older than the first. And he too was armed. He stopped short upon viewing the fire.

"How come—?" he was beginning, when the other turned on him.

"Now don't you go on like Manny. He thinks this fella musta had him a buddy."

"But we ain't seen no one else!" protested Ras. His hair and skin were dark; he was plainly of a different nationality, even race, than his freckled face companion whose tangled mop of hair was light brown.

"Sure. Only a fire don't lay more wood on itself. Let's look for the stuff and get outta here on the double. I don't like spooky tricks."

They proceeded to the search with a thoroughness and precision which told Blake that this was not the first time they had carried out such a duty. And upon kicking aside the pile of rags in the corner they found what they sought, a loose stone which, when clawed from its place, revealed a cubby filled with tins. Ras gave a sigh of relief.

"That's it. But—looky, he had a lot more'n we thought."

"So that wasn't the first cache he'd trapped!" snapped the other. "We ain't cryin' over gettin' back more, are we?"

He had been pulling the spoil out of the improvised hiding place and now he had a good collection of tins. He straightened up, frowning.

"You go tell Manny," he ordered. "We can't lug all these back to camp—not and watch out for hiders, too."

The gray-haired man returned to inspect the find.

"Good haul. Most of our stuff back again and maybe as much more. No wonder that Limey was gunnin' for him. This woulda been a rich take for a hider," was his comment.

"We can't lug it all back now," protested the younger boy. "We couldn't even pack it across the big hole without help."

"Sure, sure. You take it easy, Bill. Nobody's makin' a pack horse outta you yet, are they? You'n Ras carry what you can. Me—I'll go on point here. If this joker *did* have him a buddy we don't want him comin' back to make trouble by movin' this stuff on us. Get on with it, Bill."

Bill produced a bag which he had carried folded through his belt and stuffed in a collection of tins. Then he went out and Ras came in to copy his action. When Ras had left in his turn, Manny paced restlessly about the cleared space, pausing now and again to listen. He kicked once at the pile of tins, sending one spinning close to Blake's shelter.

"Bait," he speculated aloud. "This here could be bait to bring him back—if there *was* another guy." He took up his position just within the door.

But the cans drew Blake's attention. Food? If he had only had the good fortune to find them first! Manny was alone, but he was armed with a rifle and two knives, and his whole attitude suggested that he knew very well how to use that assortment of weapons.

Blake licked his lips and winced. Food lay only a few inches out of his reach. He longed for the power Kittson had demonstrated days and worlds ago when the agent had drawn the pack of cigarettes across the room to his hand. He could not do that, nor could he enforce his will on Manny as Erskine had manipulated Beneirs. Or could he?

Close to his hand was ammunition of a sort. Blake picked up a brick. Now, if he could get Manny to move just a foot or so. He had managed to use a stone skillfully just an hour back. Blake jerked away from that memory and concentrated on the action at hand.

He fixed both sight and mind on the guard, willing him to walk away from the door—to move a little to the left—just a step or two . . . He must!

Whether Blake's struggles with Pranj had built up his slight psi power, or whether it was only chance, he could not tell, but Manny seemed uneasy. The man kept glancing at the fire now smoldering into coals once more, shifting his feet.

"Bait—" his lips shaped the word plainly enough for Blake to read. "Bait—"

But he did not turn his back on the door. Instead he sidled to the left, and in that moment Blake hurled the brick. It struck the other on the temple. He gave a startled grunt, falling back against the wall and scraping down it to the floor.

Blake lurched into the open. He could not drag the man away, but he could and did disarm him. Then, scooping up one of those tins, he went to sit on the other side of the fire he again built up.

His prize was an army field ration kit. And he worried off the cover to ram the contents into his mouth. He was chewing vigorously when he noted that Manny's eyes were open and watching him. For some reason the other did not seem surprised.

"You a tech?"

Not knowing whether it was better to claim or deny that label Blake drank from Manny's canteen and waited for another lead.

"You must be—that swell fur jacket and all. We don't get us stuff like that around here. And you ain't no hider; you'd show up too well. You'd be picked off on your first squirm."

Blake glanced down at the parka which was his legacy from Pakahini's world. The fur was a startling black and white and about the skirt of the long tunic was a band of vivid scarlet cloth worked with brilliant threads in the dot and circle patterns of the hunter's people. No, it was not a garment in which one could be inconspicuous. Manny's clothing was drab in shade, fading into the background. Even his salt and pepper hair added to that protective coloring.

"A real live tech! But how'd you get here? Were you livin' with the guy that Limey picked off? Long did say as how he was sure there was more'n one fella holed up here. But if our fellas had seen you before they'd have said so. Say," his eyes lit up as he wriggled into a more comfortable position, "have you guys got planes again? Them kind what you can sit down right where you want 'em—the 'copters? Baldy reported seein' a big one, but we thought it was likely a Nasty and we took to the deeps for two-three days 'til we was sure they weren't unloadin' any more stuff."

Blake picked that up, it would be as good an explanation for his mode of arrival here as any. "Yes, I came in on a helicopter. But it crashed. Where is this anyway?"

Manny hunched forward. "You ain't a Nasty," he remarked with conviction. "I never did hold with them stories about the Nastys still hangin' around up north somewheres. They never got more'n a toe-hold, and them last radio messages said that nothin' was gonna come 'cross sea to help them. They sure gave us a pastin' here. You musta seen that when you flew in. But that weren't nothin' to what we gave them back. This here is—" he gave the name of the city.

Blake stopped eating. Of course, inside him, he had known all along that that was true—ever since he had heard the familiar speech of Manny and his crew. Same city—but plainly a different level—though one not so far from his own. This one was in ruins—what had happened here?

"Where you from? I heard once that there was bunches of techs hid out—'way off in the mountains and such places. Sarge has been tryin' to contact them, talkin' about doin' it after we get the hiders cleared out and can live peaceable without gettin' shot at every time we make a move outta our own holes. You a tech scout, eh, comin' down to see what's what?"

Blake decided to agree to that with a nod.

"What happened here?" he dared to ask now, trying to guess how far this level world might be removed from his own. The decision from which it had been born could not be too far in the past. The idiom Manny used was of his own time; the rifle was familiar. This was not as alien as the world into which Pranj had taken him, as the world in which Pakahini hunted his white furred prey and smashed metallic worms.

"Oh, we got plastered in the big raids. Guided rockets and such all over the place. Then all at once they stopped comin'. Guess our boys was givin' them as good as we got," Manny laughed dryly. "Me, I was with the city guard. Would you believe it, I used to push a hack right through these here streets. Seems funny to remember it now—like a crazy mixed up dream or somethin'. Some of the streets ain't even here no more. There's the Big Hole where the subways blew up and then got filled with water.

"Well, I was with the city guard when them Nasty paratroopers came in. We had a bunch of Free British gangin' along with us. And were those Limeys ever tough! Lord, they knew how to scrag the Nastys right and proper! We fought it out buildin' to buildin'. I can't even remember now how it went, so much goin' on a fellow stopped thinkin' and just fought—then hid out to fight again when he'd have a patch of better luck. Time gets so it don't mean nothin' when you're livin' just from one minute to the next.

"First thing I knew I was leggin' it with the Sarge's Mob. He knows his stuff, the Sarge does. You stick with him and you eat, and you live. He's regular army—came out of a hospital when the fight started and rounded up a gang. We was mixed all right: Free British and regular army, city guards, some Navy guys what pulled outta the bombing of the Navy Yard in time, and a bunch of women what could handle a gun as good as a guy. We dug in up around the park and there we've stayed. Them Nastys—we cleaned them up—took us some time to do it proper, though.

"Now we're after the hiders, the guys what went out for themselves and snipe everybody what comes into their territory. Once we get ridda them we can expand like and start huntin' down the things that'll help us start over again. That's what the Sarge's lookin' forward to—startin' up again. Why," Manny's voice was proud, "we growed corn last summer and eatin' stuff in the park. And them deer outta the zoo, we're takin' care of them. Sometime we'll use them like cows—for meat. But mostly we live off supplies we find around." He gestured to the tins. "How's your mob been makin' out?"

"A little better than that," Blake gave what he hoped would be the right answer. He wondered if he dared open another ration tin.

"What th'—!" Manny's bemused stare was aimed over Blake's shoulder, his exclamation made the other's head turn.

The man was staring at the pile of rubble behind which was the carrier. Blake leaped to his feet with a cry of disbelief. Forgetting the other, he plunged forward, climbing over the bricks just in time to witness full disaster.

The carrier was still visible, but around it thickened a wall of green haze; It couldn't be true—there was no one on it at the control—yet it was about to vanish before his eyes!

And the lever moved. No hand held it, yet it was being drawn down in its slot. The green haze curdled fast into a wall. Blake, his heart pounding, watched it shimmer, shimmer and snuff out. The floor of the basement was empty—the carrier had vanished!

"So that there was your crashed plane, eh? Now you just turn around slow and easy, fella. And keep your hands up while you're doin' it!"

The words reached Blake through bewilderment and shock. The carrier was gone; he was marooned! Slowly, dazedly, he obeyed the order. He turned to face Manny, a transformed Manny with the rifle back in his hands, a Manny who watched him through narrowed and menacing eyes.

"You techs sure ain't very smart, even if you can cook up contraptions like that one what just pulled the disappearin' act on you. Never take your eyes off a fella you've jumped. Now supposin' you take that rat tickler outta your belt and toss it here. And don't try any tricks like you did with the brick or you'll get a bullet right between those big wide eyes of yours what'll finish you off for good!"

Blake tossed the stained dagger blade across the floor. Manny slapped his foot down on the weapon but did not stoop to pick it up. Blake was still more engrossed with the fact that he was marooned; to him it was more important at the moment than the fact Manny was now in control.

"You can sit down," Manny informed him. "Looks like you need to before you fall, but right there on that block and keep your paws out where I can see them. What's the matter with your left one?"

"My shoulder's hurt," Blake informed him dully.

"Huh? Hider get you—or trouble back where you came from? Looks to me like you was makin' a quick getaway from somewhere with that spook flyer."

Blake did not answer. There was no use in trying to explain all the wild events of the past few days. And he had an idea that Manny would not believe any of it, even if he did tell the truth. The ex-hackie had again taken a station by the door where he could not only keep his eye on his prisoner but on the scene without as well.

"Beats me where you come from." Manny was inclined to be talkative. "Wearin' them clothes you ain't no hider. 'Less you found some new warehouse to loot. But you'd be a fool to squirm around with that coat on you, just a sittin' duck for the first sniper who gets sights on you. So you must be a tech. Anyway—Sarge'll get it outta you. Fellas don't clam up when he says 'talk'; they talk and talk fast. How long you been here?"

Blake stared into the fire feeling nothing but a dull discouragement. Through his adventures, so far, even in Pakahini's nightmare world, he had always been sustained by the feeling that he was, in a manner, in control of the situation, that escape via the carrier was at hand. But now his exile might be permanent. He was certain that Pranj had, in some way, managed to locate the level traveling device and summon it back to him.

"I said, fella, how long have you been here?" Manny's voice carried a snap.

"What? Oh, just a little while; I don't know," Blake replied absently.

"And what was that thing that went off by itself?"

"A new type of transportation."

"Only it wasn't supposed to leave without your being on it," Manny observed shrewdly. "What about it? Set on some sort of an alarm and you didn't get back in time? Now you're stuck here. Well, Sarge'll sure be glad we picked you up. *We* could use one of them disappearin' machines—we sure could!"

He was interrupted by a shrill whistle, three times repeated. And he puckered his lips to answer it with a single trill. A moment later four of his fellows crowded through the door. Two were the boys who had been there before, the other two were a tall blond man, too thin for his frame, and a Chinese.

"Well, whatta you know!" Bill exploded. "So he did have a buddy!"

Manny shook his head. "This here's some kinda tech. He was tryin' out a travelin' machine. Only it took off and left him stuck right here with the rest of us ruin rats."

All four stared at Blake as if he had suddenly grown horns and a pale blue skin before their eyes.

"A tech!" breathed Ras. "Where'd he come from? There ain't no techs near here."

"You been personally all over this here city?" Manny demanded. "We can go about three square miles—and the rest we don't know. Anyway, you, Sam and Alf, get yourselves a loada cans and help us take this guy back to Sarge. He'll sure be glad to get his hands on a real live Tech!"

The Chinese and the tall man packed cans into bags and then closed in on Blake.

"He's got a bum shoulder and his left fin's no good," Manny informed them. "I took his knife. Hey you, stand up and let Alf see if you have any booby traps under that fur tent of yours."

Blake got wearily to his feet and stood passively for the search. All the other discovered was the sealed jar he had brought from the laboratory. Seeing the demon's head on the knob, Manny promptly ordered that that be presented to the Sarge.

"All right, mate," the blond Alf spoke for the first time, "you move along now—easy does it." He had an accent Blake could not place, but the out of time man suspected that much of the big man's slowness might be a pose.

"Don't get no funny ideas about heavin' no more rocks, neither," Manny warned him. "Sam's a sniper and Alf—I've seen him break a guy's neck for him, usin' just his hands—as easy as snappin' a stick."

One of the boys went out first, rifle ready. Behind him scrambled Manny, then Alf waved for Blake to follow.

The door opening was below the surface of the ground, but a series of toe hollows for steps led them up into the full light of day, a cold winter day. There was some snow, melting where the sun struck full upon it, but even such drifts as he had battled among the towers that morning could not have concealed the awful desolation Blake now faced. Before its fate had come upon it, this city must have been close twin to the one of his own time. Another clue that the decision which had split their time stream levels had been of recent origin.

If he had not been so weary and sick at heart he might have asked questions. But now he dumbly obeyed orders to travel along the narrow path which wound among the mounds of debris.

Chapter Eleven

They split up as might an army patrol in dangerous territory—the boys scouting ahead. Sometimes they paused while one or two prowled away, taking cover, and they did not march on until a signal was whistled. Blake gathered that the Sarge's "Mob" did not control this particular section of the city, and must move through it ever on guard.

Whole blocks of buildings had been leveled off well above the original position of the street. And in other places there were empty gaps, deep pits in the ground, marked with reed vegetation, some with frozen ponds in their centers. This condition had plainly existed for several years.

Blake deduced that they were traveling uptown, but distances were difficult to measure when it was necessary to make so many detours. Sometimes they took paths beaten through the rubble by steady use, at other intervals they scrambled precariously over barriers of sand and stone.

"Big mess." Sam gave his prisoner a steadying hand as they crossed one such patch.

Blake managed a tired grin. "It sure is."

"No mess, your place?"

"No," was all the reply Blake had breath for.

"Better some day here, too. We got good place. Sarge—he fix."

They came out into an open space between two mountains of

torn and wrenched stone. Before them was the lacework of bare tree branches against a very clear blue sky. Blake made a startling discovery—he knew this under very different circumstances. This was the park! And they were about to enter it not far from the road he had taken with the TV repair truck!

He had been right, he knew this city. But it couldn't be his own level. One did not go forward or backward in time by the route of the successor worlds—only across it. The agents had sworn to that. However, merely because he did recognize it Blake felt a new spark of hope. If he could only discover what historical decision had triggered this!

The party passed a formidable barrier thrown up at what had once been one of the main entrances to the park. Sentries on duty there exchanged news with the party who had been out on a "squirm." But Blake was more intent in trying to pick out landmarks. If he had only known the city better before he had been taken by Scappa's men!

Were the agents tracing Pranj now through the bands of worlds? Had they any information as to which the outlaw fancied, or did they just visit the likely ones? And would they sooner or later appear in this one to investigate?

Saxton had said that certain possibility worlds would attract Pranj, those "disturbed" levels where chaotic conditions fostered dictatorships. Well, this one, judging even by the limited view Blake had had of it, was certainly "disturbed" to a high degree. Enough to attract Pranj and so the agents? He might not be as helplessly lost as he first feared.

Blake was hustled on down a badly kept road toward the center of the park. He was not in the least surprised to discover that they were bound for the same summer-theater restaurant he had seen in his own time. He glanced at the parking lot. Two battered jeeps rusted in one corner and several large trucks had sunk almost hub deep in the cinders. But there was no TV repair van.

On the other side of the building was a circle of cabin-huts, rude, one story shelters combining in their walls tree trunks and plundered brick and stone—from the chimneys of which puffed blue wood smoke. The taint of that smoke was thick on the air, together with the effluvium of human beings, none too clean, dwelling in a limited amount of space. But the huts were set in a straight line, an equal amount of ground about each, and the settlement had an air of permanence, almost of efficiency, which contrasted sharply with the chaos of the city.

A flag drooped limply from a pole outside the large building: Red, white and blue. Right enough! Yet there was something odd about the way those colors were combined. Blake was not sure that it was the stars and stripes he had always known. Below it was another—a smaller, squared banner which Sam indicated with a thumb as they passed beneath it.

"That belongs to Tenth Cavalry. Sarge—he was Tenth Cavalry in regulars."

They went up the steps and entered what had been the lobby of the theater. Battered desks in a military line occupied much of the space. But only two were now in use. At one sat a man whose scanty hair was white and yet whose shoulders were squared by years of army drill. And at the other was a young man who glanced up from a study of a torn map to survey Blake with astonished eyes.

"Tell the Sarge," Manny swaggered to the fore of his small command, "that we've got us a tech!"

Now the man was attentive, his open wonder plain as he saw Blake's clothing. He left his desk and vanished into the auditorium, to return shortly.

"Take him in."

Only Manny and Alf accompanied Blake into the main room. Most of the seats had been ripped out, only four rows close to the stage remaining intact. Crossing that wide expanse of floor, knowing that he was the center of attention, awoke self-consciousness in Blake. On the stage were three more desks, the middle one slightly ahead. Behind it sat the man who must be the ruler of the settlement—Manny's Sarge.

And so impressive was he that he dwarfed the other two men who shared the platform. Blake had met and seen men of assurance since this wild adventure had begun: Kittson and his teammates, the nobles who had visited Pranj in the alien world, Pranj himself, Pakahini. But none of those had been of Blake's world or kind. There existed a difference of which he had always been aware.

The Sarge was no arrogant noble, no psi man a little overpowering with his self-confidence, no hunter of a tribe who dominated his world. Always the superior who dealt only with inferiors when it came to action, the Sarge was a born leader of ordinary men—men like Blake—understandably human, whom chance and the right time had brought into his own.

His assurance held no hint of arrogance; his self-confidence no hint of superiority. He was ready and willing to face any test fate might present. When he looked down at Blake, there was something almost gentle in the smile which revealed strong white teeth, contrasting the coffee brown skin.

"You look," his voice was smooth, warm, "as if you've come a long way, Mistuh."

Blake relaxed. Manny and his men had inspired little trust. But the Sarge was a different proposition. He might have been Kittson.

"Rather," he replied.

Those dark eyes were assessing his clothing, missing no detail of the parka, of the slacks and boots. Manny stepped up to place the gemmed dagger and the sealed jar before his commander. But the Sarge gave each exhibit only a passing glance.

"You techs robbin' museums now?" he chuckled. "Where you from, Mistuh, up Canada way? Seems like I've seen fur coats like yours from there. On a tour to see how the ruin rats are makin' out?"

"He had some kinda machine. It just disappeared and left him," Manny reported importantly.

The Sarge sat very still, only his eyes moved from the ex-hackie to Blake and back again.

"Plane? 'copter?"

Manny shook his head. "This here was somethin' new. Flat platform, not even a motor I could see. It was in this here cellar where we traced the looter. This tech was hidin' there. Knocked me out before I saw him. Ate rations like he was half starved. Then I saw this green light over in a corner. He looks, too, gives a yell and runs. In the middle of that light was this here machine. Light went off and the machine with it, just snuffed out like a candle."

"At which point you took over, Manny?"

"Sure, Sarge. He was a greenie. Left my gun lyin' right there on the floor for me."

"And now you're gonna tell us how your machine got in that

there cellar," the voice was a velvety, cushioned purr. But below its liquid softness was steel. "We could use a neat trick like that ourselves."

Blake saw no possible reply, except an honest, "I don't know how it works."

The Sarge still smiled. "That's too bad, Mistuh. Seems like you techs and the big guys who got theirselves out before the smashup want to write us off as no goods, while you plan the future. Only, we're still around and we've got somethin' to say. Anyway, Mistuh, you're gonna stay here with us for awhile 'til we decide what to do about you. Manny, lock him up."

"He's got a bum shoulder, Sarge. Shouldn't he see Doc first?"

"Huh? You techs fightin' each other now, maybe?" The Sarge laughed as if he found that thought highly amusing. "Take him to Doc, and then lock him up," His eyes moved to the pile of papers before him; it was as if they were now invisible.

"This way, tech."

They did not go back through the lobby, but out a side door into what had once been the restaurant. Here partitions had been set up to cut the large room into a series of cubbys, mostly lighted with candles and oil lamps, though the walls did not reach to the high ceiling.

"Doc around?" Manny demanded of a girl they met just inside the door.

"In his office."

A narrow hall ended in a door which was only a curtain of canvas rigged over a pole. Manny stopped.

"You there, Doc?"

"Come in."

The ex-hackie pulled aside the drapery and waved Blake in.

"What is it now?" The gray haired man at the table did not look up at once from his microscope. "You or one of your boys get punctured by a hider, Manny?"

"No. We just got us a prisoner who needs patchin' up."

"A prisoner!" Now he did turn to view them. "Since when has the Sarge been taking prisoners." Then as his eyes rested on Blake they showed real surprise. "Tech!" he almost whispered. "By all the Saints, a tech! So they've contacted us at last!"

"Maybe yes, maybe no," Manny poured cold water on his enthusiasm. "We've found just this one and he's on the lam from his own crowd; the signs point to that. Sarge says to patch him up and then put him in storage."

Blake with the doctor's help stripped to the waist, exposing the raw red mark on his shoulder.

"That wasn't made by no bullet!" observed Manny, watching the proceedings with interest.

"Burn," was the doctor's diagnosis. "Almost like some form of radiation."

Blake shivered. In his own time that word had an ominous meaning which allied it with the worst of disasters.

"How did you get it?" the doctor was continuing.

"New kind of weapon," Blake returned. "But it didn't hit me full blast."

The doctor was looking over an array of jars. "Just as well it didn't. I'd say it might have been able to eat a hole through you. Burn . . . sure enough, and we'll treat it like one. We don't," a note of bitterness crept into his voice, "have the wealth of supplies you techs laid up before the smash, but we do our best. See here, Manny, I don't like the look of this. Suppose you leave him with us. I'll bed him down in one of the inner rooms; he can't elope out of there. And I want to keep an eye on him for a time."

When the other hesitated the doctor added impatiently:

"Put a guard at the door if it'll make you and the Sarge any happier. That's the only exit and he isn't going to get past it unseen. And, if I'm any judge, he's in no shape to make a run for it anyway."

Manny shrugged. "Okay, Doc. He's all yours. I'll tell the Sarge that. So long."

Blake watched him go. He was more conscious now of the constant dull ache in his shoulder. The doctor had started a new worry.

"How bad is it really, doctor?"

"Just bad enough to keep a tech here where I can ask him a few pertinent questions," replied the other. "By the look of you, you've had a pretty rugged time. What would you say to a hot bath, a good meal, and some conversation. Better than being stuck in a detention cell—eh?"

Blake brightened. "Decidedly!"

The bath must be taken in a tin tub supplied by buckets, but it was hot enough to draw the chill out of his bones. And presented with fresh though worn and patched clothing, he sat down to eat with the doctor, a soothing dressing on his shoulder, really comfortable for the first time in several days.

"Where's your tech headquarters? Somewhere in the north I'd say, from that spectacular fur jacket of yours—"

Blake was greatly tempted to tell the truth. But caution prevailed and he answered with the best evasion he could produce.

"Frankly, I don't know. I was getting away from there in a hurry and landed here. I can't tell you how or why."

The doctor's shrewd eyes met his. "That almost sounds like the truth. You say you were getting away in a hurry. Is Manny right? Are you an outlaw? You have a burn made by an unknown weapon. Are the techs fighting among themselves, or have the Nastys taken on a new lease of life and jumped you?"

"Neither as far as I know. I was dealing with—well, you might call him a renegade," Blake began slowly, trying to fit facts into a framework the other would believe. "He's trying to set himself up as a dictator."

"Pocket Hitler, eh?" the doctor did not appear surprised. "We've had plenty of them ever since the real article stopped riding the air waves out of London. They come and go—just nuisances mostly—"

"From *London*!" Blake seized on the one piece of information which was startling. "Hitler in London! When?"

"Didn't your crowd catch that last broadcast before the 'No Return' attack was launched?" the doctor wanted to know. When Blake shook his head he continued, "Yes, I remember now, things were a bit disorganized along about then and your tech holes were cut off from the rest of us. I was on duty in the fourth district, defense area, then. We heard him screaming out his nonsense. Then he was cut off right in the middle and we knew our boys had plastered London, but right. Never a peep from there since. Someday, maybe five, ten years from now, if Sarge and those like him can get us on our feet again, we'll get a plane into the air or send a ship over and discover what really happened to Adolf and his friends."

Historical decision; Blake concentrated on that. Something to do with World War II; he could pin it down that far. But what decision?

Hurriedly he tried to remember fateful points in a conflict now more than ten years behind him. And then thought he might have it.

"Then here Hitler *did* win the Battle of Britain," he half-whispered, forgetting the doctor.

August and September, 1940. This world had taken one fork in the road; his the other.

Later, when he had the privacy to think, Blake lay at ease on a bunk, staring up at a cracked and grimed ceiling far above him. The sounds of the hospital annex were muted, his body warm and well fed, he might have drowsed away the late afternoon had it not been for those thoughts.

Hints and names fell into place now, fitted like a giant jigsaw. "Nastys" were the now vanished Nazis of his own world. "Free British," Hitler's broadcast from London—it was all explained. He knew the history of this ruined city. But he had a suspicion that his strange ignorance might have given him away in part.

"Of course Hitler won the Battle of Britain. Surely even the men of a sector experimental station must know that!" had been the doctor's reply to Blake's impulsive speech. "You are well fed, your clothes are good—except for some incidental wear and tear—better than we've seen for years. You appear suddenly and are ignorant of the plainest historical events. You offer an intriguing puzzle, young man."

Blake squirmed. "I can't explain."

"Your 'can't' is probably nearer to 'won't,'" snapped the doctor. "But I'm not going to press you. And I'll accept your story about a renegade tech causing trouble. Mainly because *that does* fit in with a rumor which has been circulating lately. But I'll stage my reputation that you are *not* a tech yourself. Not one of the variety I've known in the past. And right now you are adrift from your own world."

That had probably been intended as a figure of speech. But Blake feared that the doctor had detected the start with which he heard it. How much did that keen-eyed man know, or suspect?

"I wish—" he had begun.

But the doctor was continuing. "Let us assume that you come from a secret project, one which was so well screened that it has been cut off from the outside for some time. I can imagine that one newly emerging from such a cocoon would find a great deal to amaze him. What do you want to ask first?"

Blake accepted that, or fell into the trap, now he was not certain which. The other might not believe that he was a tech, but for some reason of his own, the doctor was ready to provide him with the orientation he needed to function in this world. Blake might have to remain here for the rest of his life and the more he could learn the better.

"What if I don't know any history since—" he had groped for a point which might be common to both of their worlds, "Dunkirk?"

"Dunkirk—the end of May, beginning of June, 1940, the last gasp of Britain," mused the doctor. "Well, early in August the pressure came—air attack all out on the British Isles around the clock. The Nastys wiped out most of the air fields by the end of September. The English used their fleet to try a withdrawal to Canada. We weren't in the war then," he laughed bitterly. "Nothing like being too late with too little. The Limeys managed to bring off some of their fighting men and a few civilians. In October we sent in ships to help. But on the 10th, the Battle of the Channel began and with it the airborne invasion of the islands. And on the 15th, the Japs struck us in the West."

"Pearl Harbor!" Blake supplied but the doctor shook his head impatiently.

"Hawaii had nothing to do with it. The Japs sent in waves of carrier based planes all up and down our west coast. Then there was a howl raised to bring our fleet back from dying England. But San Francisco, Los Angeles, Seattle—they'd had it and good. Japs exploded all over the Pacific. I don't know what happened in Australia; they were still fighting a desperate rear guard action along the salt deserts there last we heard. But invasion forces landed in Alaska and lower California. We beat them back to the sea only in time to get it in the east from German raiders. Mix that with sabotage on a grand scale, and a few other tricks."

Blake, recalling every word of that, moved uneasily on his bunk. That flow of news all bad, and all so close to what might have been true. It was all the nightmare of his own world brought into daylight. And this was no dream—this world was real!

Chapter Twelve

"... germ warfare," the doctor had continued. "Though we can't be sure now. There was a virus infection in the second year. About one in five recovered. It could have been planted and it first broke out about the time the Nastys flattened Washington and made two airborne landings: one here and one in the south. We were hanging on by our fingernails right about then and the virus really smacked us into the ropes.

"Then something happened. What, we'll never know unless we can get across to explore someday. We sent a 'No Return' bombing raid—heavy bombers, carrier stuff, everything which could have the faintest chance of making a one way trip to London when we heard that Hitler and his high ranks had gathered there for conquest ceremonies. Maybe we *did* get all their top brass then, broke their chain of command. Or perhaps they went to fighting elsewhere. We always wondered how long their love feast with the Russians was going to last.

"We don't know what happened. Only the Nastys stopped coming over. Their ships vanished from off our coast and their troops here were abandoned. But that didn't happen until everything was in an unholy mess as far as we were concerned.

"That was—let's see—five—six year back. One begins to lose track of time living like this. We'd proved a harder nut to crack than they thought we would be, in spite of virus and everything they could dump on our heads. But you can't keep factories running when they've been largely bombed out of existence, not with a mechanical setup as complex as ours was. Take a city of this size, knock out the gas, light, water, service of supplies, add an epidemic and you have chaos in less than a week—without any assistance of air attack.

"One factory depends upon raw materials brought from a distance and complicated tools transported from the opposite direction by rail. Smash those rails or either source of supply, and you have a factory unable to function. It's easy to upset the applecart in a highly mechanized civilization.

"Communication went. Radios gave out when parts couldn't be produced or replaced, when there were not enough technicians to run them. We have a ham operator here. He spends ten hours a day listening, and for the past two years he's been unable to pick up another signal anywhere!

"Meanwhile in this city, which is the section I can speak of with authority, we had two attacks of the virus. I can show you places uptown black from fire. That's where we burned bodies—not by the hundreds but by the thousands! Those days were nightmares out of hell! And through it all we fought off a paratroop invasion. Since then we've managed to keep alive by being a little quicker on the trigger than the others."

"What others?" Blake had prompted.

"Deserters, Nastys who escaped the mop-up gangs, criminals who took to open outlawry when law enforcement collapsed. They hid out, preying on us, raiding for supplies. We've driven them out of this western section of the city, though they still sneak in to plunder our caches. The Sarge hopes to organize a big expedition which will rid us of them. He made contact with another Mob of Free British just last week. They're over on the government island in the bay and have two useable launches. So they're willing to give us naval support along the shore, if and when. We can thank our lucky stars for the Sarge!"

"Who is he?"

"Old army—really old army of the traditional style. Ever hear of the Tenth Cavalry?"

Blake had not.

"It was a regiment with traditions, could split honors with

Custer's famous Seventh. And it was never massacred because its commanding officer was a glory-grabber. They were part of the old Indian Fighting Army with a list of battle honors to make your hair curl. The Indians called them 'Buffalo Soldiers' and they didn't tangle with them any more than they could help. It was one of the first Negro cavalry troops.

"The Sarge's grandfather joined up right after the Civil War, and his father went in as soon as he was old enough. He never thought of any other career for himself, being born into the regiment as were the Roman legionnaires in their day. The Tenth is gone, but the Sarge is still with us—otherwise we wouldn't be here!"

Under the rule of the Sarge the settlement in the park had obtained a measure of security. The inhabitants drew on the contents of stores and warehouses for food and clothing. They clung to a shadow of the civilization they could remember and there was already a second generation growing up to whom the park village was the only way of life. And, Blake learned from the doctor, that in spite of lacking that which would have seemed to them several years earlier the necessities of life, they were not only thriving, but cherished detailed plans for future expansion. It was a community on the way back, inspired by the driving will power and genius of one man.

Foreseeing the eventual uselessness of rifles for which there was no ammunition, they had made bows. Grain had been planted in the park area, along with seed found in the ruins of a department store. Deer liberated from the zoo and horses from a riding academy were being bred.

Blake, enthused by the doctor's story, could understand the advantages of being a member of this community, of becoming one of the Sarge's "Mob." If he were sure that there was no chance of his ever being able to win back to his own level, he would count himself lucky to stay here.

In the meantime it seemed that he was forgotten by all but the doctor. He slept and ate, and then slept again. But by the middle of the next morning he was restless. Most of the pain had gone out of his shoulder and he was able to use his left hand and arm almost normally. He dressed in the drab clothing provided him and was sitting on the edge of his bunk when Manny appeared in the doorway.

"Hi," his greeting lacked ceremony, "the Sarge wants to see you."

Blake went with him willingly enough. This time the big man was engrossed with a map on which marched a series of small red dots. He was verifying the position of these from some notes on a sheaf of loose and finger marked papers. But he pushed them aside as Blake and his guard came up.

"What's this you been tellin' Doc about a renegade tech?" he demanded.

"He's the one responsible for my being here," Blake returned. "He kidnapped me, I escaped, and landed in this city."

"And this machine? You don't know how it works? Does it belong to this tech, maybe?"

"Yes, it does. No. I can't tell you how it works. I was able to get away on it, but that's all."

"What's this tech's name?" the question came bullet fashion.

"He has several as far as I know—Lefty Conners, Pranj—" The Sarge showed no sign of recognizing either.

"Ever hear of a guy called 'Ares?'"

Memory of a paragraph from an old school book was triggered by that. "He was the Greek god of war—"

"This one ain't no god," the Sarge's smile was grim, "but he sure does mix into war! For about four months now," he leaned back in his chair, locking his fingers behind his head, "we've been gatherin' in a crop of stories about this here 'Ares'. He's been dickerin' with the hiders, tryin' to organize 'em. And we've been told—if the story's straight it's bad stuff—that he's promised 'em some new arms. Now here you come along with a tale of a tech gone to the bad and causin' trouble. Seems like our Ares and your renegade tech might have somethin' in common, don't it now? You say that your man has this new travelin' contraption and a new kinda gun he shot you with. Yeah, it all fits in nice and smooth. Where's this here Pranj or Conners holed up now?"

"I only wish I knew. He's probably not in this city at all."

The Sarge frowned. "But likely he'll be comin' here?"

Blake himself wanted the answer to that. He understood so little about level traveling. If the carrier could only base in one spot, then Pranj might very well turn up in the cellar where he himself had been captured. And Blake had a strong conviction that the platform had, in a manner of speaking, been fixed while the other level worlds had formed and vanished about it during those incredible trips. So, if the carrier materialized on this level, it would do so there. But would Pranj come here? Was he in truth "Ares?" Knowing that Blake had been marooned here, would he come? Or would Blake's presence be an additional lure? There were so many ifs, and Blake felt he could not judge the other's reactions by his own. Pranj was psi—and an outlaw psi at that.

There was the other chance, for himself, for the eventual capture of Pranj. The sight of the map on the Sarge's desk had reminded him of that. What about the agents? Blake had no idea of where their carrier might be located or whether they were now using it to cruise the worlds they suspected Pranj of visiting. But the outlaw's discovery of their warehouse hideout had driven them to Patroon Place. Suppose that move had taken them to their point of contact with other levels. Again. . . . If . . . And . . . Maybe. But it gave Blake something to aim at.

"He may turn up in the place where I was found," he said.

"Because you landed there?" the other caught that quickly. "Was that thing you came on set on a homin' device?"

"I tell you I don't know!"

"But you can guess a little, is that it? That the only place you can think of?" The Sarge's voice was lazy, but the deep set brown eyes boring into Blake were alert, almost as compelling as Kittson's had been.

"Well, Pranj is on the run. There're some others after him."

"So?" The Sarge's lids drooped, half-veiling his eyes. "And you would like to meet up with the guys after him? Friends of yours, eh? And where do we go around lookin' for 'em?"

"I'd have to see a map," Blake countered. "And I'm not sure they're here either."

"Cagey, aren't you?" The Sarge pushed back his chair from the desk and beckoned. "Come around and take a look. This here's the best map we got."

The creased paper was torn and had been mended, and there were stains disfiguring its surface. But Blake traced the route he had taken up town by bus. The legend of "Mount Union" had been almost obliterated by a black smear, but he found it and then centered on Patroon Place. Had he been able to tell the full truth perhaps the quest would have been easier. But belief might not have followed his story. They would have to accept him on trust. Or, if and when he could leave this settlement, he must make for that point by himself.

The Sarge looked at the map. "That where these friends of yours hang out?"

"That's where I hope they do," Blake corrected. "But they may not be there. There's only one chance in perhaps a thousand."

"So." The Sarge rested his square jaw on a pile driver fist. "You sure don't tell a man much do you? But we've been bettin' our roles on a hellva lot of slim chances lately. Only maybe we'll take a look at that downtown place first—we know that territory. This," he licked a finger on Patroon Place, "is new; and after all you landed in that other joint."

"When the machine is in use there is a green glow."

"Sure is," Manny broke in for the first time. "Lights up the whole place, Sarge. I saw it."

"In daytime even, eh? Your friends have them a gimmick like that too?"

Blake had to believe that all carriers were alike. "Yes."

"Then we can set two points." The Sarge became brisk. "One down one up. You," he spoke to Blake, "go along with the uptown picket. You know your friends. We can take care of Ares if he turns up. You're going to save us time and trouble all around."

"If Ares is Pranj he's—" Blake began a warning.

"If he's your renegade tech he's trouble with a capital 'T.' Boy," the Sarge laughed, "we don't need no tellin' about that. We've been up against some tough men lately."

But not as tough as the outlaw level traveler, Blake wanted to say. Not against a man who would turn an enemy's brain inside out and control him as if he were a robot! He could only hope that he would reach the agents before the Sarge's men reached Pranj.

So, without being able to impress his warning more strongly, Blake found himself one of a party organized to explore uptown. He was, however, not offered arms, not even the gemmed dagger Manny had taken from him.

They kept to the overgrown wilderness of the park for their trek west. As they passed the empty cages of the zoo, Blake asked what had happened to the other animals besides the deer. The birds, he was told, had been freed to hang about the settlement, those which had survived the winters. The bears and felines had been shot.

"Not them wolves though," commented one of the men. "We got two hides curin' now. Some run and joined up with the dog packs for huntin'. In winter they're worse'n snipers if a man's alone."

Large portions of the park, which had originally been a long strip of greenery running two-thirds of the city's length, had relapsed into a jungle of matted shrubbery. The once well-kept roads had shrunk to rutted tracks between banks of impenetrable brush.

They rounded the end of an ice bordered lake, sending waterfowl squawking hysterically into the air, exchanging rude pleasantries with the gang hauling water in tanks. Even about such homely tasks the park dwellers went armed, with either bows or rifles. Blake learned that the rifles were given to those who by marksmanship proved themselves worthy, while less skilled "fighting men" (a category which included all males from the age of twelve and some women) had to be content with bows, though the younger boys had shown so much aptitude with those more antique weapons that they preferred rifles only as a matter of prestige. When the last bullet was fired, the transition to bow would not find the next generation untrained or unarmed.

The purpose of the present expedition was not only to test Blake's theory concerning the agents' base, but also for the regular occupation of foraging. Manny explained how, using old directories of the city and the Sarge's maps, the settlement was able to locate the sites of stores or warehouses which furnished them with supplies. Too often, a promising lead brought them to a district completely burnt out or reduced to hopeless rubble. However, this systematic plan of looting had paid off during the lean years of the immediate past. Every expedition had the glamor of a treasure hunt.

"Drugs for the Doc, material, clothes if they ain't too bad rotted to be any good, tinned stuff—anything what we can use. If we could just move along the streets better, get some trucks runnin', we'd do more," Manny observed. "But when you gotta stop drivin', and break your back every three or four feet luggin' stone outta the way only to run into another pile, well, it ain't worth tryin'. Once we get them hiders cleaned out so as a guy don't hafta keep lookin' over his shoulder every minute or get a bullet in his guts, then we can do this lootin' right. 'Til then we gotta lug stuff in the hard way—mostly on our backs."

"There was a drugstore on the corner of Mount Union," Blake offered.

Three—four days ago he had lingered in that drugstore, enjoying its light and warmth, protection against the storm without. But how many years had it been in this world since that building had been able to offer shelter?

"Yeah? Say, maybe we can make this trip pay off good then. Jack," he called over his shoulder to a lanky boy who was arguing with his companion, a smaller Negro lad, "you got that there list of stuff Doc told us to be on the lookout for?"

The boy put a hand into the front of his shabby lumberjacket. "Yessir. Pinned in. Why, Manny?"

"Used to be a drugstore up where we're goin'. If there's anything left of it, you and Bob cut in and see what you can find. Don't try for nothin' but doc's stuff—that's the most important."

"Yessir," the boy agreed and dropped back into the amicable dispute which dealt with the possibility of tracking down the dog pack whose trail had been seen further to the west. Wolf and dog pelts were esteemed goods at the settlement.

"Jack's quick on the uptake. He may learn Doc's business when he gets older," Manny reported. "Sarge is sortin' out all the young ones. Some—they kinda take natural to readin' and writin'—though they all gotta learn that—along with their numbers. Last month he had us haul books over from the library—let us take a coupla horses he thought it was so important to bring back big loads. Sarge says them boys may hafta fight all the resta their lives, but they ain't gonna be more ignorant than they hafta. When a boy shows talent for some-thin', well, the Sarge puts him to learnin' that as good as he can now. Someday," Manny's eyes shone with warm eagerness, "when them hiders is all cleared out and we can live without fightin' all the time, then we'll spread out more. Get outta this rat trap and see what's happened to the rest of the country. We was on top once, we'll be again—just you wait'n see!"

Something within Blake responded to that. Given a free hand, a reasonably stable future and these people would build again, build something perhaps better than that which had been blasted from under them. But how stable would be the future if Pranj broke in here? What if the rumor Sarge had heard was true, and the psi outlaw was importing new weapons—say the heat guns of the laboratory world—to equip mad dog fighters here? Those hiders who resisted the return of civilization would be so armed they could easily wipe out this nucleus of a new world to set up one of their own in which Pranj would be overlord.

At that moment Blake's struggle against Pranj went beyond the personal. It was no longer a contest between the two, a contest in which he felt the inferior, but a war against all that the outlaw psi man stood for. Sarge's people must be left unhampered to work out their own destiny, saved from one who could so easily ruin their hopes. Now he was able to understand the real mission of the agents and the web of protection they tried to spread across the other level worlds, the reason for their grim hunt for Pranj. Each world must be left to stand by itself, to rise or fall by the actions of its own inhabitants, and not be enslaved by an outsider.

If he could not return to his own world, Blake decided now, he must tell Sarge the truth—let him know the full menace facing them. But if it was possible to contact the agents, that must be done speedily before Pranj had a chance to strike here.

They left the park and turned into a street where the rows of houses appeared intact. Even a few windows still held unshattered glass in dusty panes, reflecting the chill winter sun.

"Know where you are?" Manny asked.

Blake halted. He had been here only at night but he was sure they were close to their goal.

"Hey, Manny, there's a drugstore for sure!" Jack had scouted ahead.

"Any street signs?" asked Blake.

"Wait—" Jack's voice drifted back. "Yeah, says 'Union'. That mean anything?"

Blake drew a deep breath. "This is it," he said more to himself than to Manny.

Chapter Thirteen

To enter this Patroon Place was a weird experience. The world of the laboratory, the world of the towers, had both been so far removed from the things which he knew that Blake could accept them. But here, where he had been before (or so it seemed), it was different. The same house, the same street—yet here was desolation, the desolation of the long abandoned, the ruined. Broken window panes, battered doors, were everywhere.

Manny jerked his thumb at one. "This here was raided," he remarked. "Rich joints like that got it bad from the looters in the early days. Which house you want?"

Blake stepped into the drive and gazed up at the right house, the exact counterpart of the one in which he had left the agents on his own level. To all appearances, save for the evidences of violence and time, it was the same. He felt as if he walked slowly through some nightmare. The nagging idea that this *was* the same house, that somehow he had traveled forward or backward in time instead of across it, persisted. He shivered as he advanced.

The front door was gone and there were scars about it.

"Bullet holes," Manny identified matter-of-factly. "Guy in here musta put up a scrap."

Within, a barricade of broken furniture fronted them. From somewhere Manny produced a battered flashlight, and its circle of radiance picked out a pile of white bones in the far corner. For one sickening moment, Blake wondered if that could be—? But this wasn't the same world, he must keep reminding himself of that.

"What are we huntin' for?" Manny wanted to know.

"Should be in the cellar," Blake gave a half answer. Since the site of the carrier must be hidden, it would be most easily concealed there—as Pranj's had been.

Manny went from room to room, opening the few doors left. There were other bones, many signs of a battle fought from room to room years before. Once the ex-hackie turned the light on the floor and Blake saw the track of an animal boldly printed in the dust.

"Wolf . . . or dog. They roam about uptown."

"What do they live on?"

"Us—when they can get at us," Manny replied flatly. "They do run deer and horses. That's why we don't go out alone in winter, and why we take cover at nightfall 'less it's an emergency. We've found the remains of hiders that weren't lucky or smart. Cal took the body of a dead pony up to the far west end of the park for bait four, five weeks back. He got him five dogs and a wolf before sun down. They're mean and vicious and smart, too, and gettin' even smarter. Here's the cellar—"

The last door he had opened gave on a flight of stairs and they descended into heavy gloom. A wine storage section, its contents smashed and plundered by the early raiders, lay behind another shelved space where dusty, empty jars stood in rows. They passed through a laundry and a furnace room to come to the last door of all. Manny had been counting paces under his breath, and now he said:

"This here cellar's bigger than the house. I'd say this part's out under the front yard, maybe runnin' out under the street."

Blake's spirits rose. The need for extra space was promising. Space for what? A base for a carrier?

Manny pulled at the door, but it failed to give as the others had done.

"Locked!"

Blake joined in the effort to force it. But it *was* locked, and the heavy wood did not yield. Blake ran one finger across a hinge and brought it away slick with oil. There could be only one reason for oiling a door in a long-deserted house. His guess had been right, this was a transfer point for the agents. He had only to keep watch here and sooner or later he could contact them, be able to return to his own world. But that would mean camping here, a cat at a mousehole. And would Sarge and his men permit that?

"Oiled? Your friends, tech?"

"I hope so. But I don't know when they'll be back."

"We'll set up a point here," Manny declared. "If they show, we'll know it. Why in cellars?" He added that last question as if he were thinking aloud, and Blake did not try to reply.

That shrill whistle which was the rallying call of the Sarge's forces sounded as they climbed the cellar stairs. Out in the yard were the remainder of the party, Jack and his younger companion with filled bags on their backs, the taciturn Gorham peering into the garage.

"Say, Manny," Jack greeted them, "that store's hardly been touched! We've got loads for the Doc and there's canned food, too. Worth sending a horse for. Tell Sarge that."

Manny glanced at the sky. It was well past noon by the position of the pale sun. "We grub now," he decided, "then Bob and Gorham pack back to camp and see if the Sarge thinks it's worth sendin' up a horse. We gotta set a point here—you can tell Sarge that. Afterwards, Jack, you sort out the food down at the store. Some might be left to grub the point—save 'em luggin' in supplies. There's some scoutin' to be done. How about it, Gorham, any sign of hiders?"

Gorham shook his shaggy head. "These places were raided, sure, but back in the early days. Lots of things smashed but not much taken. I'd say nobody's been back since."

"We're in luck, then." Manny sat down on the back steps. "Let's eat."

They chewed the rations they had brought with them and drank from the canteens of purified lake water they all carried. A flake or two of snow sailed lazily through the crisp air. Gorham inspected the gathering clouds. "Gonna get it by night," he warned. "Look at all that dark in the east!"

There were billows of dark gray gathering there, piling up in an ominous barrier. Blake thought they might promise a real storm. If the party was trapped in such a one they might be prevented from establishing a post here. Perhaps Manny had the same thought, for he moved uneasily and finished his meal with a couple of hasty gulps.

"Gorham, you and Bob better hit the trail," he advised. "If you can get a horse, cut back here on the double and strip that store. We don't want to get caught out in a bad storm. Jack, go down to the store and pile up stuff for easy packin'. Me, I'm gonna take a little squirm. H'm," for the first time he remembered Blake, "you go 'long with Jack."

That had the ring of an order. Blake wanted to stay right where he was; at any moment the agents might appear. But he was unarmed and his status, free and easy as Manny and the rest had been all morning, was still that of a prisoner. He lingered as long as he could, watching Gorham and Bob depart and Manny slip away into the backyard of the next house. Jack hovered impatiently and *he* had a rifle.

"Let's get going!"

Blake whirled. The sensation of immediate danger struck him like a bullet. For a moment he stared at the silent house, at the yard. Something was wrong—horribly wrong! Danger was building up to an explosive point, behind him!

With a wordless cry he flung himself at Jack, grabbing the boy by the shoulder, jerking him away from the house. Jack twisted in his hold to fight. But Blake, losing his balance, went on in a lunge which carried them both into the garage, and so saved both their lives.

There was a roar of ear-splitting sound, a flash of fire, and the world seemed to fly apart about them. Blake heard a scream of half-fear, half-pain, and then, deafened, half-conscious, he lay where he was and waited for the end.

Dust filled his eyes and mouth, choking and blinding him. He sat up and wiped his hands across his face, blinking tears which cleared his smarting eyes. There was a dull humming in his head, but through it he became aware of moaning.

Jack lay face down, his lower legs pinned under a timber, a splotch of red spreading across one thigh. Slowly Blake turned his head. Where the house had stood, there was now nothing but a ragged hole in the ground.

He crawled over to the boy and went quickly to work. The timber could be levered off, but beneath it was a raw, torn wound where metal had cut deep into the flesh. Blake labored to stop the pumping blood. He was almost sure the bone was intact and that the damage was confined to that tear.

"What—what happened—?" Jack's voice was thin, his hands swept through the dust and debris. "My rifle, where's my rifle?"

The weapon was nowhere in sight. And Blake was in no mood to search for it at that moment. But his viewpoint changed a minute later when the crack of a shot broke the silence which had followed the explosion.

"Two—three—" he counted aloud as the sharp clap of rifle fire sounded through the curtain of falling snow. Either Manny or Gorham and his companion had run into trouble.

"Rifle—" Jack pulled himself up on his elbows, "Hiders—"

Blake investigated the wreckage feverishly, now as eager as the other to find the gun, but he also ordered:

"Lie down! Get that blood started again and we're licked!"

Jack's knowledge of Doc's trade was a help, for now he obeyed at once, turning his head only to watch Blake's hunt. The rifle showed at last, unharmed as far as Blake could determine. With it in his hands he felt more secure, prepared to face whatever might come at them out of the swiftly gathering murk of the snow storm. With the explosion, his sense of warning had vanished and he thought that for the present they were safe.

"What happened?" Jack asked again in a firmer voice.

"I'd say a bomb went off."

Jack accepted that calmly. "If it was one of those delayed action babies, we were lucky." Again he raised his head for a survey. "Say—the house is gone!"

"Yes." But Blake was more occupied with the present than the immediate past. He could not leave Jack now, and the snow was growing thicker. Although the garage had saved their lives from the blast, it was no proper shelter in a storm. These shots might mean that the rest of their party were dead; that hunters would be out to sniff along their trail. He looked down the street.

The adjacent houses had suffered from the blast. And if they were cut off from the settlement in the park, they would need more than shelter; they would need food, warmth, and medical supplies. There was just one place to find those. Blake was on his own again, in a strange world, and in addition responsible for Jack.

"Look here," he turned around. Jack lived in this world, he knew all the risks, could face a dark future squarely. If he had been tough enough to survive until now, he was tough enough to assess the present odds. "Do you think that with my help you can reach the drugstore?"

He saw the boy's tongue move across his lips and Jack did not answer at once. When he did it was to ask a counter-question:

"You think Manny's had it?"

"How can we know? But the storm's growing worse and we can't spend the night here."

The snowfall had powdered the broken sidewalk, was beginning to build drifts around corners.

"Okay. And the store's tight," Jack agreed. "Sure, I can make it. A guy can do anything he has to." He repeated that last as if it were an axiom which had become a law of his kind.

But had Blake known what that trip would entail, he might never have tried it. Theirs was a snail's progress, interrupted by frequent halts to inspect the improvised bandages on Jack's thigh, to make sure that the bleeding had not broken out afresh. Taking most of the boy's weight, Blake was weaving with fatigue as they reached the store. But he got Jack inside to a storeroom in the back before he sat with hanging head, each breath drawing a knife of red hot agony through his side.

Outside, the snowfall had assumed blizzard proportions, curtaining the broken show windows, piling on the floor at the front of the long room. But where the fugitives sheltered, both roof and walls and even two small back windows were in good condition.

"Even if they weren't shot," Jack said suddenly, "the gang's going to have a tough time getting back through this."

Blake realized that his companion still hoped for rescue. But he had something else to ask.

"Won't this storm drive hiders to shelter, too?"

"Should," Jack returned. "Too easy to blunder into a shell pit or one of those places where the old gas and water mains blew up. We generally keep under cover in storms."

Blake regained his breath. And now he began to forage, blessing the custom which dictated that the wares sold by a "drugstore" be so varied. One box gave up a pack of pink and blue baby blankets, and with these he made up a pallet on the floor and, having re-dressed Jack's leg with supplies at hand, settled his patient in some degree of comfort.

When he spoke of the necessity of a fire, Jack objected. The light would attract the very attention they must avoid. But Blake pointed out that the length of the store which separated their hiding place from the street and the heavy fall of snow would hide the flames; and they must have warmth.

The marble top of the soda bar had been broken in pieces by the first raiders of years ago. He was able to pry out one section and drag it into the back room for a hearth. Wood torn from cases provided fuel and he piled it up by the armload.

Meanwhile Jack sat up and sorted through supplies he had gathered earlier, setting apart those they had immediate use for. Blake, on impulse, brought a cigarette lighter from the wreckage of the display case toward the front, and tried to ignite the crumpled pasteboard he was using as tinder. To his surprise the tiny flicker of flames answered and caught. When he was sure the fire was going well, he went back to scoop up containers of snow, using tall soda glasses, pans, anything which would hold this promise of water.

Into a pan from the lunch counter, now full of snow water, he dumped cocoa, sniffing the resulting odor with a feeling of well-being. Jack lay back under the incongruous covering of blankets patterned with cavorting panda bears, and there was a ghost of a smile on his drawn face.

"We're sure covered with luck to have it so good," he observed. "Why, we couldn't have it better at camp." He moved and a twitch of pain crossed his face.

"Leg hurting again?"

"Just when I forget and kick around. And I'm not going to do that. Brother, if Manny and Bob were only here, this would be first rate—just super! What's in that one?"

Blake read the label on the can he had picked up. "Bean soup. That's good. Wait 'til it's heated."

He emptied the contents into another pan, added a small portion of water and set it to heat. Then he poured half the cocoa into a mug and gave it to Jack. The warmth of the fire and the hot drink revived them. But their ease was swept away an instant later.

A howl, low and mournful, carrying even through the deadening curtain of the snow storm, pierced the gathering night. The liquid in Jack's mug slopped over his fingers when that cry was answered by another. His hand went out to the rifle he kept beside the pallet.

"The pack!"

Blake had only the other's concern to warn him, though that howl had sent a trickle of cold down his spine, man's age-old reaction to the cry of a hunt in which he too often had been the quarry. He must know what they could expect.

"Will they attack us?"

"The fire—they don't like fire," Jack admitted. "And they can't get at us except across it. But—" his teeth closed upon his lower lip before he added, "I have only ten shots left."

Blake got up. If the fire must be their main defense, it was up to him to keep it burning. He went out and began harvesting all the flammable material he could find in the store, stacking some of it so that Jack could feed the flames from where he lay. During his quest Blake discovered another storeroom which held mainly cartons of food, and he ripped open the cases hastily, throwing their contents on the floor, adding the boxes to his haul. There was a door there, but it was locked with a bar across it. He did not stop to explore, but he was sure that it opened upon a delivery alley in the back. One of his best finds was a hammer, which had been used to open cases, the clawed end unusually long and heavy. Blake slung it in his belt. In close fighting it would be a nasty weapon.

He was crossing the main room with as much wood as he could stagger under when he glimpsed movement by the street door. Running the last step or two, he hurled his burden into their quarters and then turned to investigate. A dark shadow slunk through the snow. It had been a dog . . . or—?

Outside, the wind whistled, driving snow before it. Blake watched the door, striving to see what might lurk in the street. He could smell the steaming soup; was its scent drawing those shadows? But the fugitives had to eat and Jack needed the warm food—he could not move about to avoid the clutch of the cold.

Somewhere, not too far away, there was a rumbling crash. Blake stepped back into the firelight.

"The wind" Jack's voice kept up the brave pretense of life as usual, "it's bringing down pieces of the ruins. That always happens in a storm."

Blake's eyes went to the roof over their heads, but it showed no cracks. And he knew that the store was well away from any taller building. At least they were safe from being buried alive, no matter what other danger the night and the storm could loose.

He was restless, unable to settle down except for short intervals. Having stacked the firewood, he busied himself bringing in cans and jars of food, until they were well prepared to stand siege. Jack drifted off into uneasy slumber and Blake took up the rifle. He was sure that the shadows flitting around the outer door were real, that only the fire was holding them at bay. So he fought his drowsiness and kept up the flames, plagued within the past hour by a faint trace of the old uneasiness. It did not stab him with the sharp thrust of immediate danger, but he was certain that there was trouble brewing, a more serious trouble than that offered by the slinking pack in the street.

The wall, which formed the back of the store, was broken only by two small windows close to the ceiling; Blake pulled boxes under the nearest, building a vantage point. He climbed, to crouch with his nose pressed against the icy glass, his hands cupped around his eyes to shut out the light. But beyond the pane was only dark and the snow which whispered as it fell. He tried to remember whether the store was situated so that he could see Patroon Place from this back window, and he rather thought that it was.

Now the wind was dying and with it some of the fury of the snowfall. Jack awoke with a cry, as if he didn't know where he was, and Blake went back to him.

"Wolves!" the boy's eyes, too bright, too wide in the firelight, did not quite focus on Blake's face.

"Not here," the other returned soothingly.

Jack's face was flushed and Blake's testing fingers found it hot. He went to the packets of medical supplies. Antibiotics . . . But did this level have the miracle drugs? There were no familiar labels on the bottles he held up in the firelight.

He was still examining the array when he was startled.

Was it a vibration in the air, to be sensed only by one who had known its like before? That strange flash of weakness, the feeling of disorientation, of whirling away—! Blake got to his feet and lunged toward the box stair. He scrambled up and tried to see through the dark. Had he in that moment caught the distant hum of a carrier voyaging between worlds?

Chapter Fourteen

Had Blake been alone he would have dashed into the night, back to Patroon Place. He did come down from the pile of boxes with a rush which toppled several from their places, but when his eyes encountered Jack he stopped.

He owed no allegiance to Jack—to this world. But he could not walk out of here, even if he were positive that such a move would return him to his own place and time.

Jack's eyes were open and this time the boy was semi-conscious. "The pack—they're going. Manny—Manny's coming!"

Was that true or only a dream which had held into Jack's waking? Before Blake could stop him, the boy's lips shaped that whistle which was the signal for Sarge's men. There was a faint noise from the other room.

One of the pack? Or some man? Blake snatched up the rifle, squeezing past Jack's pallet to search the gloom beyond. Could the agents be exploring? Holding to that faint hope, Blake went into the main room of the store.

A black shape close to the street entrance padded away, another slinked in its tracks. On impulse Blake picked up a can and hurled it after that retreat. There was a startled bark, and a third invader leaped into the night, sending snow fountaining from a drift across the doorway. The pack was withdrawing. Why? Because of his movements, or because they did not wish to face some new menace?

Blake was uneasy, but his private warning was not working. Though he lingered in the outer room for a while, none of the pack returned, and at last the cold drove him back to the fire. No one had answered Jack's whistle. But that did not prove that some hider had not marked them down, and was that very moment creeping up on them with the craft taught by years of such employment.

The night wore on leadenly. Blake kept the fire going and did sentry duty, rising to pace the end of the outer room whenever sleep dogged him. Toward morning Jack's uneasy and feverish sleep deepened into real rest and the boy's skin was no longer so hot. Blake knew a weary relief when dawn grayed the sky and brought a pale light into the cluttered room.

Snow melted in pans and he prepared a hot meal, soup, stew—the most filling food he could find among the cans. The two of them could hold out, he reckoned by supplies, for a week or more. And in that length of time the Sarge should send a rescue party whether or not Bob and Gorham got back to the settlement.

"Smells good!" Jack surveyed the warming food wistfully.

Blake washed the boy's hands and face. His nursing had few refinements but Jack submitted to his ministrations with a sigh of relief.

"The pack still out there?"

Blake shook his head. "They moved out in the night. I don't know why."

Jack frowned. "That's not natural."

But Blake refused to worry about the pack now. "If you can stay alone for awhile, I'll go out the back door and look around."

Jack glanced at the rifle Blake had left leaning against the pile of boxes. Blake smiled. "I'll leave that with you. I have this," he displayed the hammer.

"Maybe you can find Manny. You don't have to worry about me, I have the fire and the rifle. I'll do fine—"

Blake couldn't suppress a yawn as he held a mug of soup in both hands.

"Shouldn't you get some sleep?" asked the other. "I bet you didn't sleep any last night."

"No."

Jack was right; he needed rest. And an hour or two of sleep now might mean all the difference later on. If they were to hold the fort here for another night, he must be prepared to stand guard during the dark.

Exploration of storage boxes provided him with padded beach mats, the makings of a second pallet. And he curled up on it, having given Jack strict orders to call him at the first hint of trouble.

But sleep came only in fitful snatches. It was as if his precognition had been triggered below the level of consciousness. At last he gave up the struggle, heated food for them both, and decided to take advantage of the daylight and explore. Also, before nightfall, he must gather more firewood.

A last trip through the store rounded up all flammable material he could wrench loose. And the number of tracks in the snow inside the entrance were a mute warning not to be disregarded. Blake was not woodsman enough to judge the number of animals making up the pack or to distinguish one set of prints from another. But the beaten space they had left was sobering, and another day of hunger might drive the beasts to the point where fear of fire would not balk their attack.

Blake forced the lock on the back door, leaving Jack, the rifle across his lap, braced against a box, close enough to the fire to feed the flames, with food and water within easy reach. The boy urged him to go. He was certain that Manny was in some trouble and that Blake could find and help him. Blake agreed to this as a soothing measure but he was convinced that if the explosion had not brought Manny back the day before, it was because those shots had made sure that the ex-hackie would never return.

He did not go far from the store at first, conscientiously hunting wood and dragging it back to the stack within, calling out cheerfully to Jack and being answered with the same determined lightheartedness. But all the time he was curbing his impatience to be away—to get to Patroon Place and see if there was any indication that the agents had been there the night before.

"I'm going to go back to the house," he told Jack at last.

"To hunt Manny? That's great! I'll be all right. I have the rifle and the fire and you won't be away long."

"No. I'll make it a quick trip."

As he left the store, Blake's attention roved over the street and the houses. He kept to cover. There were tracks in the snow left by the pack, making aimless patterns. But there were no signs that any human being had walked that way since the end of the storm. The sky was clear and the day crisply cold. His hands, covered only by the crude mittens of the settlement, were numb and he beat them against his sides as he walked, wanting the parka's warmth.

There was the house, or rather the blast hole where yesterday it had stood. Blake broke into a trot, floundering through drifts across the drive.

Then, seeing what was written on the snow, he stopped short. These were no paw marks, but the tracks of men, and they came out of the cellar hole: out of the hole—to go back into it. He stared at the evidence dully, trying not to believe that it meant he was too late.

The footprints were anonymous. He could not be certain that any of them had been made by Saxton, or Kittson, Hoyt or Erskine. But they took him straight to the edge of the cellar and he stared down into the jumbled wreckage. Here the snow was scuffed, pushed away by the passage of feet and bodies. But on one flat surface was the final answer. More prints—tiny, distinct, made by a kitten, and ending abruptly where someone had gathered up their maker.

Black depression settled upon Blake. They had been here last night! He had been so close, so very close and now—. He kicked at a brick, sent it flying into the hole. They had not lingered; they were gone, which might be because they saw no reason to explore here—that they would not come back. He had missed his one chance!

His frustration flamed into anger. But that did not last when he heard the crackle of rifle fire. He spun around, knowing that he was not the target. Loud as they were, those shots had come from some distance away—the store!

Blake ran down the street, skidding in the snow, the hammer ready in his hand. Jack was alone. Another shot informed him that the end had not come. He rounded into the alley onto which the back door opened. No one here. The door was as he had left it. They must be attacking from the front. He clawed open the door, skirted the woodpile and made for the main room.

"Jus' one—a kid—an' he's hurt." The voice rang hollowly through the wrecked store.

"Sneak up on him."

On the floor, just within the streetdoor, a man lay on his face and from beneath his body trickled a dark stream. But two more were on their feet, plastered against the walls, out of line of Jack's fire. One held an automatic, the other a knife.

Blake's eyes narrowed. The knife man luckily was on the other side of the room. But the gunman had crept by where he was crouched. A slim chance—but perhaps their only one. Gathering his feet under him like a cat, Blake sprang, the hammer up for the single blow luck might give him.

Something made his quarry half turn and the blow did not land true, but struck glancingly, the claw of the hammer tearing loose a flap of flesh above the man's ear.

With a scream, he staggered back, one hand to his head. But he did not drop the automatic and a shot burned by Blake's jaw. There was a hoarse shout from the other side of the room as Blake threw caution to the wind and jumped to strike a second time.

The man went down, in silent limpness, flopping to the floor as might a doll from which the sawdust had been drained. Blake whirled, but not to face attack. The knife man had remembered in time that in going to his fellow's defense he must cross Jack's line of fire, and he showed a healthy respect for the boy's marksmanship.

For the moment it was a stalemate. Then Blake noted the automatic his victim had dropped. With that in his hand he would be in command of the field. But the man across the room knew that too. His bearded lips snarled; his eyes darted from side to side. When Blake moved, so did he, scrambling to safety behind a counter.

"Look out!" Jack called. "There's more of 'em!"

Blake went to earth behind a barrier of his own and glanced uneasily at the street entrance.

"How many?" he asked, estimating the chance of crawling from one point of protection to another and so joining Jack. Or would it be better to stay where he was to meet opposition when it came?

". . . don't know," was Jack's discouraging reply.

If there were more of them why hadn't they arrived by now? Had the rest of the gang gone on, or were they otherwise engaged? If they had gone beyond earshot the knifeman must be prevented from escaping with his story.

Blake's line of crawl took a new direction as the knifeman sprinted from one counter to the next. Blake snapped a shot which tore a splinter from the floor—too late.

The counter line ended a good distance short of the door. If the man was planning to run for it, he would have several feet of open to cross. This would be a test of patience. Unless the others Jack warned against came to investigate, Blake was inclined to wait.

There was the crash of broken glass from the counter concealing the knifeman. Was he heading to the door? Blake steadied the automatic across his arm. But the hunter did not make the expected dash for freedom. Through small sounds, the crunch of broken glass, a rustling, Blake knew that the man was moving. And since it was not to the entrance, he must be heading back, probably trying to find a position from which he could launch an attack at Blake.

For a while Blake hesitated. Should he move to meet the other, or remain where he was to cut off his escape? Either choice might prove the wrong one. But the frustration which had built up in him since he had learned of the agents' visit spurred him into action. He began to edge toward the rear of the long room.

"Look out!" Jack's shout of warning froze him.

Blake had just time to get to his feet and plant his shoulders against the wall before the knife wielder was on him. The blade skinned across his shoulder and the fist holding the weapon struck hard upon the half-healed burn. The agony of that shook Blake long enough for the other's fingers to vise about his wrist so that he could not use the automatic.

They went down to roll from behind the counter out onto the littered floor until they brought up sharply against the skeleton of a table. Blake kicked out, the point of his boot bringing a grunt of pain from the other. But his gun hand remained locked in an iron grip. The knife! The man's other hand was empty; he had dropped the knife!

With renewed spirit, Blake worked to twist his wrist free as the other brought up his knee in a vicious in-fighting jab, grinding it into the pit of Blake's stomach, expelling his breath in an explosive gasp. Paralyzed with pain he sprawled, staring up as the other raised the automatic for a finishing shot, his mouth split in a sadistic leer. He was prolonging the moment of the kill for the pleasure it gave him, as one portion of Blake's numbed mind realized.

But the man's preoccupation with his helpless prey undid him. For the rifle cracked first. An almost ludicrous expression of surprise crossed his face. He coughed and blood spurted over Blake. But he was still conscious, conscious and hating. He put the barrel of the automatic against Blake's forehead, his finger was on the trigger. Blake summoned up his last rags of strength and heaved. He was deafened by a shot and the room darkened and spun around him.

"Please . . . please. . . ."

Words coming out of the mist, hurting his head. Blake's eyes opened. He saw far above him cracked plaster. Frowning, he tried to remember. Where was he? How had he come—?

"Please . . ." the monotonous plaint compelled him to move.

He ached, his whole middle was a red pit of pain, but he pulled himself up. Another body lay across his knees, pinning him to the floor, and his chest was sticky with blood. He'd been shot!

Still gasping for breath, he tugged and wriggled free of the body and then he heard a dragging sound. Pulling himself by his hands, pushing the rifle before him, Jack was making a painful progress out of the storeroom. With the inflection of a prayer, he repeated over and over his "please," his terror-filled eyes on Blake. But when the latter sat up, Jack huddled together, giving vent to long shuddering sobs.

Although it was still torture to draw a deep breath, Blake took stock of his injuries. The blood on him was not his own. But he could hardly move his bad shoulder and the numbness spreading from the burn there was affecting his arm. It was an effort to act—but time was important! Jack had said there were more of these jackals. But at least these three were safely dead.

"They—they have Manny." Jack got out the words between sobs and his eyes were naked with appeal.

"How do you know?" Blake crawled over to the boy, wincing as his palm came down on a splinter of glass. He was afraid to try walking; the walls still showed a tendency to whirl when he straightened.

"Went by—outside—prisoner." Jack was regaining control. "Saw fire—three of them stayed. I shot the first one in the doorway; then they split so I couldn't see them . . ."

"You're sure it was Manny they had?" Blake persisted. He put his good arm about Jack's shoulders and supported the boy's shivering body.

"Who else could it be?"

But Blake still wondered. "You didn't see his face?"

"No. I was surprised, the snow muffled their steps. They were past almost before I sighted them."

"And you're not sure how many there were in the gang?"

"I don't know whether three or four went by before these turned in. They'll be back!" His fingers tightened convulsively on Blake's sleeve.

"If they do, they'll regret it. We're ready and waiting this time." Blake's hand went gingerly to his aching middle and then he wished he had not made that experiment. "Look here, Jack, you've ripped your leg open again—"

There was red seeping through the bandage.

"Now we'll see to that first."

Somehow he managed to half-carry, half-drag the boy back to the pallet and tend the reopened wound. Ordering Jack to stay put, Blake searched the bodies in the outer room. It was a nasty job, one he might have shrunk from a week earlier. But this world certainly hardened one fast.

The body by the door was equipped with both a knife and a shot-gun. Blake speculated as to why the man had not made sure of Jack with a blast from the very start. The automatic now thrust into his own belt appeared to be the sole weapon of the man he had downed with the hammer. But when Blake found the knife the last man had used, he shaped a whistle: the hilt was gemmed; the jewels were a sparkling fire. And he had once had the twin of this. It had come from the laboratory world. Limping, Blake turned and gave a closer examination to each dead face. But their tangled beards were real. There was no indication that they were anything but this world's equivalent of Scappa and his goons. Pranj had his forces on each level and they must be pretty much of a type. Perhaps the finely dressed, arrogant noblemen of the laboratory level were the Scappas of their world.

He went back to Jack. "Ever seen any of these men before?"

The boy was surprised. "They're just hiders. Look alike, all of them."

Blake showed him the dagger. "One of them had this. Seen one like it before?"

Jack ran a forefinger over the hilt. "Out of a museum?" he asked doubtfully. "Sarge had one something like this, one of the scouts brought it in from a museum. But it was too old, the blade snapped when he tried to use it."

"I think it is proof that these men have been in contact with the renegade tech."

"But the hiders working for him are downtown."

"One reason to bring them up here," Blake spoke his thoughts aloud. "They're hunting for the agents' base—they must be!"

"It doesn't matter why they came," Jack said impatiently, intent on his own problem, "they have Manny. He wasn't even hurt bad, because he was walking. We've got to get him away from them. You don't know how they treat us when they take us alive. And Manny— he's the kind who'll stand up and dare them to do it!" Jack's face was gray. "I can't get away on this bum leg. But you can go—you've got to go after them and free Manny!"

Blake looked down at the shotgun. How was he going to explain to Jack the impossibility of doing what he asked? Three, maybe four armed men who knew the city and its ways better than he did: they could take cover anywhere and pick him off long before he caught up with their trail. And with his left arm close to useless again, he dared not just start off into the blue. To say nothing of the folly of leaving Jack helpless and alone.

"You going after Manny now?"

Blake raised his head. "I don't see how—" he began and then was interrupted by a sound which left him wondering if he wasn't dreaming all this.

The faint cry from the outer room came again, fretful, demanding. Blake got up and went to the door. It was true—his eyes supported the evidence of his ears.

Picking her way daintily through the debris, heading straight for him, came a well-fed black kitten!

Chapter Fifteen

Blake held out his hand and the kitten approached to sniff at his fingers. But it was only when he touched that soft woolly fur that Blake believed his eyes. He turned to Jack eagerly.

"Are you sure the man they had was Manny? What color was his hair?"

Jack, staring at the kitten as if it were a four-footed time bomb, answered absently:

"Of course it was Manny. And I told you they went by here fast, I didn't notice his hair."

"Or his size?" persisted Blake. "Was he short or tall?"

"Manny's short, you know that," Jack couldn't be sure; he admitted he had not had a good look at the prisoner. And, with this living evidence now purring as he stroked it, Blake was inclined to think that one of the agents might have been that captive. If so, he must have been a voluntary prisoner. Blake would never forget how easily Erskine had handled Beneirs. Unless the hiders were all shielded by Pranj's device. Blake frowned.

Had Jack not been helpless he would have gone after that party. He should know better than to interfere in the agents' business. On the other hand his intervention at the proper moment saved the game as it had at the Shelborne back at the beginning of this crazy adventure. But he dared not leave Jack.

The kitten climbed up Blake's arm and settled on his shoulder, rubbing its head against his chin and purring. He recalled the way Hoyt had trained it—the rapport the agent had established. Had Hoyt deliberately dispatched the little creature as a messenger? It was well-fed, sleek and unafraid. By those signs it had not been abandoned in the ruins.

"I must find out." Blake spoke more to himself than to Jack. But the boy raised himself on the pallet, his eyes shining.

"You're going after Manny!"

Blake evaded a direct answer. "I'll look around."

Before he left, he laid the rifle and the shotgun within Jack's reach, built up the fire and, across the doorway, erected a waist-high barricade. With the automatic and both knives as his own weapons, he was ready to start. But when he tried to leave the kitten with Jack, it uttered cat squeaks and clung to him with every claw so he had to keep it.

"Good luck!" Jack waved him off as Blake still hesitated.

"I'll be back soon . . ."

"Stay all day if it means getting Manny!" retorted the boy.

But when he went through the outer door Blake did not turn east in the direction the hiders and their prisoner had taken. Instead he searched the snow for the trail he wanted. Neat and straight, the line of tiny paw prints led up town. Half a block he traced them before they made a right turn between two houses. Crossing the backyard of one, they continued on over a rubble filled street, heading for a derelict gas station.

"How far did you come anyway?" Blake asked the bundle of fur whose bullet head protruded from the front of his jacket.

The kitten turned its round eyes up to his and squeaked politely. Blake gazed up and down the street. He had seen no tracks except those left by the dog pack and the kitten. The hiders had not come from this direction. And he dared not venture too far away from Jack.

Those paw marks in the snow beckoned him on, adding fuel to the hope he cherished. He need go no farther than just across the street, from there he could still hear any warning of an attack on the store.

The kitten's trail led to the smashed-in door of the service station. A tall figure stepped out to greet him as casually as if they had only parted five minutes before.

"Hello, Walker."

Hoyt! And behind him Kittson. Blake found himself clutching at an arm with his good hand.

"You've been through the wars," someone said.

"Come in, son, and tell us all about it," that was Kittson.

But Blake had control of himself once more. At least over his voice, though he couldn't keep his hands from shaking.

"There's a boy back there—badly hurt," he got out. "I can't leave him—"

Kittson's dark brows drew together in a frown. "Native?"

Blake nodded. Hoyt transferred the kitten to the front of his own jacket where it rode happily, showing the half-closed eyes of complete feline bliss.

"Is he able to walk?"

"No."

Kittson gave a resigned shrug. "We'll do what we can."

Blake felt a vast relief as the burden was lifted from his shoulders. Hoyt came out of the station, a pair of high-powered rifles on his arm, and both men started back to the store with Blake.

When he tried to give them an account of his past few days, Kittson stopped him. "Time enough for that later," he was told. "We'll see to the native first . . ."

That withdrawn concentration was on both their faces and Blake went silent. Were they working on Jack at a distance as Erskine had worked on Beneirs face to face? Because of his own shield he would never know.

They gave no attention to the three bodies in the outer room but went straight to where Jack lay quiet on the pallet. His eyes were open but he did not appear to see the agents and he showed no consciousness when Kittson knelt beside him. With quick, skilled hands the agent uncovered and examined the wound.

"Well?" Hoyt asked as Kittson rewound the bandage.

"He needs attention all right. We'll take him through to the base for treatment and return him with false memories, no trouble with his type of receptiveness."

Hoyt greeted that with a sigh of relief. "Suppose I take him through. That'll give Walker a chance to brief you. I can be back," he consulted his watch, "in about an hour. Agreed?"

"You'll find us here."

As if Jack were a small child, Hoyt swept him up and strode easily out of the store.

"Hoyt will take him back to our own level. We have medical training which has outstripped that of most of the other worlds. The boy'll be cured and returned here with a false memory to cover the immediate past. He'll never know that he was out of his own world. Now—what happened to you?"

Blake spilled out the details, trying to sort out facts as if he were making a report to a superior officer. Kittson made no comments, but that aura of calm competence which surrounded the senior agent had its effect on Blake. He examined the dagger the other had taken from the dead hider, the one Blake was sure had come from the laboratory world.

"Ming Hawn," was his first remark. "So Ixanilia is one of his stops. That tower world, though, that's a totally new level—unknown on our recordings as far as I can tell. We'll investigate that later." He stuck the dagger point deep into a nearby piece of firewood. "You're infernally lucky, Walker. This may seem like a dangerous level, but I assure you that the comparative quiet of Ixanilia is far more deadly for the unwary invader. There is a hereditary nobility ruling there who have certain unpleasant pastimes—" the agent did not elaborate. "Pranj would be right at home in such a culture and we have suspected he'd head for there. But this importing of weapons . . . You say that that is a rumor among the natives here?"

"Yes, sir."

"Hmm. Well, Erskine has allowed himself to be captured by a group of hiders we believe to be Pranj's men. We would rather not contact the Sarge if we can help it. You seem to have done fairly well covering your own background with his people. In fact it's surprising—" but whatever Kittson had been about to say he did not voice. Instead he changed the subject. "Do you think you can find your way back to this cellar where the carrier left you?"

"I can try." But Blake was doubtful. "About all I know is the general direction."

"If they are taking Erskine there we shall not have to hunt." Blake guessed that Kittson must be in mental touch with the agent playing the prisoner's role.

"Are those hiders, the ones who took Erskine, wearing shields?"

Kittson smiled grimly. "No. We are hoping that that indicates Pranj's supply is exhausted."

Blake fed the fire and noticed the cans of food. He was suddenly aware of hunger. Now he pushed a pan of water closer to the flames and reached for a can opener and Kittson started to read labels.

"Rather a varied menu," murmured the agent.

"Mostly soups," Blake admitted. He measured chocolate powder into the bubbling water and opened another can. When he had the meal heating he sat back on his heels and asked a question of his own.

"*Is* your point of entry through that house on Patroon Place? And how did you get through after the explosion?"

"Yes to your first inquiry. The explosion, I believe, was a rude greeting arranged by our friends from Pranj's hideout. But chance brought your party there first and you must have triggered the bomb in some way so it did not catch us coming through as they had planned. The mop-up squad who collected Erskine will believe, when he gets through rearranging their memories for them, that the rest of us were caught in the blast. That does smell good."

He accepted the mug of soup Blake handed him and sipped it slowly. Then he began questioning the other searchingly as to what he had learned from the Doctor and other members of Sarge's forces.

"I wish you could give the Sarge some help," Blake burst out, "some of the wonder drugs for Doc; they haven't developed them here. To clean up this city and rebuild. . . ."

But refusal was plain to read on Kittson's face.

"The basic rule of our Service is not to interfere. We're after Pranj because he *is* doing just that. If we did the same—even for good— how dare we arrest him?"

"But he wants to take over the world and run it," Blake protested. "You would only be helping a people who had it tough, giving them a better chance for the future."

"One can always discover good reasons for interference," Kittson replied. "We cannot and dare not meddle, either for good or evil. What can we tell about the influence even a good act may have on the future here? Suppose we give temporary relief to a small group of people? In that world that action will be like tossing a stone into a pool: spreading waves from it will circle out and out. We could save a single life and by doing so wreck thousands in years to come. We might prevent a war which would lead through exhaustion to eventual world peace on that level. It is not for us to judge or act. We swear to that when we enter the Service. We are observers only and our training fits us for that end. The other levels provide endless changes of action, but it is action in which we dare take very little part.

"Even such a mission as that we are now engaged upon, the eradication of a man who does strive to meddle in the other worlds, comes perilously close to the boundaries past which we dare not venture, not for our own good, but for the good of others. Yes, we could give the Sarge better weapons, the drugs, supplies, the assistance of a superior stable civilization. But by doing so we would defeat his cherished dream. What he builds slowly out of the wreckage through his own efforts and those of his followers will endure far longer than anything he could achieve with our aid. We must not lend crutches and so produce cripples. If you can accept that point of view—" Again Kittson broke off, almost as if he feared he had said too much. He swallowed the last of the soup. "Better put out the fire. It's time to go."

Blake obeyed, not surprised to have Hoyt enter a moment later. Their telepathic communication he now accepted as a matter of course. His only wish was that he could share it.

"Everything's under control," Hoyt announced. "The boy's going to be all right. Hakal will keep him dreaming until we are able to bring him back. Shall we move?"

Blake hesitated between rifle and shotgun. In the end, not knowing the worth of his marksmanship, he chose the latter.

"Contact?"

Hoyt nodded in answer to that clipped question from his superior. "They are keeping out of the park. Saxton's trailing and relaying. Stan's detected only one shield. The rest of the gang are malleable."

Blake offered information: "Jack says that everyone holes up at night. It's getting late."

They had come out into the street and Kittson glanced up at the clear blue of the winter sky. "Then we'd better make time while we've the light with us."

The agents, too, avoided the park, working their way downtown along a street a block away from its border. Birds called and wheeled above them, and once or twice they heard a muffled crash as wreckage thudded to the earth. Here and there, the snow was disturbed by the tracks of animals; the dog pack left their signature along with those of other furred dwellers in the ruins.

It was eerie, weird, to thread a path through all this when only days before he had walked through the same city—or its double— alive and vigorous with activity.

They had to make a wide detour about a bomb crater and then another where a pit which had once been part of the subway lay open to the sky. Kittson wheeled to the right and hastened his pace. The shadows of the buildings were as thick as the snowdrifts between them. Blake wondered how far they would go before darkness would make travel dangerous. He was startled when a blob of white detached itself from a nearby snowbank and came to join them.

Above the baggy, white covering, Saxton's face was as imperturbable as ever, though the rest of him bore little resemblance to the conventional businessman of Blake's level.

"Quite a gathering," he smiled at Blake. "We are heading into a meeting of some kind."

Kittson grunted and Hoyt asked eagerly: "They are getting ready to start something?"

"Not only they," Saxton brushed snow from his white covering, "I'd say that there is a small but lively war shaping up. Our gang was joined about fifteen minutes ago by a second party with another prisoner and they're headed straight for that group of ruins to the east. But we're not the only ones trailing them. I've counted at least three other scouting parties."

"That must be the Sarge!" broke in Blake. "I heard that he was going to have a big scale operation against the hiders."

"Complications," observed Hoyt.

Kittson made no comment but headed on, down what had once been an alley kept free of debris by some freak of fate. At its end was a barrier fronting on the wide boulevard rimming the parkway. Once they reached that the agents made no attempt to go on; in fact, Kittson dragged Blake down into the shadows.

The late afternoon sun glinted on metal moving among the

winter-stripped brush on the other side of the wide street. A party of Sarge's men on the prowl?

"Ten," Hoyt's lips shaped the word rather than spoke it aloud.

Kittson's gloved fingers played with a broken brick from the mass before him. Blake gained a fleeting impression that the senior agent was annoyed at this development.

"We must reach there first," Kittson said, getting to his feet.

They crawled, they climbed, and at times they ran across open spaces. But for the most part they kept under cover, always boring into the choked core of what had once been the central section of the city. The tall towers were now mostly gone, their debris filling whole streets to second story level. But there were ways to be found through the stone jungle and the agents unerringly sped along these.

Blake noted that no matter how obstructions made them turn and retreat, they always eventually came back to a course which centered on a shattered tower suggesting in its outline the Medieval—a church. He wondered at this choice of landmark, but the others were certain of it.

Winter twilight was closing in as they paused in a cave which had been the display window of a large department store. Blake sniffed. There was a faint taint in the air, an unclean odor he could not identify. His three companions had frozen into the strange "listening" attitude, intent upon a telepathic search of the neighborhood.

"It is the church," that was Saxton. "They've posted sentries." His whisper was swallowed up in the emptiness of the ruins.

Blake heard nothing at all. If there were others moving nearby they were so skillful in that progress that a non-psi could not locate them.

"Take care of those two—the ones in the north!" Kittson ordered. "Pick their minds first though!"

"Yes," Hoyt answered. "And I'll take the tangle-head three streets over."

Saxton pulled up the hood of his white robe. Against a snow patch he became invisible. "One Eye's mine." He made his bid mildly.

Kittson gave no verbal assent, but both men vanished in the dusk as if sucked away by the rising wind. The senior agent stood still, "listening." Blake was chilled through. The patched and wadded garments supplied by the park dwellers did not keep out this wind.

He held first one hand and then the other to his mouth blowing on stiff fingers which the mittens did not keep warm.

At last Kittson moved. He did not speak, but a jerk of his hand brought Blake after him. They crept along the edge of a building, keeping to the shadows wherever possible. Then the agent paused before a round mound of debris, molded by years of storms into a hillock of respectable size. This had to be climbed worm-fashion, wriggling their bodies from one projection to the next until they were able to lie at its summit and gain a view of the surrounding territory.

By some odd freak, a single building stood in the center of a flattened and devastated area. The Gothic outlines were unmistakable—this had been a church of cathedral size. And now its dark sides were glittering with gems of light where shreds of its stained glass windows were illuminated from within.

As the two watchers settled themselves for a cold vigil on the top of the mound, they saw a group of men emerge from the ruins on the other side and walk, with the confidence of those safe in home territory, across to the door of the church. Blake asked a question:

"Is this Pranj's headquarters? It's not where the carrier landed."

"It's a headquarters of some kind." Kittson pulled out field glasses and focused them on the church door.

Chapter Sixteen

The snowstorms of the past days had left a wide carpet of white around the church to throw into sharp relief all parties crossing the expanse. It would be difficult, if not impossible, to make a surprise attack over that.

Kittson used the glasses on the doorway with concentration, but Blake shivered in the cold and wished they had chosen some less exposed spot from which to spy on the meeting place. He gave a start as a white figure detached from the ground and oozed up to join them. But Kittson did not turn his head.

"We'll have to move quickly." Some trace of preciseness still clung to Saxton's voice. "The group from the park are infiltrating the whole district. We could take over one or two squads, but it would require a parapsychologist to hold them all."

Kittson answered that with an impatient exclamation in a tongue Blake did not understand, though the profane meaning was easy to deduce.

"You located Stan?" he asked a moment later.

"Within six blocks," that was Hoyt. "What's going on down there?"

"Some sort of a conclave—they haven't started business yet."

"Maybe we have come at just the right time," Saxton suggested. "Could he have gathered them here to pass out arms?"

"Your guess is as good as mine. From what I've picked up so far, none of them know why they've been called in. Rumor has it that there is a big deal on." Kittson restored his glasses to their case.

"Our cue to go around and collect the star performer before he appears?" asked Saxton and then his voice was drowned out.

What Blake heard had at first no meaning, and then one so horrifying that his mind refused to accept the explanation. The howling of the tower hags had been terrifying in its alien bestiality— the scream which carried from the church was even worse, for it could only have been born out of a human throat in the highest extremity of agony.

"Erskine!" He was on his knees, the shotgun in his cold-numbed hands. Then a steel grip dragged him down again.

At a second shriek, Blake tried to tear loose. They could not just stay there—listen to that—and know that their own friend was. . . .

"Not Erskine," the words reached through the red fog in his head. "That's some native they're amusing themselves with." Kittson's voice was ice, hinting at depths of controlled passion beyond Blake's comprehension.

"We must—!" But in spite of his struggles, the other pinned him flat on the mound.

"We do nothing." Kittson was curt. "We'd be dead before we covered two feet of that stretch out there. The door sentries are shielded."

"Mark!"

But Kittson's head had turned even before that warning from Saxton. He was "listening," and then his breath hissed between his teeth.

"Good enough," he half whispered, "they'll mop up."

"*If* we can keep Pranj away!"

Kittson laughed, a humorless bark with the menace of a wolf's snarl. "Let the Sarge's men have a free chance to use that little surprise they're dragging in from the south, eh? Right you are, Jason. We'll attend to Pranj. He isn't down there, so we'll keep him from arriving."

Blake glanced from one man to the other. The dark was not yet so complete that he could not see their faces; there was the same emotion mirrored on their very dissimilar visages. They were hunters watching a dangerous beast stalk straight down a path leading to a trap. And now he was able to hear noises in the night. The scrape of an incautious boot, a smothered cough.

"What—?" he whispered.

It was Saxton, not Kittson who took time to explain: "The men from the park are moving in to attack. We disposed of the sentries for our own purpose and they have been able to get through the gaps undetected. They have a field piece with them and are manhandling it into position where they can knock the church to rubble. This is shaping up into a battle. They have the enemy cornered and will try to finish them off in one operation."

"Your doing?" Blake thought he understood.

He heard Saxton's chuckle, as warmly human as Kittson's mirth was not.

"After a fashion. We dare not really interfere, you know; but we introduced a few ideas into their heads so they believe the thoughts their own. If we can keep Pranj from getting control of the hiders long enough for the engagement to begin, we may drive him from this level and leave the natives to work out their own destiny."

Blake could hear other movements in the dark, or thought he heard them. But he longed for the others' power to follow the unseen forces mentally.

"Time to go," Kittson announced. "You between us, Walker. Hook onto Saxton's belt and let him guide you."

They crept, they hurried, they hid, breathless, to let bodies of men pass them in the dark. The agents used all their powers to keep their small party from being discovered by the army gathering for the attack—all the while working their way from the vicinity of the church. Saxton knew the trail and they slipped from one dark pool of shadow to the next, avoiding the open and the wide patches of snow against which all but their guide would be visible.

Blake was not prepared for the sudden halt and bumped into Saxton as the three agents drew together.

"A sonic barrier!" That was Kittson.

"It went on full force ten minutes ago," Hoyt answered. "Pranj is in there. He's made at least three trips with cargo, according to Erskine's report, before we were cut off. They're holding Stan for Pranj to finish off later."

"We should have been prepared for this." Kittson's voice was self-accusing.

"Even if we had believed he could get a sonic through," Saxton pointed out, "what could we have done in the way of a counter move? There is nothing to break that kind of a barrier."

If there was discouragement in Saxton's voice, Kittson was not yet defeated.

"I wonder." He turned to Hoyt. "Where is the barrier?"

"End of this street."

Kittson spoke to Blake. "See if you can go to the end of the street and cross the space there. If you can, report back at once."

Not understanding, Blake obeyed orders. As far as he could see there was no barrier of any kind before him. The piles of rubble were no higher, no more forbidding than many they had already crossed that evening, and the night was quiet.

He stepped out onto the cracked and buckled pavement of the intersecting street. For an instant there was a shrill scream in his head, a noise which was also pain. But at his next quick stride that vanished, and he walked without hesitation to the other side, stood there for a moment, and came back to the three waiting for him a few feet from the point where the noise had struck him.

As he came up Kittson spoke to the others. "There's your answer. I didn't think Pranj would have it on the lower range. He couldn't if he wants to keep contact with the hiders."

"And he does that," Hoyt replied. "Erskine reports cases of weapons coming through and there are five Ixanilians there: three nobles and two red-cloaks."

"What do you want me to do?" asked Blake.

"Pranj has set up a sonic barrier no telepath can cross. Did you have any trouble?" Kittson wanted to know.

"Just a noise; it hurt my head."

"He'd feel something," Saxton cut in. "He's enough psi to be troubled by it."

"But he *can* cross it." Kittson returned impatiently to the most important point. "Somebody has to turn off that sonic and we can't get in there until it's done."

Blake was tired; his mind as well as his body ached with that tiredness. He had no desire to walk into the range of Pranj's power. And yet Kittson expected him to do that, as though he were another of the agents.

"Your shield," Kittson was continuing, "the one you used when he tried to get at you before. Can you use it again? Think of yourself as a frightened fugitive lost in an alien world. He knows you were marooned here; he may well expect you to turn up."

"Expect that I'd be hanging around in hopes of finding the carrier again?"

"That's it!" Hoyt supplied the enthusiasm Blake could not match.

"All right," he agreed wearily. "What does a sonic look like and how do I shut it off?"

Saxton provided the description. "It will be a black metal box about a foot square. There is a small crystal bulb protruding from the lid. Your easiest move will be to smash that. The minute you do it we can follow you in."

Hoyt unzipped the front of his jacket and brought out the kitten. "Pranj has a horror of cats; it amounts to a mania. The kitten will do as it has been trained. You may not go armed, but Missus will help."

Blake laid aside the shotgun, the knives and the automatic, to put the kitten inside his jacket. Feeling remarkably naked, he started out along the way Hoyt pointed. He was across the barrier once more when, ahead, a faint green radiance and a distant hum proved that the carrier was in use not too far away.

He wrenched his mind from that thought; instead he concentrated with all his strength upon being lost, frightened, and alone—very much alone, striving to build up a picture of the past few days which would satisfy Pranj if only for an important moment or two, long enough for him to bring the agents to the scene.

Blake rounded a pile of rubbish and saw before him the half-hole which led to the cellar from which he had made his entrance into this world. Light streamed from the opening and he could hear the murmur of voices. He drew a deep breath. Then he staggered, testing out how much he could waver without losing his balance.

Hunger, cold, loneliness, fear: he attempted to marshal all those sensations, think only of them, feel only them, as he stumbled toward the hole from which spread that alien, green light.

The Ixanilians were not sensitive and not one of them was prepared for the arrival of that ragged figure which half-fell across the threshold. Blake blinked at light from portable lamps, dazzled until he was able to sort out the men staring at him in amazement. There were the brown skinned, arrogant noblemen he had last seen talking with Pranj in the laboratory building and two of their red-cloaked servants. And, his arms lashed to one of the pillars, Erskine stood, blood trickling from a battered mouth, his face black with bruises.

One of the red-cloaks caught Blake's wrists, forcing his arms behind his back in a practiced motion. The nobles conferred and their guttural speech was unenlightening to their new prisoner. Blake tried a trick Dan Walker had taught him long ago, stiffening his wrists as the red-cloak tied them. He was almost certain that with a little effort he could work free from those bonds. A contemptuous shove sent him not only halfway across the cellar, but to his knees, facing Erskine. One of the red-cloaks lounged nearby, but he gave neither prisoner strict attention. It was plain that the Ixanilians did not fear trouble from either captive.

Blake looked up at Erskine. Those pale eyes caught his and held for an instant, and then swept in a compelling message over his shoulder. Blake allowed himself to collapse. The red-cloak stepped forward, stared down into his face, and favored him with a kick in the ribs, which the captive greeted with a yelp of pain. But Blake gained what he wanted. At the edge of the rubble, which had concealed the arrival point of the carrier, flanked by a pile of boxes which the other red-cloak was methodically opening, was just such a machine as Saxton had described.

How he was going to get to it undetected was the problem Blake must now solve. The kitten moved against his chest; he felt the needle points of its tiny claws sink into his skin through his clothing.

The Ixanilian servant took guns from the boxes, odd looking stubby weapons which were the counterpart of the flame thrower he had seen. Armed with those, the hiders could make a clean sweep of the settlement in the park.

Blake tested the strength of the cords about his wrists, turning and pulling, feeling them yield just as Dan had promised. The kitten was growing restless and he was afraid that one of the others would see its movements under his jacket.

His captors talked among themselves. One of the nobles passed long, dark cigarettes to his friends and the acrid smoke puffed across the low-ceilinged space. But beneath their assumption of ease they were tense, wary, they did not relish this period of waiting.

Blake fought to relax. His warning stabbed knife-wise into his brain. Pranj must be on the way!

Green light behind the rubble . . . the hum. . . . The two red-cloaks jumped into action as the green vanished. Blake took advantage of their preoccupation to wrest his hands free. Then, his slim body encased in the clothing of an Ixanilian noble, Pranj came out into the cleared portion of the cellar.

The mask he had worn as Lefty Conners was gone. Now he was the man whose image the agents had shown Blake so long ago. Power, self-confidence, radiated from him. He was smiling faintly, as if amused at playing at some task beneath his powers.

A word from the Ixanilians drew his attention to Blake. On cat feet he came to stand over the prostrate American. Blake winced physically as well as mentally as the other's mind dark-struck. But he had had time to prepare: Alone—afraid—hungry—alone. . . .

He shut off all thought and tried only to feel. Fear—fear of this man, of the "Lefty" who had changed—fear—alone.

Pranj laughed. Had Blake heard only that laughter, he might have believed it harmless mirth. But it did not match the cruel smile which was a matter of eyes rather than lips.

"Right back into the net."

Had he heard those words spoken aloud? Cold—hungry—fear—Feel: don't think, just feel. . . .

"Time for you later."

As Pranj turned away, Blake made his supreme effort and choked down a tiny spark of triumph. His hands were free. Now he must have a chance to use them—just one chance!

The excited voices of the Ixanilians were not high enough to cover the noise the red-cloaks made dragging more cases from behind the rubble. Pranj had transported a very full load.

But the interruption Blake had been praying for came almost on cue. A distant boom—dull, ominous, sounded. Those in the cellar were struck silent. Blake's hand flew to his breast and jerked open his jacket as guards and nobles clustered about the door peering out into the night. The Sarge's men must be firing on the church.

A second shot roared across the ruins, re-echoing until it sounded like ten. Blake, one hand grasping the struggling kitten, drew his feet under him, ready to spring for the sonic.

Pranj whirled. And in that same instant Blake exploded. He released the kitten before the outlaw and jumped to the left.

There was a scream, but Blake had only eyes for the sonic. Though he stumbled, he flung out one arm and his fingers rapped its edge. The blow, slight as it was, jarred the machine back against the pile of half-open gun boxes and one of the weapons crashed down upon it. Blake tried to reach it, then a stab of torturing pain cut across the small of his back and he fell into blackness.

Battering waves of sound sorted themselves into a blaring pattern. Blake was conscious of cries, of a series of shouts. Someone stumbled and fell over his burned body, bringing a moan from him. And then the one who so held him captive writhed and screamed through a stench of burning cloth and flesh.

Blake lay still, aware that a battle was raging across the cellar. He dared not move; the least change of position added to his pain. But he tried to turn his head to see. Within the limited range of his vision lay one of the Ixanilian nobles and a second had crumpled in the door hole. Hoyt leaped that body.

So he had been successful. The gun falling on the sonic must have shattered the crystal!

The dull boom of the distant field gun was broken by the spiteful crackle of rifle fire. Blake wished he could ooze into the stone floor under him. But the dead weight across his body held him and he could not struggle for freedom.

Pranj backed into his view. He held one hand stiffly before him, and on its palm rested a bright blue ovoid. His lips were drawn back in a snarl of maniacal rage. The contorted face was no longer that of a sane man. The outlaw was doubly dangerous.

He supported the hand carrying the ovoid with his other, as if what he held was so precious or dangerous that it must not be shaken. A quiet had fallen on the cellar. It might be that those still alive were as concerned with the safety of that blue sphere as was he who bore it.

Pranj backed toward the carrier. Hoyt moved as slowly after him and then came Kittson. They had guns in their hands, but the muzzles pointed to the floor.

The outlaw laughed crazily. Then he tossed the ovoid into the air and leaped for the carrier. Hoyt sprang after him with the cry of a hunting feline about to kill. But Kittson remained where he was, his eyes focused on the blue sphere. It flashed toward him and then halted in mid-air as if enclosed by an invisible net. There was a runnel of sweat down the cheek turned toward Blake, but the agent continued to stare fixedly at the blue ball. He might be holding it suspended there by the power of his will alone.

The green glow and hum of the carrier in action did not disturb his stance. Erskine lurched into view, backing toward the door. With one hand he nursed a singed and spitting kitten. Then the weight across Blake was shifted and hands caught in his arm pits, bringing a choked cry of pain out of him as they dragged him up. Saxton hauled him to the door where Erskine, spent as he was, helped to pull him through. The Ixanilians sprawled motionless. Kittson still stood before the ovoid.

"I'm taking over," that was Saxton. "Now!"

Kittson leaped back as the ovoid wavered, dropped an inch floor-ward and then held steady once more. He picked up Blake, as if the American were no more of a burden than Jack, and went into the outer air in two great strides. Erskine awaited them there and now Saxton came too, backing up the slope, his gaze still fixed on a point in the cellar.

With Blake, Kittson went flat behind a neighboring wall and Erskine joined them. As Saxton tumbled in beside the other three, the world came apart with a terrific burst of light and sound.

Chapter Seventeen

The distant booming of the field piece was regular, broken now and then by the crackle of small arms. Blake lay face down on an unstable support which swung and tilted under him. He did not try to understand what he heard or note his surroundings, being content to await what would happen next.

"*That has the sound of a full size war.*" The words were spoken above him.

"*It should keep their attention safely fixed there—for a while at least,*" was the answering comment.

"*The D-bomb must have sealed off this entrance for him.*"

"*We hope!*" There was a note of distrust in that. "*The sooner we can get to Ixanilia the better.*"

Blake lapsed into a semi-conscious state. From time to time he roused enough to catch a glimpse of a light held on the path ahead, guiding those who carried him on the improvised stretcher. They were making better time through the maze of ruins than he would have believed possible. Yet the gray light of dawn touched them before they reached their goal. When the stretcher was set down and his bearers moved away, Blake struggled up.

"With us again?" That was Erskine somewhere out of his line of vision.

"Where are we? What happened?" he asked the two questions foremost in his mind and Erskine answered the last one first.

"Pranj blew up his own station. We're now going after him."

Blake caught his breath at the stab of pain between his shoulders, felt when he moved, bracing himself on his hands, waiting for the walls about him to stop that sickening whirl. Though above was only open sky with a powdery snow drifting down, before him was a square cube of dull metal as large as a small room. And, even as he managed to fight off his faintness and center his attention on it, an opening appeared in its side to allow Kittson out. There was an air of impatience about the senior agent.

"Any message from Hoyt?" inquired Erskine.

"He's in Ixanilia."

"Time—"

Kittson nodded. "Yes, it's a matter of time now. If Hoyt weren't with him, it would be worse. Well, we have no choice but to follow."

Then he stepped over to Blake as though the American were some necessary piece of luggage not to be abandoned, rather than a person. He held out his hand but Blake had already wavered to his feet. When Erskine went through the door in the cube, Blake, supported against his will by Kittson, made the same journey. Once inside the structure, he discovered that it bore little likeness to Pranj's carrier. Here was a control board, cushioned seats, lockers for supplies.

Blake dropped into the nearest of the seats, hunching forward so that his back would not touch its surface. The hum was familiar, but here was no green radiance. Kittson took his place before the controls watching a dial with frowning intentness.

Erskine, his battered face still bloodstained, sprawled in another seat as though he did not care where they were now bound. But Saxton was alert, eager, nursing on his knee a weapon like the Ixanilian flame guns.

"Landings clear all the way?" he asked.

"Should be," Kittson made an absent reply. "Aloon tested them on a trial run along these levels before we went on this case."

"It would be just our luck," Erskine threw in tartly, "if the Ixanilian one wasn't. I'd rather not materialize in the middle of a block of concrete. And it's half-past five in the morning; you may not have more than a half hour to get around without observation."

Although Blake could not see beyond the walls of the cube, he experienced once more that weird sensation of not being one with stable time or space. And he knew that they must be voyaging across the levels. Kittson pressed a button and the sensation subsided. They were fixed in time once more.

"We're in the clear," the senior agent announced. He picked up the twin to Saxton's flame gun before he opened the door of the cube.

"Warehouse," he informed the others. Saxton was ready to march. But Erskine pulled himself together more slowly.

Kittson came back to Blake. For a long moment he studied the American. Blake made an effort to straighten his hunched back, to give back that stare with authority. Then Kittson helped him out of his seat, transferring him without much volition on Blake's part to a place before the controls. Having settled the younger man there, the agent took from his pocket a small tube and shook out a capsule.

"Hold that under your tongue," he ordered. "Let it dissolve slowly."

Blake mouthed the capsule. But Kittson was not yet done with him. He caught up Blake's right hand and rested it on the control panel just below a button which gleamed with an inner spot of fire.

"If you get the order," he said emphatically, "you push that. Understand?"

Blake, his lips closed on the capsule, expended a small fraction of strength on a nod and Kittson appeared satisfied. The three left and Blake was alone.

Strangely enough, as the long minutes passed, his head grew clearer, the pain in his back fading as he shifted position. He tried to recall all that had happened, but most of his memories of the night remained a jumble. Meanwhile he was tired of sitting there, watching the button, waiting. He was tired, hungry. He wanted nothing more than just to be allowed to sleep . . . sleep . . .

The cube rocked under him. Blake clutched at the chair with one hand and dug the fingers of the other into the board. Earthquake! The force of the upset could come from nothing less than an earthquake! Had he by some terrible mistake pressed the button and sent the cube traveling? No, his fingers were still a good three inches from it.

A clatter made him look around. Erskine half-fell through the door, and behind him burst Saxton, stopping to aid the slighter man as he came, hurling him at one of the chairs. He was gasping for breath as he spoke to Blake.

"Be ready!"

But their impetuous entrance was warning enough. Blake's finger was on the button as Kittson came in more soberly and jerked the door to. He gave the awaited order. "All right. Let's go!"

Again the hum, the whirl, the faint nausea.

"Two sealed," Erskine had recovered his breath. "Number three, now?"

"We've got him really on the run," Saxton agreed.

"You mean Hoyt has," was Erskine's reply. And there was a hint of worry in his voice.

Feeling more normal with every passing moment, Blake wanted to ask a few questions, but a glance told him that all three of the agents were now in their trance of speechless communication. Were they maintaining some thread of contact with Hoyt? Where were they bound now? To his own level?

Blake did not notice that they had reached their destination until Kittson stood up; then he was able to walk without assistance, after the others, into a very normal basement. The senior agent was consulting his watch.

"Eight-twenty. The Crystal Bird is closed. But there's that shop Lake rents out across the square."

Erskine leaned wearily against the wall. "He thinks it's all legitimate. Pranj had him under control, but good."

Kittson spoke to Blake. "When they picked you up, did they take you to a dress shop on the other side of the square?"

Blake blinked. His adventure with the Scappa mob was so far in the past that he had to make an effort to recall details.

"I think so. But I was taken in there in a box of some kind. I couldn't swear to it."

"Those shops don't usually open until ten." Kittson looked at his watch again and then went on, the others trailing after him.

They came out of the cellar to the upper floor of the house on Patroon Place. The kitchen was empty and there was no sign of either cook or maid. The whole dwelling had the peculiar silence of a deserted house. At the windows, the shades were drawn, making the interior dusky, as the agents did not bother to switch on lights.

Boxes stood about as if the inhabitants were packing to leave. They edged among them into a room on the main hall near the front.

Erskine snapped on electricity both there and in a small bathroom beyond. Catching sight of his own battered face in the mirror, he whistled.

"Butcher's meat," he muttered and began to strip, having put the now sleeping kitten down on a cushioned chair.

Kittson set a first aid box on a table top while Saxton with surprisingly gentle touch helped Blake out of his clothes. Then he was pushed face down on the couch while the senior agent worked on his back. The comfort that the capsule had given him held and he scarcely felt their ministrations. Finally, with a thick padding strapped over the burn, he was left to rest.

"He couldn't have caught more than the edge of the beam," Erskine observed.

"Luckily. He'll do now until Klaven can see him," Kittson answered.

"Klaven?" Erskine sounded surprised.

"Can you suggest any other solution?" demanded the senior agent impatiently. And to that there was no reply.

"Breakfast." Saxton came back with a loaded tray.

Blake sat up. Much of his fatigue had vanished and he was more hungry now than tired. The food was strange; he guessed it consisted of rations from their home level. But the coffee was of his own world and he sipped the scalding stuff gratefully.

Refreshed he dressed in clothes Kittson provided: slacks and flannel shirt, with a heavy jacket loose enough not to fret his back. Erskine's delicate features were slightly more normal, though one eye was puffed shut and his lips badly swollen.

They ate swiftly and Kittson kept consulting his watch. Before they had quite swallowed the last bites, he was on his feet, leading the way to the garage.

He backed out a station wagon and they got in. They must be about to invade Pranj's base here, Blake decided for himself. The other three were all armed. But he had had no warning from his private source. Had the drug they had given him nullified that?

Kittson turned the car in the park and Blake wondered, for a bemused moment, if they were to overtake the Sarge's forces. It was difficult to drive along this road and remember that he was not in the other world—that there were two such stretches of artificial woodland.

The square which housed both the Crystal Bird and the dress shop was quiet in the early morning. One or two pedestrians were at the bus stop but there were no signs of life at either night club or shop. It was before the latter that Kittson pulled to the curb.

"All clear," Erskine reported aloud. "No one inside."

The senior agent went up the short flight of stairs to the main entrance. He cupped his palm over the lock for a second and then confidently opened the door. A long hall running clear to the back of the house faced them. Paying no attention to the rooms on either side, they went down this to the back stairs, descending to what had once been the kitchen and service quarters. In turn, they discovered and used the steps to a second cellar, Saxton playing a flashlight along the floor, centering it at last on the well-opening in the floor.

Kittson stooped and passed his hand slowly around the rim of its cover before he gave it a sharp tug. One by one they dropped to the passage below. The way was roughly walled with brick and it ran straight ahead. They were perhaps two-thirds of the way toward their goal when Blake knew that his warning had not been nullified. He reached out to Erskine's arm.

"Pranj must be ahead."

None of them answered him, nor did they slacken pace. But, as they turned an angle in the passage, there was light ahead and Blake recognized the opening into the place where Pranj based his carrier.

"Two—shielded—coming—" Erskine warned.

Kittson strode into the carrier room and Saxton was at his heels. Blake hesitated. He alone carried no gun. Erskine was beyond, leaning against the wall with flame gun ready. Blake could see no way of playing sentry himself and stepped back to follow the others.

There was the level carrier. On it crouched Pranj, his lips shrunken against his teeth, a reddish spark in his eyes. Across his knee he balanced one of the flame guns, pointed at Hoyt. The red-haired agent's face was drawn and haggard. He had the look of a man close to the end of endurance. But his compelling gaze never left the outlaw.

Blake began to understand. The psi strength of the one held the other in invisible bonds. As long as either stood firm his opponent could not move. And neither of those silent, motionless figures paid any heed to the new arrivals.

What followed was a battle, the wildest, most improbable engagement one could conceive. No nightmare had prepared Blake for its moves. The agents did not try to overpower Pranj physically; they did not even advance to the carrier. But Blake was sensitive to the unleashing of vast forces.

Once, the gun was sucked out of Saxton's hands, whirled about in the air until it faced its owner, only to crash to the floor a second later. But Saxton made no move to pick it up again. A ball of orange-red light materialized in the center of the room, skimmed at Kittson's head, only to explode in a fountain of sparks which winked out. The light in the room dimmed, was almost extinguished, and then flared up again.

Then a creature crawled from beneath the carrier, a foul mixture of lizard and snake, talons on its feet, a forked tongue playing from fanged jaws. As it advanced, it grew more solid, more menacing. At last that flickering tongue scraped Hoyt's boot. But he gave it no heed. Then it sprang at him with a hissing scream, and was gone!

Blake shrank back against the wall. He was sure that they were illusions, weird weapons. But what purpose did they serve? Unless they were intended to distract the fighters.

Pranj still squatted on the raft, grinning his rat's snarl. He was not defeated; he was still able to hold at bay the agents. The final attack came from the passage. A shot, and then another—a scream. None of the three agents within moved.

Erskine! Had Erskine been—?

But whatever had happened out there meant something to the outlaw. He hurled himself at the doorway, at the same time shouting:

"In here, Scappa!"

But his lunge brought him up flat against some invisible barrier, against which he crashed with force enough to send him to the floor. The agents, snapping out of their trances, went to work swiftly. Hoyt jerked Pranj's hands behind him, fettering them with a hoop of metal Kittson had ready. Then the senior agent pulled over the prisoner's head a hood of silvery fabric.

Erskine loomed in the doorway. "Finished?"

"How many out there?" Kittson countered.

"Three. I think we have all those wearing shields."

"If we haven't we can mop up later," his commanding officer

decided. "Once Pranj is back in Vroom they can send over a secondary squad."

Saxton slipped the carrying strap of his flame gun over his shoulder. With Hoyt, he carried the limp body of the outlaw over to the carrier. When the three of them were aboard, the older man gave a casual wave of his hand and took the control. The green mist shimmered and machine and men disappeared from view.

Erskine stretched. "Ready to go?"

Kittson nodded. They went out into the passage where the contorted bodies of three men lay. The two agents did not look at Pranj's dead henchmen any more than they had regarded the dead Ixanilian nobles. Kittson faced the door of the carrier station. He raised his hand and traced the edge of the steel portal which closed it from the passage. It fused tight, sealing the door so that Blake doubted if it ever could be forced open again.

They went back to the basement of the shop. And again Kittson sealed the well-entrance for all time. There were footsteps above, now, and the faint murmur of voices, but neither of the agents appeared uneasy. The fatigue Blake had felt earlier was closing in on him again and he dragged behind as they went up to the next floor.

A woman walked along the hall which led to the street door. But she gazed straight through the three of them, turning into a side room with no sign of alarm. They found the station wagon still outside, and got in.

"A clean 'solution satisfactory,'" was Erskine's comment.

"Not quite," corrected his commander.

Blake leaned forward, his elbows on his knees, his chin supported by his cupped hands. He was sleepy, his eyelids heavy as lead. From the moment Pranj and his captors had vanished this lassitude had spread, not only through his body, but through his mind. Now he was interested in nothing but rest.

But when they returned to Patroon Place, he was jarred out of a doze and for the first time wondered what was going to happen to him now. On his fingers he counted off the days of the week. Only last Monday this adventure had begun; how far had he traveled since then? And now he was somehow sure that he would never return to the life he had had before he opened that hotel room door.

Once inside the house again, Kittson went directly to the cellar, his companions following him. It was not until they reached the level-traveling device that the senior agent spoke to Blake:

"We can't leave you here."

He did not try to answer that.

"We can handle an open mind like Jack's. He'll be returned to his own world remembering that you died in the explosion of the house. But that barrier of yours prevents us doing the same for you. And, with the information you have, we just can't leave you here. So," he hesitated, and for the first time since Blake had known him, appeared somewhat ill at ease, "so we have to break the first rule of the Service and take you along."

He waited as if expecting a hot protest. But between fatigue and the odd feeling that now this decision was the only one, Blake said nothing. They entered the cube; the door closed upon the world Blake knew. But he did not turn his head for a last look at it.

Epilogue

The Inspector gave his full attention to the information on the desk reading-plate. By rights, the file was closed. Only plain curiosity had made him trigger it this morning. He had a weakness for wanting to know the ends of stories.

Case 4678—when the 'Solution Satisfactory' had come through for that, he had wanted to learn the rest. And at the document he was now reading, he shaped a soundless whistle. It *was* a unique case after all! They had better watch that it didn't set a regrettable precedent.

> ". . . as the Council has been advised—reports of progress nine through twelve, filed by this group—we had no choice but to bring this individual from World E641 to Vroom. Report of Senior Parapsychologist Avan To Kimal (attached) agrees that subject possesses, along with power of precognition, a natural mind barrier to the 10th strength, a force hitherto undiscovered. There is also reason to suspect that subject may be from unexplored level EX508, which was destroyed in a chain-reaction explosion some twenty years ago. Circumstances of subject's introduction in E641 suspicious and EX508 was on the verge of discovering level travel for themselves when last disastrous war broke out. S.P. Kimal now investigating this.

However, being unable to leave him in E641 with false memories, we transported him to Vroom. The subject, though young, is discreet, preserving our secret as well as any recruit. He is responsible for the discovery of level Neo 14 as yet unexplored. In addition he displays the ability to adapt and other useful qualities.

It is the considered opinion of this group that he is agent material, though not of our time or race. We unite in recommending him for further training and enrollment."

Quite a departure. The Inspector made a mental note—Blake Walker. It might be interesting to watch for that name on the rolls from now on.

He pressed a button and the plate cleared. "Solution Satisfactory," that was the way the Service liked them. The more such files they could present to the Council, the better. He yawned and prepared to close the office. Blake Walker—watch for that name in, say, three, four years from now . . .

QUEST CROSSTIME

For Richard Benyo,
who first visualized the "sterile" world

Chapter One

The land repelled. Not because of any raw breakage, for the rocky waste was contoured by wind and storm, the wind and water of passing centuries. But those gray, red-brown, lime-white strata were only that: bare stone. And their colors were muted, somber. Even the sea waves, washing with constant booming force at the foot of the cliff, were a steely shade today under the massing clouds of another storm. It was a world completely alienated from the present struggle centered in a cluster of green hemispheres in the river valley below; a world which had had no dealing with humankind, nor with animals, nor birds, nor reptiles, nor even the simplest forms of celled life such as might float in the water. For this was a world in which no spore of life had ever dwelt—sterile rock—until man, with his restless drive for change, had chosen to trouble its austerity.

The storm now gathering would be a bad one. Marfy Rogan looked up at the piling clouds, assessed the growing twilight they brought. She was a fool to linger here. Still . . .

She did not get to her feet. Instead, she leaned forward in the niche she had found, rested her forehead on the crook of her arm, pressing her shoulder against the harsh surface of the supporting rock. Her body was tense with the effort she put into her searching probe. In her, what had begun as a momentary uneasiness had long since grown into a fire of fear.

"Marva!" Her lips moved soundlessly as she sent that cry, by another method than speech, out into the vast wilderness of this life-less successor world. The sea's clamor might even have drowned out a shout, but it could not deter the call she sent mind to mind. Only—that receptive other mind was not there!

And that silence meant a contradiction which was the root of her fear. For among the other equipment fastened to the belt of her work suit was a small instrument ticking serenely away, reporting that all was well, that Marva, to whose body it was—or had been—tuned, was going about her business in a normal way. Had been tuned . . .

Any change in that personality setting would indicate willful interference. What would be the cause of such a starkly mad act? Naturally, those on the field trip would take cover when they saw the storm warnings and not try to return to Headquarters. But distance was no barrier to the tie between the twin sisters, no reasonable distance. And the 'copter was neither supplied nor prepared to make any long trek over the unending desert of rock.

Marva's personnel disk reported all well with her, but Marfy's mind and inner sense denied that vehemently. And of the two, she depended first upon her own senses. Yet the disk testified against her.

Had there been anyone down in the camp other than Isin Kutur, Marfy would have been spilling out her worries an hour ago. But he made it so plain that he resented their arrival, that he would joyfully and speedily seize any means that would allow him to bundle them back into the level shuttle and be rid of them, that she had not gone down. And in that she had been a coward. Because if what she was beginning to suspect was true . . .

Marfy lifted her head. Her fine, fair hair was netted against the wind's violence, her face now bare of all the conventional cheek- and forehead-stenciling fashionable in her set. She closed her eyes, the better to "see" with that other sense roving in frantic search. Delicate features, a skin which was ivory pale, with only closely pressed lips providing color, her face had the elegance of line that came from centuries of breeding, tending, and cherishing. So that in her present rocky setting she was as fantastically placed as a flower growing from the stone.

"Marva!" Her voiceless summons was a scream. But there was no answer.

The questing fingers of the wind pulled at her. Marfy opened her eyes just as the first spattering drops of rain hit the rocks with increasing force. She could not descend the cliff path to camp now, she dare not set her strength against the force of that rising gale, the drowning downpour; in her desire to get away from observation in the camp, she had both chosen worse and better than she had been aware of at the time: worse, in that she must be hidden from sight below and temporarily lost as far as they were concerned; better, in that, by squirming farther back into the niche, she had shelter from the worst of the storm.

So, hidden in the depths of that crevice, she could no longer see the rush of wind-lashed sea or anything else, beyond a slice of gray sky now and then traced with the brilliance of unleashed lightning. Judging by her past experience of these storms, she had perhaps an hour or so to remain here.

"Marva!" She loosed a last appeal, waited with dulled and dying hope.

Marva, contrary to all "rightness," was beyond contacting. Yet the disk said she was present, not too far away, and all was well with her. Thus—the disk lied. And yet that, by everything Marfy had been told or taught, was impossible!

When they had come crosstime to this Project, they had been given the most careful briefing, indoctrinated with the need for protection devices. And Marva—as adventurous, as impatient of control as she sometimes was—was not ever really reckless. Nor would her sister have begun a new adventure without Marfy; they had always acted together in any important thing.

Also, there was no reason in the world—this world or any other of the myriad ones open to their people—why their activities would be interfered with to the extent of making a personnel disk lie. Why, as much as Kutur resented them, it was to his own advantage to see they had Hundred treatment. They were Erc Rogan's daughters, traveling with his official permission on a carefully charted crosstime quest for knowledge.

Unless—Marfy's head jerked as a sudden thought startled her. Unless the Limiters . . . She licked raindrops from her lips. Marva oftentimes accused her of having a suspicious mind. As twin sisters they might be one in most things, but there were basic differences of emotion, spirit, intellect; they were individuals, not just two halves of a split whole. The Limiters was the party behind the growing demand that crosstime travel be placed under strict control. Supervised and controlled, of course, by Saur To'Kekrops' proposed committee—which was the same as saying To'Kekrops and his liege men alone. If there was an incident which could be used for public report, proving the dangerous quality of crosstime exploration, the need for rigid supervision; an accident to some member of the Hundred or to the family of such a member—Marfy sucked in her breath, went rigid. But To'Kekrops would not *dare*! And how could he interfere?

There was no possible entrance into this successor world except right down there in the midst of camp. And no possible travel vehicle except the official shuttles. Also, the Project personnel would and did have no sympathy with the Limiters. Their experiments here would be among the first to be canceled under such a regimen.

Marva . . .

The fury of the storm was a battle over and around Marfy's small crack of safety. She had witnessed by proxy such explosions of nature pictured on the record tapes in the library of crosstime Headquarters. It had been four centuries—no, five now—since her people had unlocked the gates of Vroom's time and had gone, not backward nor forward, but across the fabric of counted years to visit other successor worlds whose history followed tracks varying further and further from that of Vroom. For, from decisions made in history, sometimes even from the death of a single man, separated worlds split, divided, and re-divided, to make a littering web of time roads, some so divergent that those who used them were no longer wholly human as she and her kind defined human.

And this was one of the oddest of those alternate worlds, one in which the first cells of life had never come into being at all: water, stone, soil, wind, rain, sun. But nothing living or growing. Then the Project had moved in to sow life, or attempt to do so, under controlled conditions. And the experiment was the pride of one of the great scientific groups electing twenty of the ruling Hundred. No, Project personnel would do nothing to jeopardize what they were attempting to accomplish here.

Marva had been restless during the past few days. She liked people. The thrill of crosstime travel was allied in her with a chance to study other levels which were not barren deserts. The sisters had made two such trips, having sworn to obey orders, and both times Marva had been disappointed at the narrow path they had been constrained to walk. Here they had been afforded more freedom, simply because there were no other-world natives to whom they could inadvertently reveal themselves.

So—But there was no use in speculating, although Marfy's imagination continued to supply her with a series of explanations drawn from the few facts she knew, each perhaps a little more exotic than the one preceding it. Only one decision for her, once the storm was over: she was going straight to Kutur. Then she was going to demand what she had been so careful not to request since they had arrived and had learned that Kutur's compliance with Erc Rogan's request for their visit had been a very unwilling one: she was going to demand a message right, and report directly to—to whom?

Erc Rogan was level-hopping, inspecting successor depots, making sure the Limiters had no laxness of regulation, no possible excuse to enter a "contrary" at the next conference. She might catch him in any of half a hundred stations. But also she would have to leave calls at each, and she dared not tie up the message lines unless it was a matter of dire importance. The very leaving of those calls would cause comment and stir across the whole crosstime system.

Then, to whom? Com—Com Varlt perhaps? She had known Com since he had been an Aptwardsman just out of training, when she and Marva had been taken, at the age of six, to see the animals on the Forest Level. Com Varlt's family holdings marched with Rogan's; they had inter-familied twice in the not too-distant past. And Varlt was on home duty this month. Yes, a message to Varlt, though they would wonder about that, too. Unless Marva . . . Marfy shook her head in answer to her own thoughts, willing away that hot, tight feeling inside that threatened to take over her emotions whenever she thought of her sister and the unanswered mind call. She would wait out the storm up here; the time would give her a chance to think out just the right message for Varlt. Then, once the worst of the wind and rain was over, she would go back to camp, face up to Kutur, and claim her right of communication.

⊕ ⊕ ⊕

It was a small shuttle but compact. Not with all the latest fixtures, of course, but well fitted for such a routine run. Blake Walker glanced about the small cabin. Two cushioned and shielded seats were in place before the control board; behind them, the lockers of emergency supplies, recording equipment, tools. It was as safe a method of crosstime travel as the experts—and they were expert—had been able to devise to date. A satisfactory standing at his passout from instruction into the corps allowed him to make this routine run alone.

In a package wedged behind his seat was the ostensible reason for his trip: special scientific equipment to be delivered to a project attempting to seed life on a sterile world. His other mission had been delivered orally by Master Wardsman Com Varlt: to check on the Rogan twins.

Not too long ago, before the Limiters had become so vocal—and why had their reactionary party become suddenly so important, backed by a huge increase in membership—crosstime travel had provided holidaying for responsible parties, field trips for students, and the usual business of trades. But there had been a cutback in permits when the Limiters began fulminating opposition. Now word had come down the line with emphasis: no more pleasure travel save to "empty" forest worlds, nothing to cause incidents. And that had not been too smart a move, for it played into To'Kekrops' hands in the other direction. He now demanded why, if crosstiming was so safe, did they refuse permits? Rogan had fought the cutback in outgo permissions, had declared it the wrong answer to To'Kekrops' insinuations, and, to prove that, had pointedly defied the order, sending his daughters on a student permission to the Project. He had had to answer one Question for that, but he had stuck to his beliefs, and was using his position to reinstate the normal traffic.

Blake wriggled against the protecting cushions of his seat. He had worked out his own travel code and had it checked. Now he proceeded to put the pattern into action on the board. Even veteran master wardsmen were never hasty about coding, and the requirement of making three checks before the pattern was loosed did not make any shuttle pilot impatient. A fraction of an inch either way might not only land him on the wrong level, but might also mean death because the shuttle might well materialize in a position of space already firmly occupied by some massive solid object.

So Blake took his time, made three checks before playing out the pattern on the hand keys. There was a whir, the sickening lurch to break free from stable time on Vroom's level and go voyaging across the worlds of alternate destinies.

Sealed in the cabin, Blake caught no glimpse of those worlds, not even as shadows flowing about him, although the first time he had so traveled, on the secret shuttle of a level-hopping criminal, he had seen them gather, break, reform, change beyond the bare rim of the platform on which he had huddled. He himself had come out of one of those other worlds, caught up, through no will of his own but because of a psi gift, in the affairs of Com Varlt's team of man hunters. They had played out a wild game then, and in the end the team had had no choice but to take Blake on to Vroom, since his defensive inborn mind-block made false memory grafting impossible.

A stranger in his own world, where he had been found as a baby in an alley and fostered by those who had died before he was fully grown, Blake accepted Vroom's friendship and the offer of a career as wardsman. And he knew that, though it had never been fully proved, Com Varlt believed that he, Blake, came from yet another level, one close to Vroom and on the verge of discovering cross timing itself when a chain atomic reaction had destroyed it utterly. Was he the only survivor of that world? Had he been the child of some experimenter there who had seen a slim chance of survival for his son by putting him through a yet untested "door"? Perhaps. But his possible parentage was no longer of any consequence to Blake. He was well content with what Vroom had to offer, and secretly more than satisfied with the chance to make this solo run.

Once set up and in progress, the code pattern acted independently of the shuttle's pilot. He had a little more than an hour, if time was to be reckoned under such circumstances. But speculation on that point did not bother Blake.

No wardsman wore uniform save for ceremonial occasions at Vroom. You might possess the short maroon jacket, the tight-fitting breeches, metal-latched boots for all your days of service in the corps and perhaps appear only three or four times with those articles of dress on your back and body. Blake's lean, six-foot frame was clothed now in the same drab coveralls as he would find the Project men wearing when the shuttle reached his destination. Above this monotone of color, his brown skin, a smooth brown which was its natural pigment rather than any tan, seemed even darker. Sharp in contrast, in the bright interior light of the shuttle cabin, was his hair, a dark red. He wore the equipment belt of an explorer, its various gadgets for defense or survival use. And around his neck the corps identification tag slipped, cool against his flesh, as he moved.

He had made three runs since he passed out of instruction, all as the least important member of temporary crews on routine missions. And he had yet to serve as a "passer" or part of a contact crew more or less permanently in residence on any foreign level. Sometimes such a stint called for plastic surgery and study techniques that altered the team beyond the point of any return, so its members had to pass through a reversal of procedure when their tour of duty was finished. But one had to be at least two steps higher in rank and well tested before one could qualify for that. Also, one had to be really "talented." All the fabled psi gifts of his native level were known to the wardsmen, some of whom possessed two or even more. Levitation, telepathy, telekinesis, precognition—Blake had seen them all in action and also in testing. But compared with most of his fellow corpsmen in service or training, he had but meager natural equipment.

His two "talents," if so they might be termed, were precognition of danger, which he had experienced all his life—in the past to his uneasy concern—and another which he had not known he possessed until he had met the wardsmen during their hunt for the escaped criminal. But in this second talent Blake was not only the equal of his new companions—he was their superior. For without willing it or training, he had developed a mind block to the degree that no one he had yet met—and in the course of training he had been confronted with the best his commanding officers could throw at him—might influence his thinking or read his thoughts. In a telepathic society he possessed a natural defense better than any perfected by mechanical means.

Blake had tried to develop other talents, hoping that esper powers might be latent. But his most rigorous struggles had ended in failure. It was the lack of these talents that might keep him grounded when it came to regular crosstime missions. Like the ache of a long-suffered wound, suppressed but ever there, that thought lay at the back of Blake's mind.

However, there would be no call for esper talents at the Project. He would deliver this package, observe the situation as far as the Rogan girls were concerned, and be on his way back in a matter of hours. A dull task all around. Next tour ought to be Forest Level and that was better. A world without men, where animals were free and without fear, the Forest Level was a favorite with children and family groups for camping. Three wardsmen accompanied each so-arranged tour and all protective "waves" were always on. So far no protest from the Limiters for a close-down there had been voiced. Forest World was too popular. To'Kekrops' party would risk a vast amount of adverse reaction if they tried making that level out of bounds.

Light flashed on his board. Blake's hand hovered over the key as he counted up to ten and then down again, giving the double amount of time to assure himself complete arrival. Then he flicked the hatch release. The shuttle ceased to quiver, a portion of the wall moved, and Blake looked out into the faintly bluish light of the level terminal.

Blake blinked as he recognized the man facing him—Tursha Scylias, second-in-command of the whole Project. Whatever he transported must be more important than he had been informed. He pulled the package out of its tight fittings, lifting it with the care he supposed it deserved.

But Scylias accepted the burden almost absently, continuing to eye Blake.

"You are new." Not a question but a flat statement.

"On this run, yes," Blake answered, refusing to admit to this man how new he was. Because there was a metallic taste in his mouth, a prickle of roughening skin between his shoulders. Trouble! Here—or very close! He was alerted by his talent, and instantly, in only half-conscious effort, his mind shield went up. This much he had learned under tuition, to maintain before that shield a defense of camouflage surface thought. And, in times of stress, a second and deeper layer would deceive all but the expert into thinking he was not shielded at all.

Now he stepped from the hatch, his boots stamping on the undisguised rock that formed the floor of the camp structure, wishing he had some telepathic power to pick up from Scylias a hint of what the trouble was.

"Reports." The assistant Project leader whipped out two rolls of tape in a carrying case. He made no move to step out of Blake's way; it was as if he had to keep a tight hold on himself to avoid herding the wardsman straight back into the machine. Then perhaps he himself recognized that suspicious attitude, for he did not demur when Blake set the record case within the hatch and turned once more to his greeter.

"Everything satisfactory?" Blake fell back on the official report terms.

"Entirely so," Scylias replied and then added harshly, "You will eat with us? It is the mid hour."

"Good enough. Thank you. I'll just check the message station . . ."

Scylias moved as if to block Blake's movement toward the outward entrance of the terminal and to guide it instead to the tunnel connecting that room with other parts of the camp.

"Storming out." His tone was flat. "You cannot reach the rods until that is over."

Trouble . . . trouble . . . The pulse was beating heavily behind Blake's eyes now. Not the storm, no, but perhaps the rods . . . But why? No sane project leader or member would allow any trouble with the rods! To be cut off with no chance of getting a message through. They could not want that. But what was wrong with Scylias? The man was definitely on edge. And there was danger here—bad—from the way Blake felt now.

Chapter Two

Perhaps because there was no vegetation to act as wind breaks, the storm seemed to have more force than on a normal world. Blake stared out of a viewport at the rush of wind-driven rain striking against the camp shelters. They were located in a valley, the only break between cliff walls for a long stretch of territory. Blake need only turn his head to see the map of the Project set out on the curving wall. The valley was cut by an unusually slow-flowing river which formed a small delta of silt at its sea mouth. And the sea itself was provided with a breakwater of curving reef, turning the river-mouth coast into a partly sheltered bay.

Along the nearer bank of the river were the growth tanks, carefully sown and now housing the algae and other primitive life imported from the Vroom laboratories. This was only the beginning of the Project, but Blake knew that a fantastic amount of labor and capital had already gone into it.

Crosstime travel was largely trade, discreet trade, and the real foundation of all Vroom's economy. Trade from one successor world to another, natural resources from underdeveloped and primitive levels, luxuries from more sophisticated civilizations—never enough taken to cause native comment or investigation. And if now useless levels such as this could be harvested, then Vroom, apart from the knowledge gained in experimentation, would be that much richer and more securely buttressed against the future.

Outside the viewport the rain was forming so thick a curtain that Blake could not see the neighboring shelter as more than a vague outline. He turned to the map with some interest, and then passed along to view the series of taped scenes mounted in a panorama of color: always only rock, or sea, or rivers and lakes in stone settings. The color of that rock varied, sometimes brighter and more eye-catching, but never bearing any hint of green life. And, as Blake studied those pictures, the uneasiness that had ridden him since he had disembarked from the shuttle grew sharper. Though he had ostensibly been viewing the outer world since he had been shown into this lounge by Scylias, he had been listening with all the effort he could muster for any sound.

So far Blake had seen none of the other personnel. He was trying to recall all he knew of the fellowship of the Project. Isin Kutur headed it. The man had a reputation for being a driver, single-minded, one who bulled through shaky causes but shed friends, or rather acquaintances, along the way. His standing with the Hundred was high. Twice he had pulled out of difficulty, or salvaged, expensive projects about to be written off as failures. Blake had seen him on a televised cast, a stolid, thick-shouldered man, with a shock of prematurely white hair, who had given impatient, monosyllabic answers to the interview questions.

Isin Kutur, Scylias—Blake searched his memory and found that was the extent of his acquaintance with the Project personnel. Except, of course, the Rogan twins, and them he knew only through Varlt's briefing. Daughters of a four-generation Hundred family. Blake had studied the picture of them Varlt had shown him, and in his mind he could not match the stark utility of this background with the girls who had appeared there.

"Wardsman?" A woman stood in the doorway. But not one of the Rogan girls. She was at least two decades older, and her rather sharp-featured face bore the crease of a permanent frown between thick brows. "If you will come, we are about to eat." Her speech was stilted; she was clearly not at ease.

Blake followed her into a larger division of the structure from which came the smell of food, largely synthetics of the ration type. But those gathering about the table were apparently welcoming the Spartan fare with gusto. Kutur was seated with one elbow cushioned on a note board. From time to time he scribbled quickly on that archaic writing aid; otherwise he paid no attention to his surroundings.

There were five other staff members present: the woman who had ushered Blake into the room, Scylias, three more, one of them also a woman. But of the Rogan girls there was no sign. And since none of his tablemates seemed disposed to talk, the wardsman hesitated to break the silence. Kutur had not even looked up from his scribble block. Blake sipped at the container of hot drink and waited.

Trouble rang his inner alarm. But that was the difficulty with his talent, he could not define the danger or its source. That it was imminent he was sure. And it was all he could do to curb his unease and continue to sit at the table, nibble his unappetizing rations, and wait for enlightenment.

Kutur shoved the pad aside, raised his head and looked about. His attention flickered down one side of the table and up the other. When his glance reached Blake, he gave a sharp nod which might have been intended as a curt greeting or merely recognition of the younger man's place in the general scheme of things.

"Where is the girl?" It was not the voice one expected from that bull chest and thick throat. In place of a growl or a husky rumble, the words were delivered as a cultivated, almost melodious query. Blake had heard actors and orators with less natural ability to shape speech into rhythm.

"Marfy?" The woman who had been Blake's guide shot a glance to her left as if she expected to see someone there. The crease between her brows sharpened, her mouth twisted. She dropped the wafer she had been holding to her lips and swiftly detached a small disk from her belt, bringing it to her ear as she replied to Kutur. "She went up the cliff just before the storm, Head. But the signal is in order. The recall, we all heard the warning recall. She must have heard it too!"

Kutur surveyed them again, beginning with Scylias and following along the line. He even favored Blake with his searching stare.

"Evidently she did not hear it, or else she chose to disregard it. There is no place here for such foolishness. I have said it. I now repeat it many times, and loud enough for all fools to take it through their ear holes into their brains: there is no place in crosstime for foolishness! We have no time to hunt lost ones." Deliberately his thick fingers went to his own belt and he unhooked a twin to the coin-shaped object the woman still held. With one fingernail he gave it a vigorous tapping, then held it to his ear.

"She is in no danger," he stated. "Perhaps a wet skin and some discomfort will make her think next time. We cannot watch after children who will not obey the simplest and most obvious rules. So will you state this afternoon, Tursha, to the authorities. I shall have no further troubling from such visitors, no matter how many official cards they carry!"

One of the Rogans, Blake deduced, was out in the storm. But apparently the staff had some check on her which reassured Kutur, even if that did not testify to her exact whereabouts. But what of her sister? No one had mentioned the other girl at all.

They sat at a long table; there was plenty of unoccupied space around it. Blake tried to estimate who, beyond the two girls, might be missing. Dared he ask questions?

Chance seemed to be aiding him for Kutur spoke again. "The 'copter sheltered safely, I trust. No more foolishness to be reported?"

Scylias nodded. "Yes, they grounded at the first cloud massing. Garglos said they were running under a ledge big enough for full cover."

Kutur grunted. "For any trace of intelligence in one's subordinates one must offer thanks, exceedingly great thanks—or so it seems to me at present. You, wardsman, have you been given any orders for me? Any more limits to be set on what we may or may not do lest we, in some fashion, influence this stretch of rock into future ill behavior?"

From some men that might have been an attempt at humor, but to Blake it sounded like ponderous sarcasm. "Routine inspection of the rods, Head," he replied tersely.

Kutur nodded. "Very well. Do your duty, wardsman. But see me before you go. I will have a message, a personal message to be delivered to Hundredman Rogan. I will not"—he drove his pen spearfashion into the surface of the scribble block—"I will not be bothered by school girls. This I am deciding now and for all time!"

Again he stared at each of the company in turn as if expecting someone to refuse what was clearly an ultimatum. But no one demurred.

A clearing of a throat brought all their attention to one of the men who had accompanied Scylias. "Storm is slacking off."

For a moment Blake wondered how the other could be sure of that in this windowless chamber. Then he was aware that the steady beat of rain, which had been a low drumming during all his time in Project Headquarters, was lessening. Kutur was already on his feet, ready for action.

"Ulad, Kyogle, down to the flats with me! We shall be most favored by fortune if the water has not ruined half twenty days' work."

"But Marfy?" the woman leaned forward to ask.

Kutur glared. His head swung around as if counting his followers. Then his finger stabbed at Blake.

"You! Your duty is to keep an eye on travelers, is it not? Then get out there and find this fool of a girl and bring her back, even if you have to drag her all the way!" He reached the door in a couple of strides and left Blake with the woman. In a way he was right, the wardsmen were primarily a protection force for Vroom's people in the network of alternate worlds. But where would he start here? The danger he sensed waiting around some shadowy corner, was it concerned with Marfy Rogan?

"She—she has been most foolish, you know," the woman said. "These storms are very severe, and we always sound a recall before they break. Every one of us carries one of these tuned to our personality." She indicated the disk at her belt. "If we are in trouble, it broadcasts a call for help to be picked up by every other disk. This is the best protection we have found in case of accident. Marfy is not in any danger. And there is a locater tuned to these which will guide you. Wait, I will get it for you from Head Kutur's office."

She trotted off and Blake fell in behind her. Then she darted into a door which she closed firmly in his face, to return a few moments later with a slightly larger disk equipped with a swinging, nervous needle.

"I have set it. I do not believe Head Kutur will mind my taking the liberty. He would have ordered it to be given to you had he had the time. But this rain . . . And if the river rises again, it may, as he said, wipe out much of our labor. We have had three of these rains in one week, and never before so many so close together. The problem of the excess water is becoming acute. Marfy has chosen the worst possible time to irritate Head Kutur when his mind must hold and solve so many problems! See, the needle is already swinging. Follow that and you will find her. Oh, take these also." She jerked open another door and pulled out two stormcoats complete with hoods.

Bundling both of these into Blake's hold, she thrust her long arms into the sleeves of a third, hurrying away from him as she adjusted the hood. So protected against the elements, with the extra coat under his arm and the homing device in his hand, Blake followed in her wake.

The terrific force of the storm might have slackened a little, but the rain still poured, hitting the rocks and then cascading in runnels down any inclined surface. The eye place in Blake's hood gave him a curtailed field of vision, and the needle on the dial swung away from the cluster of shelters by the river, pointing to the rocky cliff at his right.

Mud was glue to catch his boots, and Blake made the cliffward march with grim determination, finding few kindly thoughts for the object of his search. If this was a sample of the Rogan girls' behavior in the field, he did not wonder at Kutur's impatience. Only—his inner alert was still warning him.

The clouds parted to the west and thin sunshine made a pallid struggle against the gloom. Blake threw back the hood of his coat. The stark nature of the country was depressing in spite of the now clearing sky and the sun. One did not miss vegetation until there was a complete lack of it. One small struggling plant would have provided a very welcome break in this bleak landscape. If the Project succeeded in its experiments, there would be more than one plant in the river valley, but such a triumph of man over reluctant nature was still far in the future.

There were shouts in the valley, the purr of motors. Blake glanced back. Machinery was moving out from under cover, heading for the swollen river and the walled pens, the barriers of which were now nearly hidden under the flooding waters. It would certainly appear that Kutur and his people had hard work before them.

Ahead of Blake was a path of sorts, more nearly a ladder where it climbed the heights. But before his boots were fairly set on that way there was movement above. Blake saw a slight figure in drab field dress, dark patches molding the fabric to upper arms and shoulders, hurrying along a ledge at what seemed to Blake a reckless pace. The girl was coming in his direction.

"Hoy!" The call was thin, distorted by faint echoes. An arm waved vigorously, signaling him to stay where he was.

She was surefooted, graceful, and competent as she descended that wet and perhaps treacherous ladder path. While she was still some distance away, he saw her stare at him, her eyes widen. Then she took the last drop with the ease of one following a known path.

Such was the difference between this wet and windblown figure and Varlt's picture that Blake might not have recognized her save under these circumstances. Her hair was braided and netted close to her head; she had none of the elaborate and exotic patterns stenciled on cheek and forehead after the latest fashion of Vroom. In spite of that, she looked older than he expected.

"You—you are not from the Project!" She had halted, her left arm flung out about a stone outcrop to break her last descent. Now she eyed him with something approaching suspicion.

"Walker, Ap-W 7105," he answered formally.

"Walker," she repeated as if the foreign-sounding name was in itself a matter for suspicion. "Walker!" That was recognition he had not expected. "Blake Walker! By the teeth of Pharses! Did Com Varlt send you? But how could he have known—Father! Something has happened to Father!" She left her rock anchor, skidded forward across a mud patch to catch at his arm with force enough nearly to send him off balance in turn.

"No, I'm making a routine run," Blake answered. "They found you missing from the camp, asked me to find you. Here, it looks as if there's another shower on the way. You had better get into this." He shook out the spare coat, swung it around her already soaked shoulders.

However, it was clear his reassurance had not relieved her concern. Through the hand still clutching his arm, Blake could feel her tension.

"What is it?" he asked in turn. She seemed to be unharmed, but he knew that Marfy Rogan was in more trouble than merely being caught in a storm.

"Marva! She went on a field trip in the 'copter this morning. And she is missing!"

Blake recalled the conversation at the table. "There was a message. The 'copter took shelter before the storm, perfectly safe—" Blake began, but the girl was determinedly shaking her head.

"She is not safe. Or at least she is not here."

"But these things"—Blake touched the disk on her belt—"would you not know about—"

Marfy tore the device from its hook, held it to his ear. "Listen!" She spoke with a fierce demand for immediate obedience. "Tell me, what do you hear?"

A throbbing beat, as steady as his own heart.

"Steady beating," he replied with the exact truth.

"Yes. And that is supposed to mean that there is nothing wrong, that Marva's out there somewhere"—she made a sweeping gesture— "sitting under a rock, maybe eating rations with Nagen Garglos, waiting for the storm to clear so they can be back in time for evening meal. Only that is not the truth, not even a shadow of the truth!"

This was it, or part of it, his talent told him; this is what that inner alarm meant. And, so knowing, Blake was more than willing to listen. But what did she have to offer in the way of concrete fact?

"How do you know?"

Marfy Rogan frowned at him; there was something of Kutur's unshaken self-confidence and arrogance in that expression. "Because we are twins, and we can mindspeak. We always have. I was down in camp this morning, in half-touch with Marva. Then—nothing!" She snapped her fingers. "Just like that—nothing at all! It has never happened before and—well—I thought for a while that I might be under a shield. Kutur has a lot of experimental installations, other projects send him things to try out in the atmosphere of this level. So when I was cut off I got out, away from camp, up here"—she waved now to the cliff—"above the level of a broadcast. But that did not help, not even when I straight-beamed . . ."

Blake could not straight-beam himself, but in the past he had been the recipient of such probes and he knew their force. Between twins such an aimed thought must be even more potent.

"Then," Marfy again shook the disk before his eyes, "this just kept on recording that everything was fine, blue sky and open land, as it were, all the way. This thing lied and is continuing to lie! And something has happened to Marva!"

"Could this be broken?" Blake fingered the disk. "Or hers?"

"I do not see how, they are warranted without a flaw. Wait!" She snatched at the locator that had led him from camp. "Now, let us see." She turned the gadget over in her hand, cupping it in her palm as she pressed a small button in its back case in a series of quick jabs. Having done so, she turned it over again so they could both see the dial.

The needle which had held so firmly toward the cliffs now swung loosely, came to a quivering stop, spun again when Marfy purposely shook her hand.

"Marva!" Her voice was a cry tinged with fear.

"What does that mean?" Blake's hand closed on the girl's shoulder to shake her gently as she still stared as if sight and mind were locked on the dial.

"She—she is not anywhere—not here!" Again Marfy feverishly shook the gadget, watched the needle spin in a crazy, purposeless whirl. "But she could not have—"

"Have what?"

"Gone off level! I was down there, right in the next room to the travel station, clear up to the moment when she lost mind touch. Our shuttle is at Vroom. There was no way for her to leave, and she would not have gone without telling me . . ." There could be one other explanation, Blake knew, but he did not voice it aloud. Somewhere out in the stone wilderness there might lie a dead girl. Yet that beat he had heard—Marfy had said it was the proper reply for a disk worn by someone in no danger. In any event, there was trouble here right enough, and it was up to him to find out just what.

"A message . . ." Marfy thrust the locater into the front of her stormcoat. "I want to send a message to Com Varlt. Something has happened to Marva."

She started to run down the slope of the valley toward the camp, and Blake went pounding after her.

Chapter Three

Only, that next and important step was denied them. For as they slipped and slid their way down to the camp, Blake suddenly slowed to a stop. On this time level where there was no need for concealment from native dwellers, installations were boldly planted in the open. The energized rods keeping communication channels open between the Project and Vroom were beacon high—or had been beacon high—against the sky. Now one leaned at a sharp angle and the other, on the far side of the camp, was not to be sighted at all!

But how . . . The importance of those would have been so paramount to the men setting up the camp that they would have based them firmly, certainly made them secure against all assaults of nature. Yet the unlikely happened.

Blake sloshed through a stream of muddy water to the inclining pole. It was correctly set in rock, but now a cavity had opened under that base, undermining it. Blake frowned. He was no tech, but the field men were neither stupid nor careless. To choose a faulty base for a com rod was completely out of character. There would be an investigation of this when it was reported. And he would have to do the reporting, in person.

"The rod is—" Marfy Rogan splashed to join him.

"Useless. And I cannot see the other one, so that may be down all the way. But how did they make such an error in base sites?"

"Ask"—her reply was terse—"and perhaps you will also get an

answer concerning personnel disks which do not work properly either!"

The laboring sound of a machine caused Blake to look around. One of the earth-movers he had seen crawling toward the flooded pens was now lumbering in their direction, the man in the driver's seat waving them out of the way. As Blake drew Marfy back, the mover clanked by and went to packing earth in an effort to keep the standard from falling to the ground.

Even if this one was righted and its fellow raised again, it would mean hours of delicate adjustment before they could once more be synchronized to open the message channel. And Blake wondered if there was any tech on the Project capable of such work. No, he would have to make his report in person and perhaps return with the men to do the job. And the sooner he got to it, the better. Still grasping Marfy's arm, he turned to the Headquarters shelter.

"You will be going back, won't you?" she asked. "Then I go, too."

"That is up to the Head, is it not?" Even part-time visitors to such a project were under the command of the Head. They took an oath agreeing to that before their passes were issued. Only a wardsman could come and go without any check from local authorities, acting under the orders of his own officers.

For the first time Blake saw her smile, a very fleeting one, "I do not think Isin Kutur will object. He will be only too glad to see the last of me. Unless . . ." She paused.

"Unless?"

"Unless he does not want my report on Marva to be heard."

"But why—" began Blake.

She turned on him, her expression one of scorn for his stupidity. "Limiters! This could be just the kind of story they would use. Marva lost in time . . ."

"But how can you be sure of that?" It seemed to Blake that she reached conclusions in a hasty fashion, none of them being more stably rooted than the rods of the camp.

"She is not in this world! Not anywhere!"

"But you said yourself that she had not, could not have, used the shuttle out of camp."

"Which simply means that somewhere, for some reason, there is another shuttle." Marfy was prompt with her answers, delivered in the firm tone of one who has made up her mind and intends to abide by it. "Oh, so you think that is impossible?" She flung the question at Blake, apparently reading his doubt in his expression. "It has happened before, you know that!"

It had happened before: illegal shuttles swinging from level to level, such as the one that had taken him on a nightmare journey of successor worlds on his first introduction to the crosstime activities of Vroom. But since then, security had so tightened that Blake could not believe any criminal or reckless, unlisted explorer might operate.

"I want to get to Com Varlt." Marfy pulled at Blake. "He will know what to do, how to reach Father."

"But who . . ." Even as he mumbled that, Blake was able to supply a few wild guesses himself: the Limiters themselves, out to provoke some incident; illegal traders, though what would they want on this world unless they had a cache here; or an unauthorized explorer. Suppose that Marva and the 'copter pilot had stumbled on something not meant to be seen and accordingly had been gathered in to suppress their discovery?

Against such an argument he could set the report of the 'copter pilot that he had found safe shelter from the storm. That did not match such suspicions.

However, one could not dismiss Marfy's dismay at the loss of mind touch. That could not be tampered with, even if machine reports could be altered. And according to her, the break in rapport had come before the storm, before the pilot's report. And his own precognition . . . he could rely on the truth of that even if it was only a general warning. If he could only focus it, narrower it would be more of a help.

"Who?" Marfy repeated. She spread out a hand, spread her fingers, showing gray mud under the nails. "I can give you several answers without needing to search. But I want to start the hunt for Marva." Her voice caught.

"All right. We can get back and—"

"Wardsman!" Kutur swung from the seat of another machine and splashed heavily to meet them at the entrance to Headquarters. The stocky Head was smeared with mud, spatters of it freckling his face when he had thrown back his hood. "You see what has happened to the rods. Incompetence! Sheer incompetence! I shall report it. You

will take my tape back with you. I was assured of complete cooperation, and what do I get? Incompetence from those upon whom our
safety depends! And"—he swung to Marfy as if he saw her for the
first time—"reckless disregard for orders on the part of silly young
females who have no business being here in the first place! Pass or no
pass, girl, you return now to Vroom!"

"And Marva?" Marfy's voice was a little shrill as she interrupted
him.

"And Marva also. Once Garglos returns her to this camp, she will
be sent after you. No more will I have to deal with foolishness!"

"When Garglos and Marva return," Marfy persisted. "And when
will that be, Head Kutur, and where shall they return from?"

He stared at her as if she were babbling utter nonsense. "They will
return from a field flight and very soon, if Garglos follows orders,
which hitherto he has done. As to where they are coming from, it is
Sector Dot One, as you well know, girl."

Marfy shook her head. "Marva went off level this morning before
the storm, a complete time unit before."

Kutur swung his head slowly, not as an answer to her words but
as if that simple gesture would clear away some fog of thinking.
"What are you saying, girl? Nonsense, all of it. You, yourself, saw
your sister leave in the 'copter. Level-hopping, is it? Stupid nonsense!" He tapped the disk on his belt. "This tells us that all is well
with her. Why do you mouth so wild a tale?"

"I do not care what that says!" Marfy retorted. "I lost mind touch
and that I do believe. Marva went off level, and if your gadgets say
otherwise, then they lie!"

Kutur's face reddened, his shoulders hunched, his hands came
up, the fingers working a little.

"You!" he exploded at Blake, "get her away, get her away from
here. Two pens utterly lost, the rods down, and now this raving to
listen to. A man can take only so much! Take her back with you. I do
not ask that, I order it! I will listen to no more. And when her sister
returns, she will be sent also to Vroom."

"When do you expect the 'copter back?" Blake asked. "The shuttle
is a small one, but for a nonstop run, I can wait and take them both."

"Wait?" Kutur's lips puffed in an explosion of breath and word
together. "You do not wait when I say go! I want techs here, those

rods up again, we do not know how many storms lie ahead. It is not beyond reasonable belief that we may have to build from the beginning again. What can be saved now, must be. Go at once!"

"Head," Scylias stood in the doorway behind his superior, "Forkus reports no hour signal from the 'copter. He used both short and extended beam."

For a second or two it was as if Kutur did not hear his assistant, and Blake watched the other closely. If the Head was expecting such news, he could not guess it by the reaction that followed. Because Kutur went into swift action.

Under a volley of orders the second of the Project's small airexploration flyers was wheeled out. Blake shed the cumbersome stormcoat and reached the door of its cabin on the heels of the pilots, who was, in this instance, Kutur himself. The Head glowered at the wardsman.

"What do you—"

Blake cut him short, sure of his own authority in this instance. "I am responsible for—" he began.

Kutur snorted. "Get in, get in, do not waste time reciting your duties and virtues. If you linger about to use your tongue, you may be responsible for things you will not wish, wardsman!"

They were airborne almost before Blake made fast the door. Kutur had a heavy hand on the controls, bouncing the light craft up, half-jerking Blake out of his seat. Then they were heading at maximum speed away from the valley camp.

Kutur appeared to know just where he was going, and the broken, rocky terrain of the cliffs sped below them as they left the valley. Volcanic action in the past was evident and Blake thought it would be close to impossible to comb that territory at ground level. But with the 'copter they covered long stretches of it.

Another river passed beneath them, this one encased in a sharply walled gorge. The water was broken by white lacing on the rock-tattered flood. Now they lifted again to a plateau with further heights of mountain to the east. Kutur slacked speed, circling and finally touching down with a back-wracking bounce on relatively smooth surface.

Once there he did not display any great desire to leave the flyer, but hunched forward in his seat, peering through the windbreak at the beginning slopes of the mountains. Blake had his hand on the door latch, but he was determined not to leave the cabin without Kutur. His sense continued to warn him, though as yet without the sharp thrust signaling immediate peril.

"Well?" He broke the silence when the Head continued to sit there. "Which way now?"

"There!" The other pointed. "It should be sheltered under that ledge."

He was right in so much: a ledge overhung a space which might be large enough to shelter a twin to the flyer they now occupied. But if the other 'copter had been there, it was now gone. The rock was bare, like all the rest of this wilderness.

"This—this I do not believe. Look you!" Kutur's hand shot out. Held rigid between thumb and forefinger was the personnel disk from his belt. "This says that they are safe, all is well. The locater brings us along the beam to here. Yet there is nothing!"

"They could already have lifted to return to camp," Blake suggested.

"But no." Kutur pounded his fist on his knee. "There would be no reason for them not to fly straight to camp, and if they had been airborne we should have seen them. Also, they would have answered signals. Do not tell me that they have sunk into this rock. That I will not believe!"

"That was wild country over which we passed, a wreck there . . ." Blake made himself say that.

"There was no automatic distress call broadcast." Kutur shook his head. "These," again he flourished the disk, "these do not lie. All my time on Project, many projects, in places where danger ever stalked at one's heels, lying in wait, these have been our safeguards. Yet now this one says what our eyes tell us is false. I do not understand, none of this do I understand." His bewilderment was complete; he had lost his arrogance and self-assurance.

Without knowing what he was looking for, save the vague chance that some sign of the lost 'copter might indeed remain, Blake left the flyer and walked slowly into the shadow of the ledge. The storm had left pools in rock pockets and now the hot sun was already steaming them away. No chance of any tracks. A small suspicion pricked at Blake. In spite of Kutur's certainty, he was not sure that this was where the others had been.

A scratch on the stone, anything . . . Suppose Marfy was right and an illegal shuttle was in use? For one of those, there need be no such terminal as existed at camp. If its user had a travel code, was sure of an open surface for a breakthrough, he could land anywhere.

The pocket sheltered by the ledge was larger than it appeared from the flyer. The pilot of the other 'copter would have had no difficulty in running in during the storm. And—Blake went down on one knee, rubbed his finger along a scored line—that was no natural scratch and it was fresh. So . . . the 'copter might reasonably be supposed to have been here. That being so, where was it now? Any illegal shuttle— Blake's thoughts continue to return to that—would not be of a size to take aboard a flyer. Or, his imagination soared again, was there an outward trader in operation with a shuttle designed to handle cargo, perhaps operating between successor worlds and not from Vroom at all?

"What is it?" Kutur had followed, stooped to examine the scratch as Blake moved on to search the rest of the area.

"Sign that they might have been here, but nothing else."

"Here, yes. I know that! But where have they gone? Tell me that. Garglos—he is not a boy, he does not play. He does not say he will do one thing, go in one direction, and then change his mind. Garglos is a man to be depended upon. I know him. He has worked with me for years. So why is he missing? And why do these lie and tell me that he is as usual?" Again Kutur held out the personnel disk and shook it fiercely.

"But," he took control of himself, "this is not good. We can do nothing here. One does not claw answers out of rocks with one's fingernails."

"You have detectors, persona beams?" Blake cut in. "Use them for an air search."

Kutur nodded. "There is nothing else to be done. Since we can no longer depend, it would seem, upon the devices which have always served us in such cases, then, yes, we shall turn to the general alarm system. But we are not equipped with high-powered detectors. Those must be brought from wardsmen's depots. And without the rods—"

"Someone takes the message in person," Blake completed. "All right, get me back to camp, and I am on my way to do just that."

During the trip back to Project Headquarters, Kutur was sunk in thought which, to judge by his thunderous expression, was of the darkest. As they climbed from the flyer, he spoke for the first time.

"We shall rig a makeshift and search the best we can. But be you quick, also, wardsman. You have seen this country; this is a dead world. Water, yes, it is drinkable, will keep life going for awhile. But there is nothing else out there to preserve a man on foot, injured. They would have very little chance."

No hint that Kutur had any suspicions of an illegal shuttle. He was now obviously ready to believe in a wilderness crash as he had denied that possibility before. But too many things did not add up for Blake. The message from Garglos that he had his machine and presumably his passenger, Marva Rogan, in shelter. Yet that had come some time after Marfy's rapport with her sister had been broken . . . and Blake's own personal warning. He must get Com Varlt on this, and quickly!

"You did not find them." A flat statement of fact and not a question. Marfy waited just inside the Headquarters door.

Kutur shook his head. "Ulad," he pushed past her to call, "take the detector from the crawler, it must be mounted on the 'copter—"

Marfy caught at Blake's arm. "The detector?" Her voice was hardly above a thin whisper. "Could they have crashed—out there?"

Blake could not conceal what she had already guessed from Kutur's order. "It is possible . . ."

But she was shaking her head. "I know that Marva is not in this world, I knew it as soon as she left. But she did not leave it that way. Death or injury to her—I would feel it with her!" Her voice was still very low as if her words were aimed only at Blake. "You—you found no sign of anything else?"

"Of a shuttle?" Blake matched his tone to hers. "No, but any outlawed level-hopper would not have a permanent base such as this."

Marfy's reason for her conclusion concerning her sister's disappearance made better sense the longer Blake considered it. A mental bond ended by death could not be mistaken by the one who shared it. He had no personal experience of telepathic union, but when such was strengthened by close relationship and emotional ties, Blake knew it was a very deep and enduring form of communication. Had Marva died out there, Marfy, in a way, would also have suffered a taste of death, and she would have known the truth in that instant.

"Com Varlt." She pulled at his sleeve. "If she was taken to another level, the sooner he knows the better."

With that Blake was in full agreement. Kutur had rallied the rest of the Project; there was a great deal of hurrying to and fro. With the rods down, Blake's own duty was to report in and in person. Marfy was hurrying him along, pulling at him.

"Come on!" she demanded impatiently.

They went, apparently attracting no attention from the others, to the shuttle. A return course had been automatically set before the transferor had left Vroom and locked in. Sometimes such a return might be a hurried one, dictated by attack, accident, or the need for moving a wardsman unable to function with either mind or body in the best of condition. Still Blake followed procedure and checked the code, while Marfy strapped in on the companion seat.

The dials were correct as he expected. He pressed the release lever. The swirl of time-exit caught them; they were bemused momentarily by the disorientation of the pass-through.

"How long?" Marfy asked as Blake turned his head to see her.

"An hour, a little more."

But he had no more than said that than his eyes blurred; the spin once more pressed him against the cushions of the seat. But—the trip surely could not be over!

The cabin was tilting, sliding. Save for the belts that bound them to their seats, they would have been flung against its side as the shuttle started a tobogganing progress to the left.

Chapter Four

When they came to a halt, the cabin was tilted at a sharp angle, and it shook ominously when Blake moved. His first attention was for the control panel. The small light signifying that they were on a successor world and not in passage was on. For the rest, the Vroom code was clearly visible.

"What—what happened?"

"Don't move!" Blake ordered. Under them the shuttle was rocking as if it sat delicately balanced on the edge of a drop.

With infinite care Blake loosed his safety belt. Then he inched forward to press the button for the emergency viewplate so that he could see beyond the suddenly unstable cabin.

Green! A thick wall of green, so blazing in color that it took him a second or two to detect individual leaves, bits of broken branches, ground against the viewport. What had happened or where they were, Blake had no idea. But that they were neither at the Project camp nor in a ward depot, he knew.

Blake slammed his flattened palm against the lying course code. Blandly the same figures continued to show. And the shuttle shuddered.

"We—we are sliding again!"

Marfy was right. The cabin lurched and began another sidewise slip. Blake clung to his seat as the movement quickened.

"Your head," he gasped at his companion. "Get it down! We may land hard!"

He balled himself as well as he could in the padded seat. The girl followed his example, and he had a flash of relief that she had not become hysterical. Only this much he was sure of—they had not landed at any regular stop.

The impact at the end of that slide was not as severe as Blake had feared. The tilt of the cabin was less acute and there was a bouncing sensation, as if the shuttle had come to rest on some elastic surface which cushioned it. Once more Blake looked to the viewplate.

Green again, but this time, also, a palm-sized piece of blue sky. Blake drew a deep breath and turned to observe Marfy Rogan. She dropped the protecting circle of her arm to blink back at him.

"We—we are not at a depot—a real one, are we?" Her voice was a monotone as if she struggled to keep control over a boiling surge of emotion. Her face, still showing here and there a freckle of storm mud on her clear skin, wore a rigid, set expression.

"That much we can be sure of." Blake moved experimentally. There was no answering tremor in the cabin; they had reached some form of stability.

"How . . ." she began again.

Blake shook his head impatiently. "No idea. This is still set"—for the second time he gave the location device a sharp rap—"on Vroom."

He got to his feet, taking each step with caution. He pressed two buttons, then the panel lifted free so that he could see what lay behind.

Blake stiffened. The panel had hidden disaster: fused wiring, a tangled mass of installation so completely ruined that perhaps only a first-rank tech could ever make sense of it again! Behind the set code someone had deliberately made chaos of the most important part of the shuttle—its directional guide.

"You—you cannot fix it?" That was more plea than question.

"No." Blake could not change that curt negative. "I do not think anyone could outside a shop."

"Then we are lost." Marfy still sat in her seat, her hands resting on its padded arms. Her fingers clenched the supports so that the knuckles were sharp knobs under the thin skin.

"We have the emergency call." Blake turned away from the ruined direction installation. Unless, he thought, that has been sabotaged too. Of course the call was short range. Perhaps all they could contact was the Project. Which was worse than useless, for with the rods out and no second shuttle—plus the fact that they might well have landed on an unexplored world for which no code existed—they would have no help from that direction. Extreme luck might present an alternative, a roving patroller near enough to pick up a distress signal, *if* the apparatus to send such remained operative.

Blake went straight to the panel behind the sender. It took a bit of prying, but he got it off. At least to the eye there was nothing wrong here, no discernible damage. So, partially assured, he rigged a routine distress signal.

"If this is a coded level," Marfy's voice was still strained, "then . . ."

"Then we have to supply some identification," he told her.

They were close to the Project level; the time element of their interrupted trip argued that. There was a series of successor worlds at this end of the crosstime swing, none of them too well-known until one reached the Forest level. But perhaps that would be in their favor, too—there was a steady stream of traffic in that direction—if they were close enough for their call to register.

Contact was only the first step though. If they could not give a coordinate to code this level, and with the director so eviscerated that was impossible, then they would have to provide clues so the experts could "set" their present whereabouts in the master pattern at Headquarters. And all this would take time, more time than he cared to dwell upon.

Of course, there would also be a follow-up when Blake did not return on schedule from the run to the Project. No message from him would lead to a trip and a general alarm. Then the hunt would be up. But they had to provide a clue to the right world.

"How—how can we tell them?" Marty's thoughts had followed a similar road.

"Type of vegetation, landmarks, anything that will give an expert a chance to 'set' it," Blake replied. That meant he must do some exploring outside the safety of the cabin. He must take view-shots of everything out there that held any promise of being identifiable and then send them through on call, if and when they had an answer to that. But at least Marfy would have occupation to keep her busy, tending that very necessary link with their only hope of escape.

As Blake coded the distress signal and set it on as wide a range band as he could force the machine to take, he explained what must be done. "Then you are going out there?"

"We have to have views to send through when you pick up an acceptance. Those will help in identification."

If their signal was picked up, *if* he could find some level identification—if, if, if! Blake went to one of the emergency lockers and unrolled an exploration kit.

There was the thin suit, hood, mask, which, when donned over his coveralls, would give him protection from insect attack, disease, low radiation. The viewer he slung by its cord to rest on his chest, and he added one of the needlers, a weapon which shot darts tipped with a narcotic to stupefy any attacker but do no eventual harm.

Marfy watched him silently. But when his hand was on the hatch lock, she spoke. "What if something happens to you out there?"

Blake tapped the com disk set into the mask of his hood. "I am going to keep reporting all the time. It must be taped for recast when you pick up a contact. And you will hear it. Armed with this"—he showed the needler—"I have nothing really to fear. Now . . ."

She raised her hand. "Good luck!"

Blake smiled at her. "We have had fairly good fortune already. This may have been a rocky landing but we came out in one piece. And that luck may continue to hold. You call while I explore."

He was using the double hatch now, just in case. Having carefully dogged the inner portal into place, he squeezed around to face the outer. The chamber was a very narrow fit, but it spelled safety in some worlds where the atmosphere was poisoned or there was suspicion of radiation, and wardsmen did not take chances.

Beyond the outer door lay a clean scar in the soil, cut deep into the red earth and fringed by broken and torn vegetation, leading up a rather steep slope, the mark of their skidding. Blake studied that and began dictating distances as well as he could judge them. The difference between their present resting place and where they had broken into this successor world would have a vital bearing on the code. And it was the first fact he had to give.

Digging both feet and hands into the slippery soil, Blake fought his way up the ridge to where they must have first emerged into this level. By the signs, they had materialized on the very edge of the drop, over-balanced, and slid into a small ravine. There a heavy growth of brush acted as a cushion for their landing.

Just as the Project had been rooted on a bare spread of rock, here was a tangled wealth of green. It was humid, hot, full of life. Huge insects soared, buzzed over the broken moss left by the shuttle's descent. Some were butterflies, their six- and eight-inch wings a brilliant riot of color. Others were slim of body and wing, moving with a buzzing whirr. Pressing the button of his view-taker, as well as describing the scene orally, Blake recorded such scenery and examples of native life as were in range. The majority of the larger growth was fernlike, some fronds rising to the dignity of trees. There was a flash of scarlet as something about as high as his waist darted from one mass of foliage to another. Its speed of movement made it a blur to his eyes, and Blake could not determine its nature save that he retained a strong impression it had scurried on two feet. The hiding place it had darted into was on the steepest portion of the slope and he refrained from hunting it there.

Behind the crest of the drop down which they had gone was a heavily wooded strip of reasonably flat country, then cliffs again, not too different from those that had walled in the valley of the Project. In fact, if one stripped away the vegetation, the contours of this country, Blake decided, resembled those of the sterile world. The ravine into which the shuttle had toppled could mark part of the river valley. Only he did not hear the sound of the sea; and when he faced west, he could see no trace of the restless ocean, unless a creamy line along the very rim of the horizon marked the sand of distant beaches.

Again Blake caught a corner-eye view of swift movement and turned to survey the spot where that red flicker had been. Not even a trembling of leaf or twig betrayed what might have taken cover there. But his danger sense was alert, and Blake was as sure as if he had been forewarned that he was now the focal point for action to come. Stalked? Why? By what?

If he could reach the top of the cliff, he might get a better view of the countryside. But to do so meant forcing a path through thick undergrowth, and Blake was sure that that stretch of green was not devoid of life. He studied the thickets before him intently, striving to pick out the easiest breakthrough.

Still dictating, pausing now and then for a view shot, he pressed on into a fern patch which brushed about him almost waist high. He swung with vigor another explorer's tool, a keen-edged, broad-bladed knife the length of his forearm, cutting an opening, careful to toss the slashed leaves and branches to one side so he could see the ground he cleared. Yet all the time he knew that he was under observation, that there was, in this miniature fern forest, that which flickered at high speed away from his path when detection seemed imminent, only to keep pace with him.

Blake had not anticipated such action from animals. This continued and the cunning surveillance was disturbing. Twice he turned up the audio plates of his hood, striving to catch any sound of hidden pursuit. The buzz of insects, sharp cries which appeared to be from a greater distance, and the regular clunk of his machete against stems, the rustle of the leaves he threw aside, were all he heard.

For some reason the passage seemed to take a long time. And, though the physical action was moderate, Blake was sweating when he came to the foot of the cliff wall. This was rough but not so pitted with climbing holds as the one at the Project. He edged westward along its base, hunting the best ascent, and finally found a possible one.

Turning back the attached gloves of the suit, Blake began the pull up the barrier. When he reached the top, he tumbled over into another fern bed, crushing the fronds under him as he squirmed around to look back, bringing out his distance lenses. The shuttle was a silver coin, resting, not quite level, in the ravine. And that did hide water at its lowest point, for now he had glimpses of a wandering stream. And he had been right in his guess about the distant ocean, for the glasses brought the billows of dunes closer when he faced due west.

On turning the glasses south, he discovered that his vantage point allowed him to scan another valley where ran a river as broad as and seemingly like the one that housed Kutur's pens. Flats of mud banked it on both sides. But those flats—Blake stiffened. No whim of nature had ever thrown up those divisions, marked by low stone walls, on the stretches of mud. No, those had been erected for a purpose and with intelligence behind that purpose. And they lined the flats on both sides of the river as far as Blake's lenses made clear.

There was this further oddity. The divisions were all three-sided, with the portions facing the stream left unwalled. And now he made out another strange thing: at the river side of each of those three-sided fields—if fields they could be termed—there was another stone, very large, standing alone. On the river face of those near him he could see markings, lines without meaning. Yet the markings on each stone differed from those of its neighbor. Blake put a telelens on the viewer and took shots of all within registering distance.

The fields, the marking stones, the river. There was nothing else to be seen. No green of plant showed on the mud stretches. If the walled fields were intended for crop cultivation, this was either not the right season or all those farms were deserted, no longer in use.

In two of the nearer fields, close to the river, were platforms of piled stone and earth, their upper surfaces level. And from the water's edge to these led ramps of packed earth.

As Blake sighted on one of these with his viewer, there was a ripple in the slow-moving water, veeing against the current, then turning to head out of the water, moving ponderously but with vast dignity. A big head raised, the arch of a dripping carapace was fully revealed in the sun and what was now late afternoon.

The turtle must have been close to five feet in diameter, Blake estimated. Its shell displayed an elaborate design of raised whorls. The general color was a dark brown, but the scaled legs and the head were patterned with vivid yellow and red markings. And the head was the strangest of all. Far too large ever to be withdrawn for safety within the shell after the fashion of its species, it was equipped with a kind of shield shaped not unlike a broad spearhead, the point jutting out over the nose, the rest spreading wide and back to the shell.

Having pulled up on the ramp, the creature made a deliberate climb to the platform, and then turned about to face the cliff where Blake stood. Since its field of vision was of necessity limited by its head armament, Blake did not trouble to take cover but continued to run the viewer.

The longer he watched, the more the differences between this shelled monster and the turtles of his own knowledge were manifest. And its movements also mystified him. It raised one huge foot, armed with clearly visible claws, and then the other in turn to its mouth. Having done so twice, it rested.

But it was not alone for long. From the very foot of the cliff below Blake's perch shot scarlet streaks, darting toward the platform in the field. They did not mount the dais, but gathered at its foot, their crested heads all upturned, their wide jaws a little agape as they stared back at the helmed turtle.

Lizards, save that their body-covering seemed more skin than plate or scales, vividly scarlet. A series of spike excrescences gave them nearly uniform topknots. And—Blake clicked tongue against teeth—His taped words might not be given credence but the viewer would back him up: each of those red warriors trailed a polished spear, barbed with a wicked-looking point!

About to attack the turtle? No, they continued to crouch before the larger creature's platform. The reptile might almost be a general reviewing troops, though the lizards did not indulge in any marching display. In fact, as far as Blake could see, they did nothing at all but squat and stare up at the platform!

There was, after several long moments, more action. One of the lizards broke from the company of its fellows, was off in a flashing dart of speed. Weaving a way around the field walls, heading up the river valley. It could have been a messenger in search of reinforcements. Yet the rest of the troop made no move to surround the platform, or to lay siege to the ramp down which the turtle might escape into the river.

Another darting streak of red, this time toward Blake's cliff. And that was followed, seconds later, by a larger pack of its companions, while the turtle continued to rest motionless and apparently uncaring.

Blake's special sense alerted him. He shoved the lenses into the carrying case, swung around just as one of the small spears flashed through the air and was turned aside by his explorer's suit. This was only the first of a rain of spears thudding against him to clatter down about his feet. While he had been watching the actions of one company of the scarlet lizard spearmen, it was clear that a second one had attacked him from the rear.

Though his suit continued to turn those weapons, Blake did not greatly fancy the descent into the valley of the shuttle while under fire. He could not return fire with the needler, for his attackers snapped into view, loosed their weapons, and were out of sight at a rate of speed he could not match. He might not be as slow as the turtle, but neither was he lizard-swift.

"Blake!" Marfy broke silence for the first time since he had left her. "Blake! The shuttle is moving!"

He threw himself at the cliff edge. To have the machine suddenly take on life while he was gone . . . Perhaps its broken coder would hurl it into another world—if that was possible! After what had happened to so-called accident-proof installations, he could believe anything was possible.

"Level-hopping?" He demanded to know as he lowered himself to the first handholds.

"No, it is moving here, along the ground," came her answer, in one way a reassurance to quiet his overwhelming fear. He paused to look for himself.

Marfy was right. The shuttle was moving, slowly and jerkily but moving, westward in the general direction of the distant seashore. A spear struck close to his right hand, too close. Blake put on speed, intent upon reaching the valley floor. Now he could hear the rustling in the bushes made by those who were still pushing the attack, fruitless as it had been so far.

Chapter Five

Blake took the path he had hacked at a dead run. And so almost came to disaster, for he had barely time to see the barricade heaped in the narrow lane to entangle his feet before he was upon it. He leaped that, again meeting a rain of spears that rattled against the protective covering about his thighs and body. Now he heard an angry, sibilant hissing, the battle cries of his enemies.

The wardsman burst from the thick vegetation, came to the scar caused by the downward path of the shuttle. The silvery oval machine was moving westward at a slow pace, and from above he could sight no reason for that. It was as if the ground under the machine was in motion. Yet well before the bulk of the shuttle struck them, branches bent, cracked, went down to clear a path.

"Blake!" Marfy's voice sounded in his earphones.

"I am here, just above you . . ."

"Blake, they are telepathic!"

"Who?" he demanded as he angled down the slope, wanting to reach a point ahead of that weird procession of invisible road clearers and the moving shuttle.

"I cannot read them, they are on a band too low. But they consider us an enemy they have been expecting. Fear and hate—that much comes through."

If the most effective weapons this world's natives had were the spears Blake had already met, he and Marfy had nothing to fear. But to be moved too far from the shuttle's point of entry into this level was another and more potent danger. Blake slid to the bow of the crawling machine, managed to get a closer look at what was happening there. For one or two startled seconds he thought that his first impression was right, that the earth itself was rolling under the shuttle, oversetting the bushes rooted in it to insure passage of the alien machine. Then he was aware of the truth.

Turtles or tortoises—Blake knew that there was a difference but he was hazy as to what comprised it—were moving with deliberation but with concentrated determination, using their bulk to smash down and flatten the growth. There were at least six of them, massive, shelled creatures although smaller than the giant he had watched crawl out of the river and differing from it in other ways. Their shells were not so corrugated, and their feet and heads were yellow-brown and not vividly striped.

As the shuttle lurched forward another foot, Blake caught a glimpse of a horny leg thrust forward from beneath it to get a fresh hold. And he guessed that the craft must rest on the backs of an unknown number of turtles who were thus transporting it in their own fashion.

Such group effort could argue only one of two things: efficient training or intelligence itself in action. Wardsman instruction had prepared Blake for an open-minded acceptance of strange sights and action on any successor world. In a thousand alternate times man had servants, tools, friends, which were alive but of a different species. Was it so hard to accept that here turtles and lizards were so used? Yet . . .

The lizards were armed and Marfy had discovered a telepathic contact which was alien, whereas any human brain would be—or should be—open to her. No shield had discouraged communication; there had just been a clear difference in thought-range.

Blake squatted on his heels as the shuttle crawled into a relatively open space. He was right! The machine rested on the shells of a number of tortoises. One dropped out and another, one of those clearing the path, fell back to take its place. Purposeful effort.

A spear struck Blake's shoulder and clattered to the ground. His lizard escort was still in action. Now, to get at him, they had to come into the open. Blake snapped a needle shot at one slim scarlet figure drawing itself up to launch a weapon. And he was lucky, for the needle struck in the upraised arm of the reptile. It made a convulsive leap in the air, hissed, and then tumbled limply down the slope where Blake gathered it up.

Instantly a rain of spears fell about him. But he paid no attention as he fired at the slowly moving tortoise legs. He planted two darts before the shuttle shuddered to a stop; the legs which had provided his targets, pulled back into their shell protection. But, like the river turtle, this band of crawlers could not retract their over-large heads. So Blake found the targets he needed in throat and neck. He was never quite sure how many were concerned in that feat of transportation. But he continued to fire until they were all quiet. Then, carrying his lizard captive—he would have liked one of the tortoises in addition but he had neither the strength nor the equipment to move it—Blake entered the cabin.

Together with Marfy he examined the slender body. Standing on its hind legs, as they appeared to prefer locomotion, the creature was about four feet tall. It was not scaled but covered with a soft, rough skin. Nor was it uniformly scarlet; the skin bore dark markings in complicated patterns here and there. The ragged-looking topknot was hard to the touch as if, under the skin, there was some bone projection. By its lack of teeth, having only bony ridges within its jaws, they guessed it to be non-carnivorous.

"Look!" Marfy stooped to touch what hung about its neck. A cord of plaited stuff which might have been either grass or skin string, and on it a small oval of bone. Scratched deeply into that were two lines like those Blake had recorded from the river field-marker stone. For the rest, the captive could have been a wild creature.

"Turtles!" Marfy echoed when Blake told her of the motive power that had been moving the shuttle to an unknown destination.

"Turtles and armed lizards. And what is behind it or who is behind it is anyone's guess," Blake continued. "How about the distress call?"

"On, for the widest sweep. But, Blake, do you realize we have broken the first law?"

The first law of crosstime: no revelation of their presence to any natives of any time level, unless it was also possible to give that native a false memory.

"Not the first time it has happened," Blake commented, "and we had no choice. You can't contact them at all? Try."

Marfy closed her eyes as if to concentrate the better. There was a chance, if they could establish telepathic communication with a higher intelligence, they might find aid or at least make sure there would be no more attempts to take them away from their point of entry.

Blake watched the girl. Though her face lacked expression, he could sense the effort she was putting into that search. Then her eyes opened.

"Nothing, now just nothing at all!"

"You mean they have gone out of range of your band?"

"No, before I could catch them they wove in and out of my lowest range. It was unintelligible, but now there is utter silence. They—or it—are not broadcasting at all."

Blake turned to the viewport. There was a scarlet blot on the hillside marking a gathering of lizards. Even as he watched, they launched their weapons at the shuttle. But the machine was immobile; the turtles lay in drugged sleep and would continue so for some hours. The turtles—could they be the intelligences Marfy had picked up before? Intelligent turtles? He made that a vocal protest.

However, Marfy did not seem startled. "Why not? This is perhaps a world in which mankind did not develop at all. There are many of those worlds and we have not begun to explore them. What dispute can we make if another species did develop intelligence and rule nature here? Turtles are long-lived. These have abnormally large heads, perhaps more brain power than their kind ever carried on any level wherein man dwells. They are very old as a species, too, for they lived among the great reptiles before the first mammal walked the earth. Blake, this is a wonderful discovery, one that will be famous!"

If we ever get a chance to report it, Blake thought. And then, seeing the faint change of expression on her face, he knew that she shared his thought.

"Turtles, and you say they marked us down for enemies?"

"The shape of the shuttle—perhaps it looks like a giant of their own species and they were taking it prisoner," she hazarded,

"But what of these?" Blake picked up the limp lizard. The skin was not chill as he expected reptilian flesh to feel, but warm and velvety.

"Slow movers might go into partnership with another species which possesses quicker reactions. Perhaps this is a pet, a servant, or a comrade-in-arms. What are you going to do with it?"

"Take a reading, then restore it to its friends. What else?" Blake arranged the body carefully on a pull-out shelf and centered the viewer on it. The record would not be as complete as that of a laboratory report, but enough to give the authorities a good idea of this particular inhabitant of a hitherto unknown world. When Blake was done, he went out to lay the unconscious lizard on a pile of bracken the turtles had thrown to one side. He took time to inspect the still sleeping shelled ones. As far as he could determine there were no signs of their rousing, and Blake hoped that that would continue.

When he returned, he discovered that Marfy had brought out ration packs and was opening them. But Blake picked up half to stow away again.

"Sorry—" he began, but she nodded quickly.

"I know, we must be careful. Maybe I am as foolish as Head Kutur says. Drink?" She had snapped off the lid of a self-heating can of stimulating drink. At Blake's gesture she sipped several times before passing it on.

"I have been thinking." Now she nibbled at one of the unappetizing but very nutritious cakes of combinerac.

"About turtles?" he encouraged as she hesitated. Inwardly Blake was amazed at what he considered Marfy Rogan's fortitude. He knew very little about the women of her class in Vroom, but those he had seen and met at official functions had always seemed beings wrapped in luxury, very carefully sheltered by their men. For a long time in Vroom, after the atomic disasters of the distant past had nearly wiped out the total population of that successor world, men had outnumbered women. The survivors had been mainly in concealed military installations or in small mixed groups that had found refuge underground or those who had scattered to distant parts of the earth.

Radiation had given rise to mutations in the very small succeeding generation. Many of these had not survived, but others had. And then had followed the development of psi powers which set the people of Vroom on other paths of exploration, both mental and physical. The need for women had sparked the first trips crosstime after the discovery of such travel had been made. For a time Vroom men had recruited wives from other levels. Then that had been made a crime, carrying the penalty of complete mental erasure.

The women of Vroom were cherished. Few of them ever crosstimed, unless to safe levels for family holidays or as members of research teams such as in the Project they had just left. Blake knew of no instance in which women had visited an inhabited level in disguise as the wardsmen and traders did. So he was astounded at Marfy's quick adjustment to their present predicament.

"I have been thinking," she began once more, "about Marva. How did she get off-level? By an outlaw hopper? Could she and Garglos have seen such in action? Such a barren world would be a good one on which to set up a cache."

His own speculation put into words. "The 'copter vanished, too," he mused.

"Or seemed to," she broke in. "The passengers could be kidnapped, the flyer dropped down a river gorge or something of the sort. And then"—her eyes fell almost as if she did not want to say what was in her mind before she added with a rush—"Marva might be persuaded into—into an adventure."

"What do you mean?"

"You are lucky, Blake Walker." She was looking at him now and there was a blaze in her eyes, green-blue eyes the color of the ocean he had seen in his own world. "There are no doors closed to you, no one lets you listen to descriptions of all the wonders of crosstime and then refuses to let you view them for yourself! All my life I have listened to tapes, seen views of successor worlds, heard all the stories such people as Com Varlt and my father have to tell. But am I allowed a story of my own or to see for myself? No!"

"You are doing both now," Blake commented dryly, "and under circumstances anyone but a trained wardsman is usually protected from experiencing."

"Yes. I know all the warnings and the sensible reasons behind the rules. Those have been dinned into my ears for years. But suppose it is also in me not to be contented, a stay-at-home daughter of a Hundred family? Suppose I want to go crosstime so much it sometimes seems that wishing is a real pain? Well, that is true. And it is also true of Marva. And she likes rules and orders even less than I. Many times I have been able to talk her out of the foolishness of breaking those rules. Supposing she was given a chance to do so once when I was not there?"

"You believe she would level-hop voluntarily if offered the chance for what seemed like an adventure?"

Marfy answered that by her expression, leading Blake to explore new lines of speculation. Offered a short hop to be made secretly, Marva might accept, and perhaps then find herself a captive of her companions on another successor world. But that made it even more possible she was in the hands of an outlaw. For a woman to turn up at the legal depot on any successor world where a legitimate wardsman team was in control would mean instant exposure and arrest.

And tracing an outlaw crosstime—unconsciously Blake shook his head. He had taken part in such a wild hunt before. And he knew the time, energy, and the need for luck such a quest entailed. Meanwhile, the search could never begin unless their own luck took a big step from dark to light.

"If I wanted to interest Marva past the limit of prudence," Marfy gazed past Blake into space, "I would mention World E625."

Blake shook his head. No wardsman could keep track of the successor worlds in entirety. Before any crosstime patrol he was given intensive briefing on those he would visit. Blake could recall out of his own past experiences those on which he personally had been caught up in some piece of action. He would remember all his life the three worlds to which the spinning shuttle of the outlaw Pranj had carried him. But outside of such specific information, one had to apply to the general file at Headquarters.

"Last year we saw the special viewing of the commercial team from there. Marva talked about it for months. Level E625—I would know at once."

"You?"

Marfy nodded briskly. "Yes. You can't just go in and pick up someone, not if they have been purposely hidden. But once I reach the successor world where Marva is, I can beam her and learn just how to reach her. There is no one or any machine that can do that. So I will have to go."

Blake did not attempt to argue with her. If she wished to spend the present laying fantastic plans for the future, he had no quarrel with that. But the fact that they might never get a chance to put those plans or any other intentions into action did not appear to worry her in the least. That fact was forbiddingly plain to Blake.

He went to the call unit. It beamed in regular pulsations, sending their appeal for help flooding out, though whether their slide down the cliff and the subsequent alteration of site made by the determined turtles had dislocated it past an effective sending he could not be sure. From the viewplate he could see the hillside. The massed scarlet of the lizards had vanished. Either they had given up their determined attack on the shuttle or had moved out of range of the viewer. There was nothing, absolutely nothing, to be done now but wait. Outside the coming of evening was defined by the dimming of light and the lengthening of shadows.

Blake slung the chairs into recline position. Marfy settled in one but sat up again as Blake switched off the cabin illumination.

"Why?"

"No use attracting any attention in the dark," he explained. From their window plate that light could ray as a beacon.

"But if help comes, they could not see us."

"We will know if they are coming through. Time enough then to light up." Blake centered his attention on the alarm that would make that true. As time passed, their chances grew slimmer, fraction by fraction. Of course, authorities would send a patrol through to the Project. Then his own shuttle would be certified as lost—*if* the second patroller was not also sabotaged.

What was happening on the Project level that caused some member of the team there to take such a fantastic step? Or were the Rogan girls the focus of all the trouble?

Blake could go on, spinning any number of reasons, most of them highly improbable, and maybe never hit on the right one at all. The cabin suddenly shifted again. He heard an exclamation from Marfy.

"The turtles?"

Could he go out there in the dark and use the needler with any accuracy, armed with only a torch? Resignedly Blake, scrambling out of his seat, explained what he must try.

Out of the hatch and into the twilight. The ground heaved, more turtles were stirring about the immobile ones he had already shot. Blake used the torch. Beads of eyes glistened in its light, a vast pair of jaws snapped at his leg. The tough fabric of his suit tore. The jaws, even if they lacked teeth, closed with crushing force on his skin. Blake shot and saw his dart wink back and forth in the skin of a yellow lip. He staggered; the pain in his leg was a red agony shooting up to the hip. He wondered if the bone had been broken, crunched.

Somehow he got back into the hatch, pulled the door shut, half crawled into the cabin.

"Blake! The signal—help is coming!"

He levered himself up, caught the back of the seat, and with its aid got to his feet.

"Put on the cabin light," he gritted out.

When that flashed on, he blinked and then lurched to the control board. Press that button . . . pull this lever . . . turn up the com . . .

"X4-67 calling X4-39. Do you hear? Do you hear?" The voice was metallic. It might have issued from a machine, not a human throat, but the impulses which had launched it had.

Blake tried to shake off the fog spreading over him from the pain in his leg. Somehow he croaked back.

"X4-39—we hear. Unlisted level . . . unlisted level . . . damage . . . can not transfer . . ."

"X4-39—contact well established. Set full call-beam. Will ride that in."

"Difficult landing." Blake strove to marshal the warnings in order. "Have slid down hill. Also native race attack. Watch out for turtles—"

"Turtles!" He heard the incredulous note in that before he snapped the beam into continuous beacon call.

"Blake!" Marfy was on her knees, drawing the torn stuff of his suit and coveralls away from his leg. "You are hurt!"

He saw the raw flesh she bared. Whoever thought teeth were needed for biting?

"Our friends out there do not care to be put to sleep. I guess." He tried to use words to cover the pain he felt at her lightest touch. "Anyway, now the worst is over."

Or was it just beginning? demanded one unsuppressible thought through the waves of pain.

Chapter Six

Blake had been right in his suspicion that worse was to follow their return from being lost on an uncoded world. His thoughts were gloomy as he lay on the narrow bed, his left leg in a mound of dressings. The usual starkness of the wardsmen's infirmary was an echo to his forebodings. Certainly the reception he had received— what he could remember of it—upon their return to Vroom had not been promising. He had always known that excuses were not popular in the corps, and now he lay adding up all the counts that might be filed against him.

Carrying of an unauthorized passenger probably headed the list. They had been lucky, so very lucky that they had been located in the turtle world. Otherwise, danger to Marfy Rogan rested directly on him. It did not matter to regulations that the rod failure prevented any request for passenger clearance, that his shuttle had been sabotaged. The prudent wardsman would have refused to give her seatroom, even on what should have been a safe return trip. Add to that the facts that he had not checked the shuttle thoroughly when carrying a passenger and that he had made contact adversely with natives on a hitherto unexplored level. Yes, those were all prime offenses and Blake would be very lucky to remain in the corps if charges were pressed on all of them!

There was a perfunctory rap at the door and Com Varlt entered, a tape recorder in one hand. His odd yellow eyes were bleak, his expression remote as he settled himself on the one chair the cell-like room provided and placed the machine, ready to go to work, on the small table at the head of Blake's bed.

"Report." The single word was an order as the senior's forefinger triggered the machine into action.

Blake wet his lips and began in the officially prescribed manner a report which was not in the least routine even if it was couched in the style he had been taught.

"Routine report—"

Varlt made an adjustment. "Classified report," he corrected sharply.

Blake digested that. So this was . . .

"Classified report," he amended. "Routine run to Project 6471. Agent: Blake Walker, Aptwardsman, 7105, Shuttle, X4-39, under orders to . . ."

He went at it slowly, recalling each detail that might have some meaning for those by whom this report would eventually be studied. As he spoke, he could, he discovered, remember most details vividly. But it was a long task. Twice Varlt switched off while Blake took the medication which appeared in the table groove, but the senior wardsman asked no questions as Blake added fact to fact.

He came to the end with the final scene in the shuttle's cabin when, a little lightheaded with pain, he had waited with Marfy for the arrival of their crosstime rescuers, and now said the last formal words: "Attested by oath: Blake Walker, Aptwardsman, 7105."

Varlt pressed the seal button, locking the recorder until its tape might be placed in the one and only reader entitled to broadcast it. His expression had not changed; he still wore that brooding, closed-in look.

"You accepted an unauthorized passenger." His words were clipped, impatient.

"I did."

"You made contact with other-level intelligent life, subjecting them to attack?"

"I did."

"Two counts will be so charged against your conduct record." The intonation of that was formal. But still Varlt did not rise to leave.

"You offer no defense?"

Blake would have shrugged, but lying upon one's back and being bound down by bandaging makes such a gesture close to impossible.

"No excuses, sir." He gave the approved answer.

"The techs have discovered extensive sabotage in X4-39 skillfully accomplished. This shall be taken into consideration when reviewing your case." And then that aloof surface cracked and Com Varlt came alive.

"This report—" he tapped the recorder—"is full, very full, and it is all fact. Now give me surmise, not just the facts."

Blake tried to raise his head and Varlt leaned forward to adjust a back rest for him.

"Either a Limiter plot, or the actions of an outlaw level-hopper."

"And the sabotage? Or do you suggest there is a tie between the Project and a hopper?"

"More probably Limiter. But why a Project tie with that, either? If a close-down is ordered, what would happen to them?"

"Yes. That presents us with a first-rate puzzle. Any motive that fits one portion does not another. This much is the fact upon which we must build: Marva Rogan has vanished, and the X4-39 was never intended to reach Vroom. Do you realize how very lucky you were that you were found? Chance only dictated that, my young friend, the thinnest rim of chance!"

"I know. I wonder why the call system wasn't sabotaged, too."

"There was a try to do just that. Marks on the protecting encasing showed up when the techs made their examination. But either there was not enough time, which I am inclined to believe, or not the proper tools to wrench open the inner panel. This much we do know: there is someone at the Project who made every possible effort to insure your nonreturn. And why? Because you had Marfy on board? Or simply to insure that the Project would be cut off from communication with Vroom for a space? Or both together? Perhaps we may find out when the techs start work on the rods."

"The rods?"

Varlt nodded. "Yes. Why their failure also? We have checked the installation diagrams. There was no reason for their collapse, none possible—"

"Unless they were deliberately planted wrong," Blake said wearily.

His leg ached dully and there was a heavy weight pressing above and behind his eyes which was not quite pain, yet one which gnawed at him. All at once it did not matter to him, Blake Walker, as to what had happened hours ago on another successor world or what would happen here. He closed his eyes and then opened them with an effort, to see Varlt watching him.

The master wardsman rose and picked up the recorder. "What you need," he observed, "is sleep and not a puzzle to solve. See you forget all this for awhile."

Blake settled back. The heaviness in his head had progressed to pain. He swallowed a tablet the medic had left. As the dose dissolved on his tongue, he closed his eyes again, determined not to see, behind those lids, a rocky overhang hiding a betraying scratch in its shadow, scarlet lizards aiming spears, or a platoon of turtles bearing away the shuttle. And sleep engulfed him so that he did not.

For much of the next two days Blake continued to drowse, slipping in and out of sleep or a kind of bemusement which held little need for constructive thinking. But on the third morning he roused, clear-headed and restless. The medic assured him he was well on the mend and must exercise his leg. So he used crutches to reach a lounge and dropped into a chair there to see, outside a wide sweep of window, one of those fantastic gardens peculiar to this time level. With all crosstime to choose from, Vroom was a mixture of strange architecture, vegetation, ornaments, a place of magic for the eye, the ear, the nose. Plants, buildings, statues—the cities of Vroom were made up from samples taken from all the successor worlds known to their inhabitants. The garden before Blake was no exception.

He saw tree ferns, not unlike those of the turtle world, forming a backdrop to a fountain image of a winged man pouring water from a horn, while about the border of the octagonal pool were roses and scented flowers Blake could not name. Not too far away, a summer pleasure house seemed to be fashioned of lace frozen into crystal walls.

Vroom lived on crosstime. If the Limiters had their way, this life would be seriously curtailed. So much of Vroom's level had been blasted in the ancient atomic disaster that the habitable part was merely a string of oases. What moved the Limiters? What did they have to offer in place of the steady stream of supplies and trade that came via the shuttles to their home world? Strict control of such contacts was already in force; to shut down nine-tenths of those contacts as the Limiters wished would be to strangle Vroom.

"Blake!"

Shaken out of his thoughts, he looked over his shoulder.

Marfy Rogan, no longer wearing the drab coverall of the Project but in shimmering silk, with head veil, face stencils, other fashionable accessories of her set, came toward him. Behind her was a tall man whose very fair hair, green-blue eyes, and cast of countenance was the masculine duplicate of her own features and coloring.

He wore the short cloak of ceremony flung carelessly back, but Blake did not need to see the Hundred badge on the shoulder. He reached for his crutches to get to his feet, but Marfy whipped them away.

"Keep still," she ordered, and the touch of arrogance he had noted at their first meeting was back full force in her voice. "Father, this is Blake Walker."

Erc Rogan gave him the conventional greeting, hands out, palms down, wrists crossed, and then drew up two chairs, one for his daughter.

There was no one in the corps who had not seen Rogan at one time or another, sometimes in intimate comradeship during an expedition, or merely as the official who was liaison between the wardsmen and the Hundred. His nervous movements, his self-interrupted sentences, his air of being only momentarily present between bouts of furious action elsewhere, were familiar.

Now he did not settle into the seat he had chosen, but rather perched on its edge as if he could be present for seconds only. And when he spoke, it was with sharp, impatient abruptness.

"I have a full account of your adventure . . ."

The pause was only momentary. Blake made no answer because he did not see that one was needed. Erc Rogan was already speeding on.

"Marfy has told me her side of it."

Side of it? wondered Blake. That almost hinted at some difference between their stories. He glanced at the girl. In contrast to her father, she appeared utterly relaxed, at ease. There was a shadow of smile on her lips as if she found this faintly amusing.

"I am satisfied with your part in the affair, Walker." Rogan pulled at the edge of his official cape as if he would like to rid himself of it altogether. "Therefore, I have requested you to be assigned to this. They tell me you lack full psi. Complete talents are not necessary in a team man. If you are willing to take this one—"

"Erc Rogan!" Marfy said in a clear tone. "You have not yet explained, none of it!"

For a second a frown showed between her father's brows. Then he smiled.

"As usual I run before I walk, young man. Very well, I shall explain. You have talked with Com; you know the puzzle to be solved. My daughter is missing. I believe that she is level-hopping. She may have been tempted into beginning that willingly, but that cannot be the case now. Too long a time has elapsed. I do not know why. There can be more than one answer and each logical. But it is very"—he hesitated and then used a word which would have been understated and colorless save for the tone in which it was spoken— "necessary to find her. And it would seem that to do that we are faced with the dilemma of a man who drops a grain of sand into a measure of the same and then requires that original mote to be brought into view again. We have some thousand or more successor worlds on which we have contact, from regularly staffed depots to occasional visiting. We may be sure that Marva has not passed through any legal station. In all of this, there is only one clue and that is as unsubstantial as a spider's thread. Marfy knows that her sister has been fascinated by E625. There is a chance, so frail that I dare not rest any fraction of hope upon it, that she was taken there, ostensibly on a flying visit—"

"But they, whoever they are," put in Blake, "could have suggested such a goal and really stopped anywhere."

"Perfectly true." Erc Rogan gave a hard jerk and his cape loosened, slid down his arm. "But, it is all we have. And so we must follow it."

"The Project—what about whoever sabotaged the shuttle?"

"There is a ward team there now, sifting evidence. But if Marva is in the hands of an illegal hopper—I do not know why I pin any hope to this but I do—we must try it. If Marva is in E625, Marfy will know it. And once that fact is established either one way or another, we shall be ready to move on to the next step."

"Marfy?" Blake looked again to the girl.

This time she inclined her head. "I shall know if Marva is there. Therefore I am necessarily one of the party, Blake Walker. Despite all the rules, this is one time they will be broken."

"And this is a matter not to be discussed," Rogan interrupted his daughter. "Marfy is indispensable. We cannot search an entire world on any level, but she can let us know in a matter of hours of her sister's presence. Thus, we do break one of the first rules and allow her to accompany the search team. I shall be called to account for this and I am ready to answer—after you have gone. I do not risk my daughters for a matter of regulations. Marfy has lived with wardsmen's reports and accounts all her life and she has made all the crosstime trips allowed one of her sex. She is far from being ignorant of procedure. Only, until she has gone there will be no mention of this to anyone!"

"I promise." Blake felt that he was being pressured into this, but refusal to join the team was far from his mind. Rogan must know of the charges now on Blake's record. To make another trip might change the verdict concerning his future career, always supposing it was a successful one.

Rogan was out of his chair, dragging his cloak along the floor.

"Marfy," he was on his way to the door, "I have ordered the preliminary briefing tapes. You share them with Walker. The medic tells me you will be able to leave in three days, Walker. It will take perhaps six to finish indoctrination. But with a beginning—"

Marfy waved her hand. "Already we are beginning, Father. You need not worry about that."

Blake was not sure Rogan even heard that assurance. He had disappeared through the door before the last words were out of her mouth.

"So you get what you want!" Blake was not quite sure of his own reaction: irritation, a small wonder at her imperturbability, a suspicion that she might be finding this an exciting adventure without being much concerned at the cause.

"So I get what I want?" She made a question of the repetition. "Not to be a telepath, Blake Walker, must at times make one go as crooked and limping of mind as you now do of body. You require explanations where others need no words. But then, you are as a solid wall to me, and I must also depend on your words and guess from them and the tones of your voice what you think and feel. Now I believe you do truly wonder if Marfy Rogan is looking upon this as an adventure more than a plan to rescue Marva?"

Blake flushed. He might be mind-blocked as far as she was concerned, but still she read him as if he lay open to her lightest probe.

"You do not know us—Marva and me—therefore I do not find my anger greater than I can lay rein upon." Her voice was cool, a faint hint of amusement about her lips. "But without Marva, I go limping in my own way. It is not in me to wail, to act madly, without purpose. Perhaps in those first hours when I could not reach her, then fear was a poison in me, a taste in my mouth. But unless fear is built up by the imagination, as long as it remains steady, then it can be lived with, even used as a spur to action.

"Were I to remain here, unable to indulge in that action, then would I indeed know the whip of fear. And perhaps under it, I might break. But now I can do what I can to save Marva, and to that I bend my energy. I do not think that you or any of the team we join will find that I shall be the weak point. Now, shall we begin?"

From her belt bag, Marfy produced a hand-size recorder, a small and costly toy, which Blake recognized as one of the best obtainable. She moved her chair closer to his and set the machine on her knee, uncoiling from under the lid, two lines with small earphones. One she passed to him, the other she set under a loop of her elaborate headdress. When Blake nodded, she touched the lever and the tape began to spin its message for their hearing.

Later would come the viewer's pictures, the solid and detailed indoctrination, most of it taught under hypnosis. Now they merely skimmed the surface knowledge of a successor world.

Earlier in time E625 had been one with the world Blake had once called home. Then two crucial alterations of events had given it another future altogether.

The first came in 1485. Thereafter no Henry Tudor had reigned in England. Instead Richard the Third's courageous charge at his enemy during the Battle of Bosworth had carried him to the Lancastrian Pretender and, with his own hand, Richard had put an end to the Red Rose for all time.

Once firmly on the throne, Richard had developed the potentials that historians in Blake's world had come to grant him, with regret that he had never, in their own past, had a chance to show his worth as probably one of the ablest of the Plantagenet House. A marriage with a Scottish princess two years after Bosworth had provided him with both an heir and a peaceful border. And the Plantagenets had ruled England for another one hundred and fifty years. The brilliance that, in Blake's world, had marked the reign of Elizabeth Tudor, had in E625 flourished a generation earlier under Richard and his immediate successors.

Always mindful of the importance of trade, Richard had supported the Bristol merchants who sought new markets. One of the trading expeditions bound for Iceland sent two ships on into the unknown west of which the Norse had rumors, and the first fur trading station was planted on the American continent in 1505.

The second break that changed history as Blake had known it on his own level came on July 7, 1520. Cortes, driven out of Mexico City by the aroused Aztecs, fought a final battle near the village of Otumba. But this time an arrow struck down the determined and stubborn Spanish leader, and his demoralized men, already decimated during the retreat of the Noche Triste, had then, for the main part, ended their lives on the bloody altars of strange gods, leaving Quauhtemoc ruler in the land.

English traders with the Indians on the northern continent were followed by English fishermen plundering the finned wealth offshore; later, colonists spread down the Atlantic coast to form eventually the Nation of New Britain, now under only nominal control by the mother country.

Spain, lacking the gold of Mexico and Peru, had held on to a few of the West Indies until her king, deeply enmeshed in continental struggles for power, refused to send more support to his overseas subjects, and the Spanish Empire in the new world was a withered dream, over before it began.

Having, in E625, defeated the Spanish invaders, the Aztecs were confronted by troubles at home. The excessive bloodthirstiness of a religion that demanded endless sacrifices to their gods led to alliances between conquered peoples against them. And they, too, went down to defeat in a series of intertribal struggles. Some of the survivors fled northward to the southwest of what was now never to become, on this level, the United States. Spanish from the islands, adventurers from overseas, and neighboring New Britain, fished in these roiled waters and added their support first to one party and then the other.

But, by 1560, there was a sharp change in this uneasy situation. One of those leaders who sometimes rise in times of national turmoil came to the fore in Central America, reviving the ancient legends of the "white god." His antecedents were never known, but he stamped his rule so tightly on that region that his two sons and their descendants unified a collection of provinces into an empire such as the Aztec lords had never known. Under them, Mayan traders spread north, refugee colonies in the southwest were brought under control, and the territory west of the Mississippi slowly became a part of the new Empire.

New Britain and the Empire clashed in two wars, both indecisive. There had now been a period of peace, or armed neutrality, lasting about fifty years. Since then, the Empire had had frontier troubles in the north and difficulties with Russian colonists in the west. The Mississippi River made a natural boundary between two nations and two very different cultures. . . .

Merely a quick picture. There would be a great deal more to assimilate, Blake knew, before he would see that level for himself.

Chapter Seven

"William Campden, born in New Sussex at the Manor of Gildenthorp, apprenticed to Giles Goforth, accredited western merchant at the Port of Ackrone. My father is a landowner in the honor of Bradbury, and I am his third son. My brother Rufus is a Commander in the Britannic Navy; my brother Cadwalder is a merchant venturer in China; my brother Richard is the heir and acts as my father's bailiff . . ."

Blake did not have to mutter that aloud as he reeled it out of a memory which at the moment seemed overstuffed with strange lore, as if one personality had been introduced willy-nilly to cover the Blake Walker that was, leaving him with a queer feeling of being two persons at once and no longer well acquainted with either.

All the top-priority emergency processes of Headquarters had been brought to bear to turn him into this composite. Though Blake did not accept hypnosis easily, they had worked patiently and unceasingly on him, until he succumbed to allow them to plant "William Campden" and William's past well enough to pass Vroom's rigorous standards. And with William's background and history had come all the material proper to place Blake in a society that would accept him without question.

"You have this much in your favor," Varlt had said, "this cold war between the Toltec Empire and New Britain does not make for free circulation of the citizens of either in the enemy's territory. Of old, the Aztecs used their merchants as agent provocateurs, sending them into new country as forerunners of conquest, with definite orders to stir up trouble so that the military would have an excuse to take a hand. In fact, the whole social standing of the pochteca, the merchants, was based on the fact that they claimed to be soldiers in disguise. On the other hand, the way of life in the Mayan states was trade and not war, and their aristocracy was the merchants, making them highly jealous of their trade rights between one city state and the next. After the wars of uniting, Kukulc·n the Second fostered the merchant class among both peoples. Such a move cut down the power of the military lords where he might reasonably find rebels and also gradually undermined the priesthood, which had already been discredited by the series of 'miracles' Kukulc·n used to take over power at the beginning of his reign.

"During the last struggle between the two powers, New Britain had the edge to the extent that she forced through a commercial treaty with Toltec. Since then there has been a race to build up strength on both sides of the border, yet communication between them continues. Toltec has its troubles, with the frontier peoples to the north, and with the Russians in California. During the long minority of the present Emperor, Mayatzin, there has been a continuing and growing dispute between the merchants and the remnants of the old military nobility which can regain power only in times of war. There have also been rumors that the worship of Huitzilopochtli, the old Aztec god, has been secretly revived. Thus we walk a narrow ledge and we must be surefooted."

Now the team was about to plunge into E625, with only the slightest hope that what they sought there might be found. Blake looked at what lay on the table before him. The delicate beauty of that display would hold any man's attention. Even in his own world, before Charles of Spain's need for a war chest had ordered them into a common melting pot, men had marveled at the gold ornaments of Mexico. Here was the lineal descendant of that work, the original designs refined, altered, clarified, in a necklace and earrings found in Marva Rogan's jewel box in a secret compartment.

Not even Marfy had seen them before her search among her sister's possessions, for a clue had brought them into the open. Both had been identified unhesitatingly as Toltec. While Erc Rogan was sifting with care all the contacts his daughter had made during the past few months, striving to find some common denominator between E625 and his household, Marfy had become more silent and withdrawn. This proof that her tie with her sister had not been as complete as she had always believed it seemingly cut deep.

From the sterile rock gorges of the Project world had come a chilling report. The wreckage of the lost 'copter had been found, caught in the toils of river rapids. That this meant the end of their search was accepted, on the surface, by Rogan and his daughter. But they did not believe that Marva, at least, had perished there.

Blake gave an impatient tug to the front of his new coat. The citizens of New Britain had never lost their taste for color as had the men of his own world when they accepted the drab uniformity of the late Victorian era. He now wore tight trousers of a dark, rich green, a ruffled and embroidered shirt of mulberry topped by a loose, widesleeved coat collared in narrow strips of fur and fastened, when he wished, with a gold clasp at the throat.

As exotic as their clothes might be, the New British were hardy, practical men of business. And they were "modern" in their industries as well. Transportation was largely via electrically powered vehicles. Horsedrawn carriages remained, however, as status symbols. Air travel was limited to short distances via low flying "wings," mainly for military purposes. An invention some twenty years back had closed the borders of both nations to air crossing by setting up sonics no wing could penetrate.

As a merchant, William Campden carried no side-arms, though his brothers in their various activities would all be equipped with ceremonial swords, shorter than the weapon Blake knew by that name. So the broad belt about his waist had on it only the buckle which bore the arms of his family, and so established his rank. An intensive course in identifying heraldic buckles had been a part of his study lest he make some slip in paying deference where it was due.

"Walker?" Varlt, wearing clothes similar to Blake's save that he had chosen blue and yellow, his fur collar was wider, his embroidery more ornate, his belt supported the "sword" of a master merchant, and his buckle proclaimed his alliance with a noble house, stood in the door. "We are ready."

In a way the new team was a reunion of old comrades-in-arms.

Pague Lo Sige, whom Blake had once known as Stan Erskine, another of the man-hunting group which had prowled successor worlds, was one of them. His slight fairness was more pale; he seemed fragile in the bulky overcloak of a merchant.

Marfy stood a little apart. While her skirt was short, barely sweeping her knees, her legs were discreetly covered with tights of black, lavishly patterned in silver-thread designs. The dress itself was a straight sheath of silver gray, bearing no ornamentation at all save the shield on her belt. Over this she wore a slightly longer sleeveless coat of a darker shade of gray. The whole effect was one of monotone to the knees, bright decoration below. Her hair had been sacrificed to her disguise, cropped almost as short as a man's, with the tips of separate locks dyed red-brown, giving her head a curious dappled appearance, the height of fashion in New Britain.

Erc Rogan was with her, his hand clasping her forearm as if, in these last minutes, he nursed a second thought about the risk of her journey. But, though he walked so, hand upon her, he offered no protest as the team entered the shuttle cabin.

Vroom had a depot on E625—there was no "chance" in this trip—and the shuttle had been minutely examined before they took off. Yet Blake could not help tensing as the familiar dizziness gripped him. Unconsciously he awaited some disaster. Then he realized his fear and was angry. Was he going to have always a suspicion concerning time transfer?

There was no conversation in the cabin. Perhaps, like Blake, the others, too, spent the period of travel reviewing points of indoctrination, striving to make sure of their new identities of William Campden, Geoffrey Warnsted, his niece Ann Warnsted, and Matthew Lightfoot.

The warning arrival signal settled them more deeply into their seats as the spin-through began. Then they came out into a screened-off section of a warehouse. Headquarters had calculated their entrance to occur under the cover of night and only the faintest of lights guided them down a narrow aisle between crates and bales. The gleam that beckoned them was in place over a door. Varlt motioned them to a halt and opened the portal cautiously.

Outside was a walled yard paved with stone blocks, and awaiting them was a vehicle, a truck for transporting goods. Varlt and Blake took their seats in front, Marfy and Lo Sige in the curtained van. As if he carried a map in his head and had been driving such a van most of his life, Varlt started the motor, swung the car through the yard gate and then through a maze of streets, all lighted with rods set up pillar-fashion at measured intervals. The buildings about them were of stone or concrete for the first four or five stories, towering beyond that point in more floors which appeared to be made of wood. There were no advertising signs, but fanciful, ornamental lanterns marked some of the structures in blazes of color, identifying the nature of the business housed within.

"Here." Varlt brought the truck under an archway into another court as poorly illuminated as the one that had flanked the warehouse. Together they entered the building. During their swift passage through the streets, they had seen only a scattering of people and those, men. This city on the frontier had curfew laws in strict enforcement, and few women lived here permanently.

The man waiting for them inside was stout of body, his coat that of a master merchant. A pointed beard of iron gray added to his general air of unquestioned authority. Roger Arshalm, English merchant out of London, was neither "English merchant" nor "out of London," but he was accepted by all of Port Ackrone as just that.

With a few words of what seemed to Blake grudged recognition, certainly not of greeting, he hurried them up a stairway to the wood-walled upper floors, the section which, for every merchant, provided living quarters for him, his family and all of his resident staff.

Within a well-lighted, paneled room, Arshalm flung off his outer coat and waved them to a table where wine pooled in beautifully fashioned cups and there were metal plates rimmed in enameled jeweled colors, each filled with fruits, wafers, or rounds of bread spread with paste mixtures which Blake could not identify but which smelled appetizing.

"This is madness," Arshalm was blunt. "You, lady," he looked at Marfy, "are a risk here. There are so few women in town that each and every one is known, with her history reaching back three generations. To have you sighted will stir up such comment as might break cover for all of us at the depot. You," now he turned to the rest of the company, "I can make shift to account for. There is unease along the river. You can be ordered out of the Empire on some lord's whim, forced to leave with only what you have on your backs—"

"That sort of thing is happening?" Varlt cut in. "Trouble brewing?"

"It is happening, yes. Trouble has always been brewing here, but to my mind it is now coming to a seething boil!"

"Any special reason?"

Arshalm threw up his hands. "Reason? The old one of the merchants wanting peace, the lords, seeing their power and their holdings dwindling, war. With rumors of wild practices along the frontiers and in less isolated spots, too. Then, the prophecy of Huitzilopochtli's return is being mouthed. A long minority for a ruler never makes for a stable kingdom; there is more than one lord who begins to see himself wearing the Imperial green."

"But all of this has been going on for years—"

"And building up to a nasty situation through all of them. The time grows short and the lords are beginning to show such boldness as they have not displayed since the abortive uprising back in 1912. They are hauling out forgotten laws, putting them into use when and where they can. The latest is containment for foreign Allowed Merchants. They are 'allowed' out of their houses only by pass and under guard—for their own good, of course. The populace resents foreigners—that is the given reason with a few controlled riots to give it credence. Some carefully manufactured incidents and they will have an excuse for expelling all the Allowed—"

"And New Britain's stand on that?"

"With the present government?" Arshalm shrugged. "No move in the immediate future. But if there is a ground swell of public opinion, the Moderates may be thrown out of power and the Kingsrule party will be in. The Viceroy is walking a very narrow path to keep the peace. And he can only advise, he can not order. The Diversification of 1810 is complete as to the legality of home rule."

"So, unless you find what you seek in New Britain—" Arshalm was continuing when Marfy made a sudden, uncontrolled gesture, sending the goblet before her crashing over to flood the cloth with wine.

She did not even glance down at those spreading yellow ripples.

Instead her head turned, not as if she willed it but as if flesh and bone were drawn about, steel to magnet.

With her head still held to that angle, she rose from her chair, leaving them staring after her. Now she turned slowly to face completely around, walking, her eyes wide, moving to a tapestry hanging along the wall. Her hands fumbled with its folds, parted them, to uncurtain a window. The girls fingers now rose to the fastening of the casement, plucked at its latch.

Varlt moved first, covering the distance between them in a couple of wide strides, pushing aside her hands to open the casement for her. Night air swept in, cool, and with it the sound of water. Flecks of light marked the lanterns. Varlt's hands fell gently on Marfy's shoulders in a gesture that combined support and protection.

"Marfy." His voice was low, coaxing.

She swayed under his touch, but her head did not turn; she still stared out into the night. Then Blake saw the shudder that ran through her whole body, as if she had been plunged into icy water to awake roughly into the here and now. She turned under Varlt's hold and clung to the front of his loose coat; her features were worn and strained.

"I was right." Her voice was thin, low, but so still were the rest in that room that it carried easily. "Marva is here!"

"Can you find out where?" Varlt's voice was as gentle as his grasp.

"Where is Xomatl?" she asked in turn.

Arshalm made a move as uncontrolled as the one that had upset Marfy's goblet. Varlt looked at the depot officer over Marfy's head.

"It is in Empire territory, south, one of the tribute centers. If she is there in truth . . ." He shook his head.

"New Britain has no contacts there at all?" Varlt demanded.

"There is a supervised caravan of Allowed Merchants escorted there every second month, or has been in the past. What will continue to be done is any man's guess. But the credentials of such merchants, they are impossible to obtain. The same families have had that trade for generations. It would be impossible to plant anyone in such an expedition, even if there is another."

Varlt looked back at Marfy. "Are you sure?"

"Yes. She—she is kept close but they do not call her prisoner. If I can try with a full-mind probe, maybe . . ."

This time Varlt's nod was brisk. "That you shall do. Arshalm, you have the necessary privacy? Marfy, will you need a booster drug?"

"Let me try unaided first. We have never used the drug and have always done well in the past."

With Arshalm and Varlt, she left the room. Blake knew something of the ordeal facing her though he had never undergone it himself. Mind-to-mind communication on the highest level induced in the participants a condition akin to trance. They must be allowed privacy and a state of complete silence and rest. This would be given Marfy here, but would her twin have the same untroubled state from which to answer? A thousand to one chance had paid off. Marfy's guess as to her sister's whereabouts had been proven true. But where did they move now—and how?

Lo Sige finished the last of his wine. Now he smiled at Blake and shrugged as if he could read the younger man's mind.

"Guessing at our next move? Do not waste the mental energy. We will take no action until we are sure. Arshalm cries 'impossible' now, but he is already striving to pick holes in his own verdict. We have but to preserve our patience for a space. What lies immediately before you and me is bed."

And when Blake was lying in the fourposter bed with its curtains and fine, lavender-scented linen clean and cool about his body, he did relax after a fashion. There was the patina of age in this room, the feeling that time in some respects had passed less swiftly, and that some of the trappings of another, more stately, age had lingered on to provide a feeling of security and identification with one's fore-fathers which was missing in his home world.

He had flung open his casement before going to bed, and the sound of the river was a murmur in the room. One thing about Port Ackrone—there was no roar of traffic lasting through the night.

The river, and beyond it, the enemy territory. Somewhere, to the southwest, another city even more alien than this, and in it, for a purpose they could not yet fathom, Marva. When did the improbable truly ever become the impossible? They were here on the same level as Marva, when that chance had been so small as to be incredible. Would luck continue to ride with them?

The murmur of the river was soothing and Blake drifted between half sleep and waking. Then he awoke. Far off for now, a mere shadow of a shadow of a shadow, peril stalked. His talent offered him only slight irritation as yet, but it was awake. Not the natural unease to be expected under the circumstances, but a definite warning of danger lying in wait. However, it was still not a loud call to arms, just that shadow of a shadow of a shadow. Reaching from the southwest?

Chapter Eight

"Madness!" Arshalm had come up from the shop rooms below. As he strode back and forth, the skirts of his coat flapped agitatedly, giving him the semblance of a bird of ill omen about to soar. "The news has just come through, they are expelling merchants from Tonocahl and Manao."

"But still the caravan is prepared to move to Xomatl, is it not?" Varlt sat hunch-shouldered at the table, staring at a map weighted open by various pieces of tableware. "These towns you mention are both in the north. Any reason why the Toltecans should do this now?"

"They are both in the old frontier lands," Arshalm answered rather absentmindedly.

"Merchants have always been suspect there," Lo Sige commented. "The plains warriors—they were only beaten into submission about two generations ago. It was their uprising against the Empire that really turned the tide in the last war and saved western New Britain from being overrun. They have never taken kindly to Empire rule, and they could well provide a weapon for intrigue, just ready to be aimed."

Arshalm paused by the table. "That is entirely true. And the signs are all of a volcano about to erupt. If any British are across the border when it happens, Heaven help them! Nothing on this earth will! The fanatics shall want a blood feast following the old

251

customs, and it was always the rule that you first used a stranger's blood to feed the gods."

"Marva is there." Into the silence which had followed the merchant's outburst, Marfy's three words fell, oddly shrill. There were shadows under her eyes; she might have risen from a serious illness.

"But more than just that you do not know," Arshalm returned abruptly.

"I was not . . . able . . . to learn more. Why I do not know."

Marfy's struggle to communicate via mind probe had brought her no closer contact with her sister. And that disturbed them all, delivering a shock from which Marfy had not yet recovered.

"Mind block?" Lo Sige glanced from the girl to Varlt and then on to Arshalm.

"Possible," Varlt replied first.

"No one on this level is capable of that," Arshalm denied.

"Never underrate a native priesthood," remarked Lo Sige, and then added, "She did not reach this world unescorted, and she was brought here for a definite purpose. To that we are all agreed. Those who brought her here must have taken precautions."

"We must find her!" Marfy's voice held a hint of hysteria now. "What if . . . if she was brought as a . . . gift?"

Vroom consciences were not entirely clean in that direction. Too many Vroomian families had imported initially unwilling brides, kidnapped from other successor worlds, to found their clans. The Rogans probably had at least one of those in their past history, one whose story would be well known to her descendants. Marfy's guess was a logical one.

Varlt shook his head. "No, this is not a matter of wife-stealing. If that were the case, she would have been given false memories, not plunged directly into another level as a prisoner. What's more, such a gift would be unacceptable in Toltec. One of your type, Marfy, would have no interest for a member of the court or the nobility. Or . . ." He stopped abruptly; his mouth tightened into a grim line.

Marfy cried out, half rose from the table, her hands at her mouth in a gesture of horror, as if to prevent her own lips from uttering something too terrible to be said aloud. Not for the first time Blake longed for telepathic powers. Whatever idea had just flashed into Varlt's mind had sped in turn to the girl and, judging by his expression, also to Lo Sige, though Arshalm merely looked puzzled. Blake decided that the merchant's psi powers must lie in other directions.

"So"—Lo Sige's fingertips beat a tattoo on the board—"it would seem that speed is now matter of importance—"

He was interrupted as Varlt spoke to Arshalm. "That makes it imperative! We have to be on that caravan when it leaves two days from now. How can it be done?"

Arshalm pounded a fist on the table. "I have already said! It cannot be! Three British families have the hereditary trading rights in Xomatl: the Wellfords, the Frontnums, the Trelawnlys. Everyone they send is personally known to the guards, the frontier patrols, the merchants in Xomatl. No substitutions can be made; it would be known at once."

Lo Sige smiled lazily. "There is no insoluble problem," he said with deceptive mildness. "Have you a complete list, plus viewer report, on every man who will go?"

Arshalm took a packet from one of the inner pockets of his coat and threw it on the table. "Six men, every one of them known as well to those over the river as they would be known to their own brothers."

Lo Sige opened the packet, fed the tape roll within to a small viewer and aimed the machine at the wall of the room. The picture was not as clear as it would be on a real screen, but bright enough for them to see each man as he appeared. Six men, ranging from middle age to youth, with the eldest being Master Merchant James Frontnum, the rest two assistants, an apprentice, and two general packers, the latter ambitious youngsters learning their trade.

"Every one of them either a Frontnum, a Wellford, or a Trelawnly, even the packers!" Arshalm declared. "We could not supply a single newcomer."

"Thus," Lo Sige said gently, "we make a clean sweep and supply a whole company."

Blake expected Arshalm to run true to form with instant protest. But the merchant did not reply with an outburst. Instead, he sat down and surveyed them all in turn.

"You know, this not merely reckless," he stated in a mild,

conventional tone, "it is simply utter madness. Oh," he waved a hand as if to stall any replies, "we can turn you out as visual copies of these men. We can get you briefings of a sort. But none of that will hold up once you are across the river and among suspicious men who know the Allowed Merchants with the intimacy of years, who also look upon all foreigners as potential spies. They know these men," he jerked a thumb at the tape and its burden of pictures, "probably better than they know themselves."

"Granted," Varlt agreed.

"Then you admit that it cannot be tried."

Varlt frowned at the viewer. "It will have to be—if what I fear is so—it must be!"

Marfy still sat with her fingers pressed to her lips. Her eyes were very large and had some of the sheen Blake had seen in the eyes of terrified animals. He was still at a loss as to what they all feared, but he realized that it was serious enough to push Varlt past the edge of caution.

"And what is so important?" Arshalm asked almost plaintively.

"Old customs," Varlt replied with visible reluctance. "Very old customs. Think, man, why might one present a stranger—and a maiden—to certain parties over the river?"

Arshalm stopped the nervous smoothing of his coat where it lay across his knee. Under his gray brows his eyes sharpened in a gaze pinned on Varlt. Then his breath was expelled in a hiss.

"No!" His protest against his own thoughts was forceful, but against his will he now shared Varlt's forebodings.

And now Blake understood, too. A most grisly memory flashed into his mind, leaving in its wake a retching sickness so that he swallowed convulsively. There was a story out of the past, enough to turn any man's stomach.

The early-wandering Aztecs, seeking a homeland, had made a temporary alliance with a city king in the fertile valley of their dreams. Together successful in war, due to the superiority of the Aztec warriors, the Aztecs had suggested a further alliance by marriage, the king's daughter as wife for their chief. And the king, considerably impressed by the vigor and military prowess of these wild men out of the north, had agreed. But when he and his court came to attend a feast in celebration of the marriage, they had seen a priest dance before a savage and alien god, his robe of office the flayed skin of the princess! When the outraged king and his followers turned upon their late allies and drove them back into the lean wilderness, the Aztecs had not really understood, for in their eyes they had done honor to both god and princess.

Yes, there was darkness and blood in the past. And what if there was a return to those ways of horror . . .

"But that was over six hundred years ago," Blake burst out. "No one could do that now!"

"Old beliefs die hard, and they can be revived to serve the needs of desperate men. United in guilt, men may be more easily led. There have always been smoldering brands of the old religion in the Empire. They may have been forced to turn to other ways, but the power of the priests has held in some pockets. They exiled one of the greatest of their early leaders, Quetzalcoatl, because he would do away with blood sacrifice. When the chaos of the civil war back in 1624 finally tossed Kukulc·n the Second into the rule and the priesthood was put down, there was a period of religious revival or awakening. But never were the old gods totally destroyed. Oh, I know that the leaders give no personal credence to Huitzilopochtli, Xipé, or any other. But blood ceremonies have their place in uniting and exciting those they would lead. One great and relatively open ceremony might well send the whole Empire spinning into another uprising in which those who wish and will can fish for the power they are avidly seeking."

"You are right," Arshalm spoke heavily as if admitting it took some virtue out of him. "Also, the date . . ."

"Fifty-two year cycle—the ancient kindling of new fire."

Varlt glanced at Lo Sige and the chill in his look would have frozen Blake had the stare been turned on him. But the younger man only nodded at his superior as if acknowledging some silent order passed between them.

Blake's briefing supplied him with the importance of Lo Sige's remark. The ancient Kingdoms of the Sun, all of them, had been rigidly rule by astronomy and their numerical systems based upon a fifty-two-year cycle. At the end of that span of years there was a colossal "New Year" period. All debts were canceled, hostilities ended, agreements and contracts terminated. Each housewife threw out all her pots and pans and her furniture, and prepared to replace them with new. And the new fire, marking the beginning era, had been kindled on the breast of a sacrificial victim.

"Ending of old, beginning of new," Marfy said. "Then it is the time for us to chance . . . Oh, Com!"

The master wardsman did not reach across the table to take her hand; he did not nod. But from him to the girl must have flowed some reassurance, for she relaxed visibly.

"Can you pick up all the members of the caravan?" he asked Arshalm briskly.

"Yes. I could offer them a banquet here. It is often common to entertain colleagues about to embark on trading trips, to try to persuade the venturers to take some of one's specialties along. Since I am English, they would believe in such a gesture on my part. But—we have only two days."

"Let us be thankful for that much!" was Varlt's reply.

Afternoon, dusk, dawn, then the first hour of a new day. Blake peered into a mirror. He was no longer Blake Walker nor William Campden; he was now Rufus Trelawnly. His merchant's coat and other badges of some small rank were missing, save for a heraldic belt buckle. Now he wore dark rust trousers, a dull green shirt, and over it a sleeveless, tight-fitting jerkin which left him more muscle freedom for the heavy labor demanded by his present station of packer.

Varlt was now James Frontnum; Lo Sige, Richard Wellford; and Marfy, Denys Frontnum. Two wardsmen had joined them, sharing Blake's rank of packer. They were volunteers from Headquarters, not from among Arshalm's staff, since the absence of those would be noted.

The native New British they were replacing had been—first, under mental control and then in drugged sleep—removed to Vroom. When they returned, they would be supplied with false memories to cover the period of their absence. Or that was the present hope.

"There it is." A short time later Blake looked along the wharf, following the pointing finger of the man who pushed a twin package-carrier to the one he himself trundled. The river boat, intended mainly for cargo, awaited them. Her crew were darker-skinned subjects of the Empire and scarlet-legged soldiers were visible along her deck. Most of the heavy cargo had been on board for days. Those carriers Blake and his companion were responsible for contained the cream of what the caravan had to offer, most of it exotic luxuries designed for the nobility, for the court, some of it for "gifts."

Could they carry off the imposture? Their briefing in their new roles had been so speedy that it had merely scraped the surface, and Blake was not sure how long they could go undetected among the ever-suspicious enemy.

"Step lively, you!" Varlt looked back with just the proper amount of irritation, waving the carriers ahead. So that Blake and his fellows were the first on deck.

In shape the vessel was a blunt-angled triangle, with the width at the stern. There was no visible means of propulsion; whatever power sent it waddling along was hidden. And the merchant party was not encouraged to explore.

Once on board all of them had been herded astern, a latticework of bars slammed shut and locked, leaving them to their own devices in what was an effective prison. They even furnished their own food supplies. Not only were they locked in, but there was an alert pair of sentries beyond the bars, changed every four hours. However, all this was according to usual practice.

"We are on our way," Lo Sige observed. "And what is our next move?"

"If all goes well," Varlt explained, "we disembark, as always, at the Pier of the East in Xomatl. But we are not lodged near there. They march us, under guard all the way to the south of the city where we stay in the Strangers' House—more like a prison than a house! Then we set up the gifts for the Port captain, the head of the local Merchants' Guild, the resident *tonalpoulqui* who practices divination and will give us a good day for trade. All this is regular procedure. If the gifts are acceptable, we are told the trade day and the *Pochteca Flatoque* at the head of the Guild move in to inspect. We may have three days, even more, between arrival and the beginning of trade. Perhaps we can string it out even longer by lagging a little on the gifts, but we dare not arouse suspicion—"

"They will watch us every minute!" cut in one of the new team members.

"That they will," Varlt agreed.

As far as Blake could see, they did not have a chance. Yet he had faith in Varlt and Varlt's experience. Somewhere, the master wardsman must see a loophole, even if he were not yet so sure of it as to explain.

Blake's own personal warning was no stronger, just lay like a shadow within his mind, a momentary chill now and then along his spine. Having helped stow the rest of the cargo so that all would appear as usual to the guard, he finally went out on the slice of deck that was allowed them. At this point, the river was wide and they had swung diagonally across it to coast along the Empire's shore, with the flood now between them and New Britain. From all Blake could see, the wilderness they were slipping past might never have been penetrated by men at all.

Twice before dusk, breaks showed small landings in that green wall. But neither time did the boat approach them, nor could Blake sight any signs of life about the clearings. He went into the cabin for the evening meal. All were present but Lo Sige.

A moment later he appeared to say crisply, "There is a Jaguar officer on board!"

"You are sure?" Varlt asked.

"He was up on the spy deck just now watching us. And there is no mistaking his badge. You know the custom; no one can wear that insignia save men granted it in full ceremony."

"A Jaguar officer . . ." Varlt chewed upon that.

The military elite of the old Aztec kingdom carried over into the Empire two companies of proven warriors: Jaguars and Eagles. The men in each of these groups attained their positions only after winning many battle honors. Even though the Empire had not been officially at war for a generation, a series of frontier struggles gave the ambitious the means of military advancement. Very few of the merchants, for all their power, even had had their sons chosen to wear the snarling beast-mask badge or the eagle with outstretched wings. Such distinction rested mainly with the old nobility.

"He might be on frontier inspection, taking this ship by chance, and curious—"

"I do not trust such coincidences," Varlt returned.

Marfy retired early to her cabin, but Varlt, Lo Sige, and the senior of the volunteers continued to sit about the table. There was an atmosphere suggesting that juniors had better keep their distance, and Blake went back on deck. The tramp of the sentries came in a regular thud-thud. Both were armed, not only with long belt knives but also this world's equivalent of a rifle, a weapon which shot a burning ray rather than a solid projectile.

Blake sought the rail on the landward side. Here, too, a net or grill rising some six feet or more above the deck made it clear that those inside were to stay there. Not that landing anywhere along that dark shore would avail a man. Any skulker would be hunted down by trained war hounds and equally savage men should he attempt to travel through what appeared to be a tangled wilderness.

"*TeyaualouonÏme*." The word came out of the shadows masking the upper deck, sounding almost like a snake hiss. Something plopped to the deck with a soft noise. Blake reached out a hand and caught at the half-seen object, to discover his fingers had closed on a rope ladder.

"Up!" ordered the voice from above. There had been a light there earlier, but now that whole section was dark. Blake could make out only a shadowy figure near the top of the ladder. "Up!" came the order again, this time more imperatively.

Someone had addressed him by the old name indicating a merchant spy in the service of the Empire and now had ordered him to climb out of what was legal confinement much as if he expected such a summons. If he refused, it might well be that he would endanger the disguise of the whole party. But who? And why?

Blake climbed up over the rail above to the deck sacred to the officers of the guard and the vessel.

"The Day is nine. Who runs through the streets with a blackened face?" The words were in the English of New Britain but delivered with a hissing intonation. And Blake, totally unable to answer the gibberish which must have some meaning both to his accoster and the real Trelawny, dared not answer.

"The Day is nine—" the other began again. Then Blake caught the sound of boot soles striking heavily against the decking.

At the same moment Blake's sense of danger was no longer only a lurking shadow; it flared into a demand for instant defense. He dodged back, away from the inner rail where the ladder still held. But the other, still only a shadow, sprang after, either in attack or an effort to get Blake undercover. The wardsman's hips met the side rail; he grabbed wildly for a hold. There was a rush. No—this other meant to aid! Blake's ankles were seized in a fierce grip and he was dumped over and down, into the swirl of the river below. . . .

Chapter Nine

Blake sprawled face down in sticky mud, the smell of rotting vegetation chokingly strong, the slime of a many-times flooded reed bank smeared on arms and body. He was not quite sure just how he had reached this spit in the dark. Some instinct of self-preservation had brought him through the madness out on the river when rays had lashed the water about his flailing arms as he had tried to keep from drowning. They must have thought that they had got him, or else they did not greatly care, content to leave him to the shore patrols.

He roused enough to crawl on, farther out of the tug of the river water, up into the crackling reed bed. Then he ventured to sit up and try to sort out the happenings on the boat. Clearly he had been summoned to a secret meeting, greeted with a password to which he had no key. Then someone probably not in the secret had come along the deck, and his half-seen companion had taken a drastic means of getting rid of a possible betrayer by dumping Blake overboard. That might not be the reason for his present plight, but as an explanation it held together sensibly.

Now he was ashore, and in territory where he was fair game for the first inhabitant who sighted him. He had two choices: to try to recross the river to New Britain, or to work his way downstream and rejoin the merchant ship. And the way he felt now, Blake was not too certain either was possible. For he had not come out of that barrage of rays untouched. Between shoulder and elbow on his left arm a raw, seared strip some three fingers wide proved that, and to move his arm at all brought a wave of sickening pain. To swim with that hurt—here where the river was so wide and the current swift—no.

On the other hand, there was drift caught all along the shore. This river, in his own successor world, was notorious for its changes of course and its floods, and the same must be true here. If he could find drift to support him, he might take to the river again and win through, even reach the boat, where, of course, he might be shot on sight.

On the other hand he might be welcomed aboard by those who would like to hear about his meeting with the stranger on the upper deck. Blake was certain that the intrigant had been an army officer. And what possible connection would there be between one of them and the foreign merchants they considered their bane and long-declared enemies?

Blake rose unsteadily to his feet. He could not go on through the reed bed, his feet were sucked deeply into its muck as he tried to walk. Better get to higher ground. But this was a moonless night and Blake only located a high bit of land by blundering face-on into a bank. Somehow he won to the top of that. He lay down and rolled over on his back, panting with the effort, his burned arm across his chest.

Small sparks of light danced under the dark curtains of bushes—fireflies. And as he lay still, Blake caught night sounds: the hoot of an owl, a splash as some animal took to the water, then—a barking which sent a shiver through him. Hound of some patrol?

To thresh about blindly in the dark was not sensible. But the longer he remained where he was, the farther away the boat would be, the greater the chance of being found by a patrol. Get to it. Get to it!

Blake stood up. The curve of the river bank here was southwest. There were trees and brush about him but not enough to form a barrier. He went on at a pace which was closer to a stumble than a walk. Twice more he heard that distant barking. And once a black blot snorted and stampeded noisily through the bushes away from his path. He began to count: five hundred; then rest for a hundred; five, then rest. It was too dark to look for drift beneath the bluff, but as soon as the first gray of morning arrived he would go down to the water's edge and find what he needed.

New Britain kept patrol cruisers on her side of the river, Blake remembered now. Find his drift for support, get across the river, well away from this dangerous and inhospitable shore. He could claim, if picked up by the British authorities, to be one of the exiles from up-river, fleeing from the hostility of Imperial nobles. Blake was proud of that piece of planning. He was too warm and his arm, thrust into the front of his jerkin for support, ached with a throb which every stumble sent jabbing up into his shoulder and across his chest. So that sometimes it seemed he could not breathe as deeply as his exertions demanded, and he was forced to stand gasping for a wasted moment or two.

The night went on forever, as if time, as a measured thing, had ceased to exist and he was doomed for eternity to waver on through the dark, sometimes tripped by roots or ground-hugging branches. Blake moved in a stupor now. His personal danger signal had faded to a general alert, just as it had in the shuttle when he approached the Project. The shuttle—Varlt—Marfy—the boat. Dully the immediate past moved through his mind, but as if none of that action had concerned him in any way. What was important was the next step, and the next, and the next—if he could continue to take them.

Blake fell again, this time landing full upon his injured arm. And he could not stifle a sharp cry, just as he had no defense against a blackness thicker than the night. So he remained where he was as the sky began to pale overhead.

Rain awoke him, blowing in chill gusts under the branches to rewet his soaked clothes. Blake blinked stupidly as he opened his eyes and tried to understand where he was. Rain—branches—he was in the open. How? What? The big drops washing his face restored a portion of memory. He was on a successor world. The boat . . . the river . . . he had been following the river. And now it was day, he could easily distinguish the vegetation about him. Drift . . . the river bank . . . he had to get away!

He was pulling himself up by the aid of a bush when he was frozen by a low snarl—and the stab of his inner alert. Blake turned very slowly to face the source of the sound. Slitted eyes, glittering green, looked at him with a calculating hunter's interest, a promise of self-confident savagery. Ears flattened to a round, feline skull, as breath hissed in warning between sharp white fangs. Puma? No, this was a jaguar, one of the spotted jungle lords of the far south, out of its home territory but very much the master of the situation.

It advanced a paw, inched forward in a stalk, with belly fur brushing the ground as it came. Around its neck was a collar set in green gems. Again that warning snarl, and Blake calculated his chances. Behind him, surely not too far away, was the edge of the river bluff. Could he make it over that drop before the cat sprang? He doubted it.

The jaguar paused, raised its head. Now it voiced a yowl which was close to a scream, and was answered by another snarl from between Blake and the lip of the bluff. He was fairly caught! Watching the stalker before him as if he could hold the beast by his will, Blake backed a little so he could see in the other direction. His inner alert was steady, as if the cats were not yet to be considered deadly.

Another sleekly furred head moved into sight. This one was less easy to distinguish in the undergrowth for the fur was black, making the white of the bared fangs stand out sharply. The second beast did not advance into the open. Water dropped from it and it snarled, shaking its head vigorously. The spotted cat was now lying down, and it, too, snarled and hissed with the rain's wetting. Neither animal showed an inclination to attack, but that they were on guard against any attempt to move on his part, Blake did not doubt.

Hunting cats. He had been warned about the hounds of the river patrols, vicious, notorious for their tracking as well as their often fatal attacks upon fugitives. But these cats were different; they had not been covered in his briefing. Personal pets of some local lord? The jaguar was a sacred animal; the Emperor sat on a throne fashioned in the likeness of one, and they had given their name to the elite military caste.

Blake did not have long for speculation. His inner alert gave a new thrust. He glanced from one animal to another. Neither had moved, nor were they crouched to spring. But from some distance away came a dull booming, repeated thrice. The black cat disappeared as if sucked back into the heart of the bushes by the call. Now came other sounds like drumbeats. Danger . . . close . . . danger . . .

He moved, and his movement was met by a crescendo snarl. The spotted cat crouched, ready to spring. Blake stiffened. Not too far away there was a yowling feline scream answered by shouts. He was clearly trapped and the cats' masters were on their way to gather him in.

A mixed crew came up to his stand. The first of them wore tanned leather breeches and sleeveless loose shirts of cotton, dyed green and brown in mottled patterns, barely covering their muscular chests and shoulders. Their hair was drawn back and tightly clubbed at the napes of their necks, and they wore splashes of paint on their foreheads. Retainers of some lord, his hunter-rangers, all of them carried the blowpipes of hunters, not the more sophisticated sidearms of the military, and each shirt also bore on the breast a crest badge.

The spotted cat rose from its crouch and paced a step or two away. None of the hunters spoke to it, but they made a path for its passing as if it were a high-born lord. It sat down on its haunches and raised a forepaw to lick.

Meanwhile, the leader of the party snapped his fingers and two of his men approached Blake, taking thongs from collections at their belts. His injured arm was twisted callously behind him and his wrists secured together in the workmanlike manner of those used to transporting game. A shove on his shoulder set him walking. So escorted by the whole party, plus the cat, he wavered on.

Blake stumbled so many times, that at last the leader, with a grunt of exasperation, told one of the others to walk beside their prisoner and keep him steady. Even if he had been unbound and fully able, Blake knew he could never equal the woodsmanship of these men. They were Amerindians of the northern tribes, the plains rovers who some generations back had been incorporated into the Empire after a series of pitched battles and guerrilla warfare. Nowadays they were drawn upon for frontier and ranger duty. All were tall, well-made, akin to the Cheyenne, Sioux, Blackfeet, who, in his own successor world, had successfully stayed the advance of the European for a half century before going down to defeat under the steamroller of a civilization that would have no part of their virtues and talents. Here the Empire had assimilated, not crushed.

Only it was those very forces which the reactionary lords, who were rumored to be ready to rise against the mechanized civilization of the south, could depend upon for their backing. And they would have little reason to favor a captive from New Britain. These were tribesmen ever ready to raid across the frontier.

"Here. Go." Blake's special guard spoke English with a kind of disdain as he gave his captive a push to the left.

They emerged upon a narrow road to face quite an impressive company. Several yards away was a large car, not unlike the vans used in Port Ackrone. But this was half fort, half hunting camp. Mounted on its roof were three guns of a type strange to Blake. The side showed an open door, giving a glimpse of comfortable living quarters in the interior. And seated on a stool beside the door was the man who was the probable commander of the whole force.

His heavy nose and flattened forehead, elongating his skull, proved him to be one of the old noble families. But here in the wilderness he wore the tanned leather breeches, boots, and simple shirt of his men, although the badge on the latter was worked in gold thread. While his hunters carried blowpipes, he had a hand laser belted on, and the two men standing not too far away wore the uniforms of a private guard. They carried not only lasers but rifles as well. At the lord's feet lay the black jaguar, its gold and ruby collar bright.

An awning projecting from the side of the car kept the drizzle from the august person of the noble. Now the spotted cat bounded forward into that patch of dry, butting its head against the man's body. He fondled the fur about its ear, paying it all his attention with none left for the captive standing among his followers.

The two guards had the unmistakable features of the south, but the few words Blake caught were unintelligible. It was only after the two cats had been given bowls of food and were eating that the nobleman looked toward Blake, sweeping the wardsman with a gaze which missed not one tear, smear of river mud, or bruise.

He beckoned with a crooked finger, his attitude one of arrogance and contempt. For a fraction of a moment Blake wondered how this Imperial lordling would face Isin Kutur, for there was a certain similarity between them, civilizations, time streams, and worlds apart though they were.

"Where are you from?" the Toltecan drawled, but as if Blake's origin was really of little importance. One of the cats lifted its head and hissed.

"Port Ackrone, *Tecuhtli,*" Blake gave the formal address due one of the old nobility. He could not fake an origin on this side of the river. Keep to the truth as much as he could; that was the wisest course. Though what means they might use to induce the whole truth out of a prisoner . . . Blake did not care to let his thoughts dwell upon that.

"So? That is well across the river and to the north. Then what do you here?"

"I was on a boat, bound for Xomatl. There was an accident and I fell overboard. When I reached shore, I did not know where I was—"

His guard made a sudden move which found Blake unprepared. He was pulled around and his bound arms jerked out so that the burn on the left could be exhibited to his questioner.

"An accident? You have been rayed, whiteskin. They say that the truth lies not within one of your kind, who speak with tongues that twist words instead of sending them straight for the hearing of honest men. But we have ways to having the truth out, even as the heart might go to Huitzilopochtli." His fingers moved in a sign, echoed by those around him.

"That you came from the river—that I can believe for you stink of it foully. Give me your name that we may send it downstream, you may be wanted."

"Rufus Trelawnly, of the Allowed Merchants, bound for Xomatl."

The noble spoke to one of the men behind him. "You have heard?" he asked in English as if he wanted Blake to understand.

"I have heard, *au cuch cabob.*"

Councilor—with a Mayan title. Might he build anything on that? Blake wondered. The Mayans had been merchants first, exploring merchants. Could that bent have lingered on, making his supposed profession more acceptable than it would be to an Aztec war noble?

The man swung up into the forepart of the camp on wheels and Blake thought he was now broadcasting a report of the affair.

"So you are of the Allowed Merchants in Xomatl, where you doubtless have had dealings with *Yacabec, Pochteca Flatoque.*" Now the Toltecan used Aztec rather than Mayan terms.

"With the *Pochteca Flatoque* does indeed my master have accord. I am not *Tecuhnenenque.* The name of the lord who is head of the merchants' guild is Npoaltzin."

The *ah cuch cabob* shrugged. He gave some order in the native tongue and Blake was urged on, past the camp to some other vehicles parked a short distance away, transportation for the rest of the party.

Several of those vans were equipped with cages built on their frames and two of these held occupants. One was a bear and the other a wolf of such size as to make Blake wonder if it would not be a formidable opponent for one of the jaguars. Into a third empty cage Blake was thrust. The enclosure smelled vilely of some former inhabitant. The wardsman sprawled on the dirty floor, trying to steady himself as the motor came to life and the truck backed onto roughly cleared space to turn around.

They drove past the camp car. The nobleman was rubbing the ears of one of the cats whose head rested on his knee. He glanced up at the caged Blake with a trace of smile that matched the snarling lip-lift of his pet.

The narrow forest track turned into a wide road, this one with a surface of crushed stone, which, in turn, became a highway paved with dressed stone blocks. Now and then they passed other trucks carrying supplies, but never anything Blake recognized as a passenger transport.

He was given nothing to eat or drink, though the two women in the driver's cab, when they paused at intervals to change places at the controls, shared out flatcakes of bread, made into saucer-sized sandwiches with a dark paste between layers, and the contents of a bottle. By bracing his feet against the bars at the opposite side of the cage, Blake managed to stay in a sitting position for some hours. But the constant tension of that became more than he could endure, and at last, the wardsman lay prone, his body all one ache, striving only to protect his injured arm as he was shaken about.

They passed through one small village along its single street. Blake caught a glimpse of the river flowing past a jetty. Their route was south, but that was all he knew. And soon he did not care about their final goal, only hoped they would reach it while he still had some consciousness left.

Darkness came as Blake fought off attacks of lightheadedness which grew longer and more sustained. He became aware of lights, of the fact that the highway was now a street running between buildings which rivaled or overtopped those of Port Ackrone.

Flashes of light showed that they were embellished with grotesque carvings. And there was traffic, enough to make him dizzy with the sounds of wheels and voices, all the rear of a good-sized town.

Deeper dark closed about him, then light once again, this time subdued, while the city sounds came faintly. The truck halted and those on the front seat got down. One stretched wide his arms while the other called.

More voices, a greater degree of light. Then a rattling at the door of the cage as it was flung back. Hands caught at Blake, dragged him out. For all his desire to front the enemy on his feet, the wardsman sagged to the ground. A boot caught him close to the burn, and that blow sent him hurtling into unconsciousness.

Cold . . . wet . . . he was helpless in the river . . . he was going to drown unless he fought. Swim . . . move arms and legs . . . but he could not. He was helpless in the current . . .

Water ran into his mouth, his hot, dry mouth. Water—that was what he had wanted for so long. The river was good. It would quench the fire inside him! Blake opened his mouth wider to drink, but the fluid dashed against his flesh, not between his parted lips.

Blake opened his eyes. There were faces hanging in the air above him. Three . . . four . . . none of them he knew. He tried to ask for water, his voice came as a rusty croaking. Hands in his armpits, jerking him up. Then the world spun and danced crazily. He shut his eyes because it made him sick to watch the spinning of the light, faces, and walls.

He could not walk, so he was dragged, his feet drumming helplessly as they pulled at him. And they were talking, but he could not understand one word they said. Then he was shoved forward, allowed to sprawl on a hard surface. He lay there gasping, until a boot toe was pushed under his body and he was rolled over on his back.

Chapter Ten

It was hard for Blake to open his eyes and focus on his surroundings. The bright light above him was searing, blanketing out the faces of his captors. Then one of them moved, dark eyes regarded him intently. A hand moved down, jerked at the heraldic buckle on his belt. There were sharp words, issuing what must be a series of orders.

Once more the wardsman was lifted and carried, but this time with a little more concern for him. And when he was dropped, it was onto a padding of mats. An old face, seamed with many wrinkles, swam out of the fog which now enclosed him. The sear burn was harsh pain, but his arms were free of bonds, leaden by his sides. His shoulders and head were raised; he was urged to drink from a bowl pressed against his lips. Bitter stuff which made him gag swilled about his mouth and finally got down his throat. He was lowered to the mats and he slept.

Blake came out of that sleep which had been dreamhaunted although he could not remember the dreams, into a sharpened awareness not only of his own mind and body, but also of his surroundings. This was precognition raised to the degree that he was a sounding board for varied impressions. Only once or twice before in his life had this happened, and each time he had drawn inner strength from that honing of the talent he possessed. A moment later as he lay there, eyes closed, giving no sign of his recovery, he felt that other thought thrusting in his mind, not such a probe as he had experienced among the men of Vroom, rather a kind of fumbling on the surface of his brain, as if the one who sought to read the secrets within his skull was not truly adept at this type of research.

He put up his briefed memories, those of Rufus Trelawnly. To select these and satisfy such a probe as this was easy, too easy. Suspicion throbbed through him with every beat of his heart. But he remained Rufus Trelawnly during that inquiry, until the clumsy seeker withdrew and he was alone in his own mind. Not—certainly not—any telepath from Vroom where such powers, trained and refined for generations, were as far beyond this clumsy invasion as the laser side-arm was beyond the obsidian-edged, wooden blades the men of the Empire had once carried into battle. But with people to whom any psi power was a wonder, the man who could read even surface thought would be a worker of magic. To this day, men of the Empire depended upon the *tonalpoulqui*—those practicing divination—and much of the privilege of their ancient priestly rank still held, especially among the lower classes. A man's horoscope, cast at birth, laid bare his life before he had breathed out his first few hours. And psi powers of any kind would make the *tonalpoulqui* possessing them notable and particularly reverenced.

Blake listened. No sound suggested that others were in the room. He opened his eyes, but did not move his head. Above him was white surface across which lay a bar of sunlight. Somewhere near there was cooking, for a spicy smell teased his nostrils. The peace of those two observations was belied by his warning.

He turned his head left and saw a wall, patterned with a mural of stylized flower-and-leaf designs in gaudy colors, broken by three uncurtained windows. The panes were opaque, letting through light but giving no sight of what lay beyond.

A table stood by the wall, its surface only a short distance from the floor. Those who used it must sit crosslegged on the mats now piled together at one end. From that he gained a scrap of knowledge; he was not in the quarters of any nobleman but in a place where the owner kept the old customs now used only by the peasants.

His left arm was bandaged, heavy by his side. With his right hand Blake explored the bed on which he lay. Another pile of mats. And when he turned his head right, he was fronted, only a foot or so away, with a second painted wall. The torn, wet clothing he had worn was gone. Now he was covered with a rough shirt and a woven blanket of bright colors and intricate designs.

He had been tended; he lay in a place that did not appear to be a prison. So much was favorable. For the rest, well, he had been warned, was being alerted at this moment.

A cadenced tramping vibrated through the floor under him. Blake sat up, put out a hand against the painted wall to brace himself when the room swung about him dizzily. As his head cleared, he faced the door. Whoever stood on the other side turning the key in the lock, for he heard the grate of metal against metal, was to be feared.

The heavy door swung inward and Blake looked up at the newcomer. He was a tall man with the harsh, beaky features characteristic of the old Aztec blood. His loose breeches were made of a material worked with bands of fine embroidery, red and blue. His full-sleeved shirt was of a clear yellow with shoulder embellishments of embroidery. And his cloak had a boldly vivid feather fringe. On his feet were calf-high boots fastened with turquoise snaps, testifying to noble birth. But it was not this resplendent visitor who had unlocked the door. He held in his hand only a bunch of flowers and herbs in a gemmed holder, at which he sniffed now and then.

The key holder wore the uniform of a private guard, and he was a plainsman not unlike those who had formed the hunter-ranger party that had captured Blake. He had a bundle under his arm which he now tossed in the general direction of the mat bed. It came apart in midair and Blake's New Britain clothing cascaded out.

"Get up!" The guard accompanied that order with a gesture to the clothing. "Dress. There is a court."

Blake did not reach for the shirt lying within a short distance. Boldness could be a weapon with a warrior race.

"You speak of a court." He drew on the most formal speech of New Britain for his reply. "That is to say there has been a crime. Of what am I accused?" He put a note of impatience in his voice and repeated, "Of what am I accused, *Tecuhtli*?" addressing himself not to the guard but his master. Nor did he miss the slight flaring in the nostrils of that prominent Aztec nose.

This lordling, whoever he might be, had not expected such a reply. But the sooner he learned Blake Walker owed him no "wood and water," the better that might be. There had always been a pessimistic acceptance of fate among those of the ancient blood; they could be baffled by any refusal to accept a decree. A people whose human sacrifices had once stood dutifully in line from sunrise to sunset, hundreds and even thousands of them, marching dully and without struggle to the fate of being cut open while yet living for the glory of many gods, were not conditioned, even generations later, to defiance.

"Up!" The officer repeated his order. "The *Teactli* waits!" He whistled and two soldiers appeared in the doorway behind the lord. "You go—or they take you."

Blake reached for his clothing. It had been roughly handled in addition to the damage suffered during his overland journey. Someone had searched every seam, slit open any portion that might have concealed something. For what had they been hunting? At least the worst of the damage had been repaired with hasty, long stitches which he hoped would hold together for the sake of his own dignity if they were about to take him into a court of law. As slowly as possible he dressed.

One of the soldiers had vanished when it appeared that his services to button a recalcitrant prisoner into his clothing were not needed. He returned with a cup and bowl which he put down on the table.

The officer gestured again. "Eat. Drink."

The contents of the cup was the ever-present Toltec drink of chocolate, which, in this case, had not been either spiced or flavored with vanilla. But it was hot and, Blake knew, sustaining. The bowl held maize cakes, spread very thinly with a paste which gave some relief to their dryness. He ate and drank to the last crumb and drop. If they were indeed taking him to a court, they would have him out in the city. He continued to speculate even when his good sense told him there was no hope of escape in this unknown city where his skin, his hair, his clothing marked him as surely as if he carried a banner in one hand inscribed "I am an escaped prisoner."

Having seen him clothed and fed, the noble stalked out, his bouquet of flowers used rather as a rod of office, which its stiff, ceremonial arrangement did not deny. The officer strode behind him, while Blake between two soldiers brought up the rear. They entered a narrow-roofed and walled passage. Through a gate-opening Blake caught a glimpse of a garden, riotous in color. But he had more attention for the man waiting at the end of the passage where it gave upon a courtyard holding several vehicles.

This—this was the would-be mind reader! As a hound might scent a natural enemy in one of the great cats, so Blake's warning gave him notice now. The man was older than the nobleman, having the same Aztec features except that these were harshened even more by a tightly set mouth and eyes sunk beneath bony skull ridges. His hair, threaded with dull gray, was worn longer, matted, dull, looking as if it had gone uncombed for years, some of it sticking into points. Unlike the others, his clothing was black, his coat so long it resembled a robe. He leaned on a polished staff which bore faint indentations and curves, as if it had once been carved and the carving had been worn away by centuries of handling.

The noble stepped quickly to one side, showing this oldster the same deference his own men displayed toward him. And the officer pressed himself against the wall of the passage as he waved Blake on to face the old man. The wardsman, meeting those deep-set eyes, knew that what he saw in them was nothing which could be a part of any sane life. The alert of his warning was reinforced by an inward repulsion, an uncontrollable shrinking.

Vroom and its people had been alien to the world in which he lived during childhood and early manhood. On other levels he had seen "people" far different from his kind, whose life patterns had varied from the road he walked until they had little or nothing in common. He had caught breaths of what was to him the rank depths of evil, a kind of evil few of his breed had ever plumbed. But here was something still different: a fanaticism rooted not only in this man but in generations upon generations behind him. He was not a man as Blake reckoned his fellows, but rather an incarnation of dark purposes, a vessel which held a power or desire or will, that was no longer human, if it ever had been.

He was power, dark power. And as he looked at Blake, he was also hunger, a hunger long denied. The inner warning in the wardsman became a need for flight, so great that Blake thought he could never control it. For a long time, or so it seemed to the younger man, they stood looking at one another. Then the staff in the oldster's hand moved, its time-smoothed top tapped Blake on the breast. The lightest of touches, and yet the wardsman felt as if the worn wood had in that instant laid some smarting brand upon him.

Without a word the man in black turned, shuffled across the courtyard and climbed stiffly into one of the cars. His use of that means of transportation was incongruous, out of character. And the mere fact he did so broke the spell for Blake. But now he was also being propelled by his guard into the back of a small van.

There were windows in the van but they were latticed, so that any glimpse he had of the streets through which they passed was fragmentary. But it was intended for passengers, since it was furnished with surprisingly comfortable and well-cushioned seats, one of which Blake shared with two guards planted firmly on either side. Nor did either man speak.

The Empire had a high form of justice; that much Blake had learned during his studies. And from the remote past the courts had been incorruptible; the penalty for any partiality was death for the judge. But why they would bring him under their jurisdiction Blake could not understand. Anyone in his predicament was usually declared a spy and turned over to the army for very summary justice, with perhaps a "hearing" that was really an interrogation, during which the prisoner might die and so save any more bother on the part of his captors. But apparently he was on his way to one of the legal courts. And the reason for that?

To prevent an "incident" which might cause trouble with New Britain? Blake doubted that. Both nations had operated for years now on the basis that their nationals traveled across the border at their own risk, and that they might expect no aid from home should those risks prove a trap.

The car turned a corner and came to a stop, the back door clanged open. Blake blinked his way into brilliant sunlight. He stood at the pavement end of an imposing flight of stairs, leading up three flights, to a building set on a pyramid base. The monumental ruins that had been found in jungles on his own successor world, ruins that awed travelers and explorers three, four, five centuries after they ceased to mark living cities, were the forerunners of this civic structure. The feathered serpents, jaguars, and god masks that had ornamented those in profusion had in the course of time become more symbolic designs. But the fine stonework still remained.

If Blake had something to stare at in the building and the brightly dressed crowd about him, so did the latter gather to gaze back at him. A volley of orders sent guards to clear the stairway. The wardsman might have been one of the Emperor's staff, judging by the speed in which that operation was carried out. Even nobles pressed back to open a path.

The stairs were steep, the treads narrow. Blake's guards kept step with him, either as supports or deterrents against some last-minute bid for freedom. Then they came through a pillared outer way into the interior.

The inner room was crowded, too. No trial in the Empire was by jury; verdict was rendered by a panel of judges who sat on a platform in the old way, crosslegged on mats. Behind them was yet another dais for the Imperial power. Centering that stood a bench carved with the legs of a jaguar, fanged heads marking the arm rests, cushioned by a mat of woven eagle feathers. Thus it stood, always waiting for a time when the Emperor might see fit to visit his court.

Now there was a scrambling hurry to clear a way to the judges' seat, that path lined with uniformed men. Blake was brought to a stand directly before the platform, his guards falling back a few steps to leave him conspicuously alone. A court official began a droning speech, consulting at intervals a roll that had been handed him. Now and again one of the judges nodded during a pause in the drone or made a comment. When the speaker had come to an end, they all looked at Blake as if expecting something from him in return. Well, he could at least ask for an explanation. Some of them must understand English, even if they did not choose to advertise the fact.

"May it please the court"—that was the first solution which came to him as proper—"I do not know what charge has been laid against me. Am I not to know the crime for which I am being tried?"

There was a moment of silence and then one of the judges spoke, his English bearing only the slightest of accents.

"You have appealed to the justice of the Great One. He of the Feather Scales." The judge bowed his head. "You have been accused before this court and the Throne of the Great One of—"

He was interrupted by a stir in the hall behind Blake. Change! His precognition told him that. There was a change coming. He was trying to assess the meaning in this warning and did not look behind.

On his left those in the body of the hall were pressing yet farther back. More soldiers filed into line. These wore scarlet cloaks and the jaguar-mask duty helmets of the elite corps. One of them, an officer by the plumed crest, leaped to the upper dais reserved for the Emperor, and draped a cloak of dramatic black and white over the cushion.

It was the sign of the *Cuiacoatl*, the Vice-Emperor, who had only one superior in the whole of Toltec territory, and that the boy Emperor himself. But the man who mounted the dais with deliberate tread was no boy. He was perhaps in his late thirties and not a warrior such as those who paid him deference. For he walked with a rocking, sidewise gait caused by a shortened left leg, and his left arm was carefully hidden in the folds of his cloak of state, while his face closely resembled one of the crystal skulls jewelers of the Empire carved with such exquisite and detailed precision.

This was Tlacaclel, the eldest brother of the late Emperor, passed over for the rulership because of his physical infirmities, but whose mental abilities had made such a mark on the circle of close councilors that they had been at last forced to grant him the vice-rulership, however much they disliked the doing. Having settled himself on the throne, he nodded sharply to his officer who brought the butt of a ceremonial "presence" spear crashing down on the stone.

Blake thought he saw the faintest of shivers hunch the shoulders of the judge now seated directly before the person of that crippled royal hawk. But without otherwise acknowledging the presence of the *Cuiacoatl*, the judge began his indictment for the second time.

"You have been brought here, Stranger, charged with seeking to ferret out the secrets of the Emperor's house, striving to cause trouble—"

The *Cuiacoatl* stared down at Blake. As the judge paused, he spoke abruptly. "What story has this over-the-river one given to explain himself?"

The judges all stirred. *Cuiacoatl* or not, living presence of the Emperor or not, this pushing aside of orderly procedure in the court was forbidden.

Tlacaclel gestured again, and once more the spear butt ordered silence and attention. Now the Vice-Emperor pointed a long nailed forefinger directly at Blake.

"Speak you. What is your tale?"

The truth, as far as it would go, Blake decided swiftly. He was depending a great deal on his new warning signal: expect change but not outright danger.

"I am of the Allowed Merchant company bound for Xomatl according to the law, Great One . . ." He made a short story of it though he spoke slowly. His fall from the boat was edited into an accident, but for the rest he kept to the facts. How much of it was understood by his listeners he did no know, although most of the nobles and the merchant class understood English.

As he talked, Blake's mind worked. One of the many facts he had learned on Vroom came to mind. When he had done, he stooped, touched his finger to the floor, and then to his lips, before he again faced the Vice-Emperor. "This do I swear by Huitzilopochtli!"

Five hundred years ago a man speaking so could never be questioned further as to the truth of what he said. Tlacaclel studied him for a moment before he answered.

"Since the Butterfly One has ceased to hold the promise of life or death in this land, Stranger, you indeed swear strangely. But still I think the need with which those words were once summoned continues to carry weight. Is there anyone you may call now to speak for you, give bond that you are what you say, to be returned to your countrymen as having meant to do no evil to this land or those who dwell therein? Who in the hearing of the judges will so speak?"

Was that question really addressed to Blake? The *Cuiacoatl* was no longer watching the prisoner, his attention swept for a telling second to the throng who stood walled away by the guards on Blake's right.

"This one so speaks."

An officer moved to the fore of the crowd. He was not one of the wearers of the Jaguar badge, his uniform was plain amid all that spread of color. And Blake did not recognize the insignia on the breast of his jacket.

"Let it be recorded that the worthy Cuauhuehuetque of the border, Thohtzin, has spoken for the prisoner, knowing that he swears to the truth of this stranger and that guilt or innocence is now equal for both!"

The *Cuiacoatl* spoke swiftly and again the judges stirred. But no one objected openly. Thohtzin stepped up to the lower dais, made some formal declaration which the others responded to, and then came directly to Blake, the guards standing aside though with visible reluctance.

"Come quickly!"

Blake needed no urging. He did not know what lay behind this, but his luck had taken a change for the better and he was willing to ride on it for now. At any rate, he went free where he had come under guard.

Chapter Eleven

It was not until they drove out on a wharf that Blake knew they had been heading for the river, since Thohtzin made no explanation and the wardsman thought it wise not to ask questions until he was surer of his ground. Their car was driven by a soldier in the same plain uniform as the officer wore, and there were two more men on the seat behind.

Tied up at the wharf was a small cruiser, one man standing at her controls, another waiting to cast off mooring ropes. For the second time Thohtzin ordered: "Come quickly!"

He pushed Blake ahead of him into the boat, glancing back up the street as if fearing to see active pursuit. It was not until they were moving into the main current of the river at a speed exceeding any Blake had seen used by water-borne traffic that the officer relaxed.

He touched the wardsman on the arm, motioning him toward the wheelhouse where he himself relieved the man on duty, taking the steering mechanism into his hands. When they were left alone, he half smiled at Blake.

"Truly you must have set out on your travels on One of the Snake, or else you were born under that favorable sign, Teyaualouanimi. We are not yet beyond a flight of darts, should those who wish you to meet Xipé or Huitzilopochtli after the old fashion move to enforce that desire. Only the Great One could so overrule the will of the Tlalogue thus. By the Nine, what ill wind brought you into this?"

Feel your way carefully, Blake warned himself. Obviously he was being taken for someone who had reason to claim aid from some of the Emperor's subjects. Was that true of the real Rufus Trelawnly?

"It was as I told the judges," he replied. "A fall from the ship—"

"Which left you scorched by a ray?" The glance at him this time was far more measuring.

"That happened after I hit the water," Blake said. "I do not know who fired at me, or why."

It was a good guess, that answer, for the officer was nodding.

"Yes, that could well be. For seeing you in the river, the guards would only follow their regular orders, and Ah Kukum dared not countermand them without bringing suspicion on us. Nactitl's eyes and ears ply those boats, both openly and secretly. Tell me, how goes the negotiations? You have good news?"

Blake looked at the swirling water through which the bow of the cruiser was cutting a swift course. "The last I heard all was proceeding smoothly. My—my superior would know more." Ambiguous, but again he apparently satisfied his questioner.

"The day . . ." Thohtzin raised one hand from the wheel, brought it down clenched into a fist. "Ah, the day when once more we can raise the standards, sound the shell trumpets!" He paused and shot Blake a look of what might be embarrassment. "That is only speaking in the old terms—we do not fight as did our forefathers."

"The courage of the Empire is well known, also the skill of her soldiers, and their ability," Blake agreed.

"Of which there shall be soon a good showing! This new law they force upon us, no more defenses, an opening of the border. Trade, ever trade . . ."

What did he mean, Blake wondered. The story at Ackrone had been of tightening of controls, of unrest aimed at perhaps eventual reopening of hostilities between the two nations. Yet here was the hint of a striving for more liberal policy.

"Tell me," Thohtzin went on, "why is it you English wish to pull down those of New Britain, make them meat for the Empire?"

That was a good question and a baffling one. Somehow Blake found words. "When have there never been factions under any rule? I am only a soldier in the ranks; to such problems my superior may have a reply."

Again Thohtzin was off on another track. "Tell me, have you seen these new weapons with your own eyes, these sounds which can shake a stone wall into rubble, bring men screaming out of any fort with no weapons in their hands, only the need to flee? And that which, when a man breathes it in the air, makes his mind an empty thing so that he will stand unknowing while his enemies march past the gate he is set to guard? Have you seen these?"

Blake groped for the edge of the windbreak before him. He was as shocked as if he had taken the full force of a laser ray dead center, save this was cold and deadly, not roasting heat.

"Yes . . ." That began as a whisper. He forced his voice higher. "Yes, I have seen such weapons!" He gazed at the water, but he did not see that, nor the cruiser, nor Thohtzin. Rather Blake drew from memory the screening of a record tape as shown in corps instruction in Vroom.

The world had had a dark and bloody history. On all the successor levels except those on which mankind had never come into being, war, rumors of war, battle and defeat, had been the way of life. Far earlier than his own successor world, Vroom had climbed to a mechanically based civilization, planet-wide. Mechanical and then atomic and then—the last blazing, terrible war sending remnants of the human race into barbarism save for small pockets of survivors. Out of that weltering chaos had come a three-quarters dead world and, eventually, the saving crosstiming. In the last frenzied days of a dying civilization, fearsome weapons had been devised, some never put to use. But they were known, their results indelibly impressed on each and every descendant of those who had been mad enough to create them. Vroom was now a peaceful level, but still there was constant surveillance so as to be sure that no warped personality could threaten that peace. Yet here, on another level, a man talked familiarly of some of those outlawed weapons! This could only leak from Vroom. No other successor world had crosstime travel, and the level in which they now were did not have the technology to produce such devices.

"You find these weapons indeed awesome, Teyaualouanimi?"

"They are of the devil!" Blake exploded, and then was too well aware of his self-betrayal.

"Devil?"

"Of great evil."

"Perhaps. But sometimes one accepts aid from the *tztizimime,* the ancient monsters of the twilight, to bring about good. For what will become of our way of life if these *tecuhnenenque,* who think more of their treasures than of their honor and that of the Great Serpent, take from us our arms and so make of us slaves? Also, we need not use such weapons, or perhaps only once, to show what we have. Then shall those who would pour poison into the water which we drink be as dogs and run about barking, knowing no safe place in which to hide. To have a keen sword in one's hand and the ability to use it makes a man walk tall and the lesser give him careful room!"

How much of that was true belief, Blake speculated, and how much the sugar-coating they were conditioned to accept?

"We would not give such arms into the hands of the extremists."

"The extremists?"

Thohtzin smiled. "You may now speak with the authority of one who has had a meeting with them. The Lord Chacxib who had you brought to judgment gives harborage, and more than half an ear, to Ihuitimal, who in the old days would have been a *cuacuacuiltin,* one of the venerable Old Ones consecrated to Huitzilopochtli. I have heard him speak concerning the wishes of his heart. Cuauhuehuetque was once not a title given to those who hold dangerous duty on the frontiers. It meant then a fighting priest of the first rank. Perhaps you of England do not study our history well enough to understand the meaning. . . ."

"I know a little," Blake responded as the other paused.

"Then you must know that ours was once a most bloody, as you would say, way of life. For each fighting man was dedicated to the capture, not the killing, of the enemy so that those captives might be given to the gods. And we had many gods, all thirsty for the lives of men. Only through the capture of many enemies might a man rise to honor, and that stairway was open to the humblest and not just to men whose fathers had been great before them.

"There are those who have always turned to the old gods and their ways, who repudiated the wishes of Quetzalcoatl when he first came to substitute grain, birds, flowers for the human hearts on the sacrifice stones. And when the second Kukulc·n arose with the same message, there were those who defied him to the last, keeping alive the old ways in secret.

"Now they begin to emerge from the shadows of secrecy, attach themselves to the party of the Return. And since every man means so much more support, they are welcome to fight on our side. But once the battle is over, the extremists will not find their dream of blood-smoking altars brought alive. Meanwhile, they are not crossed too much. Had the judgment gone against you . . . ."

Again the officer paused and looked sidewise at Blake, that moment of silence lengthening until the wardsman prompted: "Then what might have happened?"

"You could have been returned to the Lord Chacxib, on whose land you were taken, for him to render justice. And that would have brought you into the hands of Ihuitimal and his followers, to feed the god they invoke."

Varlt's fear for Marva! If Thohtzin could seriously suggest this, then Varlt had good reason for his fears. The wardsman strove to appear impassive, his tone one of interest only as he asked. "This does happen?"

"It does." Thohtzin's expression was one of disgust. "They say we must bind the extremists to us because they control the villagers and the wild men. The honor of warriors is a good thing, it is the lifeblood of the Empire, but one cannot recall the past. We should not trouble the sleep of old gods. Once we have these new weapons, then none, priest or merchant, will dare walk against us."

"We shall dock at Xomatl at dawn," he added a moment later. "Once you are again with your people you must tell your superior that we have no time to waste. The girl is safe, but how long she remains hidden without talk we cannot tell. No matter how one stops all cracks in any women's quarters, still gossip and rumor run like open streams into the city, and this is a tale worth repeating many times over. Therefore, let your party move soon lest you find you have nothing to bargain with and no one to blame but yourselves."

"I will do so."

Marva! She must be "the girl." But who—who was Rufus Trelawnly's superior? The merchant Varlt was now impersonating in Xomatl? Surely, if the Allowed Merchants were connected with a crosstime outlaw, Arshalm would have known—or suspected—as much. Unless he, too, was a part of the whole. This affair continued to widen out like the ripples from a stone thrown into a pool. Perhaps the wardsmen's team was on the edge of something far too great for the small force to handle.

Thohtzin summoned the wheelsman, and they went below to eat better rations than Blake had yet tasted this side of the river. Afterward the Imperial officer flung himself on a mat-filled bunk and signed Blake to take the one across the cabin. Even as the wardsman settled himself on the couch, he could hear the even breathing of his cabinmate, but his own slumber was light, a series of dozes from which he continued to awake, remembering and worrying.

A mist clung along the river banks in the very early morning. The speed of the cruiser had been sharply reduced as they approached the city. Save for a few scattered lights, the bulk of the buildings silhouetted against the sky was dark. And no one stirred along the dock where they moored with a precision that suggested that this might not be the first surreptitious run the craft had made to this port.

If any watchman had been stationed on the wharf, he was now elsewhere. Blake hurried along, trying to keep pace with Thohtzin. They sped the length of the jetty and then across a quayside street to a warehouse. A dim light over a small door set into a larger portal illuminated the entrance Thohtzin used.

The interior was filled with cargo, boxed and in tall baskets. At regular intervals along the high roof, lights burned, giving Blake a view of the Imperial officer on the move down the middle aisle between two walls of goods. They were almost to the far end when Thohtzin halted and began counting a row of baskets. When his finger touched one, he made the count again, this time from the other end of the line, as if to make doubly sure of his choice. Then he busied himself with the fastening and lifted the cover.

"In," he whispered. "You wait. Make no sound if you would ever get to your friends."

In the bottom of the basket were folded cloths which Thohtzin pulled up, packing them around Blake as the wardsman crouched, his arms about his bent knees, in the container. A second or so later the lid fell, leaving him a few cracks for communication with the outer world. He heard the soft fumbling of Thohtzin making tight the fastenings once again.

After that, nothing but silence and a growing cramp in his arms and legs. He might have dozed again, his forehead resting on his knees, for he roused to sound: talking, some calls, the purr of machinery.

There was conversation in the Toltec tongue just outside the basket. Then, without further warning, the basket was swung through space and was lowered again. What it rested on moved. Blake was too far from any of the light- and air-permitting cracks to see anything, but he was sure they had come out of the warehouse into the open. Another swing, and once more the basket was deposited on another surface. Abruptly the light was gone, the vibration of a motor shook him.

He could deduce nothing from the confusion of muffled sound. The basket swayed a little now and then as if the van rounded curves. Then they halted; a third swing through air, jamming him against one side of the rough basket with no chance of avoiding the bruising impact, and again he was set down with jarring force.

"That is the last of the lot." Words spoken in English! And the voice was that of one of the wardsmen pulled in to make up the last minute recruitment of the team! But was he alone? Dare Blake strive to draw his attention?

"Might as well open them up then . . ."

Lo Sige! That was Lo Sige!

Remembering the other's present cover, Blake called, "Richard—Richard Wellford!" His dust-dry voice did not sound very loud to him. But there was instant silence without. Then the lid was unfastened, lifted. Blake strove to raise his hands to the edge of the container. It swayed and fell forward so that he lay half in, half out, on a stone floor.

Hands grasped his shoulders and drew him up, although it seemed for an instant that his numbed legs might not bear his weight. Lo Sige, yes, and the other wardsman who had helped Blake store cargo—how many days ago?

"Quite a delivery." As cool as ever, Lo Sige's voice broke the silence first. "Cargo slightly damaged, but still intact, I would say. How damaged and—how intact?"

What he might mean by the last Blake had no idea. He dropped the hand he had extended to grip Lo Sige's arm, ashamed at that show of his intense relief. With Lo Sige he was most wary of any display of emotion. The other's habitual detachment divorced him from such weakness, making any such the more apparent when a companion revealed it.

Blake tried to match Sige's control. "A laser burn for damage, otherwise intact. Where is Master Frontnum?" At least he remembered to ask for Varlt by his cover name.

"Aloft. But," Lo Sige appeared pensive, "we have our own resident eyes and ears working for the Emperor. To get you above without too much remark presents a small problem. Ah, a good trick may be worked twice! We have found some grievous damage in shipment, Henry," he said to the other wardsman, "almost suggesting deliberate spoilage. To be certain, the shipment must be examined by our master in its entirety. Back into the basket, Rufus. Then we'll see how clever we can be with our own trans-shipment."

Not daring to disagree, Blake re-entered the constrained prison. There followed a great deal of grunting and shifting, bruise-raising contacts with the side of the basket. Eventually they came to a halt and Blake heard Lo Sige's low-pitched voice.

"As I said, Master Frontnum, malicious damage, surely malicious damage. A deposition must be made as we unpack. I am certain the insurance will cover this, but we should have proof."

"We shall see." Varlt sounded pontifical, the very assured master of the party, allowing no one to make decisions for him or influence his thinking. The lid lifted once again and with far less than his usual agility, Blake climbed out.

"A very novel entrance." Varlt's comment echoed Lo Sige's. "I think that it is in order we have a sharing of knowledge. Sit down, man. Richard?"

"Right here." Lo Sige materialized beside Blake, steering him to one of the stools serving as chairs, putting into his hand a cup which gave off the aromatic odor Blake knew from Vroom, an energizing stimulant that acted as a quick restorative.

"Now." Varlt had waited until half the liquid was down Blake's throat before he continued. "Suppose we hear just what happened to you since you went out on deck five nights ago."

Blake reported, carefully. There was no recorder for his words as there had been in Vroom, but he knew that both men, when he had done, could give back the substance of his report almost word for word. He made it as quick as he could, but he wanted to leave out no significant detail. And neither commented, even when he paused for more sips of the stimulant.

"Maze within maze within maze," Lo Sige observed when he had done.

Varlt plucked at the pointed beard which was the bushy identity mark for Master Frontnum.

"So they believed you to be a contact with an arms runner." He spoke as if arranging his thoughts aloud. "Yet nothing turned up during our combing of the memories of this merchant group to explain that, not a hint of anything save the legal trade. And not one of them was shielded, either."

"That password you did not respond to—which error sent you into the river—" Lo Sige said, "someone expected you, or a contact, to be aboard the boat. And they would not have taken a chance on the wrong man. Therefore, they expected, if not the real Rufus Trelawnly, a counterfeit double. Which would also explain the prompt action to get rid of you. I would wager that substitution is not exclusively our game here. We merely got in first!"

"And they did not expect us to ask any betraying questions when you turned up here again." Varlt gazed into space. "This needs thinking about. As you say, Richard, the tangle grows more twisted as we advance. I see a number of loops but no ends. Rufus, let Worsley see your arm, then rest up."

So definitely was that an order Blake dared not dispute his summary dismissal. Also, he was glad that the decisions were no longer all his. With the years of experience behind him, Varlt's choice of action should be the better.

Chapter Twelve

"Marva is here at—as far as we have been able to discover—the estate of one Otorongo who holds a unique position. It has been only for the past hundred years that the crown has descended by primogeniture. In the old days the Emperor's brothers or nephews were more eligible to succeed him than his sons. The crown was, in effect, an elective office rather than rule by divine right or inheritance. This Otorongo is a descendant of one of the earlier emperors, so possesses those ill-defined rights which every offshoot of royalty can claim in a kingdom. He has always been considered a dilettante uninterested in politics, the foremost patron of the goldsmiths, with numerous proteges in the arts, stages a concert once a year which is famous in this province. Now, in preparing for the fifty-two-year cycle he is planning a very elaborate series of both private and public entertainments."

"No tie with the military party?" Lo Sige asked when Varlt had finished.

Varlt pushed a fingertip eraser-fashion back and forth across the map of the city which lay on the table.

"When you have only superficial talk and rumor to depend on for information, you are not sure of anything. Outwardly his interests are as I have said. What under-the-cover-of-night allegiances he maintains, who can tell?"

"Marva is there," Marfy stared down at the map, "and we are

here." She stabbed a forefinger down less than an inch away from the point Varlt had indicated. But that inch represented no small distance in the city. "We must get her out!"

Varlt did not list the difficulties in such action, nor did he look up from the map he continued to smooth.

"Day after tomorrow is the beginning of the cycle. Strangers from the country are pouring into the city for the rites and general festivities after the kindling. This is one time that men may come and go unseen or undetected. Otorongo could well use his entertainment as a cover for meetings, if that is what he desires. And so . . ."

Blake stirred. "Thohtzin and whoever is behind him believed me to be their contact with this supplier of off-level arms. Could we play on that for a chance to reach Marva?"

Varlt raised his eyes, gave the younger man a long, measuring survey.

"It might have had a chance had he given you any point of contact here in Xomatl, if you knew where to locate him. But—"

"But—but—and again but!" Marfy burst out. "I tell you, I know where Marva is. I can find her within an hour. Then, with her safe here—"

"With her here—in the Allowed Merchant's quarters?" Varlt's eyebrows raised, his tone was cold. "This is the first place they would search and we have no way of retreat. There is only one chance. We must put to use the excitement of these cycle days to cover our moves. To withdraw overland would merely set hunters on our trail at once. We shall have to get a launch or river boat, be sure of that. And then, once our escape is ready, move suddenly, perhaps with only a single chance of action."

Blake rose and walked to the far wall of the room where a mirror hung, reflecting the company about the table. But he was more intent upon the image of his own face.

The radical cosmetic treatments of the Vroom technicians had lightened his skin and it would remain so if he applied the proper creams. But he had neglected to do that since his arrival in Xomatl, and the days of his captivity had already started the reversal process. He had seen lords coming in to inspect the goods on the lower shop floor whose skin was the color of his own. And, while the strong features of the Aztec and Mayan ruling caste were sharply distinguishable, he had confidence that wardsman techniques could provide those also for a short period.

Varlt's eyes met his in the mirror. Blake thought that the senior wardsman was quite able to read if not his mind, then his intentions.

"A hunter from the north could be one of the visiting strangers?" Blake made a question of that.

"To do what?" demanded Varlt bluntly.

"To try his luck at finding Thohtzin."

"Or Marva!" Marfy was on her feet. "It is right . . . get her out . . . maybe hide along the river to be picked up . . ."

"Thohtzin," Varlt repeated thoughtfully, paying no attention to the girl. "And if you find him, then what? Also, you have no briefing on the actions of a northern hunter. You could betray yourself in the first five minutes in any of fifty different ways."

"The streets are crowded, strangers are many. Choose a distant native place for me." Blake had no feeling of excitement, rather did purposeless waiting wear harder on him. And since this idea had come into mind, he had had no precognition warning. So, for the present at least, there was no danger in this.

"Say you do find him"—Lo Sige now played the devil's advocate—"what do you do?"

"Invite him here, for a meeting with my superior."

Varlt's finger no longer rubbed the map. Now he alternately crooked and straightened it as if beckoning to someone unseen.

"You are thinking that Thohtzin has access to a fast cruiser as well as information that we would be well advised to hear?"

"That's about it."

"Thohtzin," Varlt mused. "I wish we knew a little more about him. The zin name ending is honorary, and the name itself means 'hawk.' His rank is *cuauhuehuetque*—fighting priest—though that is an old title applied to a new service with a different connotation entirely. And where would you begin to look for this high-flying hawk?"

"Where I saw him last, on the docks. If the cruiser is still there—"

Lo Sige laughed. "We, who are supposed to be cautious, secretive, and all the rest, appear now to be playing the wildest of chances. Oh, don't look to me! I have nothing better to offer."

The hour was past the high of noon as Blake followed on the heels of a party drifting out of the show room on the lowest floor of the Allowed Merchants' house. There were guards at the portal, but they had not prevented the entrance of wealthy merchants and nobles eager to look over the imports, nor did they appear to check too closely on those who left; the relaxed feeling of holiday apparently was at work already. The party from New Britain could do no trading on its own, of course, only through the intermediaries provided by the city guilds.

Once in the street, Blake paused to study the landmarks. He had a good quarter of the city to cross before reaching the wharves. One of the cars for hire might pick him up; best to walk on before trying that.

A man brushed past him, thrust something into his hand. Blake controlled his desire to look until he raised his hand as if to adjust his broad-brimmed hunter's hat: a feather, barred dark on light. Again he faced the dilemma of not being able to read what should have been a plain message. But at least he had not lost sight of the messenger, and since he was headed in the same direction, Blake followed him.

It began to seem that the messenger intended to be followed. He chose, or appeared to choose, open spaces in the crowd now and then, as if seeking to remain in Blake's sight. And they continued to walk in the general direction of the wharves.

No unengaged "for hire" vehicle passed. Blake watched the red turban of the man he trailed. His headgear resembled that worn by all household servants, save that there was no family crest plainly visible against the scarlet cloth. And the violent hue, so easy to spot, was not unusual in this city where bright colors were more the rule than the exception. As Blake watched, the man in the turban slipped out of the main stream of the passing crowd into a narrow space between two buildings. Reaching that point in turn, Blake hesitated. No warning from his private signal. Discretion dictated that he keep on to the wharf. He had only a feather in his hand and the suspicion that he had been deliberately guided. Suddenly that was enough to have him take one of those risks Lo Sige had foreseen. He went into the alley.

Windowless walls cast a slice of shadow in the sunny day. No sign of red turban, either. But there was a door in the passage, two of them: one at the end of the passage, the other halfway down the wall on Blake's right. His quarry might have used either and Blake did not propose to knock to find out.

He was about to turn back when there was movement in one of the shadowed doorways; the door was swinging in silent invitation. Blake waited for his inner warning, but that did not fire in direct alarm. Soft-footedly he walked the length of that dark strip to the now half-open door.

As he stepped inside he found himself facing the man from whom Thohtzin had taken the wheel during their river voyage.

"The Cuauhuehuetque." Though he wore civilian dress now he was still unmistakably a soldier by bearing as he flattened against the wall and jerked a thumb left along the narrow hall in which they now stood. Blake went, hearing behind him the sound of a bolt being shot. If he had walked into a trap, its first defenses were now sprung, but his warning was quiet and he did not look back.

He entered a storeroom filled with strange smells of food he could not identify; other odors floated in around another door. Beyond, there was the hum of muffled noise which suggested activity.

"Here."

The limited light did not hide the man rising from a seat on a box. Thohtzin indeed, but not as Blake had seen him last. His smart uniform had been exchanged for that of a private soldier from the north. And he wore the traces of face paint some of the frontier tribes affected, which helped mask his features. Instead of an officer's laser, a long knife, guarded by a bead-decorated sheath, rested across his thigh. For a moment or two he studied Blake and then nodded.

"Clever enough, if you do not talk to the wrong man. This day will find more of your chosen disguise in Xomatl than normally walk her streets. Yes, it will serve very well."

"For what?" asked Blake and then wondered if such a question had been wise.

"There is trouble." Thohtzin plunged in at once. "The eyes and ears on the riverboat. One of them reported your mishap, but said you died in the river. With your return—and do not doubt that has already been reported, too—there will be questions asked. But time is against them, even as it hampers us. That forked-tongue frog,

Otorongo, is croaking again. He has been experimenting with the Sacred Smoke. Sacred Smoke!" Thohtzin spat the words. "We are no longer ignorant believers in all the priests tell us. A man using that sees, not visions sent by the gods who died when men ceased to believe in them, but fancies buried in his own mind, which, when he prates them to the recording priests, can be twisted in any fashion the listener chooses to set them. But once a man becomes caught in those murky 'mysteries,' then he is ripe for any suggestion whispered into his ears. Otorongo has always been a seeker of new sensations, or old ones he has not yet tasted. Since he has begun to drink smoke, he is drawn to some better forgotten, and he cannot be trusted."

"Thus?" Blake prompted as the other paused.

"Thus it is best that he no longer be allowed possession of the girl."

"You will take her away?"

Thohtzin shook his head. "No. You shall."

"Why? And how?"

"Why? Because she is rightfully the possession of those who would bargain for us, as they have told us since they first hid her here. And since you speak for them, you can also see that she must not be risked before her usefulness to us is past. And how? That shall also be your doing—in part. Otorongo throws open his garden this afternoon to the people of the city. Since it is the end of *Xiuhlolpilli*, he is minded to make a great gesture to amaze men more than anything else he has done before. He would allow his pleasure garden, the outer one, to be ravaged, devastated, before building it anew. All in the city are bidden to rob him of any treasure growing there. You will be there two hours before sunset. Slip over the wall before the gates are thrown open. Once in, you must cross to the inner way leading to the pleasure garden for those in the house of women. For the rest," Thohtzin smiled grimly, "it will be your doing. Those of the household keeping watch on the girl will have their drink spiced with new herbs, this is all I can promise you."

Blake could hardly believe this stroke of luck. He mistrusted it as being too easy. Yet . . .

"Something else," he watched Thohtzin closely, "we will need a way of escape. The Merchants' house will be suspect—"

"Otorongo cannot accuse anyone without dirtying his own shield."

"You think he will accept her disappearance without a fight?"

Thohtzin grinned. "That depends upon the mood he is in, how far he will go. What do you want?"

"A boat—say, one like your cruiser—to get away."

"To go where?" The grin disappeared. Thohtzin once more was grim under his paint.

"You name the destination, send your own guards if you will," Blake offered. Given so much of a chance, he did not doubt the efficiency of the wardsmen in making use of opportunity.

"I will have to consult my superior concerning that."

"What did you have in mind?" Blake asked and then added, "It would be very easy for Otorongo's guards to deal with us both, would it not? His prisoner, since he could no longer keep her, and the stranger who strove to steal her?"

"Well thought!" Thohtzin applauded. "Only you forget this, the girl is still necessary to our plans. Not so necessary that my superior dares reveal his identity in order to bring her forth by his own men, but enough so that we will not leave her to Otorongo's caprices. There will be someone waiting outside the gates to see you safely away from Otorongo's estate."

"To the river?"

"I make no promises," Thohtzin replied firmly. "Discuss it with your superiors. If you agree, give the hawk's feather you already hold to the guard at the warehouse in an hour's time."

"Agreed," Blake said at once.

He threaded his way back through the thronged streets, waited for another party to enter the show rooms and followed with them. Lo Sige was in charge of the display, and Blake caught his eyes as he moved behind a screen and so into the interior where he sped upstairs to their living quarters.

Marfy, wearing her merchant clothing, sat at the table there, industriously recording, by the New Britain method of a finger-key machine, the data Varlt dictated.

"What happened?" she demanded eagerly when she sighted Blake.

With some editing, omitting the hinted danger to her sister, Blake told them what he had learned from Thohtzin.

"We can get her out easily!" Marfy was out of her seat, her face lighted. "I can call her, she will come. You will not even have to enter that portion of the palace! Oh, this will be easy, Com, it will!"

"You can contact her, let her know that I am coming—"

"That we are coming," she corrected Blake sharply.

"That is impossible! Women here do not roam freely, except to travel to the docks for departure—" Blake began.

"Therefore, I shall be another hunter like you. I tell you, Blake Walker, only I can bring Marva out. But—oh! he does not know—" She looked to Varlt.

"She has not been able to reach her sister to any extent," the master wardsman explained. "We suspect that they have been keeping Marva under some type of drug control."

"Then how would your going to Otorongo's be of any aid?" Blake wanted to know.

"Because the closer I am to her, the better chance I have of reaching her. And if I cannot rouse her enough to bring her to the gate, I can guide us directly to her. Do you want to have to search the women's quarters?"

To Blake's dismay Varlt nodded approval. Before he could protest, the master wardsman said, "Lo Sige will go with you. Kragon and Laffy will also follow, under cover. You will be armed with these." He went to one of the traveling chests in the room, threw up its heavy lid, and then manipulated the underside of that until a panel slid open and Blake saw four hand weapons set into a hollow. In shape they were similar to the regulation needler, but much smaller. Wrapping a cloth about his hand, Varlt freed one from its bed and held it out to Blake.

"A new type of needler, shoots a ray instead of a dart. But it is limited by the fact it can carry only six loads. Hold it in your hand, close your fingers on it."

When Blake curled his fingers about the tiny weapon, he discovered that the originally cool substance of its material warmed. He held it so for a long moment and when he released his grip, he discovered that the silvery sheen of its surface had vanished. It was hardly distinguishable from the flesh holding it.

"Now it is sealed to you. If anyone else touches it, it will explode.

However, remember you have only six charges; it cannot be reloaded."

"Where—" Blake marveled at the weapon he had not known existed.

"These are experimental, the only ones of their kind so far. Rogan supplied them—against orders I might add. And each of them costs a small fortune."

A hand shot past Varlt, grasped the second of the four guns. Marfy's fist was not quite large enough to engulf the weapon completely, but Blake saw it changing color as it adjusted to her and her alone. Varlt moved, but the damage was already done.

"I tell you," she said defiantly, "you cannot get Marva out of there without me."

"Unfortunately," Varlt said coldly, "you are probably right. Your mental tie will help. But remember this, girl, throughout the operation orders will come from Walker; you are to depend upon his judgment or that of Lo Sige. I want your oath on that."

Marfy looked from the master wardsman to Blake and then back again. "To put ties on one going into such action is a dangerous thing, Com Varlt."

"You are under wardsman's discipline now, Marfy. And in this, Walker is your senior. He is expected; therefore he must appear there. Were it possible, I would be in his place. Lo Sige may have to take cover if he is suspected by those who will pass Blake. Thus, Walker leads and you listen to him. Understand?"

She nodded acceptance, though Blake believed she still had reservations. He himself had no liking at all for her company in the face of danger.

The hawk's feather passed them through the warehouse door and Blake breathed a little freer when, in disguise, they were on the street. Kragon and Laffy would use their own methods for following.

Outside, the crowds were thicker, and the three kept close together. There was no transportation to be had; every public conveyance that passed was full. So they walked to the borders of Otorongo's estate.

They found a spot behind a masking growth of brush and Lo Sige set his back against the wall. Blake mounted this human ladder and crouched at the top of the wall to look down into a paradise of flowers, trees, and cunningly devised vistas. He reached down and caught Marfy's hands, drew her and then Lo Sige up beside him. Then the three slid down behind a tangle of flowering vine.

Chapter Thirteen

"But why would anyone want to destroy all this?" marveled Marfy as they sought cover among ornamental shrubs, weird rock formations, and other embellishments of a garden which was a carefully tended work of art.

"A matter of prestige," returned Lo Sige. "To allow this to be broken up for the cycle celebrations advances Otorongo to the top listing of those making grand gestures. He probably thrives on such attention. What—"

Blake froze. One hand warned the others while he listened, though he depended more on his inner alert than his ears. He moved in a leap which brought him half way around, facing left. There was time for a snap shot at the furred thunderbolt aimed at him from under a trellised vine. That snarling fury struck full against his body and sent him sprawling, but the claws did not rip. By the time they both reached the ground, the jaguar was a limp weight from under which Blake edged free. One of his six shots was gone—he must keep that in mind.

Marfy shivered as she gazed down at the unconscious animal, and then, more fearfully, at the many hiding places about them that could hide similar surprises. Lo Sige pulled Blake to his feet.

"Wonder how many of those house cats are running loose here. Not that we shall take the time to count—"

"Listen!" Marfy's order was not needed. They could all hear

clearly the throbbing steady beat of drums, coming from the interior of the palace.

Lo Sige pushed ahead. They must still keep to cover, but now they must also make sure that the cover did not shelter more spotted hunters. Another wall of white stone embellished with heavy carving, the top being a conventionalized serpent with scales in heavy relief, now loomed before them.

"This is it. Now to find a gate." Blake put his hands on the surface of the barrier. Right or left? Marfy joined him, her palms also sliding along the stone. Now she turned abruptly to the right. Lo Sige watched her for a moment and then signed to Blake to follow her lead.

They were in a narrow space between the wall which was their guide and another erection of very intricately carved stone that acted as a screen between the garden and the wall. Some of the carving was pierced through so that they caught glimpses of foliage and flowers. Several yards they went before finding the door, or a door, in the wall. It was circular, deeply recessed, the portal closed, with no visible latch on their side.

Marfy turned, stood now with her hands tight against the surface of the closed door. Her eyes were shut. When Blake would have put her aside to try the door, Lo Sige caught his arm and held him back, shaking his head emphatically, as if breaking Marfy's concentration would be grave error.

Blake motioned to the wall, urging that he be given a boost up to look beyond. The other wardsman planted his shoulders as he had before, and Blake, so supported, gripped the deeply graven scales, and pulled himself up to the top. If he was now under observation from the house his dark body against the white stone would provide an excellent target.

Beyond lay a second garden, as elaborate as the first. Two long cages of fine wire mesh enclosed a number of trees and a goodly expanse of space. And within them fluttered and sang a wealth of brightly plumaged birds. But it was the door below which riveted his attention. From all appearances, it was no real door but a sealed exit no longer in use. Moreover, on the inner garden side, a bench had been set within the recess, making it a sheltered resting place for strollers.

A soft hiss brought Blake's attention back to Lo Sige. The other wardsman pointed to Marfy. She no longer stood pressed to the unopenable door but was backing from it step by step. Her right hand had gone to her head, fingertips tight to her forehead. Her eyes were still closed, her whole expression one of deep concentration. However, her left hand moved in slow, almost languid gestures toward the sealed door.

Blake looked into the other garden. There was an open path running between the bird cages; only here by the wall was there any cover. Otorongo might throw open his main garden to be despoiled in a grand gesture, but certainly he would only the more strongly protect the inner apartments of his own household.

Gripping the stone scales, Blake swung over and dropped. They must have very little time left before the crowd stormed in. That throng might afford them cover if they could locate Marva and bring her out of this second garden.

The aviary path led right and left, the bulk of the inner palace to the left. Again—danger!

Blake crouched, his stunner ready. A rustle . . . the creeping of another jaguar? His back was to the chill stone of the wall as he sifted every shadow, every suggestion of hiding place. But padded feet equipped with claws did not now steal upon him. The flicker of movement lay closer to ground level than any of the great cats could flatten its body. Blake saw beads of pitiless reptilian eyes, the lift of a spade-shaped head. And he fired, moved by all the revulsion of his species when faced by a snake.

The head went up and back in a twist, then the coils were still. Blake waited before he dared to inspect his victim more closely. A snake, yes, and probably a deadly one. But banded about its whip-like body immediately below the head was a metal ring from which glittered gem beads as cold as the eyes had been. This snake was no wild creature but one of the recognized inhabitants of the palace.

Another soft hiss. Blake raised his head. Lo Sige lay belly down on the wall above. He made a vigorous gesture towards the palace and his lips shaped words so exaggeratedly that Blake was able to catch the meaning: "Wait . . . watch . . ."

Save for the twittering birds, the garden appeared deserted. Blake could see a terrace across the front of the building, or rather a portion of its length, for trees made a screen in between. No guards stood at the doors, no servants showed; the palace might have been uninhabited.

He became aware of a murmur in the air, a distant hum. The sound must have reached and affected the birds even before he was conscious of it, for they called and some began to flutter about as if disturbed. The crowd, come to pick clean Otorongo's growing treasure, gathered beyond the outer wall.

"Look!" Again that mouthing from Lo Sige.

Movement on the terrace. Someone running down the steps, down the aviary path, running and sobbing.

Blake waited by the bench at the sealed door. A girl burst into the open and came towards him, her eyes wide, yet unseeing. If he had not caught her, she would have gone straight on to slam against the sealed door. And as he held her, she fought him, not as if she knew someone held her, but for her freedom, straining against his strength to reach the door.

It was like trying to control one of the big cats, because, as Blake struggled to hold her, she turned and raked him with her nails in a frenzy beyond any human fighting. Lo Sige leaped down, caught up one end of her cloak and whipped the material about her upper arms, pinning them to her body. And all the time her eyes were wide, unseeing, while tears trickled from them and sobs shook her.

Between them they got her up and over the wall, although Blake thought that any moment her violent struggles would alert any guard Otorongo had stationed nearby. But when they had dropped her onto the other side, she was suddenly quiet. Marfy came running, her hands outstretched, to catch her in close embrace. A second later she backed away from her sister and stared at the girl who subsided limply to the ground. Marfy had a haunted, frightened look in her eyes.

"She . . . she . . ."

Lo Sige caught Marfy by the shoulder, drew her away from her sister.

"Drugs, or some kind of induced block," he said sharply. "Take off her skirt!"

Marva was wearing a long skirt, brightly embroidered. The cloak they had twisted about her was more sober of hue, a dusky violet shade, and its only ornamentation was a band of feather work in blue and gold. Lo Sige caught at the drooping branch of a vine on the screen of carved stone. He tore portions from it. The flowers it supported gave off a heavy scent as he bruised and crushed them.

"Wait!" Blake caught his plan. Now he rounded the screen, reaching for the main roots of the vine Lo Sige had stripped. Recklessly he tore long lianas loose, choosing those with the heaviest burden of flowers, and tossed them over the screen. The natives' love of flowers, their delight in those most highly scented, would prove valuable now.

The clamor beyond the outer gates was a rising fury of sound; now separate shouts and cries could be detected. Then came a vast roar—the gates must have been thrown open! Given time, only a small portion of time, and they might get safely away.

Blake dodged once more behind the screen to aid Lo Sige. Marva, securely wrapped in the violet cloak, still lay unheeding of those about her. Her staring eyes were closed and she might have been asleep. Back and forth around her body Lo Sige was weaving the mass of flowered vine, while Marfy ranged at either side, snatching at any flower she could see, pulling them up roots and all, weaving her loot into any opening left by Lo Sige's hasty efforts.

In the end they had a bundle of vegetation which appeared to be a collection of flowers, most of them cherished rarities. A sapling thrust through the vines lengthwise provided handholds, and the men swung the bundle up between them. The shouting and singing in the garden was coming nearer. They waited at the edge of the screen until the first of the flower hunters burst into view. Men and women both, mainly of the peasant class, carried baskets or crocks or bowls; they were after not only the flowers but their roots. Several men, working together, were more ambitious; they carried spades and began uprooting small trees and tall shrubs. No, in that company the strangers were not going to be marked.

Marfy had turned her sister's skirt inside out, thus hiding the rich embroidery. Now she thrust some bulb flowers into that, fashioning a sack which she flung over one shoulder, keeping her back slightly bent under the burden and her face hidden.

"Time to go!"

Blake did not need Lo Sige's suggestion. He was already moving out. Around them the workers were far too intent on their own spoils to really notice them. One or two glanced up briefly before returning to their digging.

Slow . . . they must take it slow, no matter how much they wanted to run for the outer gate. If any guards lingered there, they must not be given the chance to wonder how this party had managed to do its looting in so short a time.

They delayed by setting their burden down at intervals. Once or twice they were questioned by some of the other looters, but Lo Sige called out slurred answers, as if they were half drunk, and the questioners shrugged or laughed.

"By the gate!" Marfy caught up with Lo Sige and gave her warning in a low voice.

By the gate indeed! It would seem that Otorongo was tasting a new sensation to the full. He was not only on hand to witness the rape of his famous pleasure grounds, he had also invited guests, or at least most of his household, to join him as spectators. By the main gate through which the looters still came, a platform was erected, with an awning canopy overhead and seats. There were the scarlets of dress uniforms, as well as the bright colors of civilian dress. Servants passed food and drink, and some of Otorongo's guests appeared to be laying wagers. All showed interest in the trickle of looters already leaving, sometimes shouting to them an order to display their finds.

"We cannot—" Marfy began.

"We have to!" Lo Sige replied. "Play tipsy, but not too drunk. And you," he ordered Marfy, "get ahead of us. If there is any trouble, run for it."

Blake picked out the man he believed to be Otorongo. He was tall and lean, wearing a very elaborate shirt which a feather cloak half hid. His boots were latched with a noble's turquoises, and his head-dress was an upstanding circlet of feathers of the same hue. He was old-fashioned enough to effect heavy earrings which dragged the lobes of his ears well out of shape.

On his harsh Aztec features was an expression of contemptuous amusement, awakening to animation only now and then when the man on his left made some remark. That one wore the dull black cloak Blake knew was the mark of the priesthood. But he did not have the wild locks of hair, the face burned by fanatic asceticism which had marked the priest of the river holding.

"Now, let us go," Lo Sige said in a low voice.

Blake waited for his private warning. There was no immediate alert. So perhaps they were going to get away with this reckless play after all. He followed Lo Sige's lead in a wavering progress toward the gate. Those on the platform were now occupied with choosing from some trays of fruit and small cakes. Other servants filled any waiting cup.

"Ay-yi-yi-yi," Lo Sige sang. His expression was that of a man enveloped in the bliss of realizing a dream.

Blake dared not attempt song, but with what small skill he possessed, he schooled his mien to match his companion's. And Marfy—Marfy was laughing, patting her improvised bag of flowers and roots.

She was safely by the platform . . . they were almost by . . .

"Ho!" The call was imperative, the words which followed it Blake did not understand.

"Walker," Lo Sige ordered in a low voice, "create a diversion. Quick!"

Blake looked up. One of the army officers was leaning over the rail of the platform beckoning to them imperiously. Behind him was Otorongo, eyes upon them.

Create a diversion? Blake rested the carrying pole on his left shoulder, steadied by his left hand. He raised his right now in the salute he had seen the lower castes use in the city. But from that hand his stunner fired. By luck, Otorongo had turned to answer some query of the priest. Now he slumped forward, caught at the rail of the platform. The officer, startled, turned just in time to catch him.

"Go!"

They were outside the gate before Blake had time to think, pushing through the crowd. It would seem that those wishing to strip the gardens were only admitted by numbers and a second group was about to enter.

Another flower-bearing party was just ahead and Lo Sige and Blake quickened step to add themselves to the tail of that procession. Thohtzin had promised assistance outside the wall. Suddenly, in spite of his distrust of the Imperial officer, Blake wanted very much to sight him. But they were still marching along behind the other party, fearfully listening for any sound of pursuit. Some quick wit on that platform might guess their connection with Otorongo's collapse if their luck ran out.

A small van stood in a side street, one of the closed, shuttered vehicles Blake now knew were used to transport ladies of noble households. This one, however, bore no family crest and was shabby, needing paint and heavily coated with dust. Its back doors opened and the soldier-messenger of Thohtzin beckoned to them.

For a moment they hesitated. To accept aid arranged by the other side might be merely postponing disaster for a bit. But to tramp on through the streets with their very conspicuous burden was to ask for attention they dared not attract. They turned, Marfy with them, and laid their vine-wrapped burden inside.

"Where do we go?" Blake asked.

"Where you wish," the man answered. "But in—in! We cannot wait. Too many have seen and of those some will remember. We must now lay a false trail."

Over his shoulder Blake saw Lo Sige nod. The other wardsman was already boosting Marfy in. As Blake entered, the doors were slammed with an emphatic click, and when he set his shoulder against them, he found them secured from without.

"Krogan was out there." Lo Sige's hand fell on Blake's arm, his voice a low whisper. "We shall be traced if they try anything. And he was right about too many people seeing us. If they can baffle the pack of hounds after us, should we protest? Now, let us get the lady out of her wrappings."

In the shuttered interior of the car the scent of flowers was thick, almost stupefying. They tore at the vines and leaves, pulling Marva out of her aromatic cocoon and bracing her up on one of the seats close to the slits which gave a fraction of fresh air. Marfy sat beside her, supporting her sister. Her twin's head lolled on her shoulder much as if Marva had been the target of one of the stunners.

"How is she?" Lo Sige demanded.

Marfy shook her head. "I reached her, enough to bring her to us at the wall. But now—it is as if she has gone away. What have they done to her?"

"Thohtzin said they would drug those who guarded her," Blake supplied. "Maybe she had some, too."

"Keep trying," Lo Sige urged Marfy. "We need her awake. There may be a need for her to help herself."

"What else would I be doing?" she snapped in return. "Where are they taking us now?"

Blake moved to one of the other seats and knelt there as he leaned against the wall of the van, striving to glimpse what lay outside the narrow window slits. These were almost closed and he could see nothing of any use. They were being driven at a slow pace, at the limited speed necessary on a crowded city thoroughfare. Twice they turned corners and now they were picking up speed. Also, whatever road the vehicle followed was certainly not as smooth as it had been earlier.

"We are not going back into the city." Blake was sure enough of that to voice his belief.

Lo Sige went to the front of the van. In the wall between the interior and the driver's seat was a closed hatch through which the passengers must have given orders. The wardsman tried to push that aside, but it did not move.

A moan drew their attention back to Marva. The sobbing that had shaken her earlier now returned as a gasping, as if she strove to fill laboring lungs with air. Lo Sige came quickly, held her head to the van wall at one of the air slits.

"Marva!" Marty's hold on her sister tightened. She looked to the wardsmen. "She believes she is dreaming."

"Can you take her under control?"

Blake searched through the debris of roots and vines on the floor and came up with a section of tough root. Using force he pushed it through one of the air slits, pried the shutter back, and then passed his improvised tool to Lo Sige who followed his example on the other side of the van. Green, the heavy green of solid woodland, slipped past them at a speed which, because of their limited range of vision, gave them little chance to see more. Blake could hardly believe that such a dense forest could exist so close to a city; it was as if they were boring into the wilds.

Chapter Fouteen

"The hunting range . . ." Lo Sige made tentative identification.

"And that is . . ." Blake asked.

"A strip of wild land preserved for ceremonial hunting. It was marked on the city maps. But if we are heading into that, we are going directly away from the river—"

"To where?" Marfy looked up from her sister.

"We have yet to find out," Lo Sige replied, a bit absently.

By the swaying and bumping of the car they knew that the road must be rapidly deteriorating. And the green approached the van until they could hear the brushing of branches against its body. Of necessity, their progress had slowed. Finally the van stopped. Blake tapped Lo Sige's shoulder.

"I stun the driver and whoever is with him with this. We take over the van . . . back to the city . . ."

"Possible—" the other wardsman agreed.

"Ahhhh-eeee!" Marva threw herself forward, out of Marfy's grasp, sprawling against the forward seat. At the same instant her sister clapped her hands to her head with a similar cry of protest and pain. And Lo Sige staggered like a man who had been struck from behind. Blake felt that mental blow, too. This was no inept, groping mind exploration such as he had been subjected to while a prisoner at the river lord's holding; it was a practiced probe, aimed at taking over minds with talent and training at Vroom level.

Lo Sige twisted, his face a mask of horror and struggle, his lips flattened against his teeth in a tortured, animal snarl. Only his eyes went to Blake. The younger man's shield held as it always had. But that very protection might warn the one who was losing those bolts that he had here an opponent who could not be controlled.

Inch by inch, unable to resist, Lo Sige was drawn to the rear door of the van. Behind him came Marva, crawling on her hands and knees, still moaning. And then Marfy staggered, keeping her feet with difficulty.

Blake jumped to the left. He could hear a fumbling at the back latch. Whoever was out there would not be prepared for trouble unless he knew of Blake's resistance. The warning—yes, that was rising in him, too—was not yet foretelling instant action.

The van door opened and Lo Sige lurched through, his movements jerky, as if not he but another's will moved his limbs. Marva rolled rather than crawled into the open, and Marfy wavered. Blake kicked at the mass of green stuff on the floor. A hand grasped inward as if to capture someone lying there. Blake fired the stunner and flung himself to the opposite side of the van for a wider range of vision.

The man he had rayed staggered back, tripped over a recumbent figure on the ground and fell. Blake fired again at the other still on his feet. One shot now—just one left! Marfy was armed and so was Lo Sige, but only they could use those weapons.

As his second victim went down, Blake saw Lo Sige and Marfy stoop, still moving in that jerky, mindless way, to raise Marva. Together the three began to stumble off away from the van. Blake edged out cautiously. Two men, Thohtzin's messenger and another, lay unconscious. Trees and shrubs walled in the vehicle and the roughest of tracks marked their back trail. But the three under compulsion were rounding the car, apparently about to vanish into the wilderness ahead.

One Blake might have managed to deter, but three he could not stop by physical means. Manifestly they were being led by mental control to some definite goal. And it could not be too far away, for such control could not operate over a lengthy distance. That meant that whoever exercised it was to be found nearby. And since this was a power out of Vroom, perhaps this was the meeting with the real enemy at long last. Whether he faced a trained adept or not. Blake might be able to use his last shot, providing he could get within firing distance. He fell in behind the staggering trio, alert to every noise, prepared to rely on his personal warning.

The track had been a road to this point. Now it was a path, likely once only a game trail. There had been recent attempts to open it, marked by slashed-back vegetation. But the shadows of twilight were gathering fast and Blake found it increasingly difficult to see ahead. They came out at last on the gravel bed of a summer-shrunken riverlet. The water was a thread in the middle of a wide expanse over which the three from Vroom wavered upstream.

Blake followed after, counterfeiting, now that he was in the open and might be under observation, the uncertain steps of those he trailed. They rounded a bend in the river and before them the twilight dimness was broken by light, not the bright and honest yellow of a fire nor even the colorful beams of this level's lamps, but a blue glimmer which not only hinted of the alien but carried sinister suggestion.

And now—Blake knew! Before them waited the spider who had woven this web, or at least the greatest menace present. There was an aura of satisfaction, of triumph which Blake could feel as well as if he heard it shouted aloud. Whoever awaited them had no doubts at all concerning his complete victory. But, why had he not realized that, in Blake, he had met a securely blocked mind? Or did he not care, believing that since he controlled three, he did not have to worry about the fourth? That meant that he might have other methods besides mental takeover of coping with potential opponents.

The building they approached was artfully camouflaged. Had it not been for the open windows and the light, Blake would not have marked it; the rough stone of its walls might well have been natural extensions of the river bank, and the brush planted on its low roof carried out the illusion of its being part of the earth.

All three controlled captives made straight for the door which was standing open. Blake dropped behind a waterworn rock. There was nothing he could do to help them by walking straight into a trap. He had only one small advantage, a chance to use effectively the shot still remaining in his stunner. If that mental force could be diverted or broken, even for an instant, he would have Lo Sige's aid also.

In the concealed hut the enemy was very confident. Not for the first time Blake longed for a share of the talents of Vroom. Any one of the wardsmen he knew could have learned the number of occupants inside and so been prepared for action. But if Blake had that power, he would also be subject to mind control; he would now be walking as blindly as the other three into that door.

The blue light appeared to conceal more than reveal. The three were silhouetted against it and then vanished as they entered. They might have pushed through a curtain. Blake waited. If the enemy had expected four to enter, there should follow some move to gather the missing one in.

What he waited for came, a blast of mind-force designed to blind, deafen, completely drive identity out of a man. Blake made his decision in that instant: to allow them to think that they had him.

He staggered out from behind the rock, lurched toward the cabin, trusting his performance was realistic enough to deceive for the few moments it would take him to get within firing distance. He came to the door, the blue light curled about his body as if it were a part of that sucking force.

The light was a fog through which he could catch only mist-blurred glimpses of objects; three shadows, one standing, the other two on the floor. Those were Lo Sige and the girls. But Blake could see no one else.

"On!" The command beat at them all.

Lo Sige stooped, lifted one of the girls with infinite labor. The other crawled ahead on hands and knees, by herself. Blake, striving to see through the confusing mist, followed lest he lose touch.

There! The warning came as sharply as it had back in the garden. Right there! But Blake could see no target. Lo Sige wavered back and forth between him and that unseen focus of force.

A barrier—in it another open door.

The warning was so acute now that Blake threw himself forward, passing beyond the blue mist into natural illumination. He avoided falling over a prone body, caught his balance, and faced the man in a cushioned seat, a man who was staring at him with an expression of complete shock. In that instant Blake fired straight into his face, letting the brain behind it have the full force of the stunray.

He heard the clang of metal against metal and then was thrown from his feet. The whole floor under him vibrated. Pushing up again, he could see the stranger. The man was slipping limply down, but one hand lay on an instrument board. That panel—it was familiar—

Blake felt the rack of time-dislocation. They were in an outlaw shuttle! And he had no idea of where they were bound or if they had any true destination at all, since that useless hand on the controls might only have sent them spinning out at random.

"What—"

Blake was making for the control seat, although of what he might do, either to halt their trip or to bring them to any level, he had no idea. It was instinct alone that made him try to do something—anything. He looked back at the sound of the other voice.

Lo Sige must have fallen when they took off. Now he braced himself up by his arms, looking about him as might a man slowly coming out of a nightmare-ridden sleep.

Blake was at the control panel, pulling the unconscious pilot away and rolling his body to the other side of the cabin. This shuttle had few of the fittings usual in those of the wardsmen. He went back to the board. A survey of the dials told him one precious fact: they were on a set course, not roaming wildly across worlds with no hope of lighting. But what course that might be and where it would land them only the man he had stunned could answer.

"Hopping?" Lo Sige had staggered after him. He, too, leaned forward to read the dials. "Hopping," he repeated and then shook his head, not in denial but in an attempt to clear his befogged thinking.

Marfy moaned and sat up, her hands pressed to her head. She retched dryly and shivered. But when she looked around, there was the light of reason in her eyes.

Blake explored the cabin. Although it was bare of the usual equipment, he hoped to find a first-aid kit with the stimulants they needed. And in a cubby he came upon the survival kit which he knew no level-hopper dared be without.

One of the tablets he mouthed himself, the rest he passed to Lo Sige who followed his example. Marfy had a third, but when she would have put one between Marva's lips, Lo Sige shook his head.

"We do not know what drugs she has been given. Better leave her alone and see if she can come out of it naturally." He went to kneel by the stranger, studying the slack face. "No one I know—"

"But I do!" Marfy joined him. "That is Garglos!"

"The Project 'copter pilot?" Blake had to reach back for that memory, it seemed so far in the past. The beginning of this venture was already dimmed by all that had happened since.

"Power to the tenth—he must have that to have been able to take over and hold all three of us," Lo Sige commented. "Why should he be acting as a 'copter pilot on a project?" Then he hastened to answer his own question. "Just a cover, perhaps. But why? Well, he should be able to answer that himself."

"When he comes to," asked Blake, "will you be able to blank against him?"

"Not without some aids we do not possess at present. If and when he recovers consciousness, he will have to be put under again at once!"

"I have used up my stunner charges," Blake announced.

Lo Sige put his hand to the sash belt about his middle, confidently at first, then searching, his fingers running swiftly between the band and his body. He looked up, astonishment more nakedly revealed on his face than Blake had ever seen it.

"Gone!"

"Yours?" Blake asked of Marfy.

Her hand went within the wider sleeve of her shirt.

"Gone!"

"But how?"

"Neat." Lo Sige regarded Garglos bleakly. "We were, without doubt, ordered to disarm ourselves on the way here, and we did so. We have one chance unless you can be sure of knocking him out at once at the first signs of his stirring. That is to get away from the shuttle the moment we are on level. I do not know how much range his control has. Did we come very far from the van?"

"I had no way of measuring it; it seemed a good distance to me," Blake replied.

"So we cannot risk just guessing. And we have to take him in!"

Lo Sige was overly optimistic, Blake thought, though he did not say that. There was no reason to believe that they would have any advantage when they reached the end of this wild voyage across time. If they were headed for Vroom, there was an excellent chance they would open the cabin door on more trouble than they could hope to handle.

"Are we going to Vroom?" It was Marfy's turn to inspect the dials.

"I do not think so." Lo Sige sat down crosslegged on the floor of the cabin. "He brought us here to him. He had a travel code set up and waiting, all prepared to hop and take us along. But I hardly think he was bound for Vroom. In the first place, your father, aware there is probably an outlaw shuttle in action, will have detectors in use. They can and will trace any crosstime-hopping near our own world or on regular lines of travel, and they will be prepared to counter such action. My guess is we are now on our way to another hideout, one that the mind behind all this believes is high security."

"An empty world," Blake said.

"Why?"

"That would be the highest security, would it not? No native population to become involved or suspicious."

"Plausible and probable. But there is more than one 'empty' level. Meanwhile . . ." Lo Sige rose and began searching the clothing of the unconscious Garglos. "No weapons. He was sure, very sure, of himself, it would seem. In fact, there is nothing to give us a clue as to our destination. Marfy, is there any chance now of getting through to your sister? Of picking up some impression? She may have the answer or a portion of it if she went to the New Britain world with Garglos."

"No. It is like trying to patch together many small pieces of something that has been smashed to bits. Will—will she continue to be like this?" Marfy gazed at Lo Sige in entreaty.

There was no ready answer from the wardsman. If he had wanted to give her some soothing denial, he could not. Marfy would have known that for deception. So when he remained silent, she stared beyond him at the bare wall of the shuttle cabin.

"There is this," he said gently a moment or two later, "this present confusion may be born of the drug plus Garglos' control. She may come out of it naturally as one awakes from a fever sleep. Otherwise, back in Vroom they will have the necessary treatment. Only, if the need arises, can you handle her? Use control?"

"I can try." Marfy did not sound very hopeful. Her attention appeared to be turned inward, concerned with her own feelings or her abiding fears for her sister.

Warning signal on the board. Blake swept her down to the floor where he lay between her and the inert Marva, his arms outflung across them both in place of the steadying belts. The dizzy spin of a level breakthrough was, he speedily discovered, far worse in this position then when one occupied the usual seat.

At least they could be sure they were not to emerge in Vroom: the interval between their take-off and arrival was not right. Lo Sige was in the pilot's seat, watching the board. Then Blake's sense of equilibrium could not hold against the dislocation of level arrival, and he had to close his eyes, fight down his illness.

There was a shock which sent a shudder through the cabin. Wherever they now were, they had not arrived in a depot. But there was no movement as there had been in the sabotaged shuttle in the turtle world. Blake swallowed and sat up as Lo Sige snapped on the viewplate.

They looked out into a world of night where moonlight cut in sharp rays. Against a starred sky reared peaks of barren rock. And the limited scope of the screen showed them no more than that.

Marfy stirred, sitting up to brush her tangled hair out of her eyes.

"That—that looks like the Project world," she said slowly.

"Might well be." Lo Sige was out of his seat, making adjustments at the door lock. "No pressure suits needed according to the register, so it is livable. We had better do a little exploring. "You"—he nodded to Blake—"keep watch on him. I do not know how long he will stay unconscious. But I have no wish to march back here under his control."

Against his will, Blake recognized the sense in that. He watched the wardsman through the lock, and then stripped off his own sash belt, tearing it into strips. He might not be able to put Garglos' mind in bonds, which was what they really needed, but he could see that the ex-pilot was otherwise secured. Hoisting him into the seat, Blake made him fast there with knots over which he spent some time and care.

Marfy continued to watch the scene on the screen. They saw the shadow which was Lo Sige appear at one corner and go off again. The girl broke the silence first.

"Garglos must have been very sure of safety when he brought us here, sure that no one was going to cause him any trouble."

"How long could he hold you under full control?" Blake asked.

"I do not honestly know. He might not have much trouble with Marva as she now is. But Lo Sige and me—together we would not be easy to hold for long."

"Which means he expected help at this end. Someone connected with the Project?" Or, he added silently, a gang of his own out here in the wilderness. Either way Lo Sige, for all his training and ingenuity, might be walking straight into the arms of the enemy. Blake's only assurance was his own absence of inner warning.

He found it hard to keep still; he prowled around the small cabin, making sure every few moments that he checked on Garglos. But to all outward appearance their prisoner was still under the influence of the stunner. Was that a knock at the outer hatch? Lo Sige on his way back or—someone else? Blake crossed to put an ear to the wall . . .

Danger! Then a mind-stab, this time aimed at him and severe enough to make him reel. Hands caught at Blake's feet and ankles, dragging him down. He glimpsed Marva's upturned face, and her dull unfocused eyes. And over her head he saw the tenseness of the bound body in the seat. Garglos had struck. Marfy, too, sprang at Blake, a spitting fury, carrying him all the way down with her weight.

Chapter Fifteen

Both girls fought him on the floor, attempting to immobilize him. Garglos had not yet opened his eyes, but the fury of his mind-stab at Blake abated. The ex-pilot could not continue to hold that pitch and still keep the girls in action. This was no time for half measures. Blake strove to free an arm. He must knock Marfy out and quickly. But she was a clawing, raging fury and he had all he could do to protect his eyes from her raking nails. Marva lay across his legs, pinning them tight with her arms, human bonds from which he could not kick free.

The sound of the hatch opening, and a face loomed over Blake: Lo Sige, but the wardsman's face was blank of any intelligence. Blake saw, too, the blow aimed at him, felt sharp pain—then nothing at all.

Blake lay in a drift of rising snow and the chill of it seeped through his body so that his hands and his feet were numb. No, it was not snow and he did not feel a chill. He lay in ashes recently raked from a bed of coals, searing him with their heat. Beyond in a wild whirl danced Marfy and Marva together with Lo Sige, while Com Varlt pounded a huge drum. When they had done, they would take his heart to feed to the great tortoise that brooded on a rock well above the fiery bed on which Blake lay.

Boom—boom—ever the drum and the whirling figures of the dancers. Snow . . . ashes . . . snow . . . Swing through time, crosstime, world after world, and in none a place for him. So, when he reached the end of that swing, he would pitch on out of time forever and be lost in blackness without end. Swing . . . boom . . . swing . . . boom . . .

Blake thought he cried out then, but there was no answer to his incoherent appeal for help. The tortoise head turned and yellow, inhuman eyes regarded him without pity. Swing . . . boom . . .

The burning was inside him, not without. Snow—if he could scoop up some of the snow to put in his mouth. Blake strove to move his hands, to grasp the wet cool snow. Snow . . . ashes . . . No, now his hands rasped across a hard, unyielding surface.

No more drumming. He no longer saw anything save darkness. Then, slowly, he became aware that that existed under the cover of his own eyelids. But the burning was still a part of him, and he made feeble motions, seeking relief. Not the boom of the drums—no—but sounds—continuous sounds and with them an urgency that he did not understand but that made him restless. At last Blake forced open his eyes.

He looked up at a gray expanse which was not open sky, for it had corners and was upheld by walls of the same color. To turn his head cost effort, but he did it, and discovered he was not alone. The three who had whirled about him in frenzied dance lay there as if they had worn out life itself in their leaping. As he watched, Marfy moved feebly, rolled her head. Her eyes looked into his.

"Blake?"

His name was the thinnest of whispers but he heard it, and, oddly enough, so hearing gave him a fraction of strength. He stiffened his hands and arms against the rocks on which he lay, pushed up into a sitting position.

The sound was a moaning, coming from Marva and Lo Sige.

"Blake—water—" Marfy's whisper came a little louder and more demanding.

He looked about the room in which they lay. The surface of the floor was smoothed rock. But the walls he had seen before, at least their like, in the Project camp.

Camp . . . supplies . . . water . . . His thinking was slow and sluggish, but Blake fitted those three words together making sense. Door . . . out . . . water . . . Turning his head was a task which made appalling demands upon his small reserve of strength. There was a door, or the outline of one. He could not get to his feet, but he could crawl—

"Blake?" The whisper was now a low wail.

He paused, turned his head and refused to surrender to the dizziness that movement caused. His mouth seemed filled with the ash of his delirious dreaming. Somehow he croaked an answer.

"Water . . . go get water . . ."

"Water?" Marfy struggled to her hands and knees.

Blake resumed his all-fours progress towards the door. Once there he set his shoulder against it and put what force he could into an outward shove. But there was no give. He tried again and then beat upon it with his fists.

They were shut into this place. There was no way out! And the thought of water had aroused his thirst fourfold. Water—he must have water!

"No—no—" Marfy joined him. She caught at one of his beating hands, her fingers weakly encircling his wrist. "This way." She flattened his hand against that unyielding surface and moved it, not outward but to the right. This time the door obeyed, sliding into the wall.

They crawled into a corridor. This must be the Project base, but . . . Blake halted to listen. Not a sound, not even the hum of machinery. Down the hall another door stood open and across its threshold lay . . .

"Oh!" Marfy cowered back against Blake, clutching at his shoulder with fingers that dug into his flesh. He freed his arm and pushed her back against the wall.

"Stay here." He had seen death before in many guises and he did not doubt that he saw it again here and now.

It was a long journey down the length of the hall to reach the body. The head was turned from him, resting on an outflung forearm. Blake had to move it to see the face. And it was a face he knew. Sarfinian! Blake had served an apprentice run with the dead man, a wardsman tech responsible for shuttle and communication installations at the depots.

Blake glanced beyond the body into the room it guarded. Equipment, mostly for communication, now a mass of wreckage—deliberately done. Much of the wiring fused, delicate installations broken. Someone had made very sure that no one would again send a message from this point!

He edged to the wall, used it as a support to get to his feet. Then, leaning heavily against it, he staggered back to where Marfy crouched.

"Who?" she asked him as he reached down to try and draw her up beside him.

"A wardsman—a com tech. Do you know, is this the Project?"

"Yes!" She was still straining to look past him at the body.

"Where . . . supplies?" It was such an effort to keep his feet and hold the girl against him that Blake had little energy left for words.

Marfy turned her head slowly, looking up and down the corridor. "There"—she pointed to the opposite end—"think . . . through there . . ."

"Stay." For the second time Blake gave that order. It would be all he could do to get himself going; he could not support her, too. But when he lurched along against the wall, she followed, and he did not waste breath protesting.

Somehow he made it to the end of the hall where there was a larger room. And this one he recognized; it was the dining place where he had once made an uncomfortable meal under Kutur's eyes. There was a muddle of dishes on the table and close to him a half-filled cup of liquid.

Never had he tasted anything so good as that cold and bitter brew. He swallowed half of it in a gulp and nursed the rest. The sound of Marfy's stumbling progress was louder. Blake turned, holding on to the table as she crept into the room. Then he offered her the cup. She had slumped to the floor, sitting there with her back against the wall. Taking the cup with both her shaking hands, she got it to her mouth.

"More? For Marva . . . Lo Sige . . . more?"

Blake made a cautious circuit of the table, peering into the cups. Two of them did hold more than just dregs and he poured that bounty together. The plates had only dried remnants of food. But somewhere beyond must be the kitchen unit with more supplies. Blake carried the second cup to Marfy.

"Where is the supply room?"

"Kitchen unit through there." She tried to stop the shaking of her hands by pressing the cup hard against her.

Blake followed her directions. The kitchen unit was an efficiency one. One fed the packaged supplies into the proper slots, watched them emerge ready for consumption on use-trays and plates. But the cupboard above the preparation unit was open, its shelves bare; none of the raw materials remained.

And that was the way it was, he knew bleakly some time later. Water, yes, they had water. With a river of it outside, those who had abandoned them had seen no reason to deny them water. But food—there was no food. Just as there was no usable form of communication, nor shuttle, nor any sign of recent occupancy except the dead man guarding the wreckage.

Lo Sige now occupied the seat which once Kutur had filled. Marva, her hands and sometimes her body trembling beyond her power to control, was still given to short periods of blankness but at other times was almost restored to their world. Marfy and Blake shared the table that was bare of all they needed to restore them.

"This is it." The senior wardsman stared down at three small packets. Not food but sustain tablets, found after an agonizing search of the private quarters, each of which had the signs of hurried evacuation. Sustain tablets were not food. The energy they supplied would be false, burning out the user when there was no proper nourishment to take with them.

"The com?" Marva was in one of her alert periods. "Can we not repair the com?"

"You saw what had been done to it," Marfy reminded her gently.

"But we cannot just sit here and—and—"

"No. It is in our breed to keep on struggling," Lo Sige said. "But the com is useless."

Blake looked up. "You have an idea?" Almost his question seemed an accusation.

The other shrugged. "It is so wild a chance that we dare not pin any hope at all on its succeeding."

"But there is a chance," Marfy caught him up. "If there is any thing we can do?"

"Like what?" Blake strove to bring them back to cold reality.

"Perhaps it may be only supposition, but—" Lo Sige broke off abruptly and then added, "I do not think that there will be any search parties sent to hunt us. After what was done here, those responsible will try in every way to erase this base. However, though, they have destroyed the com, they have not destroyed the depot terminal."

"And what good is that without a shuttle?" Blake wanted to know.

"You mean—the thin wall of time?" Marfy stared at Lo Sige. "But—but that is only a superstition, is it not?" Her question carried a pleading to be denied.

"We have always considered it so," Lo Sige agreed. "But this is a time when we must seriously test that superstition."

The "thin wall of time"? Blake had a faint memory of those words—or others like them. A discussion . . . when . . . where . . . with whom? He could not remember now. His mind was still sluggish. But he could pick out of that hazy recall some facts. No, not facts, just surmises and guesses.

The depots of the crosstime ventures were regularly established points and many of them had been maintained in constant operation for generations. There was speculation that at such depots there was a kind of thinning of the barrier of time, that constant travel from level to level caused weak points. So far the theory was supposition only, the experimentation needed to prove or disprove it too much of a risk to the whole system to be allowed.

"But this Project has not been established very long," Blake objected. "The thinning must have time to work—if it does. There needs to be a long period of constant travel."

"That is only another supposition," Lo Sige replied. "And the Project has been established for some eighteen months. There has been fairly frequent contact: check visits, shipping in and out of personnel, supply trains making regular calls. It may not have had the heavy use of such depots as Argos or Kalabria, but it has had many visits."

"What can we do?" Blake had guessed at the other's purpose: to give the girls something to think about, to revive a thread of hope to keep them from going over the edge of sanity when the full despair of their situation struck. How long could one live without food? Longer than without water, he knew.

"We'll hunt in the com room for materials to build an amplifier." Lo Sige opened one package of sustain tablets. "One each of these." He spilled out the small pills.

"Amplifier for what?" Blake was willing to go along with the other's elaborate pretense, but he could not help asking questions.

"For our signal. Linked, and with an amplifier . . ." Lo Sige looked to Marfy and her sister.

"Do—do you really think we can do it?" Marfy responded.

"Anything is worth a try, is it not?" Lo Sige swallowed his tablet. "You have one strong point of reception: Erc Rogan. His mind is tuned to yours; he must be hunting you. So he will be in excellent receptive state."

"You mean," Blake tried to keep his instant incredulity out of his voice, "that you are going to try to think yourself out?" Insane! Surely Lo Sige did not mean that. And if the girls accepted his suggestion seriously, then he, Blake Walker, was the only one still mentally stable. Their experience under control by Garglos? Had that, could that, do this to a wardsman like Lo Sige? If Blake had been asked to list those among the corps whom he knew would be the last to crack under pressure, he would have chosen this man first. That might only prove that he was a bad judge of character. But then he had no idea how deeply the stress of mental take-over could penetrate, since he had never had his own natural protective barrier forced.

"You might term it that," the other continued, "loosely." He was smiling a little. "With an amplifier we might reach someone who was attuned closely to one of us—"

"Father!" Marva broke in. Again there was a flicker of intelligence in her face.

"But if a shuttle call only reaches for a few levels . . ." Blake began and then stopped. If this was a game for the benefit of the girls, why wreck it by argument? Let them go on believing as long as they could. "You know more about it than I do." He tried to make his tone hearty, as if he did accept such lunacy as fact. "I am the deaf and dumb man in this field, remember?"

Marfy smiled at him. "Do not underrate yourself."

"I am not likely to," he replied as he swallowed his tablet ration.

They faced the disaster that was the com room after they had carried the body of the wardsman into the quarters which had once been Kutur's and sealed the door. Blake ripped, unscrewed, sorted, under Lo Sige's direction, while the senior wardsman dealt in other ways with the spoil. At intervals Marfy aided first one and then the other. Marva spent most of the time stretched on coverings taken from the bunks and piled in a heap in the corridor. They all wanted to stay together, as if something lurked within the empty shell of the Project Headquarters which was only kept at bay by their remaining in company.

Twice Blake went to the river for water. The pens built by the Project showed the scars of the storm that had broken them during his first visit. Only one had been repaired, the machinery to deal with the others standing derelict in the open.

They had to rest often. Their energy came only from the tablets. The dull cramps of hunger, their weak and shaking hands, were ever-present warnings that their labors could continue only for a short time longer.

Day became night again. They crawled into the corridor, huddled on the bedding, and rested. Blake was not sure he slept. He thought that he must be having increasing periods of blackout. Once he awakened to find himself squatting on the floor of the com room, striving to free bits of unmelted wire from a slagged mass.

It was again day, maybe the next or another even later, when Lo Sige led a halting procession into the room that had been the terminal for the shuttles. Blake subsided against the wall, watching groggily as the other wardsman, working with infinite slowness and the utmost care, set down the weird contraption on which they had labored for so long, making sure of its position by much checking.

Lo Sige was determined to carry the farce clear through to the end, Blake thought dully. They would remain here from now on, getting weaker, at last sliding into unconsciousness and the final end. Perhaps never to be found. They had no way of knowing what was happening along the crosstime routes. And they would probably never know the real reason that lay behind all that had happened to them.

"It is right?" Marfy's eyes were huge. The stain and paint used in her disguise had faded, and her face was very thin and drawn.

Lo Sige raised himself from a last check that had necessitated his lying flat before the patchwork machine.

"As far as I can tell."

"Now?" She made the single word a question.

He took the remaining packet of tablets from his belt, opened it to let the white rounds roll out on his hand. Marfy crossed the room and came back, supporting her twin against her.

"Father," she was saying clearly into Marva's ear as they came. "Think of Father. Make a mind picture of him. Call . . ."

Her sister nodded. "Yes, I know."

Lo Sige handed each of the girls one of the pellets, held another toward Blake.

The latter shook his head. "You need them more." He did not, could not, believe that what they were going to try would save them. He was content to wait out the end without any more stimulants.

The three others sat by the machine now, linked hand in hand. Maybe they would be content, even happy, in their belief that they were doing something, making a concrete effort for survival. Blake was too tired to care any longer; he did not even envy them their capacity for hope.

Perhaps he dozed. Time, as it existed here, had no meaning. Blake only knew that whenever he opened his eyes, they were always there, heads sinking forward on their chests. And slowly he came to believe that they were already gone, that only their discarded bodies were still present.

It was raining again. The battering of a heavy fall of water pounded on the roof. How long would it take such storms to demolish the deserted camp eventually and bury five bodies in the ruins? Water . . .

There was a shimmer in the center of the room—the roof must already be leaking. Some spark deep within Blake struggled to move him, to make him call a warning to the others. But it did not matter, they were gone . . . A shimmer?

NO!

Light hurt his eyes; he had to close them. Then—he looked again—a solid, gleaming surface where nothing had been a moment earlier. This was hallucination, he repeated to himself, even when he saw a hatch opening.

Chapter Sixteen

Blake sipped from the container held by both shaking hands to his parched mouth. Hallucination? Somehow his thoughts clung to that explanation of his present surroundings. Yet, for a dream, this had a reality he had never known such illusions to hold before, beginning with the taste of food in his mouth, progressing to the fact that he appeared to be seated within a shuttle, a standard two-man model used by the corps.

"That is about it, sir. Depots are being shut down all along the line on orders from Vroom." Blake heard the pilot's voice droning on over his head. "The wind-up signal is out—for what that is worth under the circumstances."

"Wind-up?" Lo Sige's voice, thin and drained, came from the other side of the cabin. "What—what does that mean?"

"To'Kekrops!" The anger in the ready answer was hot. "He forced across a Question in Council, carried it by a majority of two. Erc Rogan was not there, nor many of the others. The rumor is that opposition members were not all notified in time."

"Even so, how could he move so promptly?" Lo Sige sounded baffled.

"Oh, apparently he had been planning his coup for a long time. Squads of specially enlisted temporary wardsmen came through to the main depots and assumed control. There was trouble at at least two, but our men didn't have a chance. We never kept large crews anywhere along the line. They threatened to maroon anyone who did not surrender quietly, just as they treated your party. And I think that happened elsewhere. We have no real news, mostly just rumor. The message lines are all in their hands and all that is being broadcast is the order to come in at once and make no trouble."

"So you are on your way to Vroom?"

Blake, with food inside him, now paid closer attention to the conversation. The man in the pilot's seat was unknown to him. He had rugged features, and a small white sunburst of an old scar on one temple. His duty coveralls bore a narrow piping of green, the mark of a level explorer. And noting that, Blake was not surprised at the hesitant answer the stranger now made.

"I can run you to Vroom if that is where you really want to go."

"But you were not bound there?"

"Every shuttle reaching Vroom is impounded—that one piece of information has come down the line—and our men are taken into custody as they return. No, I was not on my way to Vroom."

"To a hideout?"

The stranger's lean hand rubbed along his chin line. "I am on exploration service, sir. Being marooned without resources on a successor world is one thing; having a base of one's own to return to is another."

"I take it you are not alone in your reaction?"

The other turned his head, looked at Blake who met his glance steadily, at the two girls, wrapped in coverings on the floor, who appeared to be asleep.

"No, I am not alone. There are others."

"And among them perhaps—Erc Rogan?"

"Yes. But just now he is in no condition to go on even if he wished. He was at the Saracossis Depot when they tried to take it over by force. We are certain they had orders to make sure of Rogan. He was rayed but made it out on a flash hop. They are using top-power mind control, and he is afraid they will make him into a puppet to mouth To'Kekrops' rot."

"Then we are not heading for Vroom. Will you take us to your hideout?"

"What about them?" The wardsman gestured to the girls. "They need medical attention. We have very little."

"They are Rogan's daughters; they can be used also. They would not choose to be in Limiters' hands."

"All right, if we can still make it. They have been slapping automatic recalls on shuttles, that was the last warning through. Unless it was just a threat . . ."

"Automatic recall? They don't care what happens to a crew, do they?" There was a savage bite in Lo Sige's demand. "In order to be safe from that you would have to disconnect part of the code director."

The other shrugged. "Which might dump you anywhere in any world, yes. But I am ready to take that chance. None of us fancies being marooned; only some things might be even worse."

"What about this hideout of yours? Coded, of course?"

The big man grinned. "That it is not! I have been on lone probe for five years now; my rank entitled me to a choice and I took it. The only record that will show up under the name of Faver Teborun, if they do any delving into assignments, is the waiver I made in order to get free rein. I have an uncounted base in the middle of Radiation Two belt."

Radiation Two belt: a series of worlds—how many no one was yet sure—where the past atomic holocaust had sent several time lines into oblivion as far as the human race was concerned. To go exploring there had taken nerve or the kind of recklessness that was thought to be beyond a qualified wardsman.

Teborun continued to smile. "It is uncoded, a wild place. Some radiation, of course, but it was not totally burned off. It's rather like Vroom. And there are a lot of queer mutations but none remotely human. At least none I have seen. It is a pocket where tracers are not likely to drop off for a look. I made two reports about it, both directly to Erc Rogan and not recorded on regular tapes. As far as the records show, I have been worlds away, doing some trading on the Icelandic-Vineland level."

"How many of our men reached it?"

"Don't know. Rogan got in with four and set up a limited call—one to New Britain and a couple more—for men he hoped to recruit before they were netted. There were about a dozen when I left just after your message got through. Say, how did you do that, anyway? The com was dead from E1045 back."

"We tried another method." Lo Sige did not elaborate. "Something new."

"Something we can use to draw in some of the other boys?" Teborun pressed. "No use letting good men walk into Limiter traps or take what they tried to give to Rogan."

"It was an experiment. I do not know whether it would work again."

Somewhat to Blake's surprise, Teborun did not push for any more details. And shortly thereafter the warning of level break-through came. Blake lay flat on the floor, close beside the girls, as the vibration shook them.

They looked through the hatch of the shuttle into what was indeed a strange place, the center of what might have been a gigantic stone globe. Well overhead was a break in its surface through which they could see the blue of what appeared to be normal sky.

The walls, sloping up and inward, were smooth as if they had been worked upon by human hands for a long time. Yet there was an alien air to the place which did not match the work of men at all.

Blake stumbled out of the hatch into a small crowd of men, some of them wearing the coveralls of wardsmen, still others a variety of strange dress as if the wearers had been hastily snatched from a number of different successor worlds. Pushed to the side of the globe, well away from the area the shuttle now occupied, were four or five more of the traveling machines. It was a rendezvous of refugees and fugitives.

"Rogan? Where is Rogan?" Lo Sige asked. "We have his daughters."

He was faced, as was Blake, with raised weapons, with closed, hostile faces. Only when Teborun dropped out of the hatch did the hostility lighten.

"What is the matter here?" demanded the probe scout.

He was shoved to one side by an armed man who looked into the cabin and then called over his shoulder, "It is the truth this time. They have a couple of women with them."

Teborun caught the man's arm and whirled him back against the wall of the shuttle. "All right, now suppose you begin to make some sense! You know why I went out—because Erc Rogan asked me to. And now I am back with his girls, plus a couple of our men who were marooned with them. Why the stunners? Where is Rogan? And just what has been going on here?"

There was a clamor of replies which was finally reduced to a disturbing story. Shortly before their own shuttle had arrived, another had appeared. The pilot had called from the hatch for Rogan, saying his daughters were on board, badly injured. The fact that Teborun was not in sight aroused suspicion in some of the men. Two had crowded into the cabin, in spite of the pilot's attempt to bar them. There had been sounds of a commotion inside and the shuttle had taken off. The trap had failed, but it had been a trap.

And the knowledge that the enemy had known just where to find them was unnerving. Events were moving so fast that the fugitives were unable to adjust to the shifting sands under them. Instead of the firm base they had known all their lives, the security of the corps, they were faced with utter chaos. The realization that they were hunted, that they might be marooned in some alien world, gnawed at their ability to think clearly.

There had never been a period when crosstiming was free from risk, and those risks these men had accepted without question for years. But those had been familiar risks, not engineered by their own people. Now return to home base was denied them if they would keep their freedom; they could not depend upon the loyalty of their own people, and certainly not upon the authorities. And they might not even be able to count on their shuttles should they be put on automatic recall.

Blake and Lo Sige sat on stools by the couch on which Rogan rested. His left leg was bandaged, his face worn with tension and pain. He looked years older than the man who had selected Blake as one of the team pledged to find Marva. That daughter and her sister now lay in an adjoining cave, one of those which led out of the sphere Teborun had chosen for his depot. Marfy had recovered to the point of talking with her father, but Marva was deep in a stupor.

"The Limiters having located this level," Rogan spoke with his normal rush of words, "they will be back, never doubt that. And what good are our few weapons against their mind control?"

"How did it all happen, sir?" Lo Sige asked. "Oh, we knew that the Limiters were trying to make trouble. But this—it blew up so suddenly!"

Rogan's mouth twisted. "We made the unforgivable mistake: we underestimated To'Kekrops! Vroom has come to depend upon crosstiming for most of the materials of life. We draw raw materials, food, the necessities of life as well as luxuries, from the successor worlds. For hundreds of years we have expanded and established depots, drawn energy from sister worlds. The Great War left us a handful of mutant survivors in a world three-quarters forbidden to human life. Only crosstiming saved us from total extinction.

"Thus, the man or men who control crosstiming also control Vroom as surely as if they hold each and every one of us here." Rogan raised his hand palm up and slowly curled his fingers inward. "To prevent any dictatorship we thought we had taken every precaution. The Hundred were selected with utmost care, the corps was sifted and sifted. But people forget when the good times go on and on. When there are no visible alarms nor enemies, swords rust, shields catch cobwebs in dark corners. I believe I can say, and be right, that the people of Vroom—except for the few who carry on the labor—do not realize just how much our world is supported by successor worlds they may never have heard of. There has always been a fanatic element among us. In the past, such people were rendered harmless by the disinterest of the rest; they were mainly talkers who feared contact with other levels. There have been wild rumors of disease, of possible importation of deadly weapons—as if any of the worlds have any worse than those we once turned upon ourselves—of ideas from abroad.

"When a people grows fat and indolent, rumors and such tales add spice to life. They are repeated as idle gossip, then they begin to be believed. A well-published disaster that affects persons from Vroom is caught up, magnified, used by shrewd troublemakers. For the past few years there has been a growing feeling that all crosstiming is dangerous.

"The reports of the corps are closed to the general public. A family from Vroom may visit the Forest Level or one of the other three approved holiday places. For the rest, they have only hearsay to depend on. And the worst is always more quickly believed and relayed than the good.

"A close-down of the corps might, in itself, accomplish two things to To'Kekrops' liking. First, it will feed the belief that danger exists crosstime to the extent that even trained men dare not risk such contact. Secondly, it will bring a pinch in our economy that will be felt by all, including those who have had no opinion concerning crosstime one way or another. Then the formation of a second corps could begin. And that corps will be, naturally, under Limiter command.

"Levels could then be looted openly under a freebooting raid system. Some of the loot, dumped in Vroom, could win To'Kekrops more and more adherents among those who have felt the pinch and would react to the plenty. Our own men, under mind control, may— probably already have—parrot what he would have them say. A few men in key positions, under his influence or direct mental control, must have begun this takeover, and the poison will spread rapidly because it comes from within corps ranks."

"But the situation cannot be hopeless." Lo Sige leaned back against the wall. "Something built with care for centuries can not just collapse overnight!"

"Disorganization at the center can work great havoc," Rogan replied. "Take a city . . . say, on your home world, Walker. What would happen if the lighting system failed, and with it the water supply, the heating, the communications? All gone in a day or part of a day. What would the result be?"

"Murder, literally murder!" Blake replied. "The city would die." He remembered a city on another level close to his own where death had come in a war it was not prepared to resist. "But afterward . . . there might be survivors—maybe one man or several who could lead the survivors and make them want to try again. But they would not have what they had before, and it would take years to gain any kind of order."

"Years we do not have!" snapped Lo Sige.

"No, years we do not have," Rogan assented. "However, we have really only one enemy, a spider at the center of the web. Bring down To'Kekrops now, before he becomes too deeply entrenched, and swift disaster can recoil upon all his party. He is not the man to delegate authority—his type never does. We have to get at him."

"And he is in Vroom, protected undoubtedly by the best guard ever assembled since the Great War," commented Lo Sige dryly.

"Just so. We are not equipped to fight war up and down

crosstime," Rogan pointed out. "We have few men, practically no supplies. We can accept marooning and save our skins, or we can try to get To'Kekrops."

"He will have mind control ready to take over anyone who sets foot on Vroom. Do you have any defense against that, sir?" asked Blake.

"I have one block—my own. Since the first reports of unrest, I have worn it. That is why he failed to pick me up."

"One man can be stunned or overpowered physically," Lo Sige pointed out, "or even rayed and removed permanently."

"I am too good a tool to kill off, at least immediately," Rogan said simply. "Mind-controlled and speaking for him, I would be worth more than he would want to throw away. Yes, they would try to take me alive. Then, stripped of my block . . ." He spread his hands in a gesture of defeat.

Rogan was talking around some idea, Blake knew, and he thought he could guess what that was. Blake Walker, alone of the men in this temporary refuge, did not have to depend on any mechanical block, could not be taken over by the Limiters' mental storm troopers. But the Limiters must already know that if Garglos had reported in as he surely must have.

"They saw you only as you were in the New Britain disguise." Though Blake knew that Lo Sige could not have read his thoughts, yet the other spoke as if he had done just that. "In Vroom you are relatively unknown. Oh, To'Kekrops will have heard of you as having been with Marfy Rogan. Whether his information goes much further—"

"It should, if he is as good as you think." Blake was emphatic.

Rogan might have been pursuing his own thoughts as they spoke, and not hearing a word, for now he broke in. "I am the only bait he will rise to, the only one who can get To'Kekrops."

"And you have not the least chance of reaching him uncontrolled." Lo Sige spoke with authority.

"But I have!" What made him say that? Blake wondered. What wild idea . . . ?

Both men were watching him now with a curious intentness as if they could will from him the answer they needed.

"You say he knows I was with Marfy. He must also know how we were marooned at the Project. Can it be possible that only because he was sure of our whereabouts he dared to try to trap you, sir? He could not have foreseen our escape."

"He now has the two men taken from here in his trap. He'll question them," Rogan said.

"Yes, but they were taken before we arrived. They know you sent for your daughters; they do not know whether we ever came. You could not be sure of our safety yourself then."

"True. And no one understood how I knew where to send for you." Rogan hitched himself up on his bed.

"What do you have in mind, Walker?" the wardsman asked.

"I imagine that when they discovered I was with Marfy on that sabotaged trip, the Limiters would have had me investigated as a matter of course."

Both men nodded agreement to that.

"Then To'Kekrops must know I am not a native of Vroom. Therefore, I represent a factor of which he cannot be sure. Would he not accept the idea that I am what is called a 'soldier of fortune' in my world, a mercenary willing to change sides for gain? I might say I was impressed into the corps because they could not erase my memory. And this is true in one way. If I approached him, and offered a deal . . ."

"You would be willing to attempt this?" Rogan was still watching him closely.

"I take it that supplies here are low," Blake counterquestioned. "How long are we prepared to sit out a search? And now they must have a code for this world. You may scatter and hide, but eventually the advantage is all theirs. Our small advantage is to move first."

"If the eventual advantage rests with them, why would To'Kekrops be ready to make any deal with you?" cut in Lo Sige.

"I think he wants quick results. Could he comb the whole of this level if you went into hiding? And you have shuttles. What is to prevent your hopping? Teborun is an experienced probe explorer; he could even find you another uncoded world."

"Good arguments. But To'Kekrops is no fool."

"You mean I'm no match for him? I do not pretend to be. But if he judges my motives by . . ."

"Those most familiar to him?" Rogan nodded. "Yes, he could

believe in you. And he could not have you mind-read to reveal any-thing else!"

"Getting to To'Kekrops is only the beginning," Lo Sige said. "What then?"

"Does he hate you enough, sir," Blake asked Rogan, "to make this a personal duel?"

Rogan twisted at the blanket covering his legs. "Of that . . . no, I am not sure."

"At least he would send a party in for you, and with me as guide. And you can lay a trap here. That would be up to you."

Lo Sige smiled faintly. "We are reduced to the thinnest of chances. Let us hope that fortune has no quarrel with us from now on!"

Chapter Seventeen

Stripped of both disguises he had worn, that of the New Britain trader and the frontier hunter of the Empire, and clad once again in service coveralls, Blake settled himself alone as the pilot of a shuttle. What had led him to make the reckless offer that had brought him here he was not sure. But he was not one to wait for any fight to come to him, that he knew. In the past waiting had always been the hardest part of discipline for him. And what he held now as a weapon was not a stunner keyed to his person, but all the information concerning his opponent that Rogan could supply: a list of those who might be of some aid—always providing they were not already under Limiter control—and a mental map of crosstime headquarters.

As soon as his machine left on the Vroom flight, the majority of the refugees would take to the outer world on that level, hiding out from a return raid. And Lo Sige would begin to set up the trap against Blake's return with Limiter forces.

Teborun had coded to run to Vroom; Blake had no fears of not arriving there safely. And once into the corps terminal, the rest would be improvisation on his part. He was no hero; he was merely the only man naturally equipped to fill this present role.

The return was like any normal trip. But when the signal told him Vroom was outside, Blake sat quietly facing the controls for a moment or two. He did not doubt that To'Kekrops would be inter-ested in him; he had only to work on that interest strongly enough to get a personal interview. And then work again, this time on the animosity between the Limiter leader and Rogan, and talk better, more persuasively then he ever had before. And maybe, if such talk did not convince, he might have to make sure of To'Kekrops somehow himself. That thought had been in the back of his mind from the first. The Limiters must be brought down! What if they did turn to level-raiding, the worst piracy the successor worlds would ever know: snatch, kill, be gone where no other level's law could follow.

Blake stood up. Better leave now or any reception committee out there would begin to suspect. He thumbed the hatch catch, stepped onto the pavement of the terminal. There he fronted rows of shuttles, more than he had ever seen gathered in one space before, not only small patrol ships such as he had just quitted, but also heavier trade carriers fitted for the moving of cargo.

Drawn up before the array of hastily parked shuttles were three men. Two were in the field dress of the corps, but Blake did not know them. The third wore civilian clothing with a wide white band conspicuous on his right sleeve.

It was the latter who aimed a mind probe at Blake.

"You will not get far with that," Blake remarked with a calculated insolence. "I am no meat for your broiling, friend."

The other's concentrated stare broke and then intensified again with a bolt of mind force that hurt Blake but did not crack his block.

The two who flanked the civilian now moved in, their faces expressionless, in their hands one of the few weapons legal on Vroom: stunners. Blake had no desire to be even momentarily subjected to darts from them, even though they had little lasting effect.

"I came through by myself. I am making you no trouble," he said. "Ask To'Kekrops if he wants to see Blake Walker. I think you will discover that any interference with me will not be welcome."

The wardsman to his left had his stunner aimed. He fired in the same instant that Blake read a dawning uncertainty in the civilian's expression. But it was too late. There was a prick at Blake's throat just above the collar line. He slumped forward; he had no defense against this kind of attack.

He awoke to the stinging slaps across his face to discover that, held upright between two men, he was being dragged back and forth while the third slapped him from time to time as a rough but effective way of bringing him back to consciousness. None of his present captors were those who had greeted him in the terminal, and he was now in an office which he recognized as being that of one of the commanders of a sector.

"Get him going." The order, marked by a note of irritation, came from behind. Then those who had supported his wavering walk turned Blake around and headed him toward the desk. He who sat there was Commander To'Frang, a credited officer of the corps. For one or two fuzzy moments Blake puzzled over that. Had the Limiters' takeover failed? Was he now in the hands of those who supported the old regime? Perhaps To'Kekrops' sweep had not been as complete as the men in the field had believed.

Yet Blake was aware not only of the actions of those striving to arouse him, but also of his warning. And on that he relied more than anything else. Danger! He could almost sniff it in this room.

"What . . ." Might as well let them know that he was conscious. But his voice sounded oddly in his own ears, thin and far away.

The man in the wardsman's uniform, who had just drawn back his hand for another slap, changed his aim and caught a handful of Blake's hair, jerking up his head.

"He is around now," he reported to To'Frang.

"About time. Bring him here."

They dragged Blake to the front of the desk. No lights reporting movements in the field played along the controls on its surface. There was only a line of dull green straight down, signaling returned shuttles. It was something Blake had never seen before.

But the question To'Frang shot at him now was not the one he had been expecting at all.

"Where is Com Varlt?"

"Varlt?" Blake repeated. It was hard, coming out of a stunner-induced daze as he now was, to adjust to the meaning of that demand. What had Com Varlt to do with his mission here?

"Varlt!" To'Frang's hands, resting on the desk surface as if he still wished to press controls and monitor reports, their fingers crooked, raised as if to claw the answer he wanted out of Blake.

"You left here with Varlt on a special mission not recorded. Now where is Varlt?"

"I don't know," Blake answered with the exact truth. The last time he had seen the master wardsman had been in the Merchant's house in Xomatl. There was a good chance that he had been marooned on that successor world.

"You do not understand." To'Frang schooled both his impatience and his tone. "We have to have Varlt. We cannot organize anything effective against these madmen without leaders such as Varlt."

"I don't know where he is—" Blake had just begun when the Commander's impatience broke its bounds. He got to his feet, leaned across the desk and gripped the front of Blake's coverall, shaking him savagely.

"We got you out of the hands of To'Kekrops' men; we can dump you right back into them, Walker! You are only important because you can lead us to Varlt and for no other reason. We are holding on here by our fingernails. Most of the senior men are now mind-controlled, shouting out Limiter poison on cue. We are trying to get in touch with those still in the field. If we can round up enough and bring them in, we may have a slim chance. Now— where is Varlt?"

"I don't know," Blake repeated for the third time. "We separated in the field. I had to level-hop. And I don't know what happened to him after that."

To'Frang released his hold on Blake, sank back in his seat. Perhaps every word the Commander had said was true. But the alert within Blake warned to walk with care, very great care. And his mission lay elsewhere. He was well recovered from the stunner-induced fog now. If To'Frang and those with him were not cooperating with the Limiters, then how was it that Blake now stood before the Commander's own desk in his assigned office? Business as usual? With crosstiming closed down and To'Kekrops' men waiting in the terminal to snag all arrivals? Hardly!

The Commander nodded, as if Blake's last answer made sense. "Clever, Walker. Play it smart. Only"—his expression now was one of a man deciding to speak frankly—"time is against us. We have been playing hide-and-seek through this building for hours. I had to get here," he slipped his hand along the surface of the desk almost caressingly, "or I had no way to recall the men still out there. The Limiters believe they have marooned them." He grimaced. "But they do not have all lines cut. Not yet. And if we can bring back men such as Varlt, then we have a chance, thin but still a chance. We need that chance, Walker. Where did you leave Varlt?"

"Well away from the local depot." Blake was willing to admit that much. "And I do not see how he could possibly have reached that before it was closed down."

"I do not associate the name Com Varlt with the word impossible." To'Frang smiled faintly. "You went to New Britain. That is one of the marooned levels; they were awaiting the return of their normal three-day shuttle and it was not dispatched. But perhaps we can send it."

"But if Limiters hold the terminal and snap mind-control on each man who comes in, then—"

"How do we plan to take over long enough to land our men? We are working on that now, Walker. And by the way, if you were level-hopping, from just which world did you come?"

"That of Kutur's Project."

"But . . ." the Commander betrayed surprise, "but Kutur has been unmasked as one of To'Kekrops' supporters. How did he—"

"Let me get away? I reached there after he left. There were indications that there had been trouble—the com had been destroyed and I could get no answers via emergency—so I came through."

Would the Commander buy that?

"And what have you to say that is so important for To'Kekrops to hear?" To'Frang pounced like a cat with prey well within paw reach. Blake did not have to act his surprise and the Commander laughed softly.

"We had eyes and ears in the terminal. We heard your words to the welcoming gang. Now you are going to tell me what you were so eager to tell elsewhere!"

If To'Frang was playing the Limiters' game deviously, then here was an excellent chance of reaching To'Kekrops' ears. But if the Commander was what he said, a leader of the opposition, then . . . Blake must walk a very perilous middle path if he could!

"The Limiters can not take me over. As you say, there were some important men of ours lost along the crosstime. If a big enough force from here could be tricked into hunting them—"

"On some inhospitable successor world?" To'Frang looked eager. "I do not think it will work. But, yes, I can see why it might be tried by men so lost. But your bait must be very good, Walker. To'Kekrops has no reason to go hunting for enemies he can dispose of merely by shutting down level-hopping. What kind of bait do you offer?"

"Erc Rogan!" Blake was forced into a corner from which the only exit was the truth. Though he would edit that truth to the best of his ability.

"Rogan? But Rogan is dead." To'Frang's tone was one of such confidence that had Blake not known the contrary he might have been convinced.

"And if he was not dead?"

"Yes." Again To'Frang stroked the surface of his desk, running his fingertips along the green line. "Yes, if Rogan were not dead, that would be bait to interest To'Kekrops, to make him send a force hunting. But Rogan is dead!"

"What proof of that have you?"

The long fingers were still. To'Frang glanced up, locked stares with Blake.

"There was a report tape. He was rayed. The man who lost his head and did it was erased two days ago."

"And the body?"

"There was no body." To'Frang's head jerked. An avid eagerness awoke in his face. "Rogan—Rogan escaped?"

"Let us think of one explanation for no body," Blake evaded. "If Rogan was almost through the hatch of a shuttle, if he was not killed, only wounded, if he made it to another level—"

"You know it—the truth!" To'Frang sprang to his feet again. For the first time the other three who had brought Blake to consciousness again crowded around, all of them intent upon what he might say. Were they eager because a failing cause might now produce a rallying point, or were they traitors avid to carry out the ultimate betrayal of the corps they had given allegiance to? At least Blake had their complete attention.

"I will tell you this much: Rogan is alive." Blake made a definite move in this blind game.

"Where?" To'Frang's hand hovered over the buttons on his desk as if he could summon the lost into this room by their prompt use.

"Safe—for now—on an uncoded level."

"Uncoded! But there is a code, there has to be! You have it?"

"With a whole world to search, what good would even having the code do?" Again Blake hedged. "Be assured that I can furnish To'Kekrops with a code and more—if I can see him personally."

"Rogan!" To'Frang breathed deeply as if he had been running. "You can get to To'Kekrops with that name, assuredly you can. And the great man himself can perhaps be sucked into a personal search. Yes, of course, yes! It is our best chance yet! Get to To'Kekrops. You will get to him with that story, Walker. Lessan!" The man who had slapped Blake moved forward another step. "Lessan, see what is going on out there, along the top floors."

The wardsman drew a wide white band from the front of his coverall, adjusted it about his right arm and slipped out into the corridor. To'Frang nodded to the others. One of them pulled seats drawer-fashion from the wall, and the other went to a dispenser and dialed meals, bringing out cover trays. In spite of the human disorganization in Headquarters, Blake saw, the machines which supplied the necessities of life were still in excellent working order. He ate heartily, the first real meal he could remember since the morning of the last day in Xomatl. And he had no idea when he would eat again. He had expected more questions from the Commander. But instead of any talk, To'Frang appeared absorbed in the code buttons on his desk, running his fingers along their rows while sometimes his lips moved as if he worked problems in his head. One might judge that he was studying out some problem of crosstiming—and not by the regular methods.

Methodically Blake chewed and swallowed. If he dared believe that To'Frang was what he claimed to be, then perhaps he had found recruits to swell the ranks of Rogan's diehards. But if the Commander was merely To'Kekrops' tool, the sooner he was uncovered the better. One comment the other had made did not ring true: Blake did not believe that the Limiter leader could be lured away to level-hop himself. But that he would send a force to search for that member of the Hundred who was his most determined enemy and who would be the rallying head of any insurrection against his rebellion—yes. And that was what Blake's own plan counted on. But backed by adepts in mental control, To'Kekrops would believe that he needed only to dispatch a take-over force. The defeat of To'Kekrops would have to be here on Vroom, and Blake had yet to see how they could do it. This was a vast gamble on chance alone.

Of course, if he were lucky enough to get hand on a stunner, and a chance to remove the rebel leader, and an open way to a shuttle . . . But each of those wishes was more fantastic than the one preceding it.

The same guard who had dialed their meals collected the now empty trays and slid them down the disposal vent. As if that act was a signal, To'Frang looked up.

"Lessan's running late," he observed.

"We go up?" one of the hitherto silent guards suggested.

"Might be wise," the Commander assented. He went to the door, opened it cautiously and looked quickly both ways into the corridor. A jerk of his head was an order and Blake got to his feet, moving behind To'Frang and sandwiched between the two guards.

Most of the Headquarters offices were soundproof, but the halls were not. And hitherto, when he had walked along them, there had been the ebb and flow of noise, muffled voices, the sounds of machinery. Now there was only an intimidating silence. Most of the doors were firmly shut and To'Frang set a good pace. He did not turn to the anti-gravity lifts but sought the seldom-used, ladderlike emergency stairs behind concealing panel entrances.

They went up two floor levels, approaching the Commandant's office at the very top of Headquarters. Crowded together on a narrow landing, they waited for To'Frang to try the door. He pushed at it, but it gave only a little until one of the others lent his strength. They looked into a small room lined with shelves crowded with supply cartons of tapes and viewer film. But the obstruction that had barred the door lay on the floor.

His white-banded arm flung across his chest as if in a vain attempt to ward off death, Lessan sprawled there. He had been rayed, just like the tech Blake had found at the Project. The Commander stared down at the body; there was no mistaking his utter surprise. So deep was that amazement that Blake was convinced that his own distrust was well-founded. The death of one of his men, caught spying on the enemy, should not have so completely astounded the Commander.

"Lessan!" The man at Blake's left pushed in, went on one knee beside the body. "But why?"

"A tape-tap!" To'Frang half whispered. "He had me tape-tapped!"

Blake was certain now concerning the other, though he strove to conceal it. So the Commander was one of the Limiter adherents! Perhaps he had played such an undercover game for a long time. But To'Kekrops, running true to form, trusted no one. He had had his subordinate's office tape-tapped, had heard or had reported to him all that passed there. And something had made the new, would-be ruler of Vroom ready to write To'Frang off.

"They left him here," To'Frang continued to stare at the body, "so we would know." The shock of his find wore off a little and he glanced at Blake. In that instant, the other knew all need for pretense was gone, that the Commander was done with acting. And he knew, too, that the Commander believed that, in Blake, he had a chance to redeem whatever mistake he had made.

"Take this one in!" He snapped the order.

The guard kneeling by Lessan merely glanced up, and then down at the body again and shrugged. His fellow was already backing to the stair door. But in To'Frang's hand flashed a laser.

"You fools!" he spat at the guards. "They will already have their orders to cut you down on sight, you will have been 'vised through-out the building. We go in there, where they will not expect us, with this one in the lead. That way we have a chance. How can To'Kekrops think we are doublecrossing him if we do that? And he wants this one. He must have heard about Rogan from the tape, and this one will lead him right to Rogan."

The man on his knees looked at the one in the doorway and that one shrugged in resignation.

"They probably have us 'vised right enough," the latter said. "And if we deliver this Walker, who knows?"

"Deliver it is," his companion agreed.

To'Frang gestured them on with the hand that still held the rayer in full sight.

There was no escape for Blake with the three of them on guard. It would seem that he was about to reach his goal.

Chapter Eighteen

To'Kekrops' features were familiar to anyone in Vroom, since they had appeared often on telecasts during the past year or so. But Blake had never seen the Limiter leader in person. And what he had expected was not quite in keeping with the man who sat stiff-backed at the end of the room that once had been dedicated to conferences between Committees of the Hundred and the Commandant of the Corps. All seats, save that now occupied by To'Kekrops, had been cleared away, leaving the center of the room open, an arrangement obviously intended to overawe those faced by the new fountainhead of law and authority.

Mind probe—far sharper and more intense than that which had greeted Blake at the terminal. But Blake had been prepared for that. To'Frang and the others halted, woodenstiff, as if the mental bolt had frozen them. But Blake walked on.

"They were right! You cannot be controlled." To'Kekrops regarded Blake, not as a man might survey an equal but as an explorer might center his attention on a new and outre form of life seen on another level.

"Turzor!"

A crackle of blue lightning cut through the air with the deadly threat, a death wall laid between them. This was no weapon of Vroom. But the man standing in the shadows by the wall plainly was adept in its use. Blake halted at that warning.

"I am told you have information for me," To'Kekrops came directly to the point, "that you told these fools you have the code of the level on which Rogan is hiding out, planning to use that as bait for me. How lackwitted do you think me, Blake Walker?"

There were two guards, the one with the flame weapon and another behind the Limiter leader; perhaps it was the second who was using the mind control. Blake had no weapon, no way of reaching the other by force, just by his wits. And at that moment he felt them singularly inept.

"If you had that via tape-tap, sir," he began, "then you heard only what I thought fit to tell those who brought me here. That is not the full truth."

To'Kekrops smiled. "So this is to be a discussion as to what is truth? I fear we have little time for philosophical subtleties, Walker."

"You want Rogan," Blake cut in baldly.

"That is true. I want Erc Rogan, preferably alive. He will provide excellent service to our cause. But—if necessary—dead. Rogan, yes, I want Rogan."

"Alive and level-hopping?"

"Alive he may be. Level-hopping? That is another question. At present we know his hideout. And if he takes to a shuttle again, well, that can be curtailed. We have already taken steps."

"And with a whole world to search while he builds up his own force in the meantime?" Blake felt overmatched; he had only To'Kekrops' hatred to play upon.

"A nuisance." The Limiter leader still smiled. "Just a nuisance, not much more. I have already admitted that, in my hands at this moment, he would have some small worth. But what is your offer? And the motive behind it?"

"If you know my name, you must know something of my past."

"That you are not of Vroom? Yes."

"That I was brought here against my will because your people could not plant false memories in me. That does not mean that I found the change altogether to my liking."

"So you harbor some resentment for those responsible? Possible—possible—"

To'Kekrops was playing with him, Blake knew. One step and the flamer would finish him as it had Lessan. Yet his inner warning held level; the Limiter Leader was not about to jump, not in the immediate future. That could only mean that he did want what Blake had to offer.

"There are rumors," Blake continued deliberately, "that once you have matters settled here, there will be a reorganization of the corps, a different method of dealing with successor worlds."

To'Kekrops' smile grew broader, was now a death's head grin.

"Rumors, rumors! We are never free of those! But do not let me interrupt you. What dazzling proposition have you to make now?"

"My own level has many opportunities for a man with backing. . . ."

"A disturbed world," To'Kekrops said, "makes for profits for those delving into its troubles, I agree. A man with backing might well rise to heights there. You build your argument on a firm base, Walker. But what of your part in the matter of Erc Rogan?"

"He is on an uncoded world—"

"To which I have the code now!"

"Have you time to search the whole world? I know where . . ."

"There are ways of learning that from you." The smile did not fade.

"I am blocked. A man can be forced to babble nonsense under pressure when he is broken. But the truth may not be in what he says."

"So once more we are back to that troublesome matter of truth. Well, what do you propose to do to facilitate matters concerning Rogan?"

"I will guide a party with a mind control. You can take him easily."

"Why you, Walker? You are not really needed."

"Because Rogan is blocked. Your control cannot take him, and the guard will not find him alive if they force it." Blake improvised feverishly. There was a slim chance of attracting To'Kekrops by such an offer to the point where the Limiter Leader might make a slip, just one slip!

"Why should Rogan trust you?"

"I brought out his daughters when your people marooned them. I volunteered to come here to contact those he thought might help him."

"Turzor!" The man with the flamer came into the center of the room. "Jargarli!" Now the one behind To'Kekrops' chair pushed forward.

"A suitable force, do you agree?" the Limiter leader asked.

Blake looked from one to the other. "Yes," he said flatly.

To'Kekrops nodded. "You are right. Jargarli can hold a dozen minds, perhaps more; he has not yet found his limit. And you have already witnessed Turzor's efficiency with a weapon imported crosstime. We have even more effective ones, of course, but as yet their production is so limited that we must depend upon these more primitive arms. You say you can deliver Rogan. Very well. Prove it!"

Blake shook his head. "No bargain is one sided. What is to prevent Turzor proving his marksmanship on me when Rogan is delivered?"

"Nothing at all, of course. Save this—a thin string on which to hang your life! You have pointed out that you have certain possibilities on your former level—"

"A very thin thread, sir, one I do not trust at all."

This was it! Either Blake won some concession now or he lost the whole game. But to accept To'Kekrops' first proposition was immediate defeat.

"Very well. I shall give you your chance. Thus." He must have pressed the summoner button in the arm of his chair, for another guard entered the far door.

To'Kekrops spoke. "Give me one of those stunners."

The man vanished, returning in moments with a box containing a weapon like that Varlt had given Blake in Xomatl.

"One of our own newer inventions," the Limiter leader explained. "It has several unusual properties. One: it can be used only by the man who first takes it into his hand. Second: it shoots a ray that is a powerful narcotic, an improvement on the stunners of general issue. Also, it has one disadvantage which its inventor has not yet mastered: it cannot be reloaded, and it has only six shots. Take it up."

Blake did so, feeling again the sensation of the weapon adapting to him alone.

"Now you will turn, having paid attention to the fact that Turzor has you in the sights of his weapon, and you will fire five times at that wall. Fire!"

There was no choice but to obey. Blake pressed the button five times, the guard who had brought the stunner watching him closely. At the man's affirmative nod, To'Kekrops spoke again.

"Now you have your defense against Turzor, and nature has provided you with one against Jargarli. Are you satisfied?"

"As much as I can hope to be, sir."

"Sensible acceptance of matters as they are. Now, bring me Rogan and we shall talk again. Assuredly we shall!"

Blake's glimmer of a plan still depended too much on luck. However, it was now in motion. They came back to the terminal, to the shuttle that had brought Blake in. Under strict survey of the two guards, Blake set the code, checked it, punched the course keys. Their quarters were cramped; Jargarli had the twin seat, Turzor was behind Blake.

No one spoke as the cabin vibrated, became quiescent again. But Blake was thinking furiously, knowing that his companions could not read his mind. How well had Lo Sige set up the welcome party at the other end? And could it function against Jargarli's mind control?

When the arrival light flashed on, he spoke to Turzor. "You had better be ready."

Jargarli sneered. "There are but three men out there; already they are under my control. They will be awaiting my orders."

Turzor watched Blake, the flamer in his hands, ready, the wardsman could see, for any hostile move.

"You first," he ordered harshly.

Blake shook his head. "No, Jargarli first if he wishes, then you. With three men under control out there and only one shot left me, how do you expect me to start anything?"

Turzor did not seem disposed to accept that reasoning. But his fellow guard nodded. "They will move at him on my words. There is no chance for any attack on us."

Now, all depended on Blake's ability to move fast. Waste his single shot and he lost everything. He might have a better chance later, but he could not depend upon that.

The hatch opened; Jargarli dropped to the rock within the hollow sphere. Blake, with split-second timing, threw himself onto the cabin floor. Turzor half turned, took the force of the stun ray at throat level. He gave a choked cry; blue flame cut across the cabin wall, ceasing when his finger slipped from the weapon's firing button. Blake grabbed for the rayer.

Teborun came scrambling through the hatch, his face blank. Plainly he was under control. He made for Blake. Under such command there would be no stopping him as long as he was conscious. Blake twisted to one side as the other wardsman rushed him. He kicked out and Teborun stumbled, banging into the seat, the stiff clumsiness of a controlled man making him awkward in the cramped confines of the cabin. Blake chopped out stiff-handed with one of the unarmed combat blows in which he had been so well trained. Teborun grunted, went down. Blake reversed the flamer and brought its butt down on the probe scout's head. One out of Jargarli's control.

But what if one of the two remaining controlled had a stunner? The odds were still in Jargarli's favor, and the Limiter could pick up and pull into the battle any other refugee within range of his mind. If they had not scattered as they planned—though surely Lo Sige must have taken care of that.

Blake turned to Turzor. The man was limp, almost impossible to handle but he would provide a shield. The wardsman tugged at the dead weight of the guard's body, propped him up with the support of his own shoulder behind him, and moved for the door.

As nearly as he could remember, the only cover out there was that of the parked shuttles—unless Jargarli could reach one of the passages leading out of the sphere. Although in that maze he would be lost unless he was able to summon a guide through the control.

Blake peered over Turzor's hunched shoulder. He heard the soft hiss of a dart, saw it sink into the stunned guardsman's flaccid arm. So, he faced at least one stunner. But he also sighted Jargarli moving backwards toward one of the other shuttles. Of course, to make sure of Blake, he would have to stay and direct his puppets in battle. And he could not do that if he removed himself from the scene.

Steadying the barrel of the flamer on Turzor's shoulder, Blake fired. The sparkling blue lanced just inches over Jargarli's head, cutting into the surface of the machine he had thought to shelter in. The Limiter ducked and Blake fired a second time.

There was the smell of ozone and of overheated metal. Jargarli would not use that machine for cover. And the next was well to his left. A figure rushed from the right, heading for the hatch of the cabin and Blake. The wardsman shoved Turzor out, straight at the attacker. Together, they crashed on the rock.

"Stand!"

Blake enforced that order with another burst of fireworks, This so close to Jargarli that he cried out, perhaps seared by the edge of the beam.

"The next goes dead center," Blake called.

Jargarli was frozen in a half-crouch. He had lost his sneer; now he showed Blake the snarl of a cornered and vicious animal. But he was far from finished.

Blake went flat, that inner warning giving him the only defense he had. He heard the metallic ping of a dart striking somewhere within the cabin. Jargarli was still playing his controlled pawn.

Blake aimed another spear of blue flame, this time running along the rock of the floor. Jargarli stumbled back, unable to stand his ground against it. Right, left, right, Blake played him, forcing the Limiter into the wreckage of the other shuttle. And then what Blake had been gambling on happened. Jargarli's own peril cracked his hold over his pawn.

There was a startled cry to Blake's left. Jargarli's head jerked in that direction. For a moment he was able to reassert control. Then he made one more jump away from the flamer, lost his balance and fell.

"Needle him!" Blake shouted. He wriggled over the edge of the hatch, got to his feet, and ran in a zigzag pattern lest some remnants of Jargarli's control still set the other at his throat. But the shot he feared did not come and he reached the fallen Limiter. Jargarli did not move. He might already be unconscious, but Blake made sure of that with the butt of the flamer.

"I don't know what you can do or if you can do it." Blake faced them: Erc Rogan; Marfy; Marva, who was pale and shrunken but more clear-eyed than he had ever seen her; Lo Sige; four of the other refugees, including Teborun who nursed an aching head. "But if you can, it is our key to Vroom and to To'Kekrops."

Rogan did not answer directly. Instead he glanced from his daughters to Lo Sige, to one or two of the others, as if awaiting their comments. It was Lo Sige who spoke first.

"We did what many claimed was impossible when we sent our call across levels. That was a uniting of power. Why could not such an effort be also a weapon? To'Kekrops is working through controllers, yes, and most of us are susceptible to control attack. But it works both ways; they can be influenced, too."

"You used the call because Marfy, Marva, and I were linked." Rogan appeared to be thinking aloud. "So you had a definite focus at which to aim."

"We shall have focuses aplenty in Vroom once we get there, and probe waves to ride back to their sources. Now we have a specimen here to practice on."

Blake could not follow their entwined thought as they consulted without words. Nor was he one of the team they finally put together after much testing. In the end, their weapon was a strange one. Lo Sige formed the center of that odd attack, Marfy and Marva his immediate backing; Rogan was one wing; and the other was another wardsman, a fantastically clad merchant from a world Blake had never heard of. Only these five could mesh and hold the strangest offense and defense that crosstime must ever have seen.

Two of the control boards of the shuttles, one of them the partially wrecked one, were cannibalized to create the thing of wires and plates Blake wore,—outside that "weapon" but still part of any battle, able to come to defend the others with the flamer and his own immunity to control. Once they disembarked in Vroom, they hoped they would be able to short-circuit the adepts To'Kekrops used to command his prisoners.

Teborun and another scout took a fourth machine, with orders to range time and pick up as many of the marooned as they could— Rogan had listed those who had special talents he needed—and ferry them into the Vroom terminal.

They had used their device on Jargarli and proved that it worked with him. Now they were ready to go.

It was a tight squeeze in the cabin of the shuttle, but this was the machine expected in Vroom and they dared take no other. As they went into a spin, all eyes but Blake's closed. He could feel the force building up around him. His head ached, he experienced the sensation of being whirled around and around in the rapids of a raging river. Yet even under this pressure he did not crack.

"Terminal," he said aloud, breaking into the trance of his companions.

"Now!" Had Blake heard that with his ears or his mind? He was not sure, but it was like a shout within him. Holding the flamer to his side in half concealment, he unfastened the hatch and jumped out.

There was a reception committee right enough. But just a little too eager. Blake had taken precautions. Needlers hissed, but Blake had already dropped to his hands and knees. He need fear assault only for those first fleeting seconds.

The men who had been waiting there, ample proof of To'Kekrops' treachery, reeled back from the shuttle as a wave of blast force was emitted from the machine. Weapons dropped as several put their hands to their heads, rolled on the ground. Blake darted forward, grabbed at the stunners, began to aim and fire, using darts even on those crying out as they lay.

"Ready," he called into the cabin.

They came out, walking as if still tranced, passing unheeding the now unconscious men. Blake realized that his task was doubled. So sunk were the five in the concentration of holding and aiming their countercontrol, that the physical defense of the party must rest with him alone.

Three men burst out of a doorway. One shouted as he sighted the bodies on the ground. Blake fired. Two of the attackers staggered out into the terminal and went down to join the earlier victims. The third jumped back within the doorway. He might escape to give the alarm.

But the spear, five minds united in one purpose, marched on. Blake attempted both to scout and protect the rear. That, he decided, was impossible. He shot twice at men in the hall ahead, bringing one down. Then they had free passage to the gravity lift. Lo Sige dialed a destination signal. They rose at the nerve-shattering speed of emergency, shooting up past all the floors and corridors to the crown of Headquarters.

"He is there, waiting," Rogan said. "He thinks of escape . . ."

"He cannot. Do not let him!" Marfy cried. Her eyes were again closed; she held to her sister with one hand, and the other, moving out blindly, grasped Blake's sleeve, anchoring him to her with tense force.

For a long moment they stood so. Blake was convinced that their will, one formed of many, was holding To'Kekrops to await their coming.

The lift came to a halt, its door grated open.

"No!" Blake interposed his body between the gate and Lo Sige's advance. "No!"

He was just in time. A pattern of violence, which could only have been woven by another flamer made a net of vicious light, but it had not caught them. These rays flew upward. Weapons, still spitting fire, moved through the air. They homed on the invaders, rose again, now pointing away, still firing, but moving ahead in some mindless life of their own, seeking now those who had earlier owned them. There were screams of terror such as Blake had never heard before. But his own warning had subsided; their path was clear.

Once before he had seen a battle of hallucination combined with the force of esper powers, that one between Lo Sige and the outlaw he had hunted across many worlds. But this was far worse. The corridor before them wavered. They might well have been marching through one successor world after another, in vivid, fantastic, and horrible sequence. Blake reeled, staggered. But Marfy still held his arm. And he sensed that the nightmares that were visible to him were not the same for her. Yet he dared not close his eyes to any of them lest they vanish and the real enemy be revealed weapon in hand, waiting.

He did not remember entering the council chamber. He was not even sure he was there, for the walls changed size and shape and the room filled and emptied with forms and figures he saw only dimly, knowing only a fierce desire not to see them clearly.

Afterward Blake could never give a successful account of that struggle. He was on the fringe of a convulsion that distorted nature, form, and substance as he knew it. The alien quality of the void in which that engagement was fought blinded him to the warfare. It was doubtful if any mortal could have witnessed that struggle with open eyes.

When he could see clearly once again there was the solid feel of floor under him and walls were no longer eddying as if they were wind-tossed smoke. Blake crouched, his hands empty of the flamer— for what weapon of metal, man-made, was useful in a battle of hallucination?

There was the chair in which To'Kekrops had sat. And in it still lolled a limp thing which pawed at itself and gave forth a thin, wailing mewl, a sound echoed by other things which crept aimlessly about on all fours or sprawled, their hands feebly beating the air.

But in the center of this room that the Limiters' leader had stripped to lend majesty to his own cause still stood those five. Now they shivered, clung to one another, displaying the faces of those who wake from bitter, heartpounding nightmares.

"It—it is done." Rogan's lips moved, but the dead tone that issued from between them was not his usual voice.

Blake gazed at the enemy, not sure just what had happened to To'Kekrops and those he had summoned to back him in the final defense. It was done if this was the last of the enemy. Done! But what had they done here, striving as they had striven? He had not been a part of the spear, but his idea had helped to forge it, his the instigation of its use. What had they done—or loosed?

"What do we do now?" Had he asked that aloud in his bewilderment or thought it? Minds . . . thoughts . . . fearful things . . . weapons . . .

"Do?" Lo Sige turned his head. A measure of sense and reason was back in the senior wardsman's eyes. It was as if he had dragged himself free of quicksand, was thankful he had won safety, yet did not quite yet believe in that safety. "Do?" he repeated. "Why, now we pick up the pieces."

"Pieces?" echoed Rogan. His arms were about his daughters' shoulders; he drew them closer to him. "Pick up the pieces, yes, and there are many of them."

Blake rose. For a moment some trick of memory brought back the alien otherness that had captured this hall for a space. But the recall was gone in a flash. Yes, there were pieces, and some of them might still exist in shapes which spelled trouble. He looked around for the flamer. It was going to be a long day or night—or whatever hour had struck now—for Vroom.